"Ava, when the shooti
to dive down."

"Okay. But what about you?"

"I'll be fine."

Oliver kept zigzagging, but the car stayed with them, the driver not moving a muscle but keeping the car close.

"We're going to keep moving and hope they'll either back off…or play chicken with us."

But the vehicle advanced and tapped the back bumper.

"Now they're getting serious," Oliver said.

New York Times Bestselling Author

Lenora Worth
and
Lynette Eason

Necessary Valor

Previously published as *Rescue Operation* and *Explosive Force*

LOVE INSPIRED
INSPIRATIONAL ROMANCE

LOVE INSPIRED®
INSPIRATIONAL ROMANCE

ISBN-13: 978-1-335-53299-2

Recycling programs
for this product may
not exist in your area.

Necessary Valor

Copyright © 2020 by Harlequin Books S.A.

Rescue Operation
First published in 2018. This edition published in 2020.
Copyright © 2018 by Harlequin Books S.A.

Explosive Force
First published in 2018. This edition published in 2020.
Copyright © 2018 by Harlequin Books S.A.

Special thanks and acknowledgment are given to Lenora Worth and Lynette Eason for their contributions to the Military K-9 Unit miniseries.

This edition published by arrangement with Harlequin Books S.A.

For questions and comments about the quality of this book,
please contact us at CustomerService@Harlequin.com.

Love Inspired
22 Adelaide St. West, 40th Floor
Toronto, Ontario M5H 4E3, Canada
www.Harlequin.com

Printed in U.S.A.

CONTENTS

With over seventy books published and millions in print, **Lenora Worth** writes award-winning romance and romantic suspense. Three of her books finaled in the ACFW Carol Awards, and her Love Inspired Suspense novel *Body of Evidence* became a *New York Times* bestseller. Her novella in *Mistletoe Kisses* made her a *USA TODAY* bestselling author. Lenora goes on adventures with her retired husband, Don, and enjoys reading, baking and shopping...especially shoe shopping.

Visit the Author Profile page
at Harlequin.com for more titles.

RESCUE OPERATION

Lenora Worth

When the host goeth forth against thine enemies,
then keep thee from every wicked thing.
—*Deuteronomy* 23:9

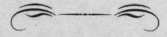

To the men and women of the US military. We respect and love all of you, and we will be forever grateful for your dedication and sacrifice. And especially to Wilberto Garcia, my air force son-in-law. Stay safe!

ONE

Ignoring the tilt and rumble of the HH-60G Pave Hawk helicopter about to hoist her down below and the dark thunderstorm approaching from the west, Senior Airman Ava Esposito adjusted the sturdy harness sleeves around the black nylon sling holding the sixty-five-pound yellow Lab that was about to rappel with her. Roscoe's trusting eyes followed her while he hovered close to her chest, always eager to work.

"That's right. It's showtime. We've got to find that little boy."

Roscoe wouldn't understand, but they were armed and ready for anything or anyone they might confront in the dense woods that belonged to Canyon Air Force Base in the Hill Country of Texas. This reserve, mostly used for training, covered hundreds of acres and could hide a person for weeks if not months. Right now, she had to find a lost little boy and watch her back for a serial killer who'd escaped from prison in the spring and was reported to be back in these woods. Boyd Sullivan, known as the Red Rose Killer because he always left one red rose to warn his victims and one after he'd killed them, was a dangerous, deranged man.

He'd killed five people over two years ago in his home-town of Dill, Texas. He'd been put in prison for those killings, but he'd escaped and made his way to Canyon Air Force Base to kill again. Two of those he'd mur-dered had been friends and coworkers of Ava's. But he hadn't left it at that. He'd also let out two hundred or so dogs from the Military Working Dog K-9 kennels lo-cated on the base. Let them out to run wild. Some that had suffered PTSD were still roaming around these woods. Now seven-year-old Turner Johnson, the son of Colonel Gregory and Mrs. Marilyn Johnson, had gone missing from his backyard this morning. The boy was up against wild animals, dogs with PTSD and a serial killer who wouldn't think twice about nabbing the kid for leverage.

Her focus humming on high alert, Ava checked her weapons and equipment one more time. Then she pat-ted the alert K-9 on his furry head. "Ready?"

Roscoe woofed his reply.

Nodding, she scooted to the open side of the chop-per and let her booted feet dangle out, Roscoe's warm breath hitting the inch or so of skin she had showing outside of her heavy camo uniform, protective combat vest, knapsack and M16 rifle.

Above her, a crew member adjusted the carabiner holding the pulleys that would hoist both Ava and Ros-coe so they could rappel down, each with their own pulley to hold them securely together.

Halfway down, she listened to the chopper's crew reporting back and forth while she hovered and checked below. Nothing but heavy woods, scattered rocks and hills, and a hint of clay here and there. But somewhere out there was a lost, scared little seven-year-old boy.

"Hold on, Roscoe."

Something whizzed past her like a gnat. But even with the chopper's bellowing roar all around her, she heard the ding of metal hitting metal.

And then she saw it. The ricochet of a bullet hitting the fuselage. Someone was shooting at them.

The chopper banked left, causing Ava to shift on the rope. Above her, the gunner motioned for her to come back up.

Then she heard the pilot. "We need to abort."

"Negative," she said through the mic attached to her helmet. "I'm going in."

With that, she steadied herself and, along with Roscoe, hurried the few yards to the ground, relieved to see that team member Chad Watson came down seconds after her. Ava dropped, unhooked the harnesses and turned on a low crouch, ready to return fire.

"Chad, take Custer to the south and wait," she said, referring to Chad's K-9 partner. "Start your search there."

"We have a situation here, ma'am," he reported back.

"*I* have a situation, and I can handle it," she replied. "And Buster will cover me, right, Buster?"

"Affirmative, ma'am. I'm about twenty yards behind you."

Buster Elliott, all two hundred and fifty pounds of him, was with Security Forces. He'd been assigned to watch her six while she searched for the boy. Good thing, too.

More shots hit all around her, and Buster returned fire while the chopper hovered.

"Don't engage," she warned the gunner and Buster through the mic. "The boy could be down here."

Heavy footsteps stomped through the woods, echoing toward her. Ava belly-crawled to an outcropping of shrubs and rocks, Roscoe doing the same behind her.

Then she lifted up to a crouch.

Letting out a gasp, Ava stared at the man standing a few feet away with what looked like an M4 aimed at her.

The Red Rose Killer.

He hadn't wasted any time in confronting her. Now her only concern was for the boy. Did this monster already have Turner?

"I'm not here to hurt you," Boyd Sullivan said, anger and annoyance singing through each word, his blue eyes cold and icy. Backing away, he held his rifle trained on her, but his gaze darted back and forth. "Tell your man to back off."

Ava lifted her fist to tell Buster to hold fire. Then she held her rifle trained on the tall blond man wearing an old beret. "What do you want?"

Roscoe hadn't moved from his alert, but the big dog's low growl indicated he was very aware of this intruder. Buster should still be nearby, too. Ava knew he'd have her back and even as big as he was, he'd use stealth while he kept his rifle trained on Boyd Sullivan. He'd also fire if he had to.

"Pretend you never saw me," Sullivan said. "That's all I need right now."

Ava didn't dare let the killer know she recognized him or ask if he'd seen the boy, in case he wasn't aware. And she didn't get a chance to react any further.

Bullets pierced the air again in a rapid explosion.

Ava hit the ground and ordered Roscoe to do the same. Buster returned fire and took off through the woods, all the while communicating with the hovering chopper above.

And then it was over. The woods went silent. Ava lifted her head and tugged at her rifle. Still lying low, she adjusted her aim. But Boyd Sullivan, the man known as the Red Rose Killer, had disappeared back into the woods.

The shooter had covered his escape.

"You saw the Red Rose Killer?"

Rain flowed like a dam had opened all around FBI Special Agent Oliver Davison. Tired and in need of about two days of uninterrupted sleep, Oliver stared at the tougher-than-nails woman who'd called him to these woods to report what she'd just been through. Tall, redheaded, brown-eyed and clearly in no mood to bicker with him, Senior Airman Ava Esposito appeared to have things under control.

A Security Forces Military Working Dog handler who was used to rappelling out of choppers alongside her K-9 partner and working with Search-and-Rescue to find injured or compromised troops the world over, she didn't seem the least bit fazed by the gully washer trying to knock them to their knees. Or the fact that she'd come face-to-face with a notorious killer.

Come face-to-face and lived, at that. Which was why Oliver had a hard time believing her.

The Red Rose Killer didn't mess around. Boyd Sullivan hadn't made it through basic training and never had a relationship last longer than a few months. The man had gone off the deep end in a way that had become very personal to Oliver. Sullivan had killed five people in Dill, Texas, where he'd grown up, including Madison Ackler, who had been Oliver's fiancée at the time of her death. His fiancée…but she'd also been involved with Boyd Sullivan when she'd died.

Oliver had been in on the hunt and the arrest for those killings two years ago and he'd been relieved when Sullivan was sent to prison. But the Red Rose Killer had escaped in April and apparently made it to the base and allegedly killed his Basic Training commander, Chief Master Sergeant Clint Lockwood, two overnight-shift K-9 trainers and a commissary cook, whose ID he had used to get him on and off the base. He'd also let most of the K-9s go in an attempt to distract the entire Security Forces unit. They'd been searching for him for months.

"I can't believe this," he said, voicing his doubts. Oliver still remembered what the Red Rose Killer was capable of.

Ava nodded, her camouflage uniform weighed down with a backpack, weapons and equipment. All wet now. "Believe it, Special Agent. I'm still in shock myself." Shaking water off her helmet, she added, "We'd expected this but I didn't think he'd show up the minute my boots hit the ground."

"Where?" Oliver asked, ready to get down to business. He had to admit, she looked a little shook-up but she was holding things together. Meanwhile, he had to tell himself to stay calm.

Pointing to a thicket behind him, she said, "Right over there."

Lightning flashed like a spotlight, followed by a

rolling thunder that stomped through the trees and shook the woods.

Figured everything would start happening during one of the worst storms of late summer.

After four years of living and working in the San Antonio FBI Bureau, Oliver still hated these Texas downpours and the humidity that always surrounded them. At times like this, he missed the New York town where he'd grown up.

Pushing away memories, Oliver focused on Ava Esposito, questions rolling through his mind.

Leaning in so he could make himself heard over the thunder and lightning putting on a show over the forest reserve behind the base, he stared at the stubborn woman standing beside him.

"So, Senior Airman Esposito, you're sure the person you saw was Boyd Sullivan—the Red Rose Killer?"

"Yes," she said on an impatient note, brown eyes making him think of how much he wanted a cup of coffee right now. "First, we were shot at when we rappelled out of the chopper. And now this."

"Who is *we*?"

"Myself, K-9 handler Chad Watson and Security Forces officer Buster Elliott. The crew wanted us to abort, but we were halfway down, so we dropped and spread out. The shots continued while the chopper circled. But our gunner couldn't fire, because of the concerns for the boy."

Turner Johnson, the seven-year-old who'd gone missing while playing in his backyard this morning. The boy's high-ranking parents were beside themselves because the whole area had been warned about an escaped convict possibly being in the vicinity. Just one more wrinkle that concerned Oliver more than a little bit. The killer had reportedly left the base a few days ago but they'd had signs over the last couple days that he might be back in the area. Now they had proof. But they also had to search for a rambunctious kid known for sneaking into the woods behind his house.

"And what happened next?"

"We hit the dirt, returned a round of fire and the shooting stopped long enough for me to come upon Sullivan. He told me to hold off my man, so he must have seen Buster and Chad rappelling down behind me and he must have known that Chad went in the other direction. Then the shooting started up again, and he got away. I called you immediately and then we went about our business. Buster searched for Sullivan but to no avail, and Chad went off on another search grid. Roscoe alerted in this spot a few minutes later."

"You were right to call me."

"Yes, but now I'm regretting that decision. We've got a whole team on the alert and you're wasting time *not* believing me."

"I'm trying to get a handle on this. Go on."

Taking a breath, she squared her shoulders. "Roscoe started digging and I tried to follow his lead until you got here. But I can assure you the man I saw was Sullivan. I certainly know his face and I know what he's capable of doing."

Oliver saw a slight tremble forming on her lips. Delayed reaction. He had to keep her talking, however. "What happened between you two? Did you try to detain him?"

Ava gave him a look that asked, *So this is how you're gonna play this?*

"Sullivan held an M4 on me. He was wearing a tight uniform that obviously didn't belong to him and a black tam. He looked me in the eye and said, 'I'm not here to hurt you.'"

Motioning behind them, she said, "He also told me to pretend I'd never seen him and ordered me to call off my guard. I didn't get to question him since more gunfire erupted and Sullivan used the distraction to get away."

"Just like that?"

"Yes, just like that," she said, grinding out each word. "Last time we saw him, he was headed west."

Oliver felt a headache coming on. His black water-resistant FBI jacket sparkled with fat raindrops. "But he told you he wasn't shooting at *you*? And he just walked away?"

"He told me he wasn't going to hurt me," she said again, her porcelain skin damp and dewy. "What part of *I stood face-to-face with the Red Rose Killer* don't you understand?"

"I don't understand any of this," Oliver replied, matching her inch for inch since she was almost as tall as him, his eyes holding hers in a stubborn stand-off that not even a torrential rain could stop. "The man killed five people in his hometown and he's gone on a killing spree on this base throughout the summer. Not to mention he has a whole target list that he *wants* to kill. And we have reason to believe he also killed Airman Drew Golosky a few days ago in order to get his uniform and ID for base access. But he tells you he's not going to hurt you?"

"Yes, Special Agent Davison," Ava Esposito said again, aggravation deeply embedded in her words.

"But someone did shoot at me and then Boyd Sullivan headed into the woods. I think that shooter, along with my K-9 partner and Buster watching my back, saved me."

Stomping water off her boots, she added, "The shooter must have been covering Sullivan. If that's the case, then he has some help. Which we've suspected all along. So let me get back to my work, and you go find the Red Rose Killer and whoever else is out there."

He wanted to find Boyd Sullivan, all right. Especially since he had a personal beef with the man. Most of the investigative team knew Oliver's history with Boyd Sullivan, even if they didn't bring it up. Oliver was the only one who knew the whole truth about Madison's past, and that she'd been briefly involved with Sullivan in high school and again a few years ago when she'd been dating Oliver. Her murder was still too personal for Oliver to talk about, and he couldn't risk being pulled off the case because of his personal interest. His SAC had approved his coming here, with the stipulation that he didn't have a personal vendetta. But how could he not?

Needing the whole picture, he asked, "Did you send your K-9 partner after him?"

"Roscoe alerted on this cave," she replied, pointing to the jagged four-foot-high rock face covered in bushes. "I kept him here because I was concerned about getting shot before I could locate the missing boy who might be inside."

A little boy missing in six hundred acres of dense thicket overgrown with clusters of trees and heavy brush. A place where dark caves and craggy hills and rocky bluffs made searching that much harder. A place where all types of predators, from poisonous snakes to wild animals of all shapes and sizes, lurked about.

Oliver worried about the worst kind of predator. The Red Rose Killer. He'd have no qualms about killing a child.

"But you haven't found the boy?"

Rain rolled off her helmet while disappointment and annoyance singed hot through her pretty eyes. "No, Turner Johnson was not inside the cave, so obviously I haven't found the boy. But I will. Roscoe is never wrong."

Oliver squinted into the wet, chilly woods. All around them, Security Forces, the Office of Special Investigations and the Military Working Dog handlers moved like hulking shadows while choppers whirled overhead. Crime-scene techs searched for evidence and bullet fragments or shell casings. Boyd Sullivan was out there somewhere. Probably long gone by now, however, since the woods had become overrun with air force personnel.

Oliver looked toward the heavens. "A missing seven-year-old and a serial killer on the loose. In the same woods. This is not good. So not good."

Her hostile gaze affirmed that summary. "No, and I really need to get back to Roscoe and his find."

Touching her arm, he glanced at the patient golden-coated Labrador retriever and said, "I understand you want to explore Roscoe's discovery. I'm anxious to catch up with the team searching for Boyd Sullivan. But I need to ask you a few more questions."

She glared at him for a moment and then checked on the K-9 eager to dig in the mud. "I've told you what happened and now I'm going to do what I came here to do. Because whatever's buried here might give us a clue to find the boy."

Special Agent Oliver Davison stared at Ava, skepticism heavy in his green eyes. The man obviously didn't believe a word of what she'd just told him. And he was seriously beginning to get on her already singed nerves.

But he did have a point. Why had Sullivan allowed her to live when he'd killed so many people already?

He'd been sent to prison for those killings a few years ago. He wanted revenge, and he was willing to kill anyone who stood in his way. He was armed and dangerous, and yes, she'd let him get away. That didn't sit well with Ava, but she had to focus on the mission at hand.

Even while the creepiness factor made her want to take off and track the killer.

Sullivan earned his name because he always left a red rose and a note stating "I'm coming for you" to warn his victims, and another note stating "Got you" after he'd killed them. Four other base personnel were targeted, so the base had been on high alert all summer. Boyd had a way on and off the base and Ava believed, along with her team members, that he was hiding out in these woods and using uniforms and IDs from some of the other airmen he'd killed to keep up the charade.

Now she'd seen the killer with her own eyes and this agent doubted her and wanted to waste her time while a child could get caught in the cross fire. Glaring up at him, Ava saw something besides a steely determination in the special agent's green eyes.

Sadness. Then it hit her. He'd been involved with

one of the victims from Dill. She didn't know the whole story, but rumors had circulated. Now was not the time to go into that, however.

"I need to get back to work," she said on a calm note, hoping to cut him some slack. "Roscoe's waiting to do his job."

"Just a few more details," he insisted, a stubborn glint in his eyes.

Remembering how her heart had gone haywire earlier, Ava thought about Boyd Sullivan's weird reaction to finding her there. Dressed in dirty, ill-fitting camouflage, he'd looked wild and disoriented, but he'd been carrying an arsenal of weapons.

Thinking about it now, she held herself rigid so she wouldn't get the shakes.

To stay focused, she stared at Oliver Davison, taking in how his green eyes matched the lush foliage all around them. "Buster went after Sullivan and tracked him, but lost him. Chad and Custer had an alert in another area due east. They couldn't make it back in time."

"Why didn't you send Roscoe after Sullivan?"

"And risk losing my partner *and* the boy's location? I sent Buster after Sullivan because I was afraid the boy might still be in the area. Turner Johnson is my first obligation."

Oliver pushed water off his thick dark hair. "So you let Boyd Sullivan slip through your fingers?"

"I don't like your tone, Special Agent."

"Well, I don't like losing a wanted serial killer, Airman Esposito."

"I'm here to find the boy. It's your job to track Boyd

Sullivan, and apparently you haven't been very successful so far."

"Ouch, that hurt."

She almost laughed, but this was not funny. She understood how he wanted to get his man, but he was stepping on her toes right now. "I'm going to see what Roscoe has found, if you don't mind. You have a whole team here to search for Sullivan."

"I guess I'm dismissed."

She turned in time to see the flare of both anger and admiration in his interesting eyes. "You could say that, yes."

But he called out to her. "Hey, if Boyd Sullivan wasn't shooting at you, then who was, and why?"

TWO

Ava wanted to find the answer to Oliver Davison's questions, too, but right now she had to get back to *her* search. Not only was she concerned for the boy's safety, but Turner's parents wielded a lot of clout. The whole base was on high alert over this. The negative press wouldn't be good either.

After Mr. FBI left, Chad Watson came bounding up, his blond hair glistening wet, K-9 Custer sloshing through the mud ahead of him. Chad had transferred from Security Forces to the Military Working Dog program and now excelled at his job.

"Nothing on the alert we had. Custer did a thorough grid but didn't find anything regarding the boy." Then he showed her a paper evidence bag inside his uniform pocket. "But we did find this."

Ava stared down into the open pocket, her hand shielding the bag from the rain. A Buff. A navy floral headband which could have gotten lost by anyone hiking through these woods, but it did look feminine. "Keep it bagged so we can give it to Forensics," she said, deciding anything could be evidence.

Chad nodded. "I'll take Custer and do a grid to the north."

"Good idea. While you do that, we'll dig here," she said. Then she radioed Buster. "Need you back at the search site."

Ava gave Roscoe the order and they both worked beside him, using their gloved hands to sift through the mud and dirt surrounding the cave, but to no avail. Yet Roscoe didn't let it go. He pawed and whined and stared at her for his next command.

"Nothing," she said. After radioing in her request and cordoning off the area where they'd already dug, they kept searching and calling out for Turner Johnson, going back over the area in every direction. But the boy didn't respond and Roscoe didn't alert anywhere else. Her partner returned to stand firm in front of the cave, so she checked inside again but didn't find anything.

"Roscoe, boy, I know you are smart and there is something here, but it's getting dark and we're gonna have to let the next shift take over."

Roscoe gave her a solemn stare and then looked toward the cave again. But he was so well trained, he didn't make a move.

Thirty minutes later, the storm raged on, thunder and lightning indicating it had stalled over these woods, lessening visibility to a minimum.

Ava got a message to return to the base with Security Forces. It was too risky to bring in the chopper but the night shift would hike in from the trail and take over.

"I don't want to leave," she said, rain slashing at her with a needle-sharp consistency. "It's getting dark. I'm so worried about that little boy."

Buster stood like a dark statue, his deep brown eyes on her. "I can stay and help the relief team, ma'am."

"It's okay, Buster. We've got a fresh second shift arriving. They'll set up camp and keep searching as long as they can. We all know the first forty-eight hours are crucial in finding a missing child."

"And it's only been a few hours," Buster replied. "With this storm, things go up a notch."

So much could happen. The boy could slip and fall into rushing water from the nearby rivers and creeks. Flash floods were common in this area during storms. She prayed he'd found a safe place to shelter. Prayed he was still alive. At least the kid was a Cub Scout. Maybe his training would kick in. The temperature would be warm, but with this rain everything took on a chill.

"We have to rest and regroup tomorrow. The Amber Alert is out on the whole base and the surrounding area. The second shift is already arriving, and Chad is briefing them."

"What if—"

"I know what you're thinking," she said to the gentle giant. "What if Boyd Sullivan has the boy and that's why he didn't shoot us? What if he had to get back to the kid?"

"Yes," Buster said. "Exactly. He sure did run fast when those other bullets started flying."

"Yes, he did, didn't he?" Ava wasn't sure if the bullets had been for Boyd or her, or both. But her gut told her the shooter was covering Sullivan. Maybe he didn't kill Ava because he'd seen the heavy activity in the woods and it was too messy and risky.

Whatever his reasons, she thanked God she was still alive.

When the second shift had arrived and she'd up-dated the head of Security Forces, Captain Justin Blackwood, Ava trudged to the trail and got in an SF SUV with Roscoe safe in a kennel and returned to the base, exhausted and disappointed.

"I'm going back out first thing in the morning," she told lead handler Master Sergeant Westley James after she'd updated several team members in the MWD training center conference room. "I promised Mrs. Johnson I wouldn't give up on finding her son."

"I agree," her boss said, his blue eyes giving away nothing as the others filed out. "We're running out of time on the boy and we now know Boyd Sullivan could be living in those woods. Which means our ear-lier reports on his whereabouts were wrong. He's back in the area."

"Yes, we are running out of time," a deep voice said from the doorway of the conference room. "And now you're in danger, too, Senior Airman Esposito."

Ava whirled to find a very wet, haggard-looking FBI agent staring over at them. "Special Agent Davi-son, I take it you didn't find Boyd Sullivan after all?"

Oliver looked as defeated as she felt. "Nope, and that storm and a pitch-dark sky brought everything to a grinding halt. But we found signs of what looked like camping areas in two different locations, so we bagged what could be evidence. I'm going to grab a shower in the locker room and then, Airman Esposito, I'd like a word with you on how we can coordinate our searches tomorrow."

"I'm off to get a shower, too," she said, thinking

she'd head in the opposite direction of him. "Meet me back here at 19:00?"

He glanced at his fancy watch. "Sounds good."

Westley James cut his gaze from Ava to the FBI agent but didn't say a word. Then he grabbed his beret. "I'm going home now to be with Felicity."

Staff Sergeant Felicity Monroe, a former K-9 handler and now the base photographer and Westley's wife, was still considered a target of the Red Rose Killer. He'd want to make sure she was safe, of course.

"Give her my best, sir."

"Will do. And, Ava, Agent Davison is right. You're in danger now, too. Sullivan might have let you go today, but you're on his radar now. He can't leave any loose threads."

Ava nodded and turned to go, conscious of Oliver Davison's green-eyed gaze following her every step.

"How 'bout we get out of here and go to the Winged Java?" she said once she was clean and dry, her damp hair curled up under her navy beret, her blue T-shirt clean and fresh against her ABUs.

"Ah, the notorious coffee shop where flyboys and air force cadets hang out and brag about their daring deeds?" he asked, his dark hair shimmering and glossy from his shower, the scent of soap all around him. "I imagine you have a lot to brag about."

Actually, she just wanted to get away from prying eyes and go over the details of the Boyd Sullivan case and how it would interfere with finding Turner Johnson.

"I don't like braggadocios."

"Did you really just say *braggadocios*?"

She laughed. "I can teach you a lot of new words."

"I suppose you can. Let's go."

She started toward the door, her keys in her hand, and tried really hard to forget that he was good-looking and overconfident. He'd changed to a white button-down shirt and dark slacks, which made him stand out like a stranger in a spaghetti Western.

He beat her to the door and opened it. "I'll drive."

Ava scooted around him and out the door. "I'll meet you there."

"Afraid to ride with me, Esposito?"

"No, Special Agent. I can go home straight from there. Since we have special permission to take our K-9 partners home until the Red Rose Killer is caught, I have Roscoe to consider."

"Of course." He nodded and jingled his key fob. "I'll see you in a few."

The Winged Java was a legendary coffee shop, just as Oliver Davison had mentioned, but it was also a great place to relax and grab a burger or the best pizza in Texas, according to Ava's way of thinking. And because she was hungry and needed coffee and maybe a slice of pie, she grinned when she pulled up in the parking lot.

"Roscoe, guess where we are?"

Roscoe loved the Winged Java, too, since K-9s were as welcome here as humans. Maybe even more so. The manager always gave her treats to give to Roscoe at her discretion. Ava could leave him in the temperature-controlled kennel in her SUV, but she preferred having him with her whenever she could.

Normally Military Working Dogs didn't go home with their handlers, but base commander Lieutenant

General Nathan Hall had given them special permission to keep the seasoned K-9s with them because of the brutal murders on base. Over the last few months, she'd gotten used to having Roscoe around. And so had several of the base restaurants. Because he was trained in search and rescue, Roscoe was more acclimated socially than the German shepherds and Belgian Malinois that did heavy battle duty, but he still had to be handled carefully in social situations.

Checking Roscoe's uniform, a vest that identified him as a Military Working Dog so people would use caution when approaching him, Ava knew Roscoe would be on his best behavior.

But she wasn't so sure about the intense man waiting for her in a corner booth. Taking a breath after spotting Oliver Davison through the window, she stared at the giant white coffee mug mural on the front of the building in an effort to stall this meeting.

Flanked by two wings that were lit up with red, white and blue lights, the cup showcased a chevron emblem. Above the cup, the café's name was done in black. The Winged Java. Inside, the walls were covered with photos and posters lauding the pride this area held for the base and the air force, some of those photos capturing shots of the Military Working Dog handlers and their dogs in training and on the job.

After sitting there for five minutes, dread weighing her down because she didn't want this man interfering in her job or her life, Ava went in and faced Oliver Davison.

"I ordered two coffees," he said, the scent of something clean and tropical hitting the air as she settled into the booth across from him. "I've seen you inhaling it in the break room."

That comment garnered him a concentrated stare. "Spying on me?"

"No, just part of the job to stay on the alert and observe people. I mean, we've never been officially introduced but you are always around."

She'd whizz through the break room with a dare to anybody who messed with her, but she'd stop on a dime to pet a dog or talk to a fellow handler. And when she smiled…

She was not smiling now, he noticed. "Does that bother you? Me always being around, that is?"

"Should it?"

She didn't look at the menu when the waitress showed up with their coffee and asked for their orders. "Cheeseburger, medium rare, with fries on the side. No mayo but loaded down."

"A woman who knows her own mind," the waitress said through a chuckle. "And for you, sir?"

Oliver glanced at the menu and looked up at Ava. "I'll have what she's having and hope I can eat the whole thing."

"Try to keep up," the freckled older woman said. Then she greeted Roscoe where he lay beside the booth with a "Hey, boy," before she walked away with a smile.

"They seem to know you here," Oliver said.

Ava's brown eyes turned a warm honey pecan. "I come here a lot."

"I've been in a few times," he offered. "But I just get a lot of stares."

"I wonder why that is," she quipped, obviously enjoying making him squirm a bit.

"Maybe they know I'm an outsider, or, worse, a dreaded Yankee from New York. Took the San Antonio Bureau a while to adjust to my accent and my bluntness."

"*We* don't judge that way," she said through a wry grin. "But they might wonder about the suit thing in the heat of summer. Here we go with jeans, T-shirts and boots when we have downtime."

"Hey, I left my coat and tie in the car, and I have a pair of boots."

"I'm guessing you've never taken 'em out of the box."

Feeling sheepish, he lowered his head. "Once... maybe."

After their food came, he leaned back and stared at the table. "What a day. Sorry you didn't find the boy."

Ava stared down at the table and then checked the parking lot. Like him, she probably never let her guard down. "I talked to Marilyn Johnson when we got back to base. The poor woman is distraught. Their only child. She's afraid Turner could have been taken but he has gone into the woods beyond their yard without permission before."

"We couldn't be sure he was still around," Oliver reminded her. "And now the killer has gone to ground. If he has the kid, this goes from bad to worse."

"We have people still looking but, like you, they had to slow things until this storm passes." Staring out into the light drizzle, she added, "I don't want to think about that little boy out in the woods in the rain and dark."

"Same with the Red Rose Killer," Oliver replied. "I sure don't want to think about him out there with the boy. He could use the boy for leverage or as a way out of here. I'm going back out first thing tomorrow."

"Me, too."

"He's left way too many threatening notes and now he's back to make good on them," Oliver said. "He's getting onto the base with other people's IDs and, just as we've suspected, he obviously has an accomplice, based on what happened today. He has to have found a way from the reserve to the base, which is probably how he got away again this time. I'm praying the boy isn't with him."

"I'm hoping the boy had the good sense to hide," Ava replied, her tone full of worry. "We couldn't get a bead on Sullivan. The chopper couldn't land in that dense area, but they did a good job of dropping us," she said. "I hope the night crew can make some headway since I didn't get anywhere."

"You're good at your job," Oliver said. "That's obvious." Then he made a snap decision. "Save the air force some money and let me give you a ride tomorrow. Unless, of course, you really do want to rappel down a rope dangling from a hovering forty-million-dollar chopper again."

"Hmm." Surprise on her pretty face, she held her hands up in the air and moved them up and down as if weighing something. "Those are my only choices?"

He laughed at that. She had a quick wit and a no-nonsense attitude that was refreshing. "You don't give an inch, do you?"

"Should I?"

"I'm trying to figure that out," he said, his eyes holding hers again. "And…while we're at it, tell me why you wanted to have this conversation away from the office, and maybe tell me a little bit about you, too."

She matched his gaze and shook her head. "I'm not sure myself why I decided to hold this meeting here, but you know how things go. Prying eyes and listening ears. I'm working to move up a rank. Right now, it's hard to trust anyone. My team is solid but we've had some major leaks with the so-called Anonymous Blogger. But one thing I can tell you—I'm here to discuss the investigation, not share the intimate details of my life. Especially with a man who seems to read people with an ease that leaves them floundering."

"Me?" Impressed that *she* could read him so well, he shrugged. "Again, part of the job. I'm curious about what makes people tick." Then to gain her trust, he leaned in. "In your case, I'd really like to get to know you. Your team is so tight, it's been hard for me to break through."

"And you think I'll be the one to crack?"

"No, I think you're the toughest one of all. But I'd appreciate knowing more about you."

Looking skeptical, she shrugged right back at him. "Not much to tell. I decided in high school to join the air force. I took a helicopter ride once out on Galveston beach when I was a preteen and fell in love. That, coupled with not knowing what to do with my life, made me want to travel and find adventure. Didn't take much from there to want to be a chopper pilot."

"Can you fly one?"

"I was headed that way but my plans changed. I love what I do now and if I work hard I just might make it to staff sergeant."

"I'd like to hear more of that story."

She took a sip of her coffee. "Since you're insisting on that, I'll need to hear more about you, too, then."

Oliver stared out into the night, wondering how much she already knew since he'd had to disclose his involvement with Madison to Ava's superiors. "Okay, but you might not like what you hear."

THREE

Ava's heart hadn't jumped this much since basic training. She'd heard enough to be cautious, of course.

Oliver Davison had been around off and on for months now and he'd barely noticed Ava, so why did she suddenly have strange currents moving through her system each time he looked at her? Probably because today, he'd focused on her and implied she'd failed. But then, he'd failed, too. And he'd lost someone he loved through a brutal murder. The team had been briefed about him before he ever arrived. His fiancée, Madison Ackler, had been the Red Rose Killer's first victim. Ava didn't know if that was a coincidence or there was a history there, but she wasn't going to grill the man on it. She did know that Madison Ackler and Boyd Sullivan had gone to high school together.

She had to remember that and try to be kind about things. But while she felt sympathy for his loss, she still had a job to do. Or maybe she was tense around him because she'd lost someone she loved, too, and they had that in common.

Stop making excuses.

They had been forced together but in the worst kind

of way. Over death and a missing child and an evil, sick man who wouldn't stop until they caught him. But that didn't make her ready to share her past or her other failures with Oliver Davison. She didn't want him to do an FBI analysis on her either.

"Hey, are you okay?" he asked, true concern in the question.

"I will be," she replied. And then to hide all the emotions boiling up inside of her, she tore into her burger. Stress eating to the rescue.

It had been a long, tough day and he'd gotten in her way and gotten *to* her. That wouldn't happen again. Dealing with an intense, dogged FBI agent one-on-one was different from watching him across the room. Not that she'd done that. Okay, maybe once or twice. And he must have noticed her, too, since he knew she guzzled coffee like a brewing machine.

But enough of that for now.

"Tomorrow, I go back to the spot Roscoe alerted on and we dig some more. Roscoe is never wrong, so there's something there we're missing. I hope whatever was buried there didn't get washed away. And, Agent Davison, I really need you to stay out of my way."

"I was in your way today?"

Yes, you with your green eyes and that messy hair and your black working T-shirt. You have those sad eyes and that bad attitude. Yes, you.

"You held me up with your repeated, pointed questions."

"Part of my job."

"Don't do it again. And please stop using that excuse."

He grinned and dipped a french fry into a glob of

ketchup. "I'll take the west end of the woods and you can take the east."

"Agreed." Then she took a sip of the water the waitress had also brought and wondered if the air-conditioning had conked out. "I'm concerned that Sullivan might have the boy. He could have easily killed me today, but he didn't. Someone shot at me, though. I don't know if that someone was with him or after him, but I'm thinking with him because that makes more sense to me."

"And protecting him from you as you suspected," Oliver replied. "They could use the boy as leverage for an escape."

"I've already considered that, but why didn't they do that today?"

"Exactly, which is why I questioned you so heavily earlier," he said, his tone apologetic now. "We have to consider every angle. You know how it goes with serial killers."

"No, I don't know how it goes, but when I saw him today I certainly understood the horror of what he's done. I could have easily died out there and he would have gotten away with murder again. I hope we find him so I can ask him why he let me live."

"I'd like to ask him a few things, too."

Ava felt that tug again. Her heartstrings were getting a workout today. "I'm sure we'll have to stand in line," she replied, trying to stay on topic.

"Maybe you just showed up at the wrong time, surprised him and caught him off guard. Or maybe he knew you had a detail on you and he'd be shot dead if he did try to kill you."

"Buster was right there, but he didn't get in a shot because everything happened so fast."

"You said it yourself. Buster's being there along with Roscoe helped to save you." Oliver dipped another fry. "And the shooter saved Boyd Sullivan. It makes sense he's had a willing accomplice all this time."

"I don't know what to think," Ava admitted. "Turner Johnson's parents are so distraught and angry right now, it's hard to watch. And I get that. First, the kid goes missing from his yard and now they find out a dangerous serial killer is out in those woods, too. Then a storm hits. I can't imagine that kind of fear."

Oliver drained his coffee, his brow furrowed in frustration. "We have to hope he's found shelter, at least."

"I have another concern to consider, too," she said. "Those missing dogs Sullivan let out of the training center that night when he killed two of my coworkers. Some of the dogs still missing suffer severe PTSD and they could be roaming those woods. If Turner Johnson happens to come upon one of them, he could get hurt."

"You need to be careful on all fronts," Oliver said, his eyes holding concern again. "You got off easy today, Airman Esposito. But I have a gut feeling the Red Rose Killer is not done with you yet."

"Call me Ava," she said. "Since you're trying to scare me to death and all, I feel as if we're bonding."

"Call me Oliver, since I can thank you for the heartburn I'm surely going to have later," he replied, his expression wry. "I'm not trying to scare you. After watching you in action today, I don't think you can be rattled. And *that* scares *me*. Sullivan's a dangerous man."

From the way Oliver said that, she was reminded of

how personal this had become for him. After all, he had a very good reason to hunt down Boyd Sullivan.

But she wasn't going to pry into the horror of that reason. She just prayed they'd both find what they were looking for.

"Okay, Roscoe, let's do this again," Ava said after Oliver had walked with her and Buster back to the marked spot the next morning. Word from the night shift wasn't good. There'd been no sign of the boy or the Red Rose Killer and no alerts from the K-9s. But they'd found several fresh campsites and patches of spent shells.

"Some from our weapons and some from whoever was shooting at you with an M4 rifle," Oliver reported. "Whoever it is, thankfully, they aren't a very good shot."

The storm had passed but it had left a lot of broken limbs and washed-over bramble in its path. Ava accepted that they wouldn't get very far today, but determination kept her from giving up. The sun was shining today, though, and even at seven in the morning, the late summer heat promised to be scalding hot.

Leaving his official SUV up on the muddy road into this area, Oliver gave instructions to a team that had arrived in another vehicle and brought off-road vehicles with them to continue the search. Then he and Ava trekked through the woods to begin another grueling day. But he'd told Ava he wanted to check around this spot again, too, since Sullivan had been in the area.

Oliver walked around the area by the cave, watching as Roscoe took up right where he'd left off after Ava had let him sniff the miniature toy and the boy's cap she'd brought back with them again today.

"Find," she told the Labrador.

Roscoe started digging again in the same spot near the entrance of the tiny cave.

Oliver hovered off to the side, doing his own search. They really hadn't shared anything much about each other last night. Ava had realized he was good at his job and determined to find Boyd Sullivan. Now she wanted to know more about him, which shouldn't be front and center on her mind today. But that sadness that shadowed him had clutched her heart.

"I thought you were leaving," she said when Oliver finished his search and came back to stand with her. "Did you find anything?"

Oliver gave her a questioning stare. "I am leaving, and no, I didn't find anything."

He looked as if he wanted to say more, but instead he nodded and turned to catch up with the team that today included Master Sergeant Westley James, Office of Special Investigations Special Officer Ian Steffen, Security Forces Captain Justin Blackwood and several others who worked with the SF, OSI or the Military Working Dog program.

Everyone wanted to capture Boyd Sullivan. But she knew they were all concerned about the boy, too.

Focusing on Roscoe and armed with a small hand-held shovel, Ava bent to help dig. Yesterday, she'd allowed Roscoe to sniff the toy and baseball cap that belonged to Turner Johnson and she'd done the same again today, praying the rain hadn't washed away the scent Roscoe had picked up then.

"Hey, be careful," Oliver said before heading out.

Ava called him back. "Oliver, hold on."

He came hurrying back, his serviceable boots kicking up mud. "Yeah?"

"Chad Watson and his partner, Custer, did find one thing yesterday. A Buff."

He looked confused. "Buff?"

"A stretchy headband-type head cover. Dark navy and floral. Chad turned it over to the crime lab."

Oliver took off his dark shades and squinted. "Possibly belonging to a woman?"

"Possibly."

"Interesting. Thanks—I'll check with Forensics later." Then he gave her a smile and put his shades back on. "Talk to you soon."

Ava ignored the warm rush of comfort that encased her and instead watched where Roscoe kept pawing away in a spot near a small rock anchored beside the entrance of the cave.

Buster stood a few feet away with his rifle held near his chest, ever vigilant. He'd been a linebacker in college, and he was six feet of solid wall with a teddy bear's heart. But fierce when it came to protecting his colleagues and his country.

"What is it?" she asked Roscoe, knowing he'd do his best to show her. Ava did another scan of the rocks and mud.

Then she saw a tiny spot of red poking out of the wet dirt. Getting on her knees, she immediately praised Roscoe. "Good find. Way to go!"

After telling him to stay, she took her shovel and managed to dig around what looked like a small toy similar to the one Turner's parents had given her yesterday.

"Got it," she said, clearing the last of the mud away so she could lift the toy out. Wedged between the small rock and the outside wall of the cave, the toy had become jammed in a corner instead of washing away along with the dirt that had covered it before. A little red-and-white robot with big black eyes and a tiny black nylon cape. A small duct-taped label was hidden underneath the cape. And the name Turner Johnson was marked across it in permanent black ink.

Roscoe woofed his approval. The plastic and the material could contain oils and epidermis particles from the boy's hands, some of which would be buried in the grooves and seams inside the toy. The rock had protected the little robot from getting too wet. So had Turner Johnson lost this toy or had he been smart enough to hide it between the rock and the cave wall?

After calling in the find, Ava and Roscoe started out again. Roscoe seemed determined to go toward the west, so Ava made sure she alerted their path to everyone patrolling and searching the woods. They started tracking again in an area called the scent cone, which worked with the breezes, temperatures and humidity to carry a scent from the last known place the missing boy had been seen. Ava started at a higher elevation just past the first cave and worked downwind from where the boy had disappeared, letting Roscoe move in a crisscross fashion back and forth through dirt, mud, rotting tree trunks, rocky terrain and dense foliage while she kept a vigilant watch for an ambush.

No one had been shot at today, so that was good. But it could also mean Sullivan had left and possibly taken the boy with him.

Even with the hot sun beaming through the pines and mesquite trees, there was a sinister darkness hanging over these woods. Remembering that Turner Johnson had been in his backyard, an area that should have been safe, Ava agreed with her superiors that now that Sullivan had been spotted, this area should be restricted until further notice. She moved toward the trail head in the more trafficked area, hoping that by going for the obvious she'd stumble on another piece of the puzzle.

It didn't take her long to come upon Oliver's team.

Buster grunted behind her and took out his canteen. "Mighty hot. Mighty hot."

"Yes, it is," she agreed, stopping to give Roscoe some water before she drank from her own rations.

Other members of their unit nodded and spoke and kept working. She wasn't sure anymore if they were looking for the child or the killer or both. Which scared her. What if they couldn't get to Turner in time?

"How you holding up?" Oliver said from behind her.

Ava whirled to greet him, noting his sweat-drenched T-shirt underneath his FBI-emblazoned bulletproof vest. "One small victory."

She showed him the toy robot she'd placed inside a paper evidence bag and stored in a pouch on her utility belt. "We reported our finding to his parents, but this doesn't mean he's still alive."

"Maybe the kid lost the toy, and he came looking for it and got lost himself," Oliver said, doing that frown-squint thing she'd noticed last night and earlier today."

"I know, and I'm wondering if he lost it or if Sullivan hid it to cover kidnapping the boy. But then, what do I know about seven-year-olds?"

"Same here," he replied, a shard of longing passing

through his eyes. Maybe, like her, he hoped to have a family one day. No matter their jobs, searching for a lost child always brought out the best in people, but it also stirred up the worst of their emotions. But they'd both been trained to school such things.

"How long have you been trying to catch Boyd Sullivan?" she asked as they pushed through bramble and called out Turner Johnson's name over and over.

"Too long," he retorted in a concise manner.

When he didn't say more, she let it go. But then, they stopped to catch their breaths underneath some mushrooming oaks and cascading mountain laurels.

"I'll explain that to you another time," he said in a gravelly voice. "How did you come into the MWD program? I mean, after you didn't become a pilot."

She shook her head. "I'll tell you that another time, too."

"I'll hold you to that."

Ava nodded. "Well, for now, we keep going." Once again, she let Roscoe sniff Turner's toy and cap. "I'll stay close by since it's getting late, but I want Roscoe to search this area, too. Maybe he'll pick up on Sullivan's scent. He's been in on most of the prior searches so you might get a break."

"I could use one."

Ava noticed the dark fatigue around his eyes. He was a good-looking man and obviously, like her, he had to stay in shape for his job. But there was a sorrow around him, as if he were searching for something other than a vicious killer. Again, she wondered how long he'd been chasing after Boyd Sullivan. He'd been in on the first arrest from what she remembered in the early briefings. But she wondered how long he could keep this up, too. That kind of tenaciousness could wear a person down.

No time now to ponder but, later, maybe he'd open up to her as he'd said.

Which meant she'd have to do the same with him, of course.

Or research his background on her own.

After they drank some water and shared an energy bar and she fed Roscoe and gave him some play time, they went in opposite directions again.

Five minutes into this new search, Roscoe alerted on another dark indention in a hill covered with overgrowth. He whined and kept glancing back at her. Not his usual alert. Something wasn't right.

Ava stepped forward and stomped through heavy vines and dense shrubs until she came to the dark crevice. Using her rifle to push back the foliage, she decided this had to be another cave.

Roscoe wouldn't let it go so she called out. "Turner? Turner Johnson? Are you in there? I'm here to help you."

She heard movement inside. Ava reported the find over the radio and before she could make her next move, Oliver was right there with her.

"It could be your boy or it could be Sullivan," he whispered, drawing his weapon. "Either way, we go in together."

Another bonding moment, she thought, still confused about how this man brought so many of her feelings out of hiding. But he was just doing his job. He wanted to be the one to capture Sullivan.

Time for her to do the same with whoever was inside that cave. She prayed it was the boy.

Help us now, Lord. Help us to find this child.

But they needed to capture the Red Rose Killer, too.

As Oliver had said, either way, they were in this thing together now.

FOUR

When they stepped into the jagged opening to the cave, Oliver heard a low growl.

Halting Roscoe, Ava turned to Oliver. "That's not a person. It's an animal."

Oliver watched as she slipped on her protective gloves. "What are you doing?"

"It might be one of the missing dogs, possibly one of the ones suffering PTSD. I'm going in to check."

"Can he harm you?"

"Yes, if he's hungry and scared. Will you radio Westley for me?"

"Of course," Oliver said, "but I'm not leaving you in this cave alone."

"Okay, make the call."

Ava turned to Roscoe while Oliver stood just outside the opening and radioed their location. He watched as she ordered the K-9 to stay. The dog glanced at the back of the cave, whimpered a protest but sank down to do as he was told.

"I think Roscoe senses that the other dog is a friendly," Ava told Oliver when he finished the call to

Westley James. "His protective instincts tend to kick in when he sees another dog."

Ava started talking quietly to the animal. "I took a PTSD course once," she whispered to Oliver. "I'm going to use what I learned on the dog to calm him down."

Cataloging that, he decided he'd ask her about it when she was out of danger. Staying quiet, he stood watch and tried to stay out of her way. When this was over, they'd have a lot to talk about.

"Hey, buddy," she said as she sank down near the door of the cave.

Oliver could see the trembling dog's shadow, but she kept talking in gentle, soft tones. "Roscoe and I are your friends. We're here to help you. You'll get to go home to the base and your warm, clean kennel and get all kinds of love, treats and good meals and chew toys. And the help you need, too."

Ava's voice wobbled, and Oliver guessed she had to be thinking of Chief Master Sergeant Clint Lockwood and her airmen friends Landon Martelli and Tamara Peterson, all of whom had died at the hands of Boyd Sullivan. He had purposely let the dogs out that night so long ago to shake everyone up and traumatize the animals.

Oliver's bones burned with the need to find the Red Rose Killer and end his reign of terror. But right now, he had to stay here with Ava.

The dog whimpered and growled low, as if Ava's changing mood had rattled him. "It's okay. No one is ever going to hurt you again. You're a hero and we're going to make you well so you can become a strong Military Working Dog." She smiled. "I have a friend named Isaac who's looking for a dog like you. A dog named Beacon saved Isaac's life over in Afghanistan. But he's lost somewhere far away. Maybe you can cheer up my friend until he can locate Beacon. How about that?"

Something inside Oliver's heart crumbled. He wanted to comfort both the hurting dog and the woman who seemed so strong but right now seemed so broken, too. But just like the dog, if he moved too fast with Ava, she'd balk. She'd bypassed flying helicopters to do this. Was that a conscious decision, or did something painful keep her from fulfilling that dream?

Maybe she was right where she should be. And then she answered his question with her words.

Talking to the dog again in a calming voice, she said, "You know, we have a family here. We take care of each other and pray for each other. We've all been praying for you, too."

Prayer. Oliver had become so far removed from the faith his parents had instilled in him, he felt out of place hearing her words. He'd turned back to God after Madison's death, but he needed to be more intentional with his faith. Now would be a good time to take up the habit of praying again. He needed help in all areas of his life to get through this case.

If this woman had a strong faith, perhaps she could be an example to him.

The dog, which looked to be one of the missing German shepherds, stopped growling but lowered on its haunches, its dark gaze on Ava and Roscoe. Oliver kept checking for Westley, holding his breath. He loved dogs. Who didn't? But seeing how Ava handled this one made him more appreciative of what the MWD team did on a daily basis.

Slowly and carefully, Ava dug into her meal supply and found a peanut-butter granola bar.

"I'm thinking you're hungry, aren't you?"

She glanced back to where Oliver leaned against the entrance of the cave, her eyes meeting his, a soft understanding and longing in their depths. Ava pivoted back to the dog, carefully opening the paper covering the bar.

But Oliver would never forget that backward glance. It told him she was gentle and caring underneath that air force bluff.

"How about a snack to tide you over?"

Breaking half of the long bar, she tossed it toward the dog. Crouching and moving on its haunches, the dog gobbled the food and inched closer.

"Hey, Westley's here," Oliver said in a low voice, his breath gushing out in relief. Why was he so worried that the animal would hurt her? She knew what she was doing, after all.

Ava slowly slid away from the trembling dark-furred dog. "I'm going to go now, okay? But I'm leaving you in the best possible hands. He's my boss, so make me look good by bragging on me, okay?"

She scooted back, her gaze on the dog. The scared animal didn't move, but Oliver saw the apprehension in its eyes. The traumatized animal didn't want Ava to go.

Oliver didn't want her to go away either. Which scared him way more than a dog attack.

When she reached Roscoe, she scooted near. "Sir, come on in."

Westley entered the cave and got down on the dog's

level. While Ava gave him a quick whispered update, he kept staring at the dog. Then he nodded to Ava. "One of our four stars." Turning back to the scared animal, he said, "We've got this, okay. You're home, soldier, and you won't ever be scared again."

Ava called to Roscoe. "Come."

The Labrador stood but turned back to the other dog, emitting a soft whimper from his throat.

Westley let out a light chuckle. "Hear that? Roscoe says chin up."

Ava made her way out. Oliver waited with his hand out to help her up. She stood on trembling legs and glanced up at him, unable to speak.

Her sweet gaze shattered him. "Hey, it's okay. The dog's safe now."

Nodding, she wiped her eyes, clearly embarrassed at the tears forming there. "But, Oliver, Boyd Sullivan did this. He sent these scared, scarred dogs out to fend for themselves. We have to find him and we have to keep looking for Turner Johnson. Because if he did this, I don't want to think about what he'd do to an innocent child."

Oliver reached out a hand and then dropped it, memories jarring him. "I feel the same way."

Then he touched her arm and looked into her eyes.

"We'll keep searching, I promise. I know firsthand what Boyd Sullivan is capable of doing. And I am not going to stop until I either put him behind bars or put a bullet in him."

"Well, Turner Johnson's parents aren't happy, and I don't blame them," Ava told Oliver an hour after they'd found the German shepherd in the cave. "But they've been waiting and wondering and I had to report back to them. Not to mention, those two base reporters, Heidi Jenks and John Robinson, are all over this and I keep telling them 'No comment.' Lieutenant General Hall will probably want to have a nice chat with me, too."

"With all of us," Oliver retorted, his expression as dark as the rain that hovered on the horizon. These pop-up storms weren't helping the situation. "You've done everything you can and you're still out here searching, so the base commander should cut you some slack." He glanced around, then lowered his voice. "I also expect that annoying Anonymous Blogger to have all the details, too. I'm wondering if that person is Sullivan's helper."

Ava had to wonder, too. For months now, someone on base had found a way to get all the details of the Red Rose Killer case and blast them online. They suspected Heidi Jenks, but Ava figured Heidi wouldn't risk her journalism career with an unsubstantiated blog full of false accusations.

"I hadn't even thought about that," she said, "but yes, we can expect some sort of cryptic, inaccurate report on that front, too."

The phone call earlier to where the Johnsons were waiting at a nearby staging site had broken Ava's heart. Turner's parents were distraught and exhausted. Their child was missing in the same area where a dangerous man had been seen, so yes, they were frightened, angry and beyond being reasonable. She'd be the same way in their position. Reporters were always hovering around, but lately they'd become even more annoying. Heidi and John both worked for the base paper, with John being the lead reporter on the Red Rose Killer case, but they were in a competition of sorts to get the scoop on the Boyd Sullivan story. But Heidi seemed the more reasonable of the two, at least. Ava figured the determined reporter was probably with Turner's parents right about now, getting their take on this turn of events.

"Well, regardless of reporters and vicious bloggers, we still have our work cut out for us. No sign of Turner Johnson or Boyd Sullivan." She did a check around them and added, "I'm so afraid that wherever they are, they might be together. But I can't bring myself to voice that to Turner's parents."

Oliver walked with her through the hot, damp woods, Roscoe back on the job just up ahead of them. "They're feeling guilty that the kid slipped away. But they're also terrified about Boyd Sullivan, too. Drew Golosky turned up dead, and we barely had time to warn anyone."

Ava watched the path ahead. "I just pray it's not too late."

"At least the base has closed down this area. It's off-limits until further notice," Oliver said, his tone solemn.

"He let me live," Ava said, her mind still reeling from the last couple of days' work. "Why do I get the feeling it's not over between us, however?"

"Because you saw him, saw that feral look in his eyes. He doesn't have much to lose right now."

"Well, I do," she said, moving ahead with Roscoe, her heart burning with the need for justice and her prayers centered on finding a lost little boy.

She was also moving away from Oliver. Somehow, they'd become too close. She didn't do close. She was single and single-minded. Work consumed most of her time, and that was good enough for her. Or at least it had been up until now. But today, he'd stood there in the cave with her and another current of awareness had sizzled between them. Like heat lightning, there but hard to understand.

In spite of the circumstances, this man whom she didn't want to like had become ingrained in her psyche. In the span of two days, they'd bonded in more ways than she'd ever bonded with anyone else. Well, maybe one other person.

Never one to rush things, Ava didn't like the confusing feelings coursing over her each time Oliver was around. And now she was thinking about the man even after she'd purposely tried to distance herself from him. No, she'd been impulsive and rash once before in the love department. Not again.

She'd served with the one man who might have taken her heart. Julian Benton had been the gunner on her crew. They'd become close but he'd died in that chopper crash and left her numb with fear and afraid of life. She and Julian had never had a chance to explore where their feelings might have taken them because protocol and war had kept them too busy to take that next step.

So she'd put love out of her mind and she'd almost walked away from the world that had given her a home and hope.

Until the Military Working Dog program had saved her by offering her a way back to justice and that hope.

Did she dare go that deep with another man?

No. Not yet.

"Hey, be careful," he said, catching up with her.

"I'm always careful," she retorted. "And so is the trained animal guiding me."

"Any alerts?"

"Not yet."

"What made you switch to the MWD program?"

Oh, he wanted her to talk now, when she'd just been giving herself a mental pep talk. Since she didn't have much of a choice, Ava replied, "A chopper crash."

He kept his eyes straight ahead, his dark shades hiding his secrets. "You were on the front lines?"

"Yes."

"And you don't want to talk about it?"

"No."

"But you survived."

"I did."

"Others didn't survive?"

"No, they died."

He didn't miss a beat. "You'll tell me later when we are clean and cool and sitting in a nice restaurant?"

"You wish."

"I do wish," he said, his tone steel edged, his voice low and husky.

"Maybe one day I'll tell you but…you might not like what you hear. Isn't that what you said to me?"

"Oh, so we're gonna play that game where we try to hold on to our secrets until the very last minute?"

"One of my favorite games."

Before he could say more, Roscoe alerted with a low growl. A sign of danger, not a frightened child.

Oliver held Ava's arm and put a finger to his lips.

"I know how this works," she whispered, drawing her own weapon. Then she gave Roscoe the signal to "Go."

The big dog moved through the underbrush and rocky hillside, still growling low.

A bullet whizzed past Ava. Another hit at Roscoe's feet.

"Come," Ava commanded, bringing Roscoe back. Ava caught a glimpse of a figure dressed in dark jogging pants and a matching hoodie holding a gun aimed toward her.

Roscoe growled low, causing the other person to halt and lift the weapon. Ava did the same, ready for a face-off.

And then Oliver was there, pushing her down, a hail of gunfire and bullets bursting out in a harsh echo through the woods.

Overhead, birds flushed out of hiding and the whole forest came alive with critters being scared away and people shouting off in the distance. The shooter pivoted and took off.

Oliver rose up to get another shot with his handgun but it hit a tree while the culprit sprinted into the thicket.

"Stay here," he told Ava as he took off through the woods, reporting through his radio.

Ava didn't intend to stay here. She needed to be in on this hunt. And he needed to remember she was trained for this. If he hadn't tackled her, she might have been able to get a clear shot.

Or she could have been killed, and Roscoe right along with her.

Moving on her hands and knees, she motioned Roscoe to do the same. Together they crouched through the woods, stopping to listen and search ahead.

Her heart hammering, her pulse on overdrive, Ava scanned the perimeter around her and kept Roscoe close.

Where was Oliver? And where was the shooter?

FIVE

Oliver saw the dark figure moving ahead in a zigzag fashion. His heart still pumped adrenaline through his bloodstream as he thought how close the shooter had come to taking out Ava and her partner.

He followed, tree limbs slapping at his face, nettles pricking his skin, a new sensation moving through his system. Fear.

Fear for Ava.

He'd become distracted by the odd feelings, but now he'd reel those feelings in and get back on track. His focus had always been finding the Red Rose Killer. But he couldn't do that if he kept losing the trail because his mind was on a woman he'd only had a few conversations with over the last day or so.

So he kept going, following, listening. Just as before, the shooter had given up and run away. But someone had Ava in their crosshairs and this wouldn't end until Oliver did his job. Was the shooter just a distraction, or some sort of bodyguard for Boyd Sullivan? Tall and slender—it could have been a woman, but with the bulky, dark clothes and dark shades, it'd been hard to tell.

Soon, he had Security Forces members and K-9 handlers all around him.

"Find anything?" Master Sergeant Caleb Streeter asked, his tone blunt and clear. Caleb had taken over as head of the K-9 training center for a while when Westley had been guarding Felicity. Now that Westley and Felicity were married and she no longer reported to Westley, he was back with the K-9 unit.

"No. Lost the shooter in that thicket about one hundred yards from here."

"We haven't located anyone either. They shoot and disappear. Odd."

Oliver nodded at Caleb, wondering if the K-9 handler doubted him. "I'm heading back to where I left Ava."

Caleb looked around. "I'll search some of the other areas where we found campsites earlier."

Winded and disappointed yet again, Oliver stopped and radioed to the rest of the team. "Lost contact north of staging area." He named the coordinates and turned to walk back to where he'd left Ava and Roscoe.

But when he got there, they were both gone.

Three hours later, Oliver had gone his own way after trying to call Ava's phone. She wasn't picking up. He knew she was okay. Caleb had come back around and informed Oliver that Ava and a couple of other handlers had gone off in another direction.

Without Oliver, apparently.

Was she feeling the same way about things between them?

Was that why she'd suddenly left him in the dust?

Sure, she was capable and competent, but he'd tried to help her and protect her. That was a big no-no, especially with a military woman. He knew that and yet, his instincts had shouted to him to do just that. Now, wanting to protect Ava seemed to be edging out everything else, even his keen need to find Boyd Sullivan.

Dusk was beginning to shadow the woods. Another day gone, and the boy was still out here somewhere, along with a serial killer and a trigger-happy, hooded interloper. Deciding he'd camp out in the woods tonight, Oliver grabbed Chad Watson and started to back out.

"We've searched every inch of these woods, Special Agent," Chad said. "Not a complaint, just an observation."

"Duly noted," Oliver replied in a clipped tone. "You have something better to do tonight?"

Chad grinned and guided Custer through the bramble. "Well, I did." He shrugged. "It wasn't going anywhere, anyway."

"Oh, so this is about a relationship with a woman," Oliver retorted, stomping harder against the slanted sun rays chasing them.

"Isn't that always the case?"

"I wouldn't know," Oliver retorted. "I'm always working."

Chad caught up with him, his eyes on the dark gold-and-black Malinois sniffing the ground and the air. "Well, you need to change that tactic. You know what they say about all work…"

"Yeah, I know," Oliver replied. "Makes for me finding a serial killer."

She was running out of daylight and time.

The longer Turner was out there, the worse off he'd

become. Ava feared he couldn't take another long night. While the temperatures were warm, the bugs, snakes and other predators could do the boy in.

Or worse, the Red Rose Killer could be holding him.

But surely by now they would have heard Boyd Sullivan's demands if he'd decided to use the boy for collateral.

Was the mysterious shooter his decoy, a distraction so Boyd could keep moving? Sullivan knew how the military dogs and their handlers worked. He could erase any signs or scents of himself. He'd broken into their headquarters and let most of their dogs escape, so the man wasn't stupid. He'd planned this attack, and he was always one step ahead of them.

Following Roscoe on yet another back-and-forth grid, Ava decided if they ever found the little boy, she wouldn't come into these woods again. She'd find a river somewhere and sit and take in the fresh air and enjoy the sun shining down on her.

In here, traipsing around with so much at stake, she'd turned her turmoil into feelings for a man who'd hovered in her peripheral vision for months now. She didn't need that kind of weakness holding her back. From now on, she'd focus on her job and forget the way Oliver Davison made her feel.

But his arms around her protecting her earlier today—that would be hard to forget. Or the way his green eyes widened when he was concerned, or the way he smelled fresh and clean even when they were out in the heat and humidity. And especially, the way his gaze had held hers when she'd looked over her shoulder at him in that cave with the K-9. He'd seen her pain. And she was pretty sure he'd felt that kind of intense pain himself.

Another crack in her armor.

But did he truly see her or notice this connection between them?

He had to have. They'd felt something that had caused them to break apart, even with someone shooting at them.

"I need to get that out of my head," she mumbled, her eyes on Roscoe. And yet she wasn't really doing her job to the max right now.

Because the next thing she knew, Roscoe took off and headed straight for the edge of a high bluff. And almost took Ava over the edge with him.

Oliver was about to call it a night when he received a call on his cell.

"Davison," he said, irritated and tired.

It was the lab. "Special Agent Davison, just wanted to report we didn't find any definitive DNA on the floral Buff your people found in the reserve behind Canyon Air Force Base."

Stomping the ground, Oliver gritted his teeth. "Okay, thank you."

Putting his phone away, he stared into the woods, wondering why he couldn't get a break on this case. And then he saw it. Just a slight opening to what looked like one of the many caves hiding in this vast reserve. And he was pretty sure he'd seen a light flaring inside.

He was headed that way when his cell buzzed again.

Glancing down, he saw Ava's number on the screen.

"Ava?" he said on a whisper, his eyes on the cave.

"I've found him, Oliver. I've found the little boy."

SIX

Ava stared down the steep incline, her heart flipping and pumping a too-fast beat. "Turner? Turner Johnson? I've come to help you, okay?"

She heard another whimper and caught sight of the little boy huddled up against the stone wall of an indention below. And then she heard something else. A yelp that sounded like a bark.

Looking down again, Ava was shocked to see a small black dog with the boy. Could it be one of the missing dogs from the kennels?

"I'm with the air force," she said, calling out again. "Search-and-Rescue. I have my K-9 partner, Roscoe, with me. He sniffed until he found you."

"I found a dog, too," Turner called out. "He stayed with me when the storm came."

The tiny figure shuffled and moved, the little dog hopping around him, and Ava's heart did another rapid thump. The indention where they were sheltered was narrow, only a foot or so wide, with craggy jagged rocks and sturdy saplings down below.

"Stay there. Don't move, okay? We'll come down to you. I've got lots of help on the way."

Roscoe woofed, and the young dog barked in reply. She took a moment to do a visual check of the boy. He was dirty and had scratches and welts all over his arms and face, but he looked okay otherwise. Alive. He was alive.

And alone, except for his furry companion. Hoping the furry little mutt was one of their missing dogs, she blinked back tears.

"Do you and the dog get along okay?" she called, amazed that the dog and Turner had found each other.

"Yes, ma'am. He's sweet, and he kept me warm. I'm keeping him."

Ava had to smile at that firm retort. They'd have to see about that later, but it made sense to her.

"How'd you get down there?" Ava asked, to keep him occupied while she tried to find the best way to get to him. Could they bring in a chopper? Possibly, but if not, she'd have to get the team to help get him out.

"I didn't want the bad guy to hurt me," the boy said. "He and that woman grabbed me and made me hide with them. But…I ran away when they started fighting and this looked like a safe place. The dog followed me 'cause I fed him some of my rations."

"You brought rations?"

Turner looked guilty. "I was playing soldier, and I snuck out the fence. I had a couple of energy bars."

"That's good. That's smart even if you did disobey your parents," Ava said, the sound of motors roaring to life echoing over the woods. She'd tried to stay away from Oliver, but she sure wanted him here now. "The bad guy is gone. He won't hurt you again."

"Promise?" Another whimper that sounded like a

sob. "'Cause he told me he'd throw me off the bluff and kill my mom and dad if I talked to anyone."

"My dog and I won't let him near you," Ava said, her tone firm and edged with anger. "You're safe now. Are you hurt?"

"No. Just sore and tired. Got a scratched knee. I'm hungry, too. And Stormy's hungry. We ate the last of my snack bars."

Stormy? The dog, of course.

"Soon you'll be with your parents and we'll feed both of you," she said. "Now, stay still while I figure a way down."

"Are they mad?"

"No, but they are sure worried."

"There's a way," Turner said, pointing past her. "I found a path."

Seeing a narrow, jagged formation that did look like steps, she motioned Roscoe. "Go," she said, indicating the path. "Guard."

Roscoe sniffed the dirt and rocks and then carefully made his way down the winding slope.

Watching his every step, she called out, "Hey, Turner, I'm sending you my buddy. He's going to watch over you and Stormy, okay?"

The scared kid glanced up. "Will he bite me?"

"No. But do me a favor and don't pet him. He's working, so let him do his job. He's going to keep you company until I can get there." And she hoped little Stormy wouldn't try to get friendly with Roscoe. "And hold tight to Stormy."

"All right."

Ava heard what sounded like an off-road vehicle coming at them. Turning, she drew her weapon, but before the ATV stopped, Oliver was out and running toward her, Chad and Custer with him.

"Where?" he asked, his hand touching her arm.

"Down here. And I think he has one of our missing dogs with him." She pointed to the overhang on the rocky bluff and then showed Oliver the treacherous rocks forming a path. "He said he'd taken that way down. I sent Roscoe down after him."

Oliver glanced back at Chad. "See if there's some rope in the ATV supply box." Then he turned to Ava. "I'm going down to get him. Cover me?"

"Cover you?" She glanced around. "Do you think they're watching?"

"Just trying to plan ahead," he said, adjusting the vest that identified him as FBI.

"I'm going down with you," she said.

He shook his head, but she held up a hand. "Look, Oliver, I've been searching for this boy for days now. I'm going down there because I told him I'm here to help him. And…it is my job."

Oliver gave her a look of admiration and frustration. "Okay, of course. I'm not trying to take over your case."

"We'll argue about this later," she said. "Let's go."

Chad came back with a coil of nylon rope. "Found this."

"Cover us," Oliver said. "And hold on to the rope in case we need some help coming up."

Chad looked down to where Turner sat with his knees held to his chest, Stormy right up against his trembling body.

"And make sure the paramedics know we're bringing him to the staging area," Ava said to Chad. "Call a chopper to medevac him to the hospital."

"Yes, ma'am." Chad threw his rifle strap over his shoulder and did as she asked, all the while watching the darkening woods, Custer at his side.

Oliver went first and Ava carefully followed, but one of her boots caught on a root and she slipped.

Right into Oliver's arms.

His gaze held hers as he righted her, but the awareness between them hit like a bolt of Texas-size lightning. "Hey, I got you."

"I'm good, thanks," she said, pulling away. Looking down, she thought how close she'd come to crashing through bramble and rocks to the gully below. Then she thanked God that Turner had made it to this secluded hiding place.

She was so glad Oliver had come, but now she wished she hadn't had that moment of weakness. After calling the proper people in the chain of command, she'd immediately called Oliver, too.

Why?

Because they'd been in this together since yesterday's rainy afternoon. He'd helped her, and she'd helped him. They'd worked to find the boy and Oliver had done so instead of rushing off to find Boyd Sullivan. He'd put his search on the line to help her.

Had he put his heart on the line, too?

So stop being so petty with him.

Feeling contrite, she took hold of his T-shirt sleeve.

Glancing over his shoulder, he gave her a soft smile. "Almost there."

Overhead, they heard the medical helicopter moving through the air.

Spotting Roscoe and the boy who sat with an arm curled around the scared puppy, Ava stepped onto the narrow ledge where the boy was perched. "Hey, Turner. I'm Ava. And this is Oliver. He's an FBI agent."

Turner's eyes widened. "Did you find the bad guy?"

Oliver shot a glance at Ava, then squatted in front of Turner. "Not yet. But we will. Did you see him?"

Turner rubbed a grimy hand across his nose and bobbed his head. "Yes, sir. I got far back in the woods and couldn't find the path home and I saw him and then he chased me. He and the woman made me go with them. The man said they'd have to kill me, but the woman didn't want to do that. She just wanted to keep me and scare me. They got real mad at each other and were screaming so I ran and found a cave and I hid my toy 'cause he was making fun of me and took one of my toys. I hid the other one so maybe somebody would find it."

Ava shuddered but got a grip on her emotions. "You were smart to hide your little robot. Roscoe and I found it, so we knew you were still lost out here."

Roscoe's ears lifted, but he kept his eyes on the boy he was ordered to guard.

Turner was wound up now, however, which only made the little black dog with him turn in circles and woof tiny barks. Ava managed to get the puppy calmed down with some treats she kept for Roscoe.

"How'd you get away?" Oliver asked, his tone conversational.

"The woman told him not to kill me 'cause I'm just a kid. She kept saying, 'Remember when you were a kid. Remember what happened.' They argued and I ran away and found another cave. Then the rain came and I had to stay there."

Oliver shot Ava a glance, then checked the dog with

Turner. "How did you and this little fellow wind up here?"

"It was first light when they started screaming at each other again, so I saw the light outside of the cave and I shoved my toy behind that rock and I ran."

Turner gulped in air while Ava checked him all over for broken bones or any odd or swollen bites or marks, the excited puppy nipping at her hands and arms. "So you spent the night in the small cave with the bad people?"

"Yeah, but I found this place and then I heard people talking and running through the woods. I had to keep Stormy quiet so they wouldn't find us."

"The bad people?" Oliver asked, looking around.

"Yeah. They sure like to fight." He shrugged and shivered all at the same time. "Me and Stormy heard voices, but I thought it was a trick. We stayed underneath the bluff. It hid us."

Oliver nodded his approval. "Sounds like you did everything right." Then he leaned close to Turner. "Listen, I'm gonna lift you up and try to get us to the top of the bluff. If we can't make it, we'll have someone else come and help, okay?"

"Okay," Turner replied, lifting his arms to Oliver's neck. "What about Stormy?"

"I've got Stormy," Ava said, scooping up the scrawny little dog that looked to be a mix between a poodle and terrier. Sneaking him another treat, she gave Roscoe an apologetic smile and turned back to Oliver and Turner.

Ava swallowed the lump in her throat. The boy looked so small in Oliver's big arms. Those same strong arms had held her close earlier, shielding her and grounding her.

"Let's go," Oliver said to Ava after he had Turner secure against his chest. "You and Roscoe go up first."

Turner glanced back at his hiding place. "I'm so glad Stormy found me."

"Me, too," Ava said, the little dog clinging to her uniform and sniffing her skin. "Stormy is safe now, too."

With darkness falling, they worked their way up the side of the bluff, rocks and dirt kicking out with each step they took. Oliver stopped midway and took a breath. "Almost there, Turner."

"I'm a scout," Turner explained. "I rationed the food in my backpack and looked for water and shelter. And I gave Stormy food so he'd like me."

"You are a trooper," Oliver said, his head close to the boy's. "I think you'll be promoted to Honorary FBI Special Agent."

Turner grinned at that.

Almost there.

Oliver had said that same thing to Ava earlier.

Thank You, God, for sending this man here to help all of us. And thank You for keeping Turner safe so we can return him to his family.

Oliver crested the last slippery chunk of rocks, gritting his teeth against the heat and the bugs. Dusk was hitting, and the mosquitoes were swarming in a mad dash to gnaw him to death.

Trying to shield Turner from any more bites, he grunted and stretched his leg to reach the summit of the tall bluff.

He made it up the last of the dangerous steps and handed the boy off to Chad so he could turn and help Ava while Roscoe moved ahead.

Chad sat Turner down on a rock and checked him over. "Hey, dude. You are one hard kid to find."

Turner bobbed his head. "Are you FBI or K-9?"

Chad chuckled and ruffled the boy's sweat-dampened hair. "I'm Chad, a member of the K-9 unit. And this is my partner, Custer."

"Another dog," Turner said, grinning. "I can't wait to tell Mom and Dad about Stormy."

"Stormy?" Chad mouthed over his head.

"Right here," Ava said, holding up the bundle of skinny black energy. "He wants to keep the puppy but we'll have to make sure he's clear to do so. This one was geared to become a service dog so…Turner might need him."

Chad nodded. "Ah, I see." Then he turned serious. "Chopper is landing at the staging area, ma'am. We are to bring the kid by ATV, provided he's uninjured and able to travel."

Ava handed Turner some water and a granola bar. "He's fine, but he'll need to be checked over."

Chad knelt by Turner and did another thorough check. "I'm finding bones, lots of bones. And I see eyes. Two very brown eyes. And yep, he has a tongue and ears."

Turner giggled. "Are you a doctor?"

"Nah," Chad replied. "I'm just pretending to be one. But seriously, bro, do you hurt bad anywhere?"

"No," Turner said. "I itch, and I need a bath." Then his big eyes filled with moisture. "And I want my mom."

Chad gave him an eye-level stare. "We can handle that."

Ava mouthed a "Thank you" to Chad and decided she'd give him a commendation as soon as they were all safe back at base.

Then she held the puppy tight and turned to Oliver. "Thank you, too."

His gaze held hers. "For what?"

"For coming to our rescue."

"You had it," he said, waving off her thanks. "But I'm glad you called me." With a shrug, he added, "We're in this together, Ava."

They stood for a moment, no words being spoken. They didn't need to talk. This very important victory held them together now.

Chad stood. "I'll go get the—"

Shots rang out and Chad spun, grabbing his shoulder. "I'm hit," he said before crumbling to the ground.

Ava dived for Turner and Oliver fell with her, covering both of them as bullets flew by them, hitting trees and bushes.

"Roscoe, search," Ava called. Both Custer and Roscoe were barking and prancing.

Chad called out a weak command to Custer and both dogs took off in the direction of the shots.

"Follow them," Ava shouted to Oliver. "Go. We'll be fine. I'll radio for help."

Oliver gave her one last look and took off through the woods, crouching to avoid being shot.

"I want my dad," Turner said, crumbling now that he was safe and the shock and adrenaline were merging in his tired little body.

"I know," Ava said, holding him close while he sobbed. "Chad, can you hear me?"

"I'm okay, ma'am. Hurts like all fire, but it's a through and through." He sat up and held his hand to his arm. "Just a lot of blood."

Ava put her arms on Turner's shoulders. "I'm going over there to help Airman Chad, okay?" After the boy bobbed his head, she said, "You stay behind this rock and hold on to Stormy, got it?"

He nodded, tears streaming down his face. "Is Chad okay? Is the FBI agent gonna be all right?"

"Sure, Chad's good," she said, praying it so. "And the FBI agent can take care of himself. He's tough like you."

Turner held to the squirming dog. "I'm okay."

Ava crawled to where Chad sat by a tree and after digging through her knapsack, found some gauze and tape. "I'll patch you up."

Chad nodded and drank some of the water she offered him. Once she had him bandaged, she asked, "Can you walk?"

"Yes, I think so," he said, sitting up, his color returning. But when he tried to stand, he wobbled.

"Okay, you're going to stay here and guard Turner, all right?"

"I can do that," Chad said, his handgun next to him.

"Then I can track FBI Agent Davison and the K-9s. They won't listen to his commands."

Chad grunted and nodded. "Yes, ma'am."

Crawling back to Turner, she said, "Here's the deal. We have help on the way and you're going to be fine. Chad will take care of you and Stormy."

"What about you?"

"I'm going to find my friend and Roscoe and Custer."

"But the bad man is shooting at us."

"Yes, but I have to follow my partner."

Before she could get going, vehicles plowed up on them, lights shining in her eyes while the sun sank down behind her to the west. Ava held her gun secure, ready to shoot.

"Esposito?"

She recognized the voice. Nick Donovan. A K-9 handler and good friend.

"Here, Lieutenant," she called, glad to see he had his bloodhound Annie with him.

After that, everything became a blur as she explained the situation and turned Chad and Turner over to Nick and the two Security Forces officers with him.

"I have to go after Oliver Davison," she said, urgency in her words.

"Why? Where is he?" Nick asked, his dark hair wet with perspiration.

"He went after the shooters. And he has Roscoe and Custer with him."

"Go," Nick said, a look of understanding in his eyes.

Ava took off but turned and hurried back to Chad. "Thank you." Then she hugged Turner. "I'll talk to you later, I promise."

Then she was off. Running and praying she'd find Oliver safe and sound.

When she heard angry barks up the path into the deep woods, Ava sprinted in that direction.

Another round of gunshots echoed like a death knell over the forest.

SEVEN

Oliver whirled when he heard footsteps behind him.

"Ava!"

"Sorry," she said, her weapon protecting her. "I didn't mean to sneak up on you, but I have to get to the dogs."

"Hear them?" Oliver said as he put his hand on her back and they both crouched low. "They've cornered someone."

She nodded. "They're doing the angry bark, which means they've sniffed out someone or something familiar but possibly hostile."

Oliver guided her into a dark copse of trees. "I was about to find them. But you're here now, so take over and do your thing. I'll back you up."

"I hear water running," she said, whirling past him and out into the open.

"Look, Oliver," she said, disappointment in her words.

Oliver saw the K-9s barking near a stream, their heads lifted to the woods beyond the water. "They lost the scent."

"Let's go see. They might have something, and if we can get across the water—"

She didn't wait on him, so Oliver took off behind Ava.

They were met with a volley of rifle shots.

Ava called back the dogs and hit the dirt.

Oliver fell down beside her. "They'll shoot all of us and end this right here."

"We need reinforcements," Ava said, reaching for her cell.

But Oliver stopped her. "No. We are getting you back to base and we are letting the next shift take over."

"This is our case to handle, Oliver."

He shook his head. "No, Ava. You were here to find the boy and you did that. Now I take over and find Sullivan."

"I'm not letting this go," she retorted, her head inching up only to be greeted with more gunfire. "They've tried to shoot me so many times I've lost count and frankly, I'm tired of it."

Oliver knew it wouldn't be wise to argue with the woman. She had fire in her eyes.

"Ava, you need to rest."

"I've been on tougher missions. I'll be okay."

"Okay, all right." He stood, causing her to grab him and yank him back before another round of shots scattered around them.

Oliver fell on the ground. "You're right. This is getting pretty tedious. Whoever this is, they obviously like using us for target practice."

"Ready to go in?" she asked, rolling away to lift up with her gun blazing.

Oliver's heart fell to his feet till he realized the

shooting had stopped, thankfully. Because this woman was way too determined for her own good. And for his blood pressure.

"They're gone," he said, tugging her back. "Ava, I've already called in my location. I'll report where we lost them and the next team can take over. Justin and Westley will send someone around the other way to this location."

She stared up at him, frustration coloring her dirty, sweaty face. "We found Turner," she whispered as the reality of it hit her.

"We did," he said, breaking all the rules by wiping his finger across the smudge of dirt on her right cheek. "You did."

Bobbing her head, she let out a breath and gazed at him, realization and longing in her wide eyes. He had to wonder how long she'd been forgetting to breathe. Then, finally, she said, "I need to check on him."

Oliver sat staring at her too long, not sure what to do with her. The woman held back tears the way a dam held back a river. But she needed to have a good cry.

This kind of work could either shut down your emotions or bring them to the breaking point. He figured Boyd Sullivan had become broken by a cruel father long before he joined the air force, but did that give him the right to kill innocent people?

And did that mean Oliver would be bitter and unhappy for the rest of his life because he couldn't bring the man to justice? His faith told him God would be the final judge for Boyd Sullivan. Maybe he should consider that and let others with a fresh approach step in.

Testing that theory, he said, "Good idea. Checking

on Turner sounds way better than following yet another dead end."

"Why can't we find them, Oliver?" she said as they stood and started back. "A whole air force base and all of our Security Forces on the ground and we can't find Boyd Sullivan and this woman that Turner mentioned."

"I know, but Sullivan lives on the fringe of being a soldier. He knows all the rules and he breaks all of them. He has someone helping him on the inside because he's charismatic and savvy. Women are drawn to him because he has that whole bad-boy thing that they think they can fix. He uses them and he's using someone from this base to keep him alive."

"Wow. You've got the man pegged," she said, her tone calm now, understanding and acceptance in her eyes. "You must eat, sleep and breathe this stuff."

"I do," he admitted. But he couldn't bring himself to tell her how his gut churned with guilt and regret. And he sure didn't want Sullivan to hurt another woman because of him. Especially this woman. "But..."

"I know, just part of the job, right?"

He laughed at that, figuring she'd given him a moment of grace. "Let's get out of these hot, sticky woods and go have that dinner I promised," he said.

"That sounds good to me, but I'm supposed to be avoiding you."

"That works since I'm trying to avoid you, too."

She gave him a surprised appraisal. "So we just avoid each other together?"

"A perfect solution."

She glanced back behind them. "At least Sullivan hasn't killed anyone else. I guess that's something to be thankful for."

* * *

"The Anonymous Blogger has struck again."

Captain Justin Blackwood stared out over the conference room, his blue eyes full of fatigue. Those same eyes zoomed in on Ava.

They'd just attended a press conference where the captain and several others had been grilled, including Ava and Oliver who had rescued Turner Johnson.

And then Heidi Jenks had brought up the latest questions from the Anonymous Blogger. "Captain, any truth to the rumors that Security Forces and the FBI aren't getting along?"

Without even a blink, the captain had handled things. "We are working closely with Special Agent Oliver Davison, but make no mistake, the FBI understands this is our jurisdiction and we are all cooperating in order to find the Red Rose Killer."

"Maybe a little too much," another reporter shouted. "Seems the FBI agent and Senior Airman Ava Esposito have become very chummy."

Again, the captain maintained a steely control. "When you're together for days in the deep woods of the Hill Country, you tend to become fast friends." Shutting the cover on his electronic tablet, he said, "No further questions. Good day."

Once the reporters exited, the team stayed behind for reports and updates.

Oliver stood up behind Ava before the captain could begin. "I have nothing but respect for your team, Captain. I'm doing my job but I'm well aware of jurisdiction and protocol. Senior Airman Esposito and I have our differences, but we're working through them. The blogger is trying to make trouble where none exists."

Justin's astute gaze moved between Oliver and Ava. "The blogger either saw you two arguing and discussing or they've overheard speculation that you either hate each other a lot or like each other a little too much."

Ava whirled to Oliver, hoping he'd play along. "Did you plant that little tidbit to make me look bad?"

Looking surprised, he said, "Excuse me?"

Giving him a meaningful "don't blow this" stare, Ava went on. "We've worked closely all week and today, you helped me when I found Turner Johnson. We agreed we'd go visit him in the hospital after this meeting, right? So tell me you didn't go and leak anything to that misinformed, annoying blogger just because I was doing my job."

Oliver tried to look justifiably confused. "I don't know the blogger and I get along with just about everyone in this room. Even you, Airman Esposito. If you ask me, you're way overdue for that promotion to staff sergeant."

Turning back to the highly interested team members gathered around them, Oliver glanced around the room. "I think the blogger is connected to Boyd Sullivan somehow. The Red Rose Killer likes to stir the pot while he gets away from us. I suggest we focus on that and not idle, unsubstantiated gossip."

Captain Blackwood cleared his throat and held tight to the rare grin he was trying to hide. "Okay, then. I believe that clears that up. Now let's hear all the real reports. This is still a serious situation."

Then he glanced at Ava. "Good work today, Airman Esposito and Special Agent Davison. You two have put yourselves on the line way too much over the last few days so I think it's to be expected that someone could misinterpret your...er...discussions. But it concerns me how they're getting their facts. I'd hate to think someone within our ranks is passing confidential information."

"Thank you, sir," Ava replied, a blush coloring her face. "That concerns me, too."

Oliver nodded and breathed a sigh of relief. Then he went over every detail of the last few days, ending with where he and Ava had last heard shooting earlier tonight.

"We never saw the shooter, but the K-9s had them on the run. The shooter took to the stream, and the dogs lost the scent. Then they shot at the dogs and us."

"I've got people combing that area all night," the captain said. "They're moving deeper into the woods and we're advancing right along with them. Sullivan will be flushed out this time."

After they were dismissed, Oliver waited for Ava at the door. But when she turned to leave he heard the captain call her back.

"Esposito, a word please?"

Ava sent Oliver a concerned stare and then turned to face the always serious Captain Blackwood.

"Sir?" Ava waited, wondering if she was going to be called on the carpet for hanging out with Oliver Davison too much.

Justin took a breath and crossed his muscular arms over his chest. "You've had a rough week, Airman. I suggest you take the rest of the week off. Come back Monday, fresh and ready to go again."

"But, sir—"

"That was not a suggestion, Esposito. You came in contact with a serial killer and in spite of that, you made every effort to find that kid. I know your history. We don't need you relapsing into depression again the way you did after you were injured in that helicopter crash."

Ava lowered her head. "Sir, I'm fine. I haven't had any symptoms of PTSD since I joined the MWD program."

Justin dropped his hands to his side. "And I'd like to keep it that way. A few days of R & R can't hurt. Besides, Sullivan has you on his radar. He's had someone shooting at you even after he told you he wouldn't hurt you. He's sneaky and he'll strike back, sooner or later."

"So you want me to hide from Sullivan?"

"No. I want you to rest and stay aware."

"And to not be so high profile on this case right now?"

"That about sums it up, yes."

Ava nodded. "Yes, sir. Thank you."

But her insides churned with worry. She rarely took a day off. What would she do with a four-day leave?

When she left the conference room, Oliver stood waiting for her by the snack machine.

Then there was the problem of him, of course.

Four days of doing nothing would leave her with too much time to think about Oliver Davison.

"What was that all about?" Oliver asked, careful to keep his voice low since the whole team now had a scope on things that might or might not be happening with them.

Ava kept walking. "I just got four days leave."

"What? Why?"

"Orders, really," she said as she headed out the door from the training facility. "So I'm going home to get a shower and I'm changing into civilian clothes before we go to see Turner."

Oliver got that she wasn't ready to talk. "Okay, I'll do the same and…pick you up at your place?"

She whirled to her SUV. "Maybe we should meet at the hospital."

"If that's what you want?"

She held a hand to the driver's-side door. "I don't know what I want. I feel as if I'm being punished, but Captain Blackwood said it was out of concern for me. That I needed to rest and go low profile for a few days."

"That makes sense because of all the attempts on your life. No one else has been threatened, you realize? The shooter is definitely targeting you."

"Yes, and you, too. I also realize that this person doesn't intend to kill me or you. Whoever it is, they are a decoy so Sullivan can move farther into the woods."

Oliver saw the frustration in her expression. "A few days off might do you good."

"I doubt that. I'll start climbing the walls. But the captain was pretty clear. I don't have a choice."

"Shower, we'll visit Turner and then I'm treating you to dinner."

"People are already talking, Oliver. The blogger must have overheard someone discussing how we operate together. Or don't operate together."

"Let them talk. We have to eat."

She opened the SUV door. "Okay, but I'm taking Roscoe so there will be no doubt that even off duty, this is only a work meeting. He can sniff out any lurkers at the hospital."

"He'll be a big help," Oliver said, wanting to reach out to her. But he held back. "I'll pick you up in forty-five minutes."

"Do you know my address?"

"Of course."

"Of course," she echoed. "Just part of the job, right?"

"No. I wanted to know where to pick you up for our first date."

She shook her head. "This is not a date, Special Agent. I want to make that perfectly clear."

"As clear as mud," he replied.

Oliver watched her drive away, worried that she was going home to an empty house. But she lived on the same street as several of the other team members. They looked out for each other, though Ava would spit nails if he tried to protect her. Still, he hurried to his car and went back to the base hotel to get cleaned up

He'd be at her house soon enough.

EIGHT

Ava heard a knock at her door and checked the peephole to be safe, Roscoe by her side. She'd gotten used to having Roscoe here and she didn't like feeling vulnerable.

But her fears were put to rest when she squinted through the tiny glass circle.

Oliver, and right on time.

She took a last look at the white cotton button-down shirt and capri jeans she'd dragged out of her closet to throw on with some bright pink sandals. Too much?

Not one to be fussy about her clothes, she smiled at the sandals. They were a birthday gift from her mom earlier this year, with a note that said, "Live bright, honey."

Her mom loved florals and prints in bright colors.

Ava, not so much. Maybe because her dark red hair always clashed with anything bright. But she wore the sandals tonight to give her strength and to put her in downtime mode. Maybe she did need a few days' rest.

Taking a breath, she tossed her hair off her shoulders, threw on some earrings and opened the door to find Oliver standing there, looking way too good in a navy blue T-shirt and jeans.

"And boots," she said, not even realizing she'd spoken out loud. "You wore your boots."

"For you," he replied, stepping inside and lifting a foot to reveal what looked like hand-tooled rich brown cowboy boots. "You live close to Boyd Sullivan's half sister, Zoe."

Ava reached for her purse, used to his blunt switches in conversation. "Yes, but she's married now. She's Zoe Colson. I barely knew her before. Now we chat a lot in passing. She kept to herself until Linc Colson came along. They had a quick ceremony in their uniforms, performed by Pastor Harmon, from what Zoe told Felicity and me—and they're happy together. I visit with them now and then. I feel sorry for her since everyone suspected her of helping her brother."

A few months ago, Linc Colson, a tech sergeant and Security Forces investigator, had become Zoe Sullivan's bodyguard after she'd been targeted by Michael Orleck, a man who'd failed her training class. Zoe, a staff sergeant and flight instructor, had been the victim of his "gaslighting" pranks. He hoped to make it look like Zoe was having a breakdown because of her half brother Boyd and his killing sprees. But Linc helped her figure things out, and Orleck and a female accomplice were apprehended.

Since Oliver knew all of this, she said, "Zoe can't help that Boyd is her half brother."

Oliver lifted his chin. "Well, we've cleared her. She has had no contact with Boyd since he escaped."

"Yes, so why that concerned look on your face?"

"Just going over the angles. He could still try to get to you through her."

"Zoe wouldn't allow that," Ava said, glancing around her tiny but tidy apartment located on Base Boulevard, where a lot of people she knew lived. "Besides, Sullivan had his chance with me in the woods— several times if I count his accomplice shooting at me. I'm sure he's moving on, and he could be miles away by now."

Oliver didn't look so sure, but he didn't pester her about it. Instead, he did a standard FBI sweep of the living room and kitchen and then stared down the short hallway to the bath and bedroom.

Her one-bedroom apartment was a single story, with a small front porch and an open patio and small backyard that opened to the common area and some woods behind. She used the place for sleeping and eating and watching sappy movies.

But now she wished it looked a little more like a home since Oliver's astute gaze had scanned the place. Was he still worried about her safety? Or checking out her sad lifestyle?

"Everything seemed okay when you got home?" he asked, confirming the answer to her question.

So maybe he didn't care about the dead plant on the table and the dust on the windowsills.

"Yes. Just stifling hot. I turned the air down so I can sleep better tonight."

"I'm glad you have Roscoe with you."

"Me, too. It'll be tough to let him go back to the kennels after this."

Oliver nodded at Roscoe. "You're a keeper." Roscoe woofed a thank-you. Oliver laughed and escorted her out, then scanned the street both ways. Seemingly satisfied after she'd put Roscoe in his kennel in the back, he opened the door to her SUV for her like a real gentleman.

Ava didn't have the heart to fuss at him for holding the door open for her. His chivalry was kind of endearing, but she didn't want to get used to it. Her work was done for a while, anyway. She'd still be part of the team searching for Sullivan, but she'd have to keep her distance from Oliver from now on.

At this dinner they needed to wrap things up and then take a step back.

Soon, they were at the base hospital, where Turner was spending the night as a precaution. The boy had been questioned by several members of the team searching for the Red Rose Killer, and Oliver had filled her in on the way over.

"He says he saw a woman and heard a woman and a man arguing about whether to kill him, but that the woman was dressed all in black, 'like a Ninja,' he says. Turner was so afraid, he wouldn't answer to anyone who called out his name."

But he'd answered to Ava, maybe because Roscoe had been with her or maybe because he didn't want to spend another night in the woods, huddling on a ledge.

After Turner's parents had thanked both of them, Ava and Oliver went into the little boy's room. Turner was sitting up in bed playing with his toys and watching an animated movie.

"Hey," he said with a grin, his bites looking clean and doctored and his scratches still evident but not as nasty looking. "You brought Roscoe?"

"Sure," Ava replied, smiling down at the boy. Roscoe woofed hello. "We just wanted to check on you."

"I'm fine," Turner said, his snaggletoothed grin doing Ava in. Since when had she thought of having her own little Cub Scout?

Since the fresh-and-clean-smelling man standing beside her had burst onto the scene.

After a few specific questions, Oliver made a big deal of calling Turner's parents back in so he could honor Turner with a plastic FBI badge. When both the agent and the little boy shot her dazzling smiles, Ava knew she was a goner.

She had to take four days away from this man, if nothing else.

They decided to have dinner at Carmen's. The Italian restaurant was intimate and quiet, with small tables covered in pretty checkered cloths and soft instrumental music playing in the background.

After the waitress put them in a back corner where Ava could keep Roscoe away from the comings and goings, Ava breathed a sigh of relief.

She could see the front door from here. Not that she worried about gossip. The base grapevine was common no matter where a person was stationed, since most military bases were like a city within a city and everyone knew everyone else.

But she did worry about the blogger, who seemed to thrive on making Security Forces, and especially the K-9 team, look bad. Why would anyone want to do that? Why stir up trouble where there wasn't any? Well, she and Oliver had grown close, but they were both toeing the line on their feelings. They'd spent the better part of their time together in the reserve behind the base, so the person had to be connected to Boyd Sullivan in some way to have even seen them together.

Unless the blogger was a member of the team?

She didn't even want to think about that.

"The scents coming out of that kitchen smell really good," Oliver said, his gaze on her instead of the menu. "Hey, are you okay with this?"

"With what?" she asked, coming out of her stupor. "Yes, I love Carmen's. The lasagna is so good. My favorite."

"No, I mean…this…us, together in public."

Ava put down her menu and stared at the artificial daisies in the center of the table. "I don't care what people think and I can't control gossip, but I wish we could figure out who the blogger is. Do you think it's Sullivan?"

"Only if he has a really good Wi-Fi signal from the woods."

"Could it be someone on the inside?"

"You mean from Security Forces?"

"I don't know. I'm just trying to figure how the blogger's reports always seem so close to the truth."

"Yeah, they nailed us. Arguing one minute and… having dinner the next."

Shaking her head, she glanced around. "It could be anyone."

"Yes, but I think it's possibly someone from Sullivan's camp, not ours," Oliver replied, his tone firm.

"So you think it could be his female helper who loves to use us for target practice?"

"Could be. Another smoke screen to distract us from him. But he hasn't made a move this time around.

We've confirmed through DNA and fingerprints that he killed Drew Golosky, but he hasn't killed since then, that we know of."

"Maybe he's bored and sent his accomplice to mess with us just to get some kicks, since that person seems to be the shooter."

"About the accomplice, the floral headband thing we found didn't pan out. No DNA, but the rain probably took care of that."

"Turner said he saw two people, a man and a woman. That confirms that the shooter could be a female."

"According to the report from Caleb Streeter, the boy described the man as looking exactly like Boyd Sullivan. You saw Sullivan, so we know he's back, but you didn't see the person with him."

"And Turner didn't get a good look at the woman."

"He saw her but, like he said, she was heavily clothed and disguised. We'd need to do a lineup of anyone we suspect and let him pick one out."

"Is that wise?" Ava asked after the waitress took their orders. "He's just a little boy."

"It's the only choice we have right now."

Ava knew he was right, but Turner had been through the wringer out there all alone. The boy seemed okay, but the hospital had brought in therapists to make sure he'd recover emotionally, too.

The waitress brought their salads and lasagna, then placed some bread and butter on the table. "Eat up."

"Let's enjoy our food," Oliver suggested. "And then we'll go over the list of female suspects we know of."

"There could be others?"

"With Sullivan, that's a distinct possibility."

He looked as if he wanted to say more, but he held

back. Instead, he took a drink of the mint iced tea they'd both ordered and grinned at her. "Go ahead. I love watching you eat."

They both dug in and Ava had to admit, the lasagna hit the spot. "I didn't realize how famished I was."

"Dessert?" he offered when the waitress cleared his empty plate and put the other half of Ava's lasagna in a to-go box.

"No, just some coffee," she told the smiling woman.

Once they had their coffee, Oliver settled back to stare at her again. "We've only really known each other a couple days," he pointed out. "Seems longer."

"Tired of me already, Special Agent?"

He looked at her—really looked at her. His gaze moved over her face, her lips, her hair, the silver feather earrings she'd put on at the last minute.

"I don't think I could ever get tired of you, Ava."

"You don't know me, really," she said to deflect the warmth spreading throughout her system. She couldn't do this. Not with him. He was too much to take in, to absorb, to understand. And what if he got hurt or killed? She'd have to go through that kind of anguish all over again.

He let out a rough sigh. "I'd like to know you, the good you and the bad you. All of you. And I have to tell you, Ava, I'm not one to be rash or impulsive. I calculate and plan and analyze. That's what I do. That's my job."

He stopped and looked down at his fingers cupped on the table. "My job has taken over my life. It's all I've had for years now, and that was fine until one day in April when you walked into the conference room and…something changed. I didn't even know it had changed until we ran up on each other in the woods."

April. That's when she'd first noticed him, too. So he had been watching her, and she had to admit she'd been keenly aware of him even if she had tried to deny that to herself over and over.

But that didn't mean anything. Or it could mean everything.

Trying hard to breathe, she bobbed her head and pushed at her hair. "Yes, Oliver, in the woods with a serial killer watching our every move. A man who kills for the pleasure of killing. You came here for him, right? You came here on a mission and my gut tells me you'll finish that mission, no matter what. No matter the cost."

Sitting up straight, she pushed back her chair. "It's a cost I'm not willing to pay. Not again."

Oliver grabbed her leftovers, threw some bills on the table to cover the meal and the tip, and hurried after Ava.

"I'm sorry," he said once they were outside. "I told you I don't do this sort of thing and I'm not about to cross that line now, not with so much at stake."

Why had he told her he'd like to know her better? Now she was running away faster than a fighter pilot doing a downward spiral. She'd just admitted she didn't want to be hurt again. Now he had to know what had happened and who had hurt her.

"It's okay," she said, waiting for Roscoe to hop into his kennel. "We've only known each other a short time and yes, it would be nice to become friends. But now I have four days off and I don't want to think about you or the woods or Boyd Sullivan."

Oliver put her food in the back seat, got in the vehicle and turned to her. "So does that mean you've *already* been thinking about me?"

Her eyes told him everything. Interested and aware, but afraid and fighting.

"I've been thinking about a lot of things," she admitted. "But I'm going to use this reprieve to regroup and remember why I'm here. I want to get to the next level. I'm ready and I've worked hard and—"

He stopped her protests with a finger to his lips. "Did you hear that?"

"What?" Ava went quiet and listened. She heard a car starting, a motor roaring to life.

"Go," Oliver said. "Hurry."

Ava backed up and peeled out of the parking lot, glad the base traffic was light. "What is it?"

"Someone was watching us," he said, his eyes on the side mirror. "There." A black sedan pulled out and turned behind them.

Oliver's heart pumped a rapid beat. "They were sitting in the car. Must have been waiting for us to come out of the restaurant."

Ava glanced into the rearview mirror. "So you think because someone else started their car and idled the motor, they were spying on us?"

"No, I think they were planning to either run us down or follow us." He checked behind them. "And now they are following us."

Ava checked the mirror. "That sedan is behind us but it's staying back."

"Don't go to your place yet," he said. "Turn toward the training center."

Ava didn't argue with him. She watched the approaching vehicle and then sped toward the K-9 compound. "Surely they wouldn't follow us into the center?"

"We'll see. They got on base somehow."

They both watched as the car gained speed. But just as Ava put on her blinker and turned toward the center, a Security Forces SUV sat waiting at the turn-in to exit into traffic. The black car moved on by. The SF presence had scared them away.

"That was close," Oliver said.

"But we still can't be sure," Ava replied. "Better to think the worst and be cautious, right?"

"Right."

They remained silent while she circled back and took the road to her house.

Oliver's thoughts swirled in confusion as Ava parked the vehicle and they got out, Roscoe leading the way to the door. He'd find Boyd Sullivan and end this thing, but now he'd do it because he'd been assigned to find a killer. Because it was his job. He'd do it for Madison. He and Madison had dated and come close to getting married. No one could ever know that she'd betrayed him by going back to a man she'd briefly dated in high school.

Boyd Sullivan. The man who'd killed her because she was with Oliver.

No one needed to know, but maybe he should tell Ava, at least. So she'd understand about him. That he had no heart left to give to anyone again.

* * *

"Dinner was nice in spite of that creepy car following us," Ava said, her tone uncertain. "I guess I'll see you tomorrow."

Glancing past her, he said, "Since you insisted on coming back here, at least let me clear the rooms again for you."

"I know how to check my apartment, Oliver."

"Yes, but…I'd feel better. I'm not trying to be all macho. I just don't want to leave without knowing you're safe."

He looked up and down the street in front of the brick apartment building. "I don't see any suspicious cars, but I'd still like to check on things inside."

"Fine, come in and we'll check the rooms together."

Ava put the food on a small counter in the open kitchen. Flipping on lights, they cleared the living room and then headed down the hallway to the bath and bedroom. Roscoe stopped at the door and growled.

"Stay." Ava walked ahead of him into her bedroom and turned on the light.

And gasped.

"Oliver?"

Oliver moved past Roscoe and her to stare at the bed.

A red rose lay across the bright blue bedspread. And a note stood against a fluffy white pillow.

You saved the kid. Good for you. Now…I'm coming for you.

NINE

Ten minutes later, Ava's house was overflowing with crime-scene techs and K-9 handlers, Oliver right in the thick of things to make sure nothing from the crime scene was compromised.

She sat on the couch holding a glass of water someone had brought her, her mind whirling with the implications of what they'd found in her bedroom.

Boyd Sullivan had let her live long enough to save Turner Johnson.

But why, when according to Turner, the man they thought to be Sullivan had threatened to kill him?

What had the boy said—that the woman reminded the bad guy about something in his own childhood?

Turner's ability to recall key elements of their heated conversation could help solve that puzzle, at least. What had happened in Boyd Sullivan's childhood to make him so evil and yet, willing to let a child live and willing to let Ava live until she'd found the child?

Someone touched her on the arm.

Vanessa Gomez, second lieutenant and critical care nurse.

And one of the women suspected of being in cahoots with Boyd Sullivan. But how would Vanessa have time to go traipsing through the woods shooting people when she worked long hours at the base hospital?

"How you doing?" Vanessa asked Ava, her brown eyes full of what looked like genuine concern.

"I'm fine," Ava said. "But every time I get up to help, someone tells me to sit down and stay out of the way."

"They've got it under control," Vanessa said. "I had just gotten home and came over when I heard about what had happened."

Ava remembered Vanessa lived down the street from her.

"How did you hear?" Ava asked, suspicion her constant companion now.

"We have scanners at the hospital to report incoming and other things. My shift had just ended, so I asked to see you, since I've been looped in on this from the beginning."

Ava tried to calculate the distance from the hospital to her house. "Thanks for checking on me. I'm kind of jittery."

"Understandable," Vanessa said. She wore her long brown hair up in a haphazard messy bun. "You know, I'm a target, too. I got a rose back in April. I have a security guard escort me out of the hospital and some of the base patrols make sure I get home. And at home, I have K-9 Eagle assigned to me until further notice, and my brother, Aiden, lives there with me. I've been watching my back for months now and let me tell you, it's not any fun."

Ava's suspicions eased. She'd heard Vanessa's younger brother had come back from deployment with a serious case of PTSD. "I'm sure it's been awful and now that the Red Rose Killer is back, it's even worse."

"Yes." Vanessa glanced around at the activity. "He's becoming bold again. We've heard he's hiding out in the woods. Quite a feat, you finding that little boy alive."

"Sullivan could have killed him."

"And you, too," Vanessa said. "Now you're on the list, so, Ava, take any precautions you can."

"I intend to," Ava answered. "But right now, I need something to do. I can't just sit here."

The front door opened and Roscoe came running in and galloped straight to her, Buster grinning behind him.

"Roscoe." She ruffled his golden fur and hugged him close. "I'm so glad you were here with me."

Her furry partner woofed his happiness, too. But Roscoe was a working dog. He lifted his head and started sniffing the air.

Oliver came in from the hallway. "I asked Buster to take him around back. They picked up a scent so we've got people combing the woods."

"He should go back over the apartment." Ava stood and ordered Roscoe down the hallway even though he'd cleared the apartment earlier. But he had alerted at her bedroom door. Oliver had rushed both of them away from the scene. Now she wanted answers. "Search."

Buster followed Oliver, along with a couple of techs and Captain Blackwood, all eager to see what else Roscoe might find. Ava thanked Vanessa for checking on her and hurried to the back of the apartment.

Roscoe stood with teeth bared and his fur standing straight up, same as he'd done earlier.

"He recognizes a scent," Oliver told her as he pulled her into the bedroom. "But we don't know who that scent belongs to."

Ava watched Roscoe, then grabbed some latex gloves and searched under her bed and all around the room. "I don't see anything out of the ordinary. And we know they came in through that window." She pointed to where they'd found a bent screen that someone had managed to put back on the window and a broken pane near the lock. "Roscoe alerted earlier and we didn't find anything else. He could be picking up a scent from someone in the house." She thought about Vanessa, but Roscoe had whizzed right past Vanessa.

Roscoe kept growling low, his fierce eyes on the window.

Oliver looked at Ava for a brief moment and then grabbed her and dived to the floor with her.

Just before a bullet pierced the wall behind where she'd been standing.

"I'm getting you out of here," Oliver said a few moments later, his body still shielding her.

Ava clung to him but tried to move away. "Oliver, I'm not going to run away scared."

He helped her sit up, and after he'd assured everyone she was all right, he leaned toward her, his dark head close to hers. "You should be scared, Ava. They're coming for you, one way or another, and sooner or later, they will get to you. Tonight was too close for comfort. They had a solid bead on you and we stopped them, but they won't miss next time."

"I'll be more careful," she said, her insides cold

with dread, the sound of that kill shot still ringing in her ears.

How she'd do that, she wasn't sure. She'd tried to be cautious, but this entire week had been one big search and rescue. The adrenaline from that assignment had receded but now her heart rate was right back up. Out of worry for her safety.

And Oliver's.

Ava couldn't believe that whoever had broken in here had been hiding out, watching and waiting the whole time while a team of trained law enforcement officers and K-9s stormed her house and the woods. Had the car following them been a distraction so the killer could get in the house and then hide in the woods?

Oliver held her arm. "The minute you came into the bedroom, they tried to kill you. He's done toying with you. The boy is safe and now Sullivan needs a new kill. This has escalated beyond being careful."

"You're scaring me."

Captain Blackwood walked in and after salutes, he turned to Ava. "I agree with the special agent, Ava. You can't stay here alone."

"I'm taking her to San Antonio," Oliver said, his tone firm and sure.

"No," Ava said, shaking her head.

"Yes," the captain said, nodding his head. "Getting her off the base without him knowing is a good idea."

"Sir, with all due respect, you haven't sent any of the others off-site," Ava replied, thinking the last place she needed to be right now was with Oliver Davison.

"No, but they've all had protection and right now, I don't have anyone to spare. Oliver can still do his job at the FBI field office by searching for any loopholes we've missed and he can protect you, away from base, for the next four days, at least."

"But, sir—"

"That's not a suggestion, Airman. We'll clear the way and make sure we sneak you out of here so they can't find you."

"Yes, sir. If I go, Roscoe goes," she said, hoping they'd both agree.

"Might be risky," the captain replied. "Roscoe isn't used to the city. What do you think?"

She didn't want to leave her partner. "Because of his breed and since he's SAR, he's more socially inclined than the hard-nosed bomb sniffers and terrorist hunters. I can handle him in crowds, sir. Besides, we probably won't venture out that much, if at all."

The captain gave her a curt nod. "Roscoe could use a break, too."

"It won't be that long," Oliver told her while she gathered some clothes. "I have a two-bedroom apartment and I'll give you all the space you need."

"What I need is my life back," she replied. "And you should be here, looking for Sullivan."

"I've got other agents scattered around and I had intended to report in and do some work from home this weekend anyway," he said. "You can help me go over the list of female suspects who might be helping Sullivan. I want to put them in that lineup I mentioned earlier."

Ava still didn't agree with that idea, but they might not have any other choice. If Turner could ID the woman, they could bring her in and question her. And maybe get a break.

"I'll help in any way I can since I'm being taken against my will."

They were alone in the room now, but the captain had stationed guards outside so they could sneak her out.

"Are you really going against your will?" Oliver asked her now, his tone soft and husky against her ear.

She couldn't answer that. Her heart wanted some time alone with this man but her head told her to sneak away from him and everyone else until she could figure this out.

"I'm going," she replied, stepping back. "That will have to be enough for now."

He nodded. "I'll take it because I'm not going to leave you alone here."

They set up a decoy—Special Agent Denise Logan, who'd been brought in not long ago to help with training one of the K-9s. Denise specialized in electronics and had worked with Senior Airman and training volunteer Chase McLear and a beagle named Queenie. Denise trained dogs in electronic detection but she was also good at surveillance and undercover work.

She'd been back on base this week to help with training again and to check on some of the missing Military Working Dogs and service dogs they'd found in the woods.

So, they brought her in disguised as a tech and then took Ava out, also disguised as the same tech.

Denise would stay in Ava's house with a trainee dog, hidden guards on the alert all around, in an effort to draw Sullivan or the shooter back to the house.

Normally, Oliver would have stayed close for such

an operation, but right now he wanted Ava away from Canyon Air Force Base. And he wanted to start from scratch and go through the whole timeline to try to figure out how Boyd Sullivan's mind worked. The man was a naturalist and an extremist, so he knew how to hide in plain sight in those dense woods. He was rubbing their noses in it.

He wanted to toy with Oliver a little bit more, but Oliver wouldn't fall for his tricks any longer.

Oliver couldn't be everywhere and his priorities had now shifted to taking care of Ava first and leaving the hunt to the highly trained pros on the base.

Now with everything in place they were on their way to San Antonio, traveling in the dead of night with a detail behind them for an extra precaution.

"So it's about a thirty-minute drive to my place. It's downtown near the Riverwalk," Oliver told Ava.

"Fine."

She'd been quiet. Too quiet. Ava didn't like being handled. She was used to handling things all by herself.

"Tell me about your family," he said.

"You're trying to draw me out, Special Agent. And I don't want to talk to you right now."

Nope, not happy. She was using that special agent thing like a weapon.

"Are you going to pout for four days and waste the time we have together?"

"Yes."

"Ava, c'mon, we're all concerned about you. Sullivan veered off the beaten path to scare you, and he follows through on his threats."

"Yes, and several other people are on that list, too."

"Yes, but several are being protected around the clock and the others are being vigilant in staying safe."

"I can keep myself safe. Roscoe is with me twenty-four-seven these days. He saved me tonight. Well, you both saved me."

"Yes, and we're both here with you. I don't doubt your abilities, Ava, but someone tried to put a bullet in you last night while you were standing in your house."

When she didn't respond, he added, "Plus, your superior ordered some R & R for you since you've been in the woods for days now with very little rest and you were shot at on several different occasions while searching for Turner Johnson."

"What if they come after Turner?" she asked, her pout session forgotten now. "Maybe we should consider that instead of my safety."

"On it."

"You've got people protecting Turner?"

"We're watching his house. They already have a state-of-the-art security system. We haven't leaked anything that he told us to the press."

"Not even to Heidi?"

"No. Especially not to Heidi. You were at the press conference last night. We never mentioned that the boy had run into Boyd Sullivan."

"What if Turner tells someone?"

"I don't think he will. He's still scared, for one thing. And his parents are encouraging him to only talk to his doctors and therapists."

"But if he has to pick someone out of a lineup—"

"It will be done in secrecy."

She went back to pouting. He watched her shut down

and lean toward the passenger-side door. Roscoe was tucked into the back, his head turning from left to right.

"Ava, I'm sorry. I can't help this need to protect you."

"And I can't help that it makes me angry. I'm not a shrinking violet, Oliver."

"I can tell," he said, trying to lighten things. "You're more of a fiery cactus flower. Pretty but prickly."

"Is that supposed to be a compliment?"

"Yes."

"Do you really think you can hide me in San Antonio?"

"It's a big city, and I know all the secret spots."

She was silent for a while and then shifted toward him. "Since we're stuck together, why don't you tell me about where you grew up?"

"Oh, so we're talking again?"

"No, I'm asking the questions now. I mean, I really don't even know you. You don't talk much about yourself, so now's your chance."

Oliver decided he'd try anything to draw her out and win her trust. Even talking about himself.

"I grew up in Yonkers, in a mostly Irish neighborhood. I thought my dad worked at a financial firm in New York City, but I found out when I was old enough to understand that he was FBI. He dealt with a lot of bad mafia people and put some of them away for a long time."

"So you followed in his footsteps?"

"Lived it and breathed it. Couldn't wait to get out of college and head to Quantico."

"How did your mother live with that? Both of you being FBI, I mean?"

Surprised at that question, he shook his head. "Not very well."

"Don't tell me he got killed while on duty?"

"No. He retired, and they moved to Florida."

She seemed to exhale after hearing that. "And your childhood?"

"Normal, fun, always running in packs with my diverse group of friends. I loved it."

"You really are too good to be true."

"You think that?"

"Why don't you tell me about what's really eating at you?"

"How do you know something is eating at me?"

"Because you get this sad look in your eyes at times, a look that I remember well. I used to see that same look each time I came upon a mirror."

"Did it go away?"

"It's getting better," she said, staring out over the highway.

"This person who died when you were in the chopper crash, was he special to you?"

"Yes."

Oliver swallowed and took a leap of faith. "I had someone special once. Or at least I thought she was special. But she lied to me and kind of ripped my heart out."

Ava didn't say a word. She waited.

Exiting the interstate, he drove a few more miles and then turned into a tree-lined street and made a left into an apartment complex. "The saddest part of it—I didn't really even love her."

TEN

Ava barely noticed the swanky gated community or the upstairs apartment that had a view of the entire city, including the nearby famous Riverwalk. The place was modern and minimalist with sleek lines and very little artwork or distractions.

But she didn't need a distraction in design. Stunned, she couldn't get past what he'd just said to her before they'd made their way up the elevator.

Oliver had been in love and he'd been betrayed? Was he referring to Madison Ackler?

But then, he hadn't really been in love?

She needed to know more about his relationship with the woman Boyd Sullivan had killed.

Much more.

"Are you hungry?" he asked, causing her to turn from the glass doors to the wide balcony.

"No. Just tired." Then she shrugged. "But I'm too wired to sleep just yet."

"You want answers."

"Of course I do. You might have tried leading with that 'I didn't love her' comment."

"I think my mom left some chamomile tea here last time they came to visit. I'll make you a cup."

"I hate hot tea." She moved across the wide, open room and sank down on a creamy leather couch by a cozy fireplace. "Stop with the patronizing. I want you to tell me the truth, Oliver. I assume you're talking about Madison, right?"

He let out a breath. "Yes, but there are things regarding this case that not many people know."

Ending the search for tea, he came and sat down on the couch then propped his booted feet on the glass coffee table.

"She and I met here in San Antonio about four years ago." Looking around, he shook his head. "She wanted it all because she came from a small Texas town. She wanted the city life and the night life and the good life."

"Did you try to give her all of that?" Ava asked, trying to picture him with that kind of woman.

"Yes, I did. But she tended to get bored easily. We lived near each other in downtown apartments and grew close pretty quickly. For a while, things were good. She worked as a paralegal with a prestigious firm and I did my job. We dated and I enjoyed her company. But Madison always held things back and she complained about my long hours."

"She hated your being FBI."

"How do you know that?"

"If she wanted it all and you had to give work your all, it doesn't add up, does it?"

Giving Ava an admiring stare, he finally said, "No."

"So she…started staying out with the girls, complaining that you never had time for her?"

"Did you know her?" he asked with a wry grin.

"No, but I know how it goes. I've seen a lot of that, being military. Anything to do with saving the world tends to take up a lot of time and energy."

"Yes, that is true. She wanted me to find a good desk job that paid more. Maybe something in the finance world."

"You'd last at that about two days, tops."

"You see, this is why we click, you and me."

They sat, eyes on each other, for a few heartbeats.

Ava blinked first. "Stop stalling and finish your story."

He cleared his throat, sat up and held his hands together. "Madison grew up in Dill, Texas. She went to high school with Boyd Sullivan. They dated briefly and went to the prom together...but Madison broke things off with him when he got too possessive after only a couple of dates."

Ava's stomach roiled while her pulse skidded to a stop. "So Boyd and Madison were close at one time and she ended it? Is that why he went back there and killed her?"

"Yes, that and the fact that she was with me."

He stood and moved to the fireplace to place a hand on the wooden mantel. "We were engaged."

Ava took in a breath and hurried to him to pull him around, her hand on his arm. "Wow. I don't remember all the details of the victims' backgrounds." Looking over at him, she asked, "How did she wind up dead back in Dill if she was living in San Antonio and engaged to you?"

"That's the rest of the story."

"Okay, I'm listening."

"He killed her first and then killed the other four. At

first, I was a suspect, being the boyfriend. But I had a solid alibi. I was doing surveillance with another agent the night she was killed."

He took Ava's hands in his. "I had asked her to marry me, but I realized after I'd asked her that I wanted to get married for all the wrong reasons. Madison wanted children and a big house and the ideal suburban life. I cared about her and thought my image of a family man would be good for my job. Then I remembered what my mother had gone through and I…kind of balked on the marriage thing. When I tried to explain to Madison, we had a horrible fight and I broke up with her because I could see we'd never make it."

Holding tight to his hands, Ava asked, "So you tried to be honest with her, but things didn't work out?"

He closed his eyes and took another breath. "No, she got really angry and called me all kinds of names. Then she left. I thought she'd gone back to her apartment and that we could talk after she calmed down. Maybe we could just hold off on the wedding for a while to see if it was right. But when I didn't hear from her, a friend told me that Madison decided to go home to Dill for the weekend. But she didn't come back to the city that Sunday. I got the call late the next day, after searching for her everywhere. He shot her and left her inside her car on a rural road just outside of town. Left the final note on her body and then he killed all the others."

Ava swallowed the lump in her throat. Oliver's fiancée, gone in an instant. "Oliver…"

He held her hands but shook his head. "No, let me finish. I need to tell you all of it."

Ava nodded and waited, holding her breath for what might be next.

"After she died, a friend came to me and told me the truth. Madison went back to Dill, all right. And right into Boyd Sullivan's waiting arms."

Ava pulled away and stepped back, her gut burning. "They had kept in touch?"

"I think Sullivan was her first love but she couldn't deal with his dark side," Oliver said. "I think that sicko killed the woman he claimed he loved because he thought *she* loved me. I can't prove any of this, but I've put together enough bits and pieces to know they met back up somehow after she left Dill the first time and she had an affair with him. But she didn't want to break off things with me because she wanted me to be the man she married, while she kept him on the side. I believe he confronted her about me and she told him she wanted to marry me. The friend who told me all of this said Madison didn't want to acknowledge her love for Sullivan because he was a loose cannon and, in Madison's mind, a loser."

The puzzle started falling together in Ava's mind, too. "So he killed her when she threw you up to him?"

"I don't know. But knowing Madison, she might have blurted that out. She wanted the good life, which he couldn't give her."

Oliver's gaze met hers and she could see the torment of this horrible burden he'd been carrying. "He must have snapped when she turned him down again and then he wanted to get even with all of us. So… in a way, my being with Madison started this whole chain of events."

"No, Oliver, no. He's sick. He would have done this eventually anyway, and Madison obviously didn't love him, or you either, for that matter. She played both of you and that's not your fault. You can't think that way."

Oliver lifted his hands and then dropped them to his side. "But I have to think of all the angles, because I helped to put him away and he managed to escape. He's not done killing and he's targeting you now. I can't let him do this all over again."

Ava understood Oliver's intense need to protect her, but she worried he was going down a slippery slope.

Looking into her eyes, he said, "I'm the real target now. It's become personal between us. But he won't kill me, because that would be too easy. He'll go after the people I care about and that means you're high up on the list."

Ava digested that, her heart splitting, but she needed to know a few other things, too. "Why haven't you told any of us this, Oliver? You're way too involved in this case."

"Because my SAC only offered me this opportunity if I'd stay focused on the whole case and not just Madison's murder. He picked me because I know the case, but he's watching me like a hawk, too. Trust me, I can't blow it again."

Pacing in front of the patio door, he turned to stare out at the city. "It's too late for me to help Madison. But I can't stand by and let this happen again. Not to you, Ava."

"He won't get to me."

"But he'll try. It's a matter of pride now. He has to win. I won't let him win again."

Ava wanted to pull him close, but that would be too tempting. He didn't need a romantic entanglement right now, and neither did she. She thought back over their time in that dense wilderness and how much the guilt must have been eating at him out there in the wild and each time he came home at night, knowing he'd let Sullivan get away yet again. No wonder he'd gone into hyper mode in trying to find the Red Rose Killer. Oliver had relived his fear and guilt when he'd seen that rose and note in her bedroom.

"I'm so sorry," she finally said. "Oliver, I'm sorry. We're going to find him, and maybe one day we'll understand why—what happened to make him so evil." Then she whispered, "But none of this is your fault. You have to keep telling yourself that."

Oliver looked at her, his gaze hungry for redemption as he stared into her eyes. "I've changed, Ava. After she died and I put together the truth, I took a long walk and wound up in a little church, and I prayed like I've never prayed before. I told the Lord I wanted to be a better man, a man who knew true love and felt things deeply, with all my soul."

"You are that man," she said, holding back tears. "Oliver, you are that man."

"I want to be," he said, his shoulders sagging. "But I keep slipping back into that old habit of doing my job and ignoring everything, including my faith. I want to bring in the Red Rose Killer, for Madison and for all the others he's killed. And now, for you."

Ava gave in and put her hands on his face and kissed him, her heart opening and accepting that something was happening between them. Something that went deeper than finding a killer.

"And for yourself," she whispered.

Oliver felt lighter, free, hopeful now. After he'd spilled the truth to her, Ava had softened. He knew she could be a good friend, if nothing else. Yes, she'd kissed him, but that only meant she had empathy for his situation. They'd discussed the case and life in general well into the dawn and finally, exhausted, he'd escorted her to her room. After making sure Roscoe was settled near her bed and the alarm was set and no suspicious cars or people were hanging around outside, Oliver had finally slept for a few hours.

Now they'd had coffee and bagels and were about to get busy with work. Roscoe sat obediently after his breakfast and a fast walk in the neighborhood doggie park, both Ava and Oliver careful that no one suspicious was around.

"In spite of the gruesome details," he said now, "I feel better having told you the truth. I've never told anyone the whole story."

"Not even your SAC?"

"Oh, he found out right away. Once I was cleared as a suspect, my SAC watched me like a hawk because I became obsessed with finding Madison's killer. Then when the reports about the other killings in Dill came in, I got sick to my stomach and worked day and night until my SAC pulled me off the case and told me to go home and sleep. But I couldn't sleep or eat or do much of anything. I went through the ordeal of packing up some more of her things and I found a note."

"A note?" Ava turned to him. "From Sullivan?"

"I believe so. A card with a dried red rose pressed inside. The note said, 'I'll find you again one day.'"

"That's the Red Rose Killer," Ava said. "He must have had it in for her after she dumped him in high school, but you had to connect him to the others, too."

"Exactly. So I explained my theory to my SAC and

he got serious about things then, but he still wanted me off the case. Of course, we had a solid case when he went to trial. Madison must have had that note since high school. I don't know."

"So you thought it was over when he went to prison?"

"Yes, I tried to give up but I'd still wake up at night in a cold sweat, thinking about how she died. He was in prison by then and I thought I had justice for Madison. Then he escaped and killed again, and now I'm back on it because I know more about the man then most, but still not nearly enough. When Sullivan escaped, my SAC came to me and asked me if I could handle it."

"The case or the fact that Sullivan escaped?"

"Both. He offered me the case, provided I took things slow and had a lot of backup. He knew the base had jurisdiction but he allowed me to consult, so to speak, since I know this investigation like the back of my hand."

But he'd failed yet again. The Red Rose Killer had been on a new killing spree, and right under Oliver's nose, at that. "I don't know if this will ever end, if I can ever get past it. Maybe I should give up the FBI."

"Oliver, you can't go back to that dark place. I won't let that happen."

He smiled over at her and remembered that gentle kiss they'd shared last night. "So you'll become *my* protector now?"

"We'll protect each other," she said, the look in her eyes making him think she remembered the kiss, too. But her words dismissed that. "And we start by doing what we came here to do. We go back over this investigation, study all the reports, news briefs, questions, answers, witnesses, friends, acquaintances, everything."

He nodded and accepted that neither of them was ready for more than finding a killer right now. And that one task could bring on a lot of burnout. No need to go beyond the here and now. Work. They had work to do.

Ava put a hand on his shoulder and gave him a determined look. "I'm here and you're stuck with me until this thing is over and done."

"And after that?"

Ava stared over at him, surprise and acceptance in her dark gaze. "And after that, you're taking me for a hamburger at the Winged Java."

"That's a date," he said.

He wanted to make that date. But Oliver wasn't sure his battered heart could go beyond friendship. He'd find justice, but he wouldn't become the obsessed, half-alive man he'd been before.

He wouldn't. This time, with prayers and a new calm about him, he'd get it right. Ava's presence had grounded him.

He'd have to hold that notion tight until he knew she was safe.

Or he'd die trying.

ELEVEN

Oliver brought out a file box from his office and then, on his laptop, opened up what he'd saved on a thumb drive. "Let's get busy."

"Wow," Ava said an hour later, her coffee cup in front of her on the small desk in the den. "You were serious about being obsessed."

Not only did he have stacks of hard copies but he also had several folders saved on his hard drive and on thumb drives.

"I have every inch of anything ever written or spoken about the Red Rose Killer," Oliver admitted. "Police reports, interviews from his family and people who knew him growing up. You name it, I've studied it. So why can't I bring him in?"

"Because he's evil," Ava said, wishing she could do more. "And you did help bring him in the first time. Somehow, he escaped and now he's managing to mess with all of us."

Oliver lifted a thick file and then let it fall back down. "So evil wins?"

"No. We have to think the way he thinks."

"I'm supposed to be the expert," Oliver replied. "I've

tried thinking the way he thinks. But he stays one step ahead of me. He knows the Canyon base better than I do, even though I've studied those woods and the fence that surrounds the base. He's getting in and out somehow. Thankfully, your commander has beefed up security at the gates and we have Wanted posters of Sullivan plastered outside of the gates and pretty much through the state of Texas." Shaking his head, he stared over at Ava. "How is he doing it?"

"He has help, for one," she reminded Oliver. "And we know he uses disguises and stolen IDs, but the gate patrols have been diligent checking IDs for months now. He's allegedly still in the woods now and he obviously has a good hiding place. Plus, he knows how to work the system and hide in plain sight."

"All correct," Oliver said. "But sooner or later, he has to slip up. I just wish with all my *expert* knowledge, I could make that happen."

"You *are* an expert, but you're too close to this," she said, putting her cup down on the desk. "Why don't you relax a little bit and I'll start going over this information. I know that base pretty well, too. I might see something that you haven't noticed."

"No, we're in this together."

"Oliver, you need to rest. Just rest."

She sat down beside him and urged him around. "Turn away from me."

"I'd rather turn toward you," he said with a questioning lift of his eyebrows.

"Just do as I say."

Oliver turned away with a shrug. "Yes, ma'am."

Ava put her hands on his neck and started kneading

his tight muscles, acutely aware of how strong those muscles were, too.

"That does feel nice," he said, his head drooping. "If you keep that up I won't be able to concentrate on work."

"That's the whole idea," she said, finishing with a few digs that went deep. He was coiled like a rope, knotted and tightly held together. Maybe by a thread.

"Now I'm sleepy."

"See that couch over there? That's a good place to take a nap."

"But we just had breakfast."

"And we were up most of the night."

He gave her a green-eyed stare that made her think of that kiss again. "And what about you?"

"I'll be fine. Go and rest for a few minutes. It might open up some memories you've forgotten."

She watched to make sure he'd really lain down on the big couch and then turned back to the laptop and the stack of files he'd dumped on the small desk.

Then Ava started reading all about Boyd Sullivan. He'd been troubled even in childhood. From interviews from friends and neighbors, she learned his father had been a hard-nosed bully who expected Boyd to do his bidding. Boyd had killed animals for fun and picked on other kids. That was never a good thing. A scrapper, highly sensitive, disturbed, a troublemaker. His family had sent him to the military as a last resort.

He'd been forced into trying to become something he could never be, even if he thought he wanted to make it work. Ava kept reading, comparing paper reports to the ones Oliver had downloaded. After she'd read over several, it became clear to her that Boyd had issues even as a child. Then his father died when he was a teen, leaving him and his half sister, Zoe, to be raised by two different women. But Zoe had turned out okay. Why hadn't Boyd?

She wanted to understand how someone could become such a horrible person, a killer who couldn't stop. A killer who would be caught and contained, one way or another.

And, she reminded herself, a killer who now had her in his sights.

Boyd Sullivan had all the hallmarks of a sociopath and a psychopath, making him a lethal combination. Charming and convincing on the one hand and a cruel monster on the other.

Ava closed her eyes to that horror. Oliver must have suffered such grief, knowing what he knew. This monster had killed Madison out of anger and a twisted passion.

A shiver moved down her spine like a warning tickle.

The Red Rose Killer could take her life.

But there was something that scared Ava more. He could easily kill Oliver in a fit of sheer rage.

She had to find a way to stop him.

Turning to Oliver, she found him sleeping, his jaw slack against a big black pillow, his face looking younger and more relaxed as his breath lifted in soft waves. Ava got up and took an old blue throw and gently laid it over Oliver.

Then she whispered to Roscoe. The big dog lay on the floor beside the sofa, his head up. "Let him rest. He needs to find some peace."

* * *

He dreamed of Madison. She was blonde and pretty, a true Texas beauty. She wore a bright red dress and pretty sandals. Then her image changed. She was pale and gray tinged, her corpse bloody and lying on a sterile, cold autopsy table.

Dead. Madison was dead.

Oliver came awake with a groan and stared up at the woman hovering over him. Not Madison.

Ava.

"Are you all right?" she asked, concern etched across her heart-shaped face.

Ava. So different from Madison.

He couldn't fall for her. He didn't want to lose her, too. Needing to distance himself from that horrible dream and from the woman he was beginning to care way too much about, he sat up and nodded.

"I'm fine. Just a dream. What time is it?"

"Almost noon," she said. "Oliver, what kind of dream?"

"I don't want to talk about it."

Ava sat down and shrugged. "Okay, then we won't. How about some lunch?"

Running a hand over his hair, he shook his head. "No. I need to get back to work."

"Oliver, listen, I think I found something."

He got up and tugged at his wrinkled shirt. "First I need coffee." He found a fresh pot and poured a big mugful. "Okay. Talk to me."

Ava led him to the desk and then pulled up another chair. "Remember that floral Buff we found in the woods?"

"Yes. But Forensics got nothing." Oliver took a long

sip of his coffee and stared at the laptop. "What did you find?"

"I hope you don't mind," Ava said, her brown eyes full of something he couldn't read—apprehension, concern? "I did some comparisons on the type of women Boyd Sullivan goes after."

"And?"

"And he seems to go for the ones who turn him down, obviously. We know that, but it becomes a quest for him and then it becomes way too personal when he thinks he's been insulted or slighted in any way."

"Yes, he's proven that with both female and male victims, so I don't see your point."

"But with the women, he seems to like the healthy, fit types."

"Okay. But the man kills at random, too, so why are you telling me this?"

Giving him a confused look after that blunt question, she said, "Back to the Buff. I pulled up photos of all the women he's hit on or been with."

Oliver's stomach recoiled, the strong coffee turning sour. He should never have told her all the intimate details about his former love life. But Ava knew everything now and there was no going back on that. "And?"

"I think I found a match to that floral Buff we found in the woods."

She pulled out a picture that Oliver recognized immediately. "This looks like the same Buff, doesn't it?" she asked.

Oliver put down his coffee mug and grabbed the picture he used to have on his dresser. "Madison," he said, his gaze moving over the image. She wore an exercise hoodie over black leggings and bright green tennis shoes. They'd been on a long run that morning and he'd snapped a picture of her downstairs right before they came up to get ready for work.

And she was wearing a floral headband that looked almost exactly like the one Ava's team had found in the woods behind the base.

Ava watched from her spot at the desk as Oliver put down his phone and stood with his hands on the back of the couch.

"Okay, I've reported in to the base and I've asked the crime techs to hold on to that headband so we can make a comparison. But I already know it's the same one."

He stayed there and looked over at Ava, the distance between them that she'd felt since he'd woken up still cold and silent. "I don't know why I didn't see it before. Madison always wore one of those when we worked out, to keep her long hair out of her eyes."

"A lot of women do," Ava said, wishing she could erase his pain. She'd worn headbands and Buffs all of her life. "And most of the women he's targeted have had long hair and they worked out a lot."

"Including you, too, now."

He said that without an ounce of intimacy. More like FBI terms. Curt and to the point.

"Yes, but this just confirms what we already know. My point and the significance of matching this headband to the one we found is that he might have kept this one hidden away and he retrieved it when he got out of prison."

"Or someone else could have just bought the same style of headband."

"Yes, but don't you think it's mighty interesting that

we found one that looks exactly like the Buff Madison is wearing in this picture?"

"I get it," Oliver said, whirling to stare out the window. Then he sat down in the chair beside her. "He loved Madison. This is all about that twisted love and his bitterness toward anyone who went up against him after she broke up with him. And the woman who is helping him could be a close match to Madison. That could be her headband. Or he might have given it to her and asked her to wear it."

"Yes, but she lost it," Ava said.

"So we go back over the list of women who've been targeted," he said, his green eyes blazing with that compulsive need to find the truth.

"Yes, just as we'd planned."

"Sullivan might also keep trophy pieces from everyone he's killed," Oliver said. "We need to look closer at the crime-scene photos as compared to the victims in other pictures before their deaths. Scarves, jewelry, medals, anything that might have gone missing. If he's regifting these trophies, we might spot something on one of these women."

Ava agreed with Oliver, but she wished that she could reach inside his heart and assure him this would all work out. But how could she guarantee that when so many people had already died at the hands of the Red Rose Killer?

She understood his putting up a wall between them. She'd wanted to do the same, and yet here they were, forced together again. Maybe God was trying to break down walls, not put more up.

After they'd studied the five victims from Dill, they didn't find much in the way of clues or missing links.

Three of the five early victims had been men who'd all wronged Sullivan in some way. The two women had both dated Sullivan briefly in high school. Why had Madison Ackler taken back up with Sullivan years later when she'd claimed to be in love with Oliver?

That question might not ever have an answer, but Ava was pretty sure it was the one puzzle Oliver needed to solve.

Putting that out of her mind, Ava moved on to other scenarios. "What about fishing and camping supplies? How is he getting them? Where would he get them?"

They searched a couple of outdoor supercenters near San Antonio where Sullivan might have gone when he'd first arrived in the area.

"But how do we prove that he might have bought supplies from either of these places?" Ava asked. "He's a wanted murderer. Anyone could have recognized him."

"Maybe he didn't buy supplies," Oliver said. "Maybe he sent someone else."

"A woman."

"Exactly."

Oliver put in an order to send an agent to the two stores in question and look at security footage first. If they found any matches, they could get an order to pull up receipts to match the time of day and purchases. Then he emailed photos of Vanessa Gomez, already on Sullivan's hit list—and Yvette Crenville—who'd dated Boyd back in basic and had a public falling out with him—to headquarters and sent a report to the team at Canyon.

"It's a start," he said, giving her another rare smile.

Ava smiled back. "If we can establish Sullivan's

tracks or his accomplice's movements, we can at least find a pattern and maybe figure out the way he's getting around right under our noses. Then we watch the targeted women and suspects for new jewelry or interesting accessories."

"Yes. We've searched the woods and some of the caves, but his accomplice might also be providing a getaway vehicle. He could be using a cave, too," Oliver said, getting up to stretch. "A tunnel under one of the fences."

Then he held up a hand. "The other day, right before you called about finding Turner, I spotted what I thought was a cave. I remember seeing a spark of light inside."

"But you didn't get to check it out because you rushed to help me."

"Yes, but I'm glad I did. Turner had to come first." Spinning, he said, "However, we do need to have someone check out that location and see if it leads to any other tunnels or caves."

"I can put someone on that," Ava said, reaching for her phone. "The base engineers can go over the infrastructure of the roads and boundaries and crosscheck that with the geography of the land to find possible entryways."

After she finished her call, Oliver turned to stare down at her. "Instead of running in circles, we've managed to take a step back and reevaluate this investigation and the hunt, and we've got others working to help us. We do make a good team."

Ava stood, too. "I think so." She wanted to say more, but she'd accepted that they might not last past this investigation.

So instead she brushed past him to clean up the kitchen.

But Oliver snagged her arm and tugged her back around. "How about we get out of here for a while?"

Surprised, she asked, "Are you sure?"

"Yes. I woke up in a foul mood and took it out on you. Let's go get some real dinner and, like you suggested earlier, take a break from all of this."

"I don't know."

"If you're worried about being exposed out there, don't. I know some out-of-the-way places to eat."

"It's not that. I'm not so sure we should socialize."

"We're stuck together here," he pointed out. "We can't help but socialize."

"But another dinner out? That takes things a step further, and I'm not sure either of us is ready for that."

He stood inches away. "Ava, don't give up on me. I have a lot to work through but I'm going to get there, sooner or later."

"I believe you will," she said, her prayers centered on seeing this through. "I hope so for your sake, not mine. But I hope it won't be too late for you to see that none of this is your fault."

Then she moved away and went into her room to change for dinner.

TWELVE

They waited until sundown to venture out.

Oliver guided Ava and Roscoe down side streets and through pretty back alleys full of quaint residential homes near the Riverwalk. He took her to a squatty little food trailer called The Taco Truck. It was brightly colored and tucked back in a secluded shopping area underneath towering oaks and ancient magnolias.

"How do you know your way around?" she asked, after they'd had some of the best tacos she'd ever eaten. She marveled at how Oliver made sure they blended in with other groups out on the street and along the winding paths of the Riverwalk. Marveled also at how he seemed to have ignored her concerns regarding the obvious guilt eating away at his soul. Ava knew all about that kind of guilt. It could cripple a person and ruin any chances of having a solid relationship.

"I jog a lot," he admitted, holding her hand and always keeping her near the buildings instead of the street. "After Madison died I walked a lot at night. Wound up once at this old church. I'll show it to you. It's not far from here."

A church.

Ava followed him in a zigzag through the city, taking in the blend of new and old that made San Antonio so unique. They came to a neighborhood of Spanish Eclectic homes built around the 1920s. Ava had read up on the city when she'd first come to Canyon, but she rarely made it into the downtown area. It had been over a year since she'd come to the Riverwalk for a night out with friends.

Now she was using this historical place as a cover from a killer.

But when Oliver stopped in front of a quaint Spanish-style creamy stone chapel, Ava took in a breath and stared up at the jutting steeple. For a moment, she forgot why she was standing here and allowed the beauty of the place to settle over her bones.

"Is this the church, Oliver? Is this your special place?"

He slowed to a stop under a giant oak tree. "Yes. This is where I turned back to God and vowed to turn my life around." Then he took her hand and held it tight. "This is how I'll find my way back, Ava. I don't want it to be too late. I want it to be right. Tell me you get that."

"I do," she said. "I'm trying, Oliver. I… I lost someone, too. So we've both been fighting our way out of the wilderness."

"Yes, we have. It's hard. But I need you to keep fighting, okay?"

Ava gave him a weak nod. "Okay." She glanced up at the tiny church. "It's beautiful. Why don't we go inside?"

Oliver looked into her eyes and saw that she really wanted to understand him, saw that her faith ran deep and fierce. Glad that she felt the same way he did about this little chapel, he smiled over at her.

"Sure. We could do that," he said, his heart thumping against his shirt in a fast beat. "It's never locked."

"That's a good sign."

She took his hand, guiding him now. Oliver swallowed back the memories of that night long ago and wondered if he'd ever truly follow through with the promise he'd made in that solitary moment. He'd tried. He'd focused on work and volunteering here and there and he'd attended church when he could, but his faith still missed that essence that made him sure and solid.

When he'd heard Boyd Sullivan had escaped, Oliver had gone back down that slippery slope of doubt and bitterness.

And then he'd met Ava. The climb back up would be worth it, if he could keep her near. So he stood quietly while her gaze moved over the old chapel with the arched stained glass windows and the Mission-style facade.

The heavy, arched wood-and-metal double doors squeaked open to a muted light that carried them up the short aisle toward the altar. A stained glass backdrop of the Last Supper shimmered in reds, greens and blues, a soft yellow halo shining down on Jesus and His disciples.

The church was hushed and quiet, filled with centuries of prayers and pain, triumph and joy, and that sense of ultimate peace he'd felt the first night he'd stumbled inside. He felt an immediate peace now.

"This place hasn't changed at all."

"That's a good thing," Ava said. "It's so pretty. So

peaceful. Safe. I can see why you considered it a refuge."

Oliver tugged her close as they sat down on a pew several rows back from the front. *"La Capilla de Los Perdidos."*

"The Chapel of the Lost," Ava interpreted.

They held hands and sat silent. Then Ava lowered her head and closed her eyes. Oliver did the same.

He prayed and while he prayed, he renewed his faith and asked God to help him live up to his promises and his pledges.

When he opened his eyes, Ava sat watching him with a soft smile on her lips. "I've decided that no matter what happens I will never forget you, Special Agent Davison."

"And I've decided that no matter what, I won't let you forget me, Senior Airman Esposito."

They strolled back toward the vestibule, the sound of Roscoe's paws against the wooden floor echoing out around them.

When they came out onto the sidewalk again, Ava turned to him. "I don't think I'll forget you. But things will be different when this is all over."

Oliver leaned in. "Yes, maybe then we can truly get to know each other."

And that's when the shooting started.

Drawing his handgun, Oliver pushed Ava around the corner of the church toward another street. "Run."

Another round of muted shots echoed through the night. Bullets danced off the trees and carved smoking grooves in the sidewalk all around them, a silencer making the shots whisper past without alerting anyone else.

Ava took off with Roscoe right on her heels. They turned a corner into an alleyway, the cadence of Oliver's footsteps hurrying behind them. Roscoe's low growls indicated he had picked up a familiar scent.

"Keep going," Oliver shouted, urging her on. "Up ahead."

Ava ran, tripped over an old root. Oliver righted her and they took off again, moving through the old, twisted oaks and tall cypress trees.

Oliver pushed her through a restaurant patio lined with colorful umbrellas and glanced back. "I see the shooter."

They came onto a street festival in full swing. Ava held tight to Roscoe's leash and gave the dog gentle commands to keep him calm. Oliver put away his weapon and tugged her close while they weaved in and out of the crowd. Pulling her into a booth of jewelry and floral hats and scarves, he peeked around the billowy dresses hanging just inside the entryway.

The crowd merged and mingled, people laughing and talking, but no sign of the shooter dressed in black.

"I think we lost them."

"Or they're staying out of sight." Ava took in air and shook her hair away from her shoulders. After telling Roscoe to stay, she turned to Oliver. "Do you think Sullivan sent someone after us?"

"Him or someone else."

"Who beside him or his accomplice would want us dead?"

"Well, I have put a lot of people away."

"I have a feeling someone knows our every move," Ava replied, glad for the cover of the stuffed booth.

The old woman sitting on a stool inside the opening gave them a quiet, considering stare, her dark eyes missing nothing.

"Is there anything I can do to help?"

Ava shook her head. "Just avoiding someone unpleasant."

"Then take your time."

They huddled there inside the booth for a few more minutes.

Oliver grabbed a colorful butterfly-embossed scarf and paid the serene woman for it, then handed it to Ava. "Wrap that over your hair."

Then he bought a dark baseball hat and put it over his head.

"Thank you," the woman said after putting away the cash. She smiled at Ava. *"Dios te bendiga."*

God bless you.

Ava nodded as she looked back. *"Gracias."*

Oliver held her close. "We'll keep close and walk back to the other side of the Riverwalk and get to my place."

Ava had ridden in the big open tour boats that served as giant taxis to the many hotels, restaurants and shops that lined the tributaries of the San Antonio River running through the city. It was a perfect night for such a ride, but too risky right now. Walking made more sense for Roscoe, too.

They circled around and crossed one of the many stone bridges over the river and then got caught in a crowd waiting for the next boat. By the time the boat was loaded with tourists and locals, they were well on their way down the path.

Oliver held her close and whispered in her ear. "Keep your head down."

Ava nodded but moved her gaze over the crowds lining the sidewalks along the waterway. Was the shooter watching them right now?

Oliver did the same, his face close to hers. Being so close only reminded her of the many reasons they needed to stay apart.

He was doing his job and just trying to protect her.

Still, one thought echoed in her head. Would he follow through on that date at the Winged Java when this was over?

"Whoever this is, they are not a trained assassin," Oliver said to Ava the next morning.

They'd made it safely back to his apartment, and Oliver had alerted the twenty-four-hour security that his female friend could possibly have a stalker. They weren't to let anyone near his apartment without calling first.

"I agree," Ava replied, staying away from the windows now. She sat in a corner away from view, Roscoe at her feet. "We'd both be dead by now if that were the case."

He came and sat down beside her at the tiny breakfast table. "And I can tell you something else. If the Red Rose Killer wanted you dead, you wouldn't be sitting here."

"So what's his plan? To toy with me and keep everyone on alert while he does something else? Hurts someone else?"

"That's how he works," Oliver replied, picking up a piece of dry toast to take a bite. "Letting the dogs out, knowing that would be a big deal. Grabbing innocent people just so he can use their identities and uniforms to hide himself. Using this mysterious woman to run interference and cover him while he slips away."

"A woman who has to be misguided and desperate," Ava replied, wishing she could have gotten a better glimpse of the shooter in the woods and tonight. "I can't believe it's Vanessa Gomez. She seemed genuinely scared when she came by my house the other night."

"Yes, but why did she come by your house at that exact time? You were shot at right after she left."

"She didn't shoot at me and we have witnesses who can vouch for that. I think she really was concerned, or maybe she was feeling me out, since she's probably heard she's on the suspect list. And on Sullivan's list, too, for that matter."

"Maybe, but she could have been a distraction to get the shooter in place."

"Or she could be the Anonymous Blogger, digging for information."

"I don't buy that," Oliver replied. "The blogger has inside information but very little facts. More Sullivan's type of thing."

"I'm just not feeling it."

"We'll keep her on the list," Oliver said. "And we will agree to disagree."

"What about Yvette Crenville?" Ava didn't know the hyper nutritionist that well, but she'd sat through a couple of Yvette's health and wellness classes and the woman seemed ditzy to the hilt, possessive and demanding, and a bit odd. Unstable, maybe? "Yvette tends to date the wrong kind of men, from what I've heard, but she has short hair and she's kind of wiry. Not Sullivan's type."

"But she is tall and athletic," Oliver said. "She could move through the woods pretty quickly."

Ava thought about what she knew. "She has an alibi the night he first showed up and killed Landon Martelli and Tamara Peterson and then let the dogs escape."

"Yes, but a lot has happened since then. I intend to watch her more closely when we get back on the base."

Ava wanted to go back to work, but for the first time in her life she also wanted more time with a man. This man.

Too antsy from being so close to Oliver and once again almost being shot, she got up to roam around. "We also need to consider Heidi Jenks. She *is* a reporter and I've noticed the stiff competition between her and her colleague John Robinson. Maybe being the blogger is her only way of staying ahead of him. Which would mean we have a mole who is feeding her information."

"Or misinformation. And *that* person could be Sullivan's girl Friday." Shrugging, he drank some water. "What better way to keep us sniping at each other and one step behind them?"

"I just can't picture Heidi as the blogger. If she were, she'd at least verify her sources." Ava let out a sigh and shook her head. "Will we ever figure this out?"

He sat across from where she stood, his gaze holding her, reminding her of being in that church with him last night. Reminding her of things she'd put out of her mind, like a nice home and two or three children.

"I'm going to figure it out," he said, his tone quiet

but firm. "I can't keep living like this, obsessed with a murderer. He killed Madison and those others in Dill. We know that. He's killed on the base. We have proof of this through DNA and other evidence. I just need to find him again and put him away for good this time."

"Would you really shoot him if you got the chance?" she asked, needing to know how far Oliver would go.

He didn't even blink. "If he tries to hurt you, yes."

Her heart tripped over itself on that one. "Oliver, you said we need to go by the book."

"I won't kill him in cold blood," Oliver said. "But I'll end this one way or another, as I've already told you. He'll either be in jail the rest of his life or he'll be six feet under."

Ava got jittery again. She couldn't trust that Oliver would be able to let this go, even if Sullivan was brought to justice again.

"We have to go back to the base tomorrow," she reminded him. "Are you still intent on doing a lineup of women?"

"If I can get Turner's parents to agree."

He stood and came around to her. "Meantime, we need to stay inside. Looks like another round of storms is coming this way."

THIRTEEN

Ava woke the next morning and came out of her room to find Oliver up and drinking coffee, his curly hair tousled and his eyes bleary.

Pulling her robe tightly against the T-shirt and leggings she'd slept in, she went to pour her own cup of brew. "Did you sleep at all?" she asked, worried about him.

"A little," he said, smiling up at her.

The reams of paper lying all around him indicated differently.

He swept a glance at her. "Did you rest?"

"Some." She'd mostly tossed and turned, but she hadn't stayed up studying videos half the night. Her thoughts had been on the man who seemed bent on protecting her and finding a killer.

He checked her over as if he didn't believe her. "You look tired."

"Not what a woman likes to hear."

He shook his head. "You have a right to be tired."

"I'll make us toast," she said, wishing she could have done a better job of tracking Boyd Sullivan, too.

She wanted to tell Oliver she *was* tired, but he

looked haggard and distressed and…obsessed. He didn't need to feel guilty about how hard she'd been working, even before they'd ever joined forces. Her priorities had shifted from trying to get a promotion to stopping a vicious killer.

And fighting against her heart and the way Oliver made her feel.

Did he have the kind of staying power she needed in her life?

She didn't have much time to consider that because Oliver got up and came over to her. "Thank you."

"For what?" she said, unable to look at him.

"Breakfast. I didn't realize what time it is."

"I don't cook much, you know."

"Is that for future reference?"

"Just warning you. I'll burn this bread within minutes."

"You know, last night we were talking about what comes after this."

"And then, we were saved by bullets. Yet again."

"Don't make jokes about that, Ava."

She looked from him to the folders and documents with what she hoped was a pointed frown. "I'm sorry. I shouldn't have said that. It must have been horrible, knowing how Madison died."

He nodded and helped her butter toast. "Still is. Which is why I don't want it to happen to you."

"Did you find anything else?"

"I've established a more solid pattern. He killed her first and then, one by one, he found and shot others who he felt had wronged him. We put that together from people who knew him and remembered his volatile temper, and verified he'd had beefs with everyone he'd killed. From high school on to joining the air force and basic training, he held grudges against everyone. And he's gone after as many of them as he can."

"So he went back to Dill first and got even with people there. I guess he was still angry from being kicked out of basic and decided that since his life was spiraling out of control, it was payback time with the air force, too."

"That sums it up," Oliver said. "Now he's on a rampage and he has help. We just have to pinpoint who else is deranged enough to go along with his schemes."

"So can we predict who'll be next? I recently got added to the list. So if he's that diligent, he might go in chronological order."

"Then why are you being stalked and shot at?"

"Because the shooter might not be Sullivan or his woman friend. Maybe it's someone else entirely. Maybe we have a copycat on our hands."

Oliver took the toast she put on a plate with some fruit she'd sliced yesterday. "Someone else who hangs out in the woods and leaves a rose and a note?"

"We have to consider that possibility since people tend to take advantage of this type of thing. But that doesn't add up, does it?"

"I don't know. You might be onto something." He took a big bite of toast. "But first, breakfast, because this is the best toast I've ever eaten."

She burst out laughing at that.

"Let's get back on to our investigation," she said. "We'll keep digging, keep tracking, keep praying."

"I like the way you think."

Ava ate her toast, wishing she could say what she was really thinking. Oliver wasn't going to give up on this investigation, and she understood his reasons. But where did that leave them?

They were on the road back to the base by noon, but Oliver wished he could prolong the weekend. The light Sunday traffic made the drive go by faster, so he couldn't stall much longer, but he sure liked being with her. At least they'd had a little downtime, if he didn't count the shooter by the Riverwalk.

"I missed church," Ava said, her gaze sweeping over Oliver. "Have you ever met Pastor Harmon? He's married with two sets of twins, one of them a girl. And all of them under the age of ten."

"I don't think I have," Oliver replied. "I… I don't go to church on base. But I'm impressed about the twins. He must have a lot of patience."

"He and his wife both. They're a great couple. Good to talk to about anything."

"Glad to hear that." He watched the road, always checking. "Do you think I need spiritual counseling?"

"Can't we all use that at times? You've been through a lot, Oliver."

"Yes. And you know all about me now. Why don't I know more about you?"

"You're turning the tables," she said. "Okay, I'll lay off for now."

His expression softened but his words were firm. "I still want to hear your story."

"One day," she promised, looking uncomfortable. Why was it so hard for her to talk about herself? No doubt changing the subject, she asked him, "Do you attend at the Chapel of the Lost?"

"When I'm not deep into a case."

They made it onto the interstate that would take them west of town. Oliver glanced back to do a check and saw a black sedan approaching at a rapid pace.

"Ava, slide down in the seat."

"Why?" she asked, turning.

"Don't look back," he said, watching the vehicle behind them. "I think our shooter has found us again."

Ava did as he asked and scooted down. "Are you serious?"

"Someone is riding my bumper and I don't think it's a little old lady coming home from church."

The vehicle sped up but Oliver couldn't make out the person inside since the driver was wearing a dark baseball hat and sunglasses. "Looks like the same car that followed us on base the other night."

"Should we call for help?" Ava asked, taking a glance in the passenger-side mirror.

"Not yet," Oliver said. He weaved his car in and out of the sparse traffic. "Let me make sure I'm not just imagining things."

The black sedan followed, quickly and expertly.

In the rear, Roscoe woofed, sensing an adventure.

"If that's our shooter, he or she seems to know how to tail people."

"Practice makes perfect," Ava said, her tone full of that fierce bravery he knew so well.

"Yeah, I'm thinking that, too."

"What are we going to do? Let them chase us all the way to the base?"

"We could."

"I can alert the gate," she said, going into action.

"Ava, wait on that," he said. "I think I'll try to lose them."

"But then we won't know who they are."

"That doesn't matter right now. I have to put your safety first."

"Forget that," she said. "We have to do something."

She unfastened her seat belt. "I'm going to the back."

"No, you are not," Oliver said, grabbing her arm. "Ava, buckle up and stay down. I'm going to find a way to get us out of this."

She glared at him but refastened her seat belt. Then she told Roscoe to lie down.

Oliver breathed a sigh of relief. "Good. I can't drive and watch out for you at the same time."

Looking contrite, she glanced in the side mirror. Then she sat up. "Oliver, I think I saw someone on the passenger side."

"Okay, stay down. When the shooting starts, I need you to dive down as low as you can."

"Okay. But what about you?"

"I'll be fine."

He didn't plan on letting them get that close.

He kept zigzagging, but the car stayed with them, the driver not moving a muscle but keeping the car close. What did the driver hope to accomplish? And how had they found Ava and him?

As if she'd read his mind she said, "They must have waited outside your apartment-complex gate."

"This is growing tedious," Oliver said. "But we're going to keep moving and hope they'll either back off or play chicken with us."

"I don't mind playing chicken as long as we win," Ava retorted.

She'd do that. Ram them and stare them down.

That worried Oliver to the point that he figured he'd need to play it safe to keep her out of the fray.

But the vehicle advanced and just tapped the back bumper.

"Now they're getting serious," Oliver said.

He made it off the main road, taking an exit that would bring them around to the base. "Hold on, Ava. I'm about to break the law."

Ava nodded and grabbed the door handle. "I'm good."

Oliver peeled out and took off to the right of the two-lane road, then passed a farmer in a pickup truck. Speeding away, he checked the rearview mirror and saw the dark car behind the farmer.

"Here they come," Ava warned, her gaze on the side mirror and her body language showing she was ready to brace for impact.

Oliver nodded. "I'll be ready for them."

He sped up and hit twenty miles over the speed limit, all the while watching for cars up ahead.

They rounded a curve and for a moment, the sedan disappeared. But Oliver looked up as they were cresting a hill. "Moving closer. He'll come after us on the long stretch."

Ava glanced in the mirror to her right. "Let's rodeo."

Oliver shook his head. Did the woman have no fear?

The car approached close enough that Oliver spotted the shooter aiming out the passenger-side window. "Stay down, Ava," he said again. "I'm going to do a spin."

"I need your gun," she said, her tone full of grit.

"No."

"Yes."

Oliver took his handgun out of the shoulder holster, but he didn't give it to her. "I can shoot and drive at the same time."

"Oliver!"

"Stay down."

Placing the gun in his lap, he hit the button to the window on his side to open it.

Oliver waited until the right moment to slow a bit. When the car approached and tapped him this time, he was ready. He hit the brakes for a split second, causing the other car to slam hard against his vehicle. Then he went into a turn that brought him into the other lane and almost ran them into the ditch. But he held the wheel and then reached for his weapon.

After that, he started shooting through the window, his other hand guiding the vehicle.

Ava held tight, her eyes wide, bullets whirling all around them.

Oliver completed the one-eighty and shot another round, which caused the driver to veer away. He and Ava watched while the other vehicle came up on a slow-moving van.

Then they heard the screeching of tires and saw the black sedan slide into the low ditch to avoid hitting the van. The car moved through a field, dust and rocks spewing up behind it.

"We've got 'em now," Ava said, triumph in her words.

But the two people in the car got out and took off running into the sparse woods behind an old barn.

"And there they go," Oliver said, hitting the steering wheel in rapid palm slaps. "I can't tell who it is since they look like ninjas. Exactly how Turner Johnson remembered them."

"Should we go after them?"

"No. Too risky out here," Oliver said. "But they left the car. We can at least take a picture of the license plate and send it in. Then we'll call the locals and report their bad driving habits."

"I hope they run across a rattlesnake," Ava said, her gaze on the now still, smoking car. "Do you think that was Boyd Sullivan and his handy helper?"

"Probably," Oliver said. "The shooting was bad."

He called in their location. "Now we wait."

"No, now I call Westley and get some help out here," Ava replied. "Meantime, I have Roscoe."

"The car is stolen," Master Sergeant Westley James told Ava an hour later. "We'll notify the owner. Maybe they can shed some light on how it went missing."

Ava held Roscoe's leash. They'd tracked a scent into the hills across from the field but lost it at the crest of the first bluff. "Nothing on the car?"

"No prints to speak of," Westley replied. "They must have both been wearing gloves."

"They were covered from head to toe," Oliver said, his frown edged with frustration. "I got off a round but I don't know if I hit one of them."

Westley looked from him to Ava. "So tell me about the shooting in San Antonio."

Ava's gaze slammed into Oliver's. "You told him about that?"

"I had to, Ava. You're still in danger."

She went through the scenario. "We got away and no civilians were hurt, thankfully."

"So much for staying safe," Westley said. "But we might be able to find something to connect that car to Boyd Sullivan."

"It had to be him driving that car," Ava said, her stomach still queasy from all the excitement. "I just want to know who his wingman is."

"Or his wing woman," Oliver added. "We need that lineup, and soon."

Ava watched him stalk away. "He's running on thin air, sir."

"I can see that," Westley said. "We'd hoped this time away with you would calm him down."

"We survived, but now we know Sullivan or someone who might be helping him is somehow tapping our every move."

Westley nodded. "Let me go talk to the locals about towing the car. It's evidence for now."

Ava saluted him and then rubbed Roscoe's head. "We make a good team, don't we?"

Roscoe woofed his agreement and stared up at her with doleful eyes.

"*We* make a good team, too," Oliver said from behind her, his expression full of a longing that tore through her.

Ava held his gaze, her whole being aware of how this man had changed her.

"But we haven't been very successful so far," she said. "And I'm not sure you can ever move on until you can find some peace and let go."

"You mean, let go of the Red Rose Killer?" he asked, following her to the row of official vehicles lined up on the highway.

"No," she said, turning her head to look him in the eyes. "I mean Madison Ackler. Are you sure you didn't really love her, Oliver?"

FOURTEEN

Ava was back at work but bored. She'd been confined to desk duty for this week. Her superiors didn't think it was a good idea to have her roaming around the woods while a shooter seemed intent on going after her. She didn't dare tell anyone until she could verify it, but each time she went out anywhere on base, she got the feeling someone was watching her. Waiting for her.

While she was away, no one came snooping at her house so the decoy didn't work. But going back there could be dangerous.

Was the killer waiting for the right opportunity to take her out?

Not today. Here she sat, doing paperwork, studying training updates and annoying the other K-9 handlers by offering to do their work for them. She and Roscoe had worked through several practice sessions, too.

She was also staying away from Oliver.

Each day, they were briefed on the status of the Red Rose Killer and other investigations. Since Ava hadn't been called out on any rescues, she stayed in the secure areas of the training center. But no one had seen any sign of Boyd Sullivan since last week, and she and

Oliver had no proof that the two people who'd chased them were Sullivan and his accomplice. The owner of the stolen car had been out of town and had come home to find his house ransacked and his car missing. No prints and no security footage. Another rabbit hole.

They'd sent people to check several outdoor superstores in the areas surrounding San Antonio, so maybe they'd get a hit from one of them and be able to go through the store security tapes and find a receipt or two. As long as the store was willing to cooperate, they wouldn't need a warrant.

Oliver went out every day, searching for any signs of Boyd Sullivan. The woods had grown quiet since they'd found Turner Johnson. Ava figured Sullivan had watched them and had either followed them into the city or had someone follow them.

Unable to get through security at Oliver's apartment building, that person, or persons, had waited until Ava and Oliver had made a move.

Now Oliver was beating himself up for taking her out of the apartment and exposing her to a shooter. Why did he seem to want to carry every kind of guilt on his shoulders?

He'd never really answered her when she'd asked if he'd loved Madison. Earlier he'd claimed he didn't, but what if he truly did? Could that be the thing that held him back? That kept him invested in finding the killer?

Now, three days later, Ava sat at her desk and thought about everything that had happened over the last couple of months. Oliver's silence seemed to prove her point. She'd stared at the map on the wall that contained all the photos of the victims and those who'd been threatened. Connected with thumb tacks and strings of colored twine, they told the tale of the Red Rose Killer's murderous rampage.

Oliver was right. This shouldn't be so hard, but Sullivan knew how to slip in and out and stay under the radar, a true trait of a serial killer. But Oliver believed in the one thing that brought down most psychopaths. Sooner or later, their egos made them slip up.

Oliver didn't want to move on, because he wanted to find the killer. But he also had a load of guilt because of Madison's death, either because he hadn't really loved her, or because he did love her and he was still grieving.

But he's the one who opened up to you.

Maybe it was time for her to take the next step. Oliver had tried so many times to get her to talk to him.

She'd call him tonight and invite him over to dinner. Except that her house was still being monitored in case her shooter returned. Oliver had made sure of that, even if he'd pulled himself off of guarding her.

It was time to confront the man.

They could meet at the Winged Java. A lot of friends met there. And that would work better. It was a less intimate setting for opening up her heart.

Her cell rang, causing Ava to sit up straight in her desk chair. "Esposito."

"We need to meet and talk."

Oliver. Did he have a built-in radar on her?

"Hello to you, too."

"Hi," he said on a long breath. "I need to see you."

"Uh, okay. The Winged Java?"

"No. I'll come there. Meet me in the parking lot."

"Okay."

* * *

"Why the subterfuge?" she asked once she and Roscoe were outside of the K-9 training center.

Oliver gave her the once-over, his eyes telling her nothing. "Have you forgotten what we've been through?"

"No, but this is different."

"I wanted privacy, but I also wanted a wide-open area so I'll know no one is listening."

"Okay." She glanced around, that creepy feeling overcoming her again, and followed him to a bench near the main building. "What's going on, Oliver?"

He placed his hands on his lap. "I tried to love her. I wanted to love her. But my job was the thing. I loved my job more than I loved Madison. She wanted more and I tried to give her that. But I didn't have strong feelings for her."

Ava absorbed that while she watched the road and the grounds. "So if you don't love her, do you resent her for lying to you?"

"Yes," he said. "Her death was horrible. I want you to know that this is my burden to bear and that not having that last conversation with her and hearing the truth has bothered me a lot. I've turned back to my faith and I'm working my way through the grief and the resentment. I try to be honest with people, but…I wasn't honest with Madison and she sure wasn't honest with me. She turned to someone else for comfort and we both made a mess of things."

Ava saw the pain and grief in his eyes. He was the type of man who needed answers, but he'd never have answers from Madison.

So he searched for the truth in his work. He wanted

to find Boyd Sullivan again to try to get those answers. Last time, the hunt had been fast and furious and had ended with Oliver being in on the arrest of the man who'd murdered the woman he'd tried to love. This time, he'd want more. He'd want to get to the bottom of things so he could finally let this go.

"Do you think saving me will be atonement for the fact that you couldn't save her? Or that you couldn't have that last conversation with her?"

"That's part of it, of course."

"What's the other part, Oliver?" she asked, her heart bursting for that truth he held so high.

"I want to protect you," he said. "It's that simple."

"You are anything but simple," she replied. "I don't know how to handle you."

"Why don't you start by being honest with me, Ava."

"About what?"

"About what really happened when that chopper went down."

Well, she had wanted to see him and tell him about the tragic helicopter crash that had changed her life. He was here and he was ready to listen. But was she ready to talk?

Ava stared down at her boots. "I don't think—" She stopped, listening. Did she hear footsteps crunching in the mulch by the crape myrtles? Or was it only squirrels frolicking?

"Do you want to go somewhere more private?" he asked.

She glanced around and understood why he needed the open air. It was hard to breathe through this. Her emotions were on edge. "No. It's better here. I can't fall apart here."

"Ava—"

"No, you need to know, Oliver. It's nothing mysterious, nothing against my record or anything like that."

"I didn't think it would be," he said. "Just talk to me, Ava."

"Nothing much to tell." She took a deep breath and began her story. "The chopper had a four-person crew and some Search-and-Rescue personnel looking for three missing soldiers in a remote part of Afghanistan. Should have been an in-and-out extraction since we had their location and had communicated with them over a secure two-way evader locator and were ready to roll. We verified their location and dropped down, and they were climbing aboard when someone launched an attack."

Oliver listened, a slight nod his only encouragement, but his hand hovered near hers on the bench.

"We got blasted and things turned nasty pretty quickly." She stopped, took in a breath, kept an eye on Roscoe. The dog's ears had gone up and he had his nose in the air. "Julian and I had become friends from the start. We were in basic training together and both wanted to be pilots. We were crew members—he was the gunner and I worked as a flight engineer. We spent our spare time together. We were both the same rank but when we…got closer, we decided to be extra careful, just in case." She shrugged. "He was as ambitious as me. So it was kind of a competition."

Oliver gave her a gentle smile. "But you were in love?"

"We fell in love, yes. But we were in the middle of a war zone." Remembering Julian's olive skin and gentle brown eyes, she shook her head. "I'll never know what might have happened once we got back stateside." Pulling away, she said, "We got hit with several rounds and then the chopper started spiraling out of control. The pilot was shot and when I looked around, Julian's eyes met mine. He gave me the sweetest smile and then... he just toppled over onto the gun."

Oliver's expression mirrored the pain that would always be inside her heart. "I'm sorry."

"Yes, me too," she said, the bitterness tasting like bile. "I don't remember much after that. I woke up in triage and then I was in and out of consciousness until we got to Germany. I had contusions and a broken leg and everything was kind of fuzzy for a while. But when they told me Julian was dead, a lot of it came rushing back."

She wiped her eyes. "I wish it hadn't. I wish I didn't remember him every day of my life."

She saw a flicker of something unattainable in Oliver's eyes. "So you need answers, too?"

"No, I need memories. Good memories. Ours were all wrapped up in death and fire and go, go, go."

"An adrenaline rush."

She nodded again, tears burning her eyes. "I'll never know about those soft, sweet memories."

"I'm sorry you had to go through that," he said. "But you pulled through and you're great at what you do now."

"I pulled through only after a lot of therapy and someone introducing me to the Working Dog program. I had to work hard to qualify and that saved me. But it didn't prepare me for someone like you walking into my life." She lifted her chin. "I've been coasting along

on a routine that kept me stable and steady and now…
I'm shaky and not so sure about my future."

"You have a future, if I can keep you alive."

"You see, that's it, right there. Your need to watch
out for me. I'm not Madison, Oliver. I can take care
of myself. What I can't risk is losing someone else I
care about."

He leaned back, his eyes going dark. "So that's why
you're avoiding me? We've been forced together and
we're dealing with the horror of a serial killer on the
prowl."

"Isn't that enough to do anyone in?"

He gave her a look that told her he understood her
now, his eyes full of a misty realization. "More than
enough. But, Ava, we're both stronger now. We've lost
a lot, been through things no one wants to go through,
but we've also gained a lot. Wisdom, caution, understanding, empathy. And I think we've both grown
stronger in our faith."

"But can we truly heal, Oliver?" she asked, her heart
doing that fast beat that told her she was close to panic.
"We signed up for this kind of life—the kind that takes
over your soul at times. I flew a lot of missions over
there and they didn't all turn out good. We saved a lot
of soldiers but we lost some, too."

"And I've put away a lot of bad people but some of
them got away," he replied. "We can't let that define
us. We have to keep fighting."

"I want to keep fighting," she admitted. "But what if
that ambition, that need to make things right, destroys
us in the process?"

"Are you worried about me? About how I won't let
go of this chase?"

"Yes, I am," she said. "I know you want to capture Boyd Sullivan and I sure want that, too. But there comes a time when you just have to give over the power and let someone else take the lead."

"But we're going to find him. And soon. That doesn't mean you and I can't be close. Friends, at least, for now."

"And what about later? Will you disappear when we come down off that rush?"

"You don't seem to understand," he said, his eyes burning with a distant fire. "You give me the same kind of rush, but in a much better way."

"I can't do that if you wear yourself down looking for a man who might not ever come out of the shadows. What then, Oliver? Will you keep on chasing him until you're the one who gets killed? Do you want that more than you want us?"

He gave her a shocked stare. "Ava, are you asking me to remove myself from the search to find the Red Rose Killer?"

FIFTEEN

Oliver waited for her to respond.

But Ava seemed distracted. She kept an eye on Roscoe.

"I can't stop midstream," he said, wishing there was some other way. "You know how this works."

She nodded and turned back to him, her eyes misty and filled with dread and concern. "Yes, I do know how it works. That's why there can't be an *us* until you're done with him."

Trying to understand, Oliver sat up straight. She wasn't in the mood for this discussion and maybe he wasn't either. "I will be done with him if I can ever find the man."

"You'll keep chasing him all over Texas. He's a survivalist, Oliver. He can stay on the lam for months, possibly years."

"I'll find him, and soon," Oliver said, determination making his tone sharp.

Ava stood up. "Okay, we'll go with that. I want him put away again, too. He's wreaked havoc on this base and the state of Texas for way too long now. But I've been shot at and harassed and I have guards outside my apartment day and night and you taking me on as your responsibility. So I'm forced to stay near the training center. Which is good, I guess, since I'm pouring over documents and electronic files. Maybe I'll find a clue that can lead us to him. Maybe not. But I'm going to do my job, too."

"Is this a brush-off, Ava?" he asked. "Are you saying you'll find him and save me the task?"

"What I'm saying is that I have a stake in this, too. I can pour myself into my work, same as you."

When she turned to leave, Oliver caught up with her. "That sounds a lot like a challenge, Ava."

"It could be. But I'm tired of sitting at my desk. If I have to drag Boyd Sullivan in by his hair, I'll do it. I can't function this way anymore."

Oliver's heart skipped a few beats. She was too reckless for her own good. "Don't say that. Don't even think it."

"I'll be careful," she said. "Meantime, you get on that lineup you're so determined to provide."

He stopped her. "I can't. The Johnsons refuse to let Turner do it. They won't put him through anything else that could add to his trauma. They say he's been through enough and he still has nightmares."

Some of the fire went out of her. "Don't we all?"

Oliver wanted to take her in his arms. "Ava…"

"Don't say it." She turned to go back inside. "Just let me work on this, Oliver. Let me figure it all out."

"Alone?" He couldn't let her go.

"Yes. Alone. Same way I've always done things."

"That's too dangerous."

"Oliver, I'll be okay. You do your job and I'll do mine, all right?"

He reached for her, his hand on her shoulder while he leaned in. "I'm sorry about Julian. He sounds like a good man."

Ava resisted pulling away. "He was a good man. He died too young. But he died doing what he loved, fighting bad guys. We lost several good people that day."

"You need to take care of yourself."

"And so do you," she said. Then she headed back to the building. But just before she reached the door, Roscoe alerted and barked a warning. Ava whirled, meeting Oliver's gaze.

"Inside," he said, drawing his gun. "Get inside."

Oliver heard someone running away.

Ava heard it, too, and ignored his warning to go inside the building. "Find," she said to Roscoe. The big dog leapt into the shrubbery near the building, his barks loud and clear. Someone had been in the bushes, listening to them.

Ava and Oliver both rushed around the corner just as a car motor revved to life. Roscoe stood at the sidewalk, barking at the vehicle that turned the corner before Oliver got a good look at the plates.

Shaking her head, Ava called Roscoe back. "I guess now even this place isn't safe for me anymore."

Ava hadn't slept well that night but at least she was back at her place, Roscoe by her side. She'd dreamed of the chopper crash and Julian's smile. But in the dream, Julian turned into Oliver and they were running through the woods with someone right on their heels. Then she saw a little boy moving through the shadows, but when she called out to him, her voice was barely above a whisper.

She'd woken in a cold sweat, fear clawing at her. Not fear for herself, but a new fear. Turner Johnson had seen the bad man and he'd heard the woman talking. He'd heard them fighting and arguing.

What if Sullivan decided to track him down after all?

Who had been listening to her and Oliver there near the training center today? They'd searched the area and found nothing. The dark compact car had disappeared into traffic.

And they'd both been too distracted even to know they were being watched. But she'd felt it. She should have been more alert.

She gave up on sleep and tried to focus on work, but she finally fell asleep on the couch. When she woke, groggy and more confused than ever, she went out to get the paper. Roscoe went along with her for a quick walk around the yard so he could have his own break. She had the paper and was halfway back up the short drive when she saw Yvette Crenville jogging by.

The other woman looked even more gaunt than last time Ava had seen her, almost malnourished in spite of her job as a nutritionist. Remembering from her research that Yvette had briefly dated Boyd Sullivan, Ava had to wonder again if Yvette could be his helper. But they'd had a horrible and very public fight right before he left basic. Besides, she and Oliver had watched Yvette's routine and found nothing out of the ordinary. But that didn't mean she wasn't sneaking out at all hours. She might be covering her tracks too well for them to see anything.

Had Sullivan rekindled things with Yvette after his escape the same way he'd rekindled things with Madison once he found her again? Would he eventually kill this woman when he was done with her?

Ava kept smiling as Yvette approached, all the while trying to figure out if Yvette had been the one shooting at her.

She certainly had the tall, slender frame of someone who could probably be a fast runner. But the shooter in the woods had been dressed in bulky sweats and a hoodie. Ava had never seen the shooter's eyes or hair. Yvette had short, choppy blond hair that stood out all around her face. Not Boyd's usual type at all. But he could have changed types to suit his purposes.

Deciding to test that theory, she waited for Yvette to pass, and then waved. "Hey, I haven't seen you around for a while."

Yvette slowed and ran in place, but stayed on the sidewalk. "Hey, Ava. You missed my last class on the low-carb diet, not that you need to worry about that."

Ava held Roscoe's leash and laughed. "Yes, I've been kind of busy."

"So I heard." Yvette stopped jogging in place and took a deep breath. "Me, too. Keeping a low profile right now." Pushing at the spikes of hair around her forehead, Yvette added, "I've had a lot of things going on. I just broke up with my boyfriend."

Ava felt Roscoe bristle, but the big dog didn't show any outward signs of distress. He'd never been around Yvette, so maybe he was reacting to her as a stranger. But then, animals picked up on hostility, too, and she'd heard Yvette complain more than once about all the "mutts" on the loose. Obviously, the woman didn't like dogs a whole lot.

"I'm sorry to hear that," Ava replied, remaining neutral. "I didn't know you were in a serious relationship."

Yvette's grunt and frown showed a hint of anger. "Apparently, neither did he."

Ava noted the grimace and the hostility of Yvette's statement. "I'm sorry, Yvette. Relationships are always complicated."

Yvette's gaze scanned the quiet street. "Yeah, I guess so. At least now I have more free time on my hands. Anyway, I heard about the incident in the woods. You rescued that little boy."

"Yes, I did," Ava said, wary of the concern in Yvette's words. "But I had a lot of help. The whole team was in on the search."

"And the search for the Red Rose Killer, too," Yvette said with a delicate shudder. "It's hard to sleep at night, knowing he might still be out there. Why hasn't that hunky FBI agent hurried up and done his job?"

"We won't give up on finding him," Ava replied, wondering if Yvette was deliberately baiting her about Oliver.

"I also heard you and what's-his-name, Owen, Olson, have grown close."

"Special Agent Oliver Davison," Ava replied. "And we're friends. Chasing someone through the woods does that to people."

"Oh, I see." Yvette winked and checked the street both ways. "Hopefully, the killer is long gone and you'll never have to go back into the woods again. It can be dangerous out there. I worry about that kid, too."

Again, Roscoe bristled. Ava felt a chill moving down her spine. Just her imagination and lack of sleep? Or did Roscoe recognize Yvette's scent?

At what sounded like a threat to both her and Turner Johnson, she stiffened her spine and stared Yvette down. "If Sullivan returns here, I'll be ready to go anywhere to bring him in."

"You're so brave," Yvette retorted with a smile. "And I need to be gone myself. Busy day, as always." Running backward, she shouted, "Let's do lunch someday soon." Then she frowned and pointed to a neighbor's trash can. "Messy around here."

Always the complainer, from what Ava had heard about Yvette. That, coupled with the cryptic conversation and the way Roscoe had silently alerted, made Ava wonder yet again about Yvette. Could she be sneaking out to help Boyd Sullivan?

Ava made a note to check into Yvette's schedule again, but for now she could report back to Oliver that she'd encountered one of their suspects.

And that she'd gotten the creeps from that encounter.

Then she remembered she'd pulled away from Oliver. How easy it had become for her to think about telling him things first.

But she was on her own now and she would report to her superiors, especially her concerns involving the boy. She had to stay away from Oliver until they were both done with the Red Rose Killer. Only then could she be sure about him, and only then could she decide if she was ready for another relationship.

Once she was back inside the house, Ava poured herself a cup of coffee, then opened her laptop to her email. And found another update from the Anonymous Blogger.

Seems the FBI Agent and the female Search-and-Rescue crew member are still at odds, even after they emerged as heroes after a dangerous rescue of a little boy a few days ago in the Canyon Base Reserve wooded area. Why are they still arguing about the Red Rose Killer? Why aren't they out there finding the man? These two appear to be more competitive than capable. And who keeps trying to shoot them? Who is on their suspect list now?

Ava let out a groan. Had the blogger been listening in on their conversation yesterday?

But this was not good. Ava was already being scrutinized and watched for her protection. This kind of attention would only bring her more into the limelight and fuel the killer's keen need to make her life go from bad to worse.

Boyd Sullivan had been jealous of Oliver Davison once before, and that had not ended well. She had to stay away from Oliver, not only for herself but for his safety, too.

Oliver had been staying in the base hotel this week so he could get out early each morning with a fresh team to scour the woods and surrounding areas. So far, he'd found no signs of the Red Rose Killer, not even a campfire or bit of trash left in a cave. Oliver had even gone back to the big cave where he'd seen a light the day Ava had found Turner Johnson. Nothing in there but bats and spiders, but it could have served as a good place to hide.

"We could go in deeper," one of his men had suggested. "Some of these caverns go far into the earth."

Working on that angle, Oliver now sat studying topography and geological maps of the Hill Country around the base and San Antonio. What if Sullivan was somehow moving through one of those caverns that lead right underneath the base's back fence?

Before he could wrap his brain around that, his cell rang.

"Davison."

"Agent Davison, this is Lieutenant Nick Donovan. The blogger has posted something new."

"What, Lieutenant?"

Nick read him the short blog post. "Have you and Ava been at odds again?"

That was an understatement. "We've been discussing this investigation a lot, as you well know," Oliver replied. "I need to call her before she hears about this."

"I reckon you do," Nick replied. "Talk to you later."

Oliver ended the call and reached for his phone.

This would set off Boyd Sullivan.

He had to stay away from Ava for her own good.

But that didn't stop him from hitting her contact number on his phone.

Ava didn't pick up. Instead, her phone rang and rang and then went to voice mail.

Rather than leave a message, Oliver finished getting dressed and headed out to find her.

SIXTEEN

"I have a special assignment for you, Esposito," Master Sergeant Westley James said to Ava when she reported for duty after seeing the blogger's latest post.

Wondering if she was going to be reprimanded, Ava nodded. "Yes, sir." He'd probably read the Anonymous Blogger's latest report and decided Ava wasn't qualified to continue the search. But she had decided that she and Oliver weren't going to be seeing much of each other outside of work from now on. Things were getting too mixed-up. So she would make that clear to her superior.

"I need you to head out to the airfield and stand by at the main hangar," Westley explained. "You'll be escorting Senior Airman Isaac Goddard to wait for a plane that should be bringing in the dog he's been trying to locate." He checked his watch. "Scheduled to arrive at 1100 hours."

"You mean they found Beacon?" she asked, excited for her friend Isaac. Beacon had saved Isaac's life and he'd been searching for the dog ever since he'd returned stateside.

"We think," Westley said. "Just stay with Isaac, will you? He's been having a hard time lately."

"Sure, sir," Ava replied. This wasn't the assignment she'd expected, but she was more than willing to help her friend who suffered from PTSD. "I'll leave Roscoe in his kennel in the car so the other dog won't get agitated."

"Good idea." Then Westley opened the office door and turned back to Ava. "Oh, and Special Agent Davison is going with you."

"May I ask why, sir?" Ava asked, shocked. So much for avoiding Oliver.

"He called looking for you," Westley replied, his tone as neutral as the paint color on the wall. "I told him you'd been over at the kennels helping tag and exercise some of the dogs we've picked up but you were about to head over to the flight line. He said he's on his way."

"I don't need Special Agent Davison to go with me, sir."

"I'm going with you whether you like it or not."

She whirled to find Oliver standing at the door to Westley's office. "That's not necessary."

"We need to talk, and we can do that on the way," Oliver replied, walking into the room. "I've been considering your concerns regarding the Johnson boy."

Ava looked back at Westley and almost protested. But he gave her a stern stare that reminded her he was her superior. "Orders, Esposito."

"Yes, sir."

Westley made to leave but stopped outside his door to speak to Captain Blackwood's sixteen-year-old daughter, Portia, who happened to be walking by. "On your way to hang with your dad?" he asked.

The girl's disdain was palatable and the expression on her face showed boredom and aggravation. Ava had heard she was a handful. But she felt some sympathy for the girl since Portia's mother had died last year and her life had changed completely when she'd come to live with Justin, the father she didn't really know.

Portia twirled and smacked her chewing gum. "Forced to hang around like I'm a kid."

Westley's smile was patient. "Your dad will enjoy that, at least."

Portia tossed her long blond hair. "I seriously doubt that." Then she glanced into the office where Ava and Oliver stood. Giving them an eye roll, she took off, her black lace-up boots clacking on the floor.

"Teenagers," Westley said with a shake of his head. "I'll want a full report on what you find at the hangar, Esposito."

"Yes, sir."

When the sergeant had left, Ava whirled to Oliver. "Why are you here?"

He pushed back his hair and gave her his own eye roll. "Because I've been looking for you all morning and I'd like to discuss some things with you."

"I've been right here, under house arrest."

"Protective custody," he corrected.

"Call it what you want. I've scrubbed kennels, gone through the obstacle courses with the dogs, caught up Roscoe on training hours, his shots and a good bath, and I've filed away more paperwork than I ever care to see again."

"So you need a diversion," Oliver said, walking with her to the parking lot, Roscoe following obediently.

"Yes, maybe. But you don't have to be a part of that diversion."

"I was concerned about you. I haven't seen you since that scare yesterday, and you haven't returned my calls."

Ava handed Roscoe up into his kennel and made sure he was secure before heading to the driver's side. "I'm okay, Oliver. Which you know, since I've seen you checking with my security detail."

"Until that brief conversation yesterday, you've been avoiding me."

"I thought that was the other way around. You've been busy searching for the Red Rose Killer and you've been avoiding me. Besides, each time we're together we make things more dangerous for everyone. Someone was here yesterday and they got away yet again."

"Another reason I wanted to talk to you yesterday, but we got interrupted."

"What about?"

"I wasn't avoiding you, Ava. I was trying to stay away from you. And I'm pretty sure you were trying to do the same for me."

She shot him a questioning look as they hopped into her SUV. "Why, besides the obvious?"

"Because the Red Rose Killer has a grudge against me and I thought if I stayed away from you—"

"He'd come after you instead and end the grudge?"

"Something like that, but he seems to have disappeared off the face of the earth."

Ava headed north on Canyon Drive. "And I was

avoiding you and staying out of sight so he wouldn't come after you while he's trying to eliminate me."

"We've got to stop avoiding each other that way," Oliver said, his eyes dark with emotion and worry. "I was stupid, okay. I thought if I threw myself back into work, I could forget you. To protect you."

"That is kind of stupid."

"What's your excuse?"

"I was trying to protect you and to let you do your thing. Because you need to get him out of your system before I can be in your life."

"You drive a hard bargain."

"Yeah, well, I guess I do. I don't like losing people."

"You won't lose me."

"You can't make that kind of promise, Oliver. Look, let's just pick up Isaac and get to the hangar."

"Okay," Oliver replied while, out of habit, they both checked for any tails behind them. "At least Isaac will get some good news. He's going to see Beacon again today."

"That's not Beacon."

Isaac Goddard's green eyes held disappointment and frustration while he stared down at the dog Ava held on a leash near the kennel he'd traveled in. "Is this some kind of joke? Is someone trying to pull one over on me and make me think this is Beacon?"

Ava glanced at Oliver and then back to Isaac. "We had confirmation that this might be your dog, but no one could say for sure until he arrived and you had a chance to look him over."

Isaac looked contrite and lowered his head, his wavy sandy-brown hair glimmering in the sunlight. "He's a German shepherd all right." He petted the curious dog's furry head and checked him up close. "But he's not Beacon."

The dog sniffed at Isaac and let out a soft cry. Isaac smiled at that, but stood and pulled away.

Oliver bent down to pet the scrawny dog's dark brown fur. The dog woofed and licked Oliver's hand. "Sorry, man," he said to Isaac. "I guess you'll have to keep trying."

Isaac shook his head and backed away. "I'm never gonna find him. It's important that I do, though." Shrugging, he said, "I know it's silly but…Beacon belongs with me."

"Then don't give up," Ava said, her hand on her friend's arm. "Isaac, remember how far you've come. You survived and Beacon saved your life. It might take a long time to find him, but you can search as long as you need to."

"Yeah, I reckon so," Isaac said. "Let's get this guy to the training center. Maybe he can be somebody's dog."

"But not yours?" Ava asked, hoping Isaac would change his mind. The dog kept looking up at him, as if eager to have someone to love.

"Not mine," he said. Then he turned and headed toward her waiting SUV outside the hangar.

Ava and Oliver helped one of the flight crew members load the dog into another vehicle so he could be taken straight to the vet's office.

Oliver joined her by the SUV. "You handled that nicely."

"He's been through a lot and he still has a long way to go. Each disappointment is just another setback."

"Sounds as if you've been there."

"I went through a hard time when I got home, but I told you that."

"You skimmed over it, yes. Maybe if you told me more—"

"Not a good time to analyze me, Oliver."

"I'm not trying to analyze you," he said, his words for her only. "Just trying to understand you." His eyes holding hers, he added, "You just told Isaac not to give up. Like him, you survived and you've come a long way. But you're afraid to take that next step. I get that. I'm afraid, too."

"Let's go," she said, not liking how he seemed to understand her too well already. "I have more work to do."

Oliver walked around and got in the front seat, a frown deepening the fatigue that seemed to cloak him these days.

From the back seat, Isaac sent Ava a long stare through the rearview mirror when she started the vehicle. Then he leaned forward and asked, "What's with you two, anyway?"

"We have no idea," she replied.

Isaac gave her that soft smile he kept hidden away. "Right."

Oliver shook his head and stared out the window.

What was with them? she wondered after she'd dropped Isaac off at his house.

Oliver must have been wondering the same thing because as soon as they were back on the road he asked, "What *is* going on with us?"

"Like I said, I have no idea."

But she did have an idea. A pretty good idea.

She was falling in love with Oliver Davison.

And that was the worst possible thing she could do.

* * *

"Can we go somewhere and talk?" Oliver asked Ava when they reached his car.

"No. I told you, I have work to do."

"You're finding work to do so you can avoid me."

"Isn't that the plan? To avoid each other?"

"It should be the plan, and yet even your immediate superior is throwing us together."

"No, he was forced to allow you to come along because you were hounding him about wanting to talk to me."

"Well, yes, I did do that."

Ava turned to face him, her hands still on the steering wheel. "Oliver, we need to take a break. The Red Rose Killer is after both of us, so let's keep him guessing by splitting up."

He knew she was right. "That's usually a good idea, but I worry about you."

Ava glanced around and then back to where his car was parked a couple of spaces over. "And I worry about you, too." Pointing to his vehicle, she said, "I think you have a flat tire."

Pivoting, Oliver took in the sight of the deflated front tire on the driver's side. "How did that happen? It was fine when I got here earlier."

Getting out, he examined it and then kicked it. "Great, just what I needed today."

"We can change it," Ava said as she came around her SUV.

"I'll take care of it," he replied, aggravation getting the best of him. "But not until I'm sure you're safely back inside the building."

"We're right here," she said, checking all around them. "No one would dare mess with me here."

"Ava, someone has already messed with people here and they didn't live to tell about it, and yesterday, someone was hiding in the bushes listening to us."

At the hurt in her eyes, he grabbed her hand. "I'm so sorry. I shouldn't remind you of your friends. I know their murders are a big part of why you're so determined to find Boyd Sullivan."

She nodded and took a deep breath. "No, you don't need to remind me of that. Everyone I work with wants to bring in the Red Rose Killer. And since that's your goal, too, why don't we do what we started out doing? Work together."

Relief washed over Oliver. Finally, they could quit pushing each other away. "I can live with that."

Lowering her head, she leveled her gaze on him. "But there is one stipulation."

So much for relief and hope. "And what's that?"

"Nothing social. We show up here and work with the rest of the team. We compare notes and go over details. We even go back into the woods and retrace our steps. Sullivan could still be out there, for all we know. Or he could have a bead on Turner Johnson."

"I don't like—"

Ava held up a hand. "I do my job, my way, same as I did before you showed up. And you do your job, your way."

She was asking too much. "I can't stop wanting to protect you, Ava."

"And I can't stop worrying about you," she replied. "But we keep those feelings compartmentalized for now."

"You mean, until this is over."

"Yes. No more dinners or forced excursions or coffee breaks." She stepped back. "Now, I'm going inside and you get that tire changed and get back to work."

"Bossy, too, aren't you?"

She didn't answer. Instead she stood her ground. "Can we agree?" she asked, her tone hopeful but firm. Was that a trace of regret he saw in her eyes?

"Do I have a choice?"

"This is the best solution for now," she said, turning to let Roscoe out of his kennel. "I'll see you later."

Oliver nodded but decided she couldn't stop him from watching her until she made it into the building.

When she reached the middle of the street, he heard the roar of a motorcycle and looked up in time to see a sleek black bike heading at full speed right toward Ava and Roscoe.

SEVENTEEN

Oliver didn't stop to think. Sprinting toward where Ava stood frozen, he called out, "Run."

But Ava appeared to be more worried about Roscoe. "Go," she ordered, her body shielding her partner. The K-9 did as he was told but he whirled and barked at Ava.

Oliver made it to her and shoved her with all his might. Ava went down, sliding across the pavement and twisting around while Oliver felt the impact of the big bike against his left thigh. Just enough impact to cause the high-powered machine to skid and slide before rolling sideways into the grass between the street and the sidewalk.

Oliver tried to stand, but his leg gave out. "Stop," he shouted as the driver managed to get up off the grass and jog away.

"I've got it," Ava called, but she winced and cried out. "Roscoe, find."

Glad for the chance, Roscoe barked and took off in a leap toward where the dark figure had headed.

Oliver grunted and tried to get to Ava. People started running out of the training yard, sirens echoed, dogs barked. Ava moaned and stood on shaky legs and moved toward him.

"Oliver?" She crumpled beside him and grabbed his hand.

"I'm okay," he said, the warmth of her hand touching his. But he also felt something else on her hand. Blood, sticky and wet from where she'd skidded onto the pavement. "You're hurt. I pushed you too hard."

"You saved my life," she replied, tears gathering like rain clouds in her eyes. "Oliver, are you all right?"

"Let us check," someone said from behind them.

"Her first," Oliver said.

And then he passed out.

Ava sat on an exam table in a tiny room at the base hospital ER, wondering what was going on with Oliver. He'd passed out and then someone had lifted her up onto a gurney and rushed her to the hospital. Now no one would tell her anything about Oliver or Roscoe and she was going to scream if she didn't hear soon.

Her hands had ointment and bandages on them and her knees were scraped, her uniform pants were torn and her whole body ached with bruises, but she was alive.

Oliver had put himself in harm's way to save her.

What if he didn't wake up? Had he hit his head when he'd gone down? It all happened so fast. The sound of a roaring motorcycle, Oliver's warning, Roscoe's fierce barking, and then the sound of a motorcycle skidding on the pavement.

She'd glanced up in a blur of confusion to see the driver dressed in all black—helmet, gloves, clothes, goggles.

Was it the same person who kept trying to shoot her and Oliver?

She didn't know. But whoever it was, they were getting closer and closer.

Too close.

Ava grabbed at the hospital gown around her and tried to slip off the table.

"Whoa, there."

Glancing up, she was ready to do battle with anyone trying to stop her. But it was Pastor Harmon, his hazel eyes bright with amusement. "Going somewhere, Senior Airman Esposito?"

Ava managed to get back up on the table, pulling the lightweight blanket after her. "I need to find out if my K-9 partner is okay and Special Agent Oliver Davison got hurt trying to protect me and…and…"

She stopped, very near tears. She refused to cry, even in front of the one man who could handle any woman's tears.

"Okay," Pastor Harmon said, his expression oscillating between pity and understanding, his neatly clipped sandy-brown hair combed into place. "Okay, why don't you rest and I'll get you some answers, how about that?"

Ava sniffed. "Thank you, Pastor. And thanks for stopping by, too. Have you heard anything?"

"I just got here," he said, calm as always. "I do know the doctors are with your special agent. Something about X-rays, but don't quote me on that."

"X-rays," Ava said, her heart bursting with too many emotions. "That could mean a lot of different things."

"Yes, and since I'm not a doctor, let's not get all

worried about that right now." He patted her hand. "Is there anything I can do for you, Ava?"

"You mean, besides the usual?"

"Oh, I'm praying for all of you, yes. Anything else? A drink or another blanket?"

"No," she replied, grateful for his calming presence. "But you did mention finding out about Roscoe."

"I'm on it," the pastor replied. "I'll track down someone who looks official."

"Thank you," Ava said, suddenly exhausted.

She was dozing off when the door opened again and Vanessa Gomez came in, her smile bright. "Ava, are you stirring up trouble with a man of God?"

"No one will tell me anything," Ava said, her suspicious mind going into overdrive. Was the nurse here to check on her, or snuff her out for good? Ava reminded herself there was a guard outside her door. Vanessa had obviously been cleared and they were obviously watching.

Vanessa gave her an overall appraisal. "I came in to tell you that you're okay. I'm on duty, but on my break, and since I'm not your regular duty nurse, I can't do anything too official, but I thought I'd sit with you while you wait to hear on Special Agent Davison."

"Can you tell me anything?" Ava asked, all the while checking for sharp needles or deadly chloroform. But all she saw was a tired nurse who seemed to want to make her feel better.

Could Vanessa be that good at hiding her connections to Boyd Sullivan? Or had she been the one on that motorcycle earlier? Ava said she was on break, so that meant she'd been here at the hospital all day.

"You look perplexed," Vanessa said. "I'm sure Oliver will be just fine. From what I heard, he's bruised badly on one hip and suffered a few contusions on his face and left arm. The X-ray is probably to make sure nothing's broken."

"Is that all you know?" Ava asked, impatient. "Did they catch the driver?"

Vanessa sighed. "I'm sorry, I don't know anything. I shouldn't have told you that much, but Pastor Harmon felt a revolt might be coming."

"He did catch me trying to get out of here."

"Why don't you just rest until someone can escort you home?"

"Where is Roscoe?" Ava asked, panic setting in.

A knock at the door brought her head up. Vanessa opened the door and saluted Captain Justin Blackwood and then excused herself. "I hope you feel better soon, Ava."

Ava nodded after saluting. "Thank you, Vanessa."

Captain Blackwood stared after the nurse. "Why was she here?"

"Checking on me and giving me a report, sort of," Ava admitted. "She said she was on break and the guard cleared her to enter."

"I see," Justin held his thoughts close to his chest, too. "I'll verify that."

Maybe they were both being too suspicious, but lately Ava had to go on the notion that anyone could be guilty.

"Roscoe is safe," the blue-eyed captain said in his no-nonsense way. "He's with Lila Fields."

"Lila's a great trainer, sir. I'm glad to hear Roscoe's in good hands."

Lila was new to the training program and a single

mother to a toddler daughter. Ava had often chatted with her in the break room.

"Yes, she's going to be an asset to us," Justin replied. "Listen, the driver of the bike managed to slip over a fence. We've got the base on lockdown but so far no sign of them. We did find one scrape of black material, probably from their pants. Sent it to the crime lab to be tested for DNA evidence."

"That's something." Ava wondered if they'd find anything at all. "But these people have managed to cover their tracks over and over. If we can't find the driver, that means it's someone who knows this base and knows where to hide."

"I agree and we're on it," Justin replied. "Special Agent Davison is okay, Ava. Badly bruised hip and left leg so he'll be out of commission for a few days. Which means if you're up to it, we'll need you back out there looking around."

"I'll be fine, sir. When can I go home?"

"That's up to the doctors," Justin replied. "I'm sure you'll hear soon, but…if you don't get cleared for duty you'll have to accept that, understood?"

"Yes, sir."

Ava talked to the captain awhile longer, going over the few details she remembered. "I don't know if the driver was male or female. It happened so quickly. But it could have been the same figure we've seen in the woods and, possibly, in San Antonio."

"You relax and we'll keep searching," Justin said. "Roscoe tried his best but that fence got between him and the runner. We lost the scent about four blocks over near the main entryway. Whoever it is left the base somehow."

Feeling her superior's frustrations, Ava waited for Captain Blackwood to leave and then managed to get dressed in her torn uniform again. By the time the ER doctor came in to release her, she was ready to go.

But she wasn't going anywhere until she talked to Oliver.

Oliver grunted and kicked his good leg. "I can't stay here overnight. I need to be out there."

"You're injured," ER doctor Trevor Knight repeated to him, his blue eyes full of authority. "You came close to a hip fracture. You can barely walk right now, let alone chase after a killer. And we need to watch that head wound, too."

"They tried to run down Ava," Oliver said, realizing too late he'd addressed her by her first name and not her rank. But Oliver was beyond caring about protocol right now.

"I know, but you saved her and she's okay. In fact, I just left her. I released her to go home."

"Not without me," Oliver said, trying to turn and stand. But the pain that shot down his leg made him break out into a cold sweat. "Not without me," he said on a weaker note.

Trevor pinned Oliver with a doctor's glare. "You do realize that Senior Airman Esposito is well trained and more than qualified to take care of herself, right?"

"Yes, I'm well aware of that fact," Oliver said, his head throbbing like a machine gun. "But thank you and everyone else for reminding me."

"Why don't you rest," Trevor suggested. "That's the best thing you can do right now. If you get out there and can't protect your...friend, then she'll have to take care of herself and you."

Oliver finally caved, knowing the doc was right. But he still worried about Ava. Closing his eyes, he said a prayer for protection. Then he lay there thinking about how much she'd come to mean to him over these last couple of weeks.

He was beginning to think he might be in love with Ava.

And he was probably the last person involved in this case to realize that.

Ava had been trained to be as quiet as possible while tracking for lost military personnel or trying to bring home a wounded soldier. Using those same tactics now, she found Oliver's room and quietly opened the door.

He was asleep, his frown evidence that he wasn't happy to be here either. Walking gingerly since she was sore all over, she made it to the bed and stared down at him. She didn't want to love the man, and yet her heart seemed to swell with something she'd never felt before, not even with Julian.

Had Julian been a crush or a distraction during a horrible time in theater? Or would she always hold him dear as her first true love?

Maybe both, but standing here now, she felt something strong and solid and unflappable for the man before her. Oliver was the real deal.

She wanted to know everything about him. How he'd handled growing up in New York State, where he'd gone to school, his first crush, his first time feeling brokenhearted and alone. What he'd seen and done out there in the tough world of the FBI.

And she wanted to share the intimate details of her life with him. Growing up without a lot of hope and no money to provide that hope, joining the air force so she could travel and finish her education and make something of herself. Almost dying while she watched the man she loved die right before her eyes. Changing in midstride from becoming a pilot to becoming a K-9 handler and a member of the Working Dog program. She wanted to share all of that with Oliver.

So she took his hand and held it tight and prayed to God to give them the strength and resources they needed to find the Red Rose Killer and his accomplice.

"We won't stop fighting," she whispered. And then she leaned down and kissed him. "I won't stop fighting for you, and soon we'll get past all of this."

Oliver sighed in his sleep. She turned to go, not wanting to wake him. But he called out, "Hey, did I hear you talking to me? Or was that a dream?"

Ava turned and headed back to the bed. "No dream. But you need to rest, okay?"

"What about you?"

"I'm okay," she said, his husky voice strumming across her soul. She wanted to say so many things, but now was not the time. She needed to get back out there. "I'll check back with you later," she said.

Oliver reached out a hand to touch her sleeve. "Be careful."

"Always."

She'd do her job, but she'd also try very hard to hold back on her growing feelings for Oliver. It was too dangerous to let her heart take over when she needed her head in the game.

EIGHTEEN

Two days later, frustration colored Oliver's words. He was obviously still in a lot of pain, and he'd been quiet. Too quiet. "Neither of these women do anything but work, shop at the BX and go straight home. You'd think they'd have social lives, at least."

Ava's disappointment matched Oliver's aggravation. Over the last couple of days, they'd set up surveillance on Vanessa Gomez and Yvette Crenville, but so far they'd heard nothing out of the ordinary from the people they'd had watching the two women. They didn't have enough evidence to delve into phone records or bank accounts at this point and no probable cause to get a warrant.

"Vanessa goes to church," she said. "Can't say the same for Yvette, but the woman sure loves to jog around the base and pay occasional surprise visits to all the refrigerators in the break rooms to fuss at us about our unhealthy eating habits."

"Or to spy," he retorted as he hobbled to the coffee pot in the training center lounge. "She's probably placed a bug in here somewhere." Then he grunted and leaned on the table. "She could easily be the Anonymous Blogger since she pops up everywhere."

"I'm liking her more and more as Sullivan's accomplice," Ava admitted. "But we have no proof. The worst we have on Yvette is that one of our people saw her wolfing down a huge chocolate bar while sitting on her front steps. And that's not a crime, or most women I know would be in jail."

Oliver shook his head at that. "And when we interviewed her months ago, she said she hated Sullivan and never wanted to see him again. Which is also not a crime."

"They did have a very public breakup from what I've heard," Ava said. "But she seemed worried when I saw her jogging the other morning. He could easily turn on her if she doesn't do his bidding."

She almost mentioned the creepy feeling Yvette had given her, but she'd reported the encounter to her superiors, so she wouldn't add to his worries now. His bruised leg was better, but he was grumpy and he worked on shouting orders over the phone, since he couldn't work off steam in the exercise room yet.

But Ava got the impression that something was bothering him beyond this investigation. The tension between them seemed to be getting worse instead of better, and she didn't want any rumors to get back to that annoying blogger.

Ava thought about Yvette's habit of jogging day and night. "It would be easy to go out and purposely be seen and then slip off the jogging trail, throw on some hidden clothes and do her dirty deeds. But that's a stretch."

"We don't discount any scenario. Still waiting on the footage from the outdoor superstores near San Antonio, too," Oliver reminded Ava. "They gave us a hard time at first, but now they're allowing one of my agents to go through sales receipts and look at surveillance footage. But that could take a while."

"We're not getting anywhere now," Ava replied. "Maybe that will bring us something."

She rubbed her eyes to get what felt like sawdust out of them. They'd been holed up here all day, waiting to hear what the lab found out about the scrap of material the motorcycle rider had left behind. If there was any trace of DNA, it could help them. Now she watched Oliver grit his teeth as he tried to pretend he was fine.

"I'm better," Oliver said, as if reading her thoughts.

"I know that," she replied.

"Then stop looking at me like that. Sympathy is beautiful in your eyes, but I don't need pity, Ava. I need to get back out there."

"You're still not able to walk very well," she pointed out. And he refused to take any pain pills. Stubborn man that he was. "Maybe you should do some of the stretches the physical therapist suggested."

"The more I move, the less pain I'll be in," he said with a grimace. "And that means I'm capable of walking around in the woods."

"But you can't run, Oliver."

"I don't plan on running. I can still use a weapon."

"Why don't we get out of here for a while?" she said. "It's a nice fall day. We can grab some food and find a bench, get some sun."

"Chase a bad guy," he added, smiling. "That sounds like a good idea."

"Chasing the bad buy or getting out of here?"

"Both."

Ava called to Roscoe and soon they were in her SUV, driving toward the Winged Java. It seemed to be their place, and since everyone had noticed them hanging out together and working together, no one dared tease them or question when they left the training center headquarters. Except to warn them to be vigilant, of course.

"We'll raise eyebrows," Oliver said, favoring his left leg while he sat back in his seat.

"We are way past raising eyebrows," Ava replied. "But you know, a lot of people around me have started dating, and some are getting engaged and even getting married. That seems to be in the air around here in spite of the horrible situation that brought them together."

At his silence, she glanced over at him. "Not that I'm hinting or anything." Then she let out a groan. "Never mind."

Oliver finally looked over at her. "It's not what you think."

"Oh, really? Lately, you've been clamming up like a tortoise. Isn't that a typical man thing?"

"Did you just call me a tortoise?"

"You act like one sometimes."

"Ava, I'm trying to do my job, same as you. I would have thought you'd be glad I'm staying quiet these days." He shrugged. "I haven't been around a woman this much since—"

"Since Madison," she finished, feeling as low as a person could sink. "I'm sorry. So sorry. I must remind you of her death and the Red Rose Killer whenever we're together."

"I didn't mean it that way." He looked even more

aggravated, so she decided to drop that thread of con-versation.

She stopped the SUV in the café parking lot and her cell went off as she was reaching for the door handle.

Oliver's buzzed at the same time.

"Esposito."

"Davison."

As soon as they answered, Ava listened on her line to Westley's voice, her eyes on Oliver. "Yes, sir, we'll be right there."

Oliver listened and then said into the phone, "Hey, somebody needs to grab my FBI jacket, my Kevlar vest and my weapon out of the locker you assigned me."

Then they both put away their phones.

"The motorcycle was stolen but the DNA on the torn fabric matches Boyd Sullivan," she said, knowing Oliver had just heard the same. "I sure thought that person could have been a woman."

"Maybe it was a woman but she borrowed Sullivan's sweatpants," Oliver said. "They've had sightings in the woods again. Let's get going."

"No," Ava said, giving Oliver one of her not-happy stares. "You can't go on this search."

"Yes, I can," he replied, adrenaline giving him a boost of confidence. "Ava, I have to be in on this. For a lot of reasons. The man tried to kill you."

"I'm fine," she said, her eyes on the highway lead-ing to the reserve. "My equipment is in the back and I'm ready to go."

"You're still bruised, too."

She shot him a frown. "And you're still limping."

"You can't take me home or back to the K-9 center. We don't have time."

"Okay, all right." She beat a hand against the wheel. "But you have to stay near this vehicle, understood?"

He slanted a stern stare her way. "I don't take orders from you."

"Oliver, please," she said. "I thought I'd lost you the other day when I saw that motorcycle hit you."

"Did that make you care?"

"You know I care, even if you don't make it easy. As I said, I thought they'd killed you."

"But they didn't. I'm hard to get rid of. I'll be okay. I'll do a ride along with one of the OSI people or Security Forces."

She gave him another headstrong stare but didn't argue anymore. They made it to the command post set up half a mile from the opening trail into the woods. All around, officers from the Office of Special Investigations, Security Forces and the K-9 unit were stalking through the woods. Sullivan could be long gone by now.

"Here we go again," Ava said. "We've got a few hours before dark."

"Then let's get cracking."

He watched as Ava put on her protective gear and strapped on her weapons. After checking her knapsack, she turned to Roscoe. "Ready, boy."

Oliver worried about her, too, but he knew better than to voice that concern. She was independent and strong and not to be reasoned with when she was on a search.

But he wasn't about to sit this one out. So he got

out of the vehicle with a shrug and gritted his teeth. "I can't sit here when the action is out there."

Surprisingly Ava didn't push back. Her mind was no doubt already on what they might find in those woods.

Captain Justin Blackwood and Master Sergeant Caleb Streeter met them as they walked up the narrow strip of road.

"Hey," Caleb said. He gave Oliver the once-over. "Are you ready for this?"

"I walked about a half mile just now," Oliver said, wishing they'd all quit worrying about him. "I'm good. Where's my gear?"

Chad Watson, now completely recovered from his gunshot wound, jogged up and helped Oliver get on his bulletproof vest and check his weapon. "We gotta stop meeting like this, Special Agent Davison."

"I couldn't agree more," Oliver said, thanking the Security Forces officer.

Ian Steffen from the Office of Special Investigations stalked up. "I just got word that someone tried to break into the Johnson house."

Oliver met Ava's apprehensive gaze. "Was Turner home?" he asked Ian. "Is the boy okay?"

"I'm waiting to hear," Ian replied. "We've sent a squad to check." He scrolled his phone. "We've had eyes on the boy since the incident out here so we expected this."

"That could be a diversion," Oliver said, "to throw us off."

"Yes, I did consider that," Ian responded.

His phone buzzed. Listening, he said, "I see. I'll alert the necessary people."

Ian ended the call and looked at Ava and Oliver, his eyes narrowed.

"Someone has taken the boy."

Oliver called the Security Forces officer who'd responded to the 911 alert at the colonel's home.

"Suspect tried to get in through a side door but was seen in the backyard," the officer explained. "Parents alerted our people. The kid was playing in his fort but tried to escape. Last Mrs. Johnson saw, someone dressed in dark clothing was carrying her son toward the woods behind the house. They held a gun on the boy and told her to back off."

"How did they get past our guards?"

"Found one knocked out and the other one is missing."

"I'm coming there myself," Oliver said, ending the call.

Caleb Streeter hurried toward Oliver. "I think I know why someone went after the boy, Special Agent."

"What now?" Oliver asked, his leg protesting each step.

"Our Anonymous Blogger leaked earlier today that Security Forces and the FBI were considering a lineup so that Turner Johnson could identify the woman he saw with the Red Rose Killer."

"What?" Oliver stomped his foot and then moaned. "That's classified."

Ava put a hand to her mouth. "Oh, no. So that's why they took Turner. Oliver, they could kill him."

"I know," he said. He went into action, making calls, giving orders, stomping and pacing. "I know," he said again after he'd done all he could do from there. "Let's go."

"I'll radio the others."

A few minutes later, they were back in her SUV. "We can have Roscoe search the house, at least. Maybe find us a trail. I can't believe this is happening again, and all because that blogger sent out misinformation."

Oliver nodded, his bruised leg on fire with pain, his stomach churning.

"We have to find the person who's been somehow listening to all of us and leaking things that cause everyone to be in danger," he said. "And we have to find Turner. Before it's too late."

NINETEEN

Colonel Johnson's home was stately and well maintained, the lush yard sloping down to a small stream that ran along the property. Tall cottonwoods and oaks lined the area near the woods while the landscaping around the house contained various shade trees and blooming shrubs. A wooden fence enclosed the backyard and a chain-link fence could be seen finishing out the enclosure about fifty feet beyond the wooded area and stream.

A good place to hold a picnic.

Also a good place for an intruder to lurk and wait.

"But we have security," Marilyn Johnson kept saying, the shock of her son missing yet again taking its toll on the woman. "How could this happen? We were so careful."

Ava held the woman's shaking hand. "Mrs. Johnson, can you tell me why Turner was out there all alone?"

"It's my fault, isn't it?" the distraught woman said, tears forming in her eyes. "He was here with me but he wanted to go outside. I got up to check on dinner and told him I'd be right back and…he'd slipped out ahead of me. I heard Stormy barking and then I ran out the door."

"So he was playing in the fort and you called to him?"

"I saw him climbing down from his little fort. Stormy kept barking." Marilyn glanced toward where the colonel was talking to Oliver. "Yes, and he came running when I called but that person jumped out of nowhere and grabbed him and held a gun on him. Told me to stay back or they'd kill my son. Stormy tried to stop it, but the intruder kicked him and then took Turner toward the stream. He must have cut the fence."

"What did this person look like? What was this person wearing?"

"I told the others already. All black, sunshades, a dark hat, long sleeves, bulky pants. All dark and unrecognizable. I can't say who I saw."

She put her hands to her ears. "I can still hear Turner screaming and Stormy barking. Why can't you people do your jobs and find this murderer?"

Hearing his name, Stormy came running. The little dog was okay, thankfully. But Ava's worries centered on Turner.

"We'll find him," Ava said, nodding to Oliver.

The sooner they got out there, the better things would be. The chain-link fence had been cut in the far back right corner. But she wouldn't burden Mrs. Johnson with the details right now.

Oliver hurried to her. "No sign of anyone down by the stream, but we found footprints leading due west."

"I'm not waiting around," Ava said. "I'm going after Turner."

"I'm with you," Oliver replied. "I've got a team here

from our Bureau already setting up phone monitors and they know the drill. They'll let us know if they receive any demands." Then he looked grim. "Not that I expect any ransom demands. They want to silence the boy."

"This has to be Sullivan or his accomplice. He has to know we'll track him," Ava said, her mind reeling with every possible scenario.

"Yes, that's exactly what he expects, but we're going to do it differently this time."

"What do you mean?"

Oliver leaned close. "I called Heidi Jenks and told her to head to the reserve and make a big to-do, taking pictures and interviewing people. The paper can post to its website immediately. And so can the televison reporters who'll hear this on their scanners and show up out there."

"But—" Ava stopped short. "But we won't be there."

"Exactly. Just you, me and Roscoe will be out in *these* woods. Less of a chance he'll know we're here."

"But if he's watching the house?"

"We came in a side door and all of the drapes are closed. He won't even know we're here. All he can see is the guard at the back door." He shrugged. "Besides, if he's smart, he's long gone by now. Bad for us but that's how he'd do it. Get the kid away and send all of us scattering like rats to find him."

"Okay, and what if he's already left the area? He might not take Turner to the woods. He might take him across state lines."

"He's an hour or so out, but we can get a fresh track on him. He'd wait until full dark to leave the area or he could be seen, so we have a window of opportunity."

"Do you think he'll hurt Turner?"

Oliver put a hand on her arm and looked into her eyes. "We don't know if it's him." But yes, he knew Sullivan would do whatever he had to do to survive. And he suspected Ava knew that, too.

She nodded. "This could be a trap, but we have to try to save Turner."

After they'd alerted Oliver's agents to the plan, Ava and Oliver took Roscoe and made their way down the street to the higher level of the stream. They'd backtrack to this spot and hope Roscoe would pick up a scent, since Oliver was pretty sure Sullivan or possibly his accomplice had followed the stream to the edge of the Johnson property and managed to get past the security cameras and knock out one of the guards. The other guard had come running when he heard the screams and the barking, but he'd been shot in the shoulder. Thankfully both guards were okay.

Oliver wanted to get out there and search.

The coming dusk was quiet, a crisp fall breeze hitting them as they moved through the heavy foliage. Oliver hung back and let Ava and Roscoe do their job. She had let the dog sniff one of Turner's T-shirts and he took off toward the stream almost immediately.

Oliver moved slowly but he didn't complain. No need to whine now and he had to stay alert, so pain pills were out of the question.

"How are you doing?" Ava said on a low whisper as they moved through the decayed leaves.

"I'm either better or too numb to care," he admitted. "Adrenaline is a good drug, you know."

"Until you come down from it."

"I'll be okay, Ava. I've been worse off than this."

She didn't respond to that. If they were to have any type of relationship, she had to accept the bad with the good. Oliver didn't know if she'd ever step over that line. She'd seen someone she loved die in a horrible place and in a horrible way. She was afraid to open her heart up to that kind of pain again.

He certainly understood that notion. The realization that he might be falling for her had sobered him and left him dazed and confused. Oliver wasn't sure how to handle all the emotions this woman brought out in him.

It wasn't too late to walk away and they both knew it.

He wanted the Red Rose Killer and his dangerous accomplice to be captured and put away for good this time. Taking a child had ratcheted things up a notch. Oliver prayed they could save Turner and find a way to keep him safe.

After that, he'd think about the woman he was falling in love with.

They walked in silence for a few minutes, Roscoe leading them along the rocky streambed. They rounded a curve where the water rushed and gurgled.

"This leads to the river," Ava said. "That makes sense since the river's not that far from here."

Roscoe alerted as the creek grew deeper.

Oliver felt the hair on the back of his neck rising. "It could be showtime."

"If he's picking up a scent, that means they haven't crossed the water yet," Ava said. "Maybe we should split up to be sure?"

Oliver shook his head. "Not a good idea."

"We can stay close but I'm going up ahead with Roscoe."

Oliver stared at her for a minute. "If something happens one of us needs to be able to call for backup."

"Yes."

He finally agreed to move higher up along the shore so he could explore and keep his eyes on her and the K-9.

Between the moonlight and their muted flashlights, he should be able to watch their backs. "I can send out an SOS over the radio at any time," he said.

"Same here," Ava replied, glancing ahead.

Oliver nodded. "Be careful."

Ava smiled and signaled Roscoe with a silent command to go. Then they took off, following the water downhill.

Oliver said a prayer for all of them.

Roscoe emitted low, soft growls. Something was happening up ahead. Ava gave the silent signal to "Find" as they carefully moved forward, her night goggles showing them the way.

They reached an outcropping of rocks where the water grew swift. Roscoe stopped and looked back at Ava.

"What's up?" she asked, wondering what the dog had smelled or heard.

Then she heard a sound. A sob.

Ava's heartbeat accelerated. "Turner?"

A dark figure stepped out from the trees. Roscoe growled low. Ava saw why the dog had remained still.

The dark figure was holding Turner Johnson.

"Let him go," Ava said, drawing her weapon.

The kidnapper shoved the boy forward, a gun at his back. "I will. But I want you to take his place. So if you try anything stupid, such as commanding that dog to attack me, I'll have to take the boy instead. Do you understand?"

Ava nodded, her eyes on Turner. "Turner, are you okay?"

The boy bobbed his head, his eyes wide, his sobs gone now. "She's been singing to me but...I don't like her."

She. The woman had disguised her voice somehow, but Turner obviously knew his captor was female. And he was smart enough to blurt that out.

Ava didn't respond or react. "I'll go with you and I'll send my dog away with the boy."

"That would work."

"Why do you want me?" Ava asked, stalling, wondering where Oliver had gone.

Or worse, what had happened to him.

Oliver heard voices a few yards ahead. He'd spotted some knocked-down shrubs and undergrowth, footsteps evident in the indentions. He'd only stopped for a couple of minutes.

Then he heard another noise not far from where he was standing. He whirled, his gun raised, and hit his foot on a protruding stone. He stumbled and fell hard, sliding about five feet down to the bank of the stream. Pain shot through his body but he managed to get up. Then he heard more voices echoing through the woods.

Oliver held on to rocks and bushes, saplings and trees, moving along the streambed so he could follow the voices.

They were moving toward the river. And the river wasn't far from where the woods behind the base picked back up. The river ran through the reserve from northwest to southeast. Sullivan and his accomplice could have been using the river to make their getaways all this time.

Oliver stopped to get his breath, the pain in his left leg throbbing like fire-tipped hammers. Then he heard someone rushing through the woods.

Managing to drop behind an old log, Oliver waited.

"C'mon, Roscoe," he heard someone saying. "You got to get me out of here."

Turner?

Lifting up his head, Oliver saw the boy, wet and dirty, holding on to Roscoe's leash. Where was Ava?

"Why are you doing this?" Ava asked, biding her time until she could make a break for it.

She'd given Roscoe the order to "Go Back" and then she'd handed the leash to Turner. Roscoe would take the boy home, she hoped. The dog had a special bond with Turner, having guarded him on that ledge and knowing his scent so well. Roscoe would know what to do.

The woman shoving her ahead on the path made it impossible for Ava to see who she really was. She'd disguised her voice and her face and she wore several layers of clothing. She used no perfume, covered her hands and face. She had to be sweating inside all that gear.

"Talk to me," Ava said, checking their location, the moonlight showing her they were headed toward the river. "Why did you take Turner?"

"He knows too much," came the muffled reply. "And so do you."

"So you're going to kill me?"

"Yes. And my boyfriend will take care of the boy."

Ava's heart lurched at that comment. The woman had tricked her. Now they'd kill both the boy and her and then they'd find Oliver. Or maybe that's why he hadn't found her.

What if Oliver was already dead?

His leg was going to give out.

Oliver stood up, hoping he wouldn't scare the boy and the K-9. "Hey, Turner, it's Agent Davison."

The boy whirled, his hand holding on to the leash. "FBI?"

"Yes, FBI," Oliver called. "We've been looking for you. Are you okay?"

The boy tried to pull Roscoe back. "I'm fine now. Roscoe is supposed to be taking me home. He won't turn back."

"What happened to Ava—Airman Esposito?"

"She took her," Turner said, his voice trembling. "Like a swap."

Oliver's chest hurt and a new rush of adrenaline gave him the strength he needed. "You need to get to safety. I'm going to call for help and alert them you're on your way home, okay?"

Roscoe barked. Not a growling bark, but more of an alert that meant "We have to keep going."

"Okay," Turner said. "I'm scared they'll come back. Will Roscoe bite them?"

"Of course," Oliver said, hoping the dog would do just that. "Meantime, I'm right behind you. So don't be scared. We're calling for backup."

He'd get the boy safely home and then he'd find Ava. He just prayed he wouldn't be too late.

Ava knew it was now or never. The closer they got to the river, the worse things would go for her. If they took her on a boat, they could easily kill her and toss her in the water. Her body would wash up downriver.

She couldn't let that happen.

"So how long have you and Boyd been an item?" she asked now, hoping to get the woman riled enough that she'd become distracted. Hoping she'd figure out who this really was. Because she was beginning to think this person definitely wasn't Vanessa Gomez or Yvette Crenville. Boyd Sullivan could have a new paramour from another town.

The woman huffed out a couple of breaths and then replied, "Off and on, years. Not that it's any of your business."

Ava bobbed her head. "No, not my business except that you keep trying to kill me."

The woman's next words chilled her to the bone. "You're the only one he's ever let live."

Ava saw an incline up ahead and hoped there would be a gully or ravine on the other side. So she worked on her strategy a little more. "You know, I did notice that. We all did. I think he has a soft spot for me. Is that why he sent you to do his dirty work?"

The woman shoved Ava hard, but Ava was ready. She pretended to trip, her body going slack as she slid down. When the woman came after her, she lifted a booted foot and shoved it into the woman's padded midsection. The woman let out scream, lost control of her weapon and went backward, her bulky clothing softening her slide down into the ravine.

Ava scooted up and took off back toward Turner's house, running for her life while she prayed that Turner and Oliver were both safe.

Oliver dragged himself through the woods toward Turner and Roscoe. When he heard footsteps approaching and someone commanding Roscoe to "Guard," he knew the cavalry had come.

Up ahead, flashlights shone on the path. Oliver waved and called out. "Agent Davison. Over here."

Caleb Streeter and Ian Steffen hurried up to Oliver, both armed to the teeth in tactical gear.

Oliver grabbed Caleb's arm. "Ava? I don't know where she is. She sent Roscoe back with the boy."

"Which way?" Ian asked.

"Down the stream, toward the river."

Oliver took a deep breath and then he passed out.

TWENTY

"I'm all right."

Oliver kept pushing at the paramedics who'd arrived to check both him and Turner.

"Take it easy," someone said. "Just a precaution."

"I can walk," Oliver said. "Now let me up."

One of the first responders glanced at Ian and Westley. Westley nodded. "It's your call, Special Agent."

"Yes, so let me get back out there so I can find Ava."

They had him on a stretcher in the Johnsons' driveway, but he slid off the stretcher. Turner was inside with his parents and Stormy.

"Is the boy okay?" Oliver asked as he tried to stand. Gritting his teeth, he favored his left leg but managed to hobble toward a waiting SUV.

"He has some cuts and bruises, but he's a real trooper. He said the woman didn't hurt him. She mostly cried and wished she didn't have to do this."

"Can he identify her?"

"I don't think so," Ian replied. "But he did wonder out loud if it was the same woman he'd heard in the woods."

"Makes sense to me," Oliver said. He began to study

the maps spread out on the hood of the vehicle, a spot-light shining on them. "We started out here and fol-lowed the stream to the river. I stayed a few yards behind Ava and Roscoe to search up high on some of the bluffs. They needed quiet and I was watching out for them. I found evidence that someone had traveled that way—broken branches, trampled grass and foot-prints in the dirt."

He pointed to the area on the map. "I think who-ever took the boy stopped here to rest and regroup. Or to wait for us to show up." He shook his head. "We thought we'd fooled Sullivan but he fooled us. He's not here and he's probably not in the woods on this side of the river. He's been crossing over to get back and forth."

Finishing, he pointed to where the stream merged with the river. "Right here. This should be the entry point."

Justin Blackwood came up and studied the map. "Call in Search-and-Rescue," he said. "We need a chopper and this time, we work around the clock and use every means we have to find Boyd Sullivan."

"And the mysterious woman who's helping him," Oliver said. "But my intent is to find Ava."

Ava was halfway back to the Johnsons' house when she heard a twig snapping up ahead. The woman had thrown her weapon into the woods, so Ava had no way of protecting herself. Sliding behind a rock, she waited, holding her breath.

Had the woman survived that fall?

Not knowing what had happened to Oliver and pray-ing Turner had made it home with Roscoe, Ava closed her eyes and held her breath, her prayers centered on the three of them.

Please, Lord, let them be safe. Roscoe knows his job.

Then she opened her eyes and searched for a weapon. Any weapon. Finding a big, aged tree branch, Ava grabbed it and waited.

Then she heard a woof. A friendly woof.

"Roscoe?"

Another woof, followed by a shout. "Ava?"

Roscoe rushed up and danced around her, woofing a happy tune.

"Oliver?" She stood, the glare of a flashlight temporarily blinding her. Then she heard a chopper overhead. "What's going on?"

Oliver hurried toward her and Ava immediately saw the pain on his face. "Oliver, are you all right?"

"I am now," he said, hugging her close. "How about you?"

"I'm fine. She had me but I got away. I kicked her off into a ravine and I ran because I was so worried about Turner and Roscoe."

"Turner is safe and doing great. He gave us a lot of details, including how she let it slip that her friend would be angry with her for doing this, but she had to get back to the river to meet him."

"Did Turner recognize her?"

"No. But he thinks it's the same woman he saw and heard in the woods."

"What are we doing?" she asked as people surrounded them.

Tech Sergeant Linc Colson came jogging up, his rottweiler, Star, with him. "Someone spotted a man who looked like Boyd Sullivan at the boat launch on the east shore of the river. We're bringing in two choppers and one found a spot to land about a mile from here. Let's get back to the house and move out."

"Can you walk?" Ava asked Oliver.

"I'm fine," he said. "I had a little tumble earlier but... I just needed to find you. The medics fixed me up and I'm good to go."

"This is serious if they're bringing in the choppers."

"Ian, Westley and Justin all agree we need to ramp things up. The woman is a problem, but she's either a big distraction so Sullivan can get away or she's gone rogue and is out to do you and me in, regardless of what the killer wants. She wanted to shut Turner up, and she didn't care who else she had to kill."

"Yes, but I pushed and she's very jealous of Sullivan. She thinks he's got a thing for me since he let me live."

"You must have struck a chord somewhere in his sick head."

"Or he's out for revenge against you."

"We need to find that woman and get the real story."

Ava sighed. "Meanwhile, Sullivan could be anywhere."

"Yes, so we're calling in more people and we'll use the chopper's technology to zoom in on any movement in the woods."

"That didn't help before."

"Well, we'll try again. I'm bringing in more agents, too. We're going to search with more intention on the other side of the river. An all-out manhunt leaving no stone unturned."

"I think we should since he slipped away last time. He's obviously been using the river to escape. The land on the other side is denser than the reserve connected to the base. We ended the search there last time because we thought he'd left the area."

Ava held his hand and guided him along through the trail, Roscoe leading the way while flashlights shone on their path out.

Once the medics had checked her over and released her, she geared up, secured new weapons and got Roscoe ready for their chopper ride.

When they made it to the rendezvous point, Oliver took her hand in his. "They won't let me get in the chopper with you. My leg is hurting and I'd slow you down. But I'll be in on the search. I'll be riding shotgun in a Jeep."

"I'll see you there," she said, wanting to kiss him.

"Stay safe," he whispered. Then he squeezed her hand. "Go."

Ava got out of the vehicle, giving him one last look before she hurried with Roscoe to the waiting helicopter.

"Okay, Roscoe, you know the drill."

Ava prepared both their harnesses and got ready to rappel down into the black hole of the dense thicket. It had been a while since she'd done such an urgent nighttime search. Using GPS and the infrared system, they'd spotted a lone figure darting from the river into the woods. They believed that figure had to be the Red Rose Killer.

Now Ava had her night vision goggles and she had Roscoe geared up, the V-ring ready to hook to his harness. His vest was Kevlar and had all kinds of gadgets she could use if necessary. Including a flashlight with a battery pack and a built-in GPS to help her keep track of him.

This search had escalated to priority status now that they had evidence that Sullivan was back in the area.

But they hadn't found the woman. Ava got word on the radio that they'd searched the spot where Ava and the suspect had fought and saw signs that indicated the woman had slid down to the stream.

But she was nowhere to be found.

Exhaustion warred with adrenaline throughout Ava's system.

The crew prepared for the mission and then Ava did one last check and gave them the thumbs-up.

The gunner stationed behind one of the two .50 caliber machine guns gave Ava a nod, making her think of Julian.

He'd want you to keep moving, keep doing what you do, keep loving life. He'd want you to love again.

With that thought in mind, she held Roscoe in front of her and let the crew members guide her partner and her down to the ground.

Oliver sat in the Jeep, watching.

He needed to be out there, but he didn't want to keep others from doing their jobs. The open Jeep could get him close, however. The driver sent the Jeep flying through the woods, taking mudholes and ravines with the ease of a fighter pilot. Oliver held on and gritted his teeth, his leg throbbing less since they'd given him a mild pain reliever.

When they found the rendezvous point with the chopper he watched in awe as Ava slipped to the ground, loaded with gear and wearing a helmet and night goggles, and then unhooked herself and Roscoe all in one efficient movement.

The Jeep hovered on the narrow, overgrown path, watching and waiting along with Security Forces, the K-9 team and OSI members.

They'd all spread out through the woods in several different directions. Oliver got reports from his agents and gave advice as needed.

But after an hour, they still had nothing.

When his cell rang, he sat up straight. "Davison."

"We got some feedback from the superstore surveillance, sir. A tall female dressed in black went to two different area stores and purchased camping and fishing supplies." The agent named the dates, times and locations. "Paid with cash."

"Description?" Oliver asked, his gaze scanning the woods.

"Negative. She wore sunshades and a big hat. Probably wearing a wig, too."

Oliver thought of all the times he and Ava had spotted Sullivan's accomplice. Always in heavy black, no matter the Texas heat. And always so covered, no one could pick her out of a lineup. No one except a scared little boy whose parents didn't want him to have to suffer any more horrors.

Oliver couldn't push them on that either.

He ended the call with little more of a lead than he'd had before. They had a scrap of material with Boyd Sullivan's DNA on it and footage of an unidentifiable woman buying the exact kind of supplies needed to survive in a hot, bug-infested Texas thicket. And the boy's report that he'd been nabbed by a man and a woman who vacillated over killing him or holding him for ransom.

He suspected either Boyd or the woman had tried to shoot Oliver and Ava in San Antonio, but he had no solid proof there. Not even on the bike the driver had abandoned. They had the make and model on that and even the store where it had been purchased. But the owner had reported the bike stolen the same night Oliver and Ava had been in San Antonio.

"I'm losing my touch," he mumbled, frustration making his head roar.

They had to get a break, and soon. The base and the entire Hill Country area were on high alert again.

When he heard a ruckus in the woods and several dogs barking, Oliver looked around for his driver. The guy was nowhere to be found. So Oliver hopped out and went around to the driver's seat of the old Jeep and started it up. He wasn't waiting around. He had to help Ava and her team.

The chopper reported two possible hostiles moving in opposite directions through the woods. One team went to the east and another one spread out across the perimeters of the forest, while Ava took Roscoe and headed toward the west, staying within sight and communicating through her earbuds.

Roscoe alerted about a half mile deep into the woods. Ava had broken away from the others, letting her partner do his job. The foliage and undergrowth was so thick Ava had spurs and sharp nettles coating the legs of her camo pants. Her boots were dusty and caked with dirt and old mud. And the bugs were out to do her in, finding every bit of uncovered flesh despite the bug spray she'd hosed down with earlier.

But now Roscoe was definitely on a scent. The big dog moved with a tenacious zest up and down the hills and crevices. Then Roscoe stopped and pawed at something in the dirt before turning back to Ava.

She hurried over and bent down.

Another headband. This one solid black and dirty.

"Good boy," Ava said, lifting the headband with a stick to drop it into a small evidence bag. Then she put the bag into one of the many pockets attached to her uniform jacket.

"Go," she told Roscoe. "Find." If he had a scent from the Buff, maybe, just maybe, they'd find the mysterious woman and maybe, just maybe, she'd lead them to Boyd Sullivan.

Other dogs started barking off in the distance. The woods came alive with action. Roscoe sniffed the air and the forest floor and then took off toward the west.

They rounded a curve where a well-beaten path brought her to a hidden stream by a wide-mouth cave.

Ava spotted a camp just inside the big cave. She could see where a fire had burned, several empty cans lying there. There was water nearby and a roomy, almost hidden, shelter, two things someone on the run would need.

I think we've found his lair.

At last.

"Good job," she told Roscoe on a low whisper. "Good find."

Ava crept around the side of the rocky cave, hoping to wait for Sullivan or his accomplice to emerge. But if they'd heard the dogs, they'd be on the run again by now. Didn't he know that sooner or later they'd corner him in the woods?

She studied the cave through her night goggles. No movement. But it could go deep into the terrain and, just as she and Oliver had suspected, the cave could open up near the fence that protected Canyon Air Force Base. Ava stepped forward for a better scan.

Roscoe growled low and gave her a warning, but too late, she whirled. And heard the click of a gun in the darkness.

"At last, we meet again," the unseen gunman said, his voice lifting out over the woods in a disembodied echo. "I've given you so many chances to live, hoping that you'd leave me alone or that possibly we might even become close."

Ava tried not to flinch. "I'm here now. What do you want with me?"

Roscoe barked, loud and angry, sensing the danger and the evil. The roar of the choppers flying off in the distance gave her hope.

He moved close but stayed behind some heavy undergrowth. "Call off that mutt and turn off your radio, or our first date will end very quickly."

Ava commanded Roscoe. "Quiet. Stay." Then she switched off her only means of contact, took a breath and tried to focus on ending this. "What do you want?"

"I want you to come with me," he said. "My former ally has suddenly deserted me and it's just so lonely in these woods."

"Did you kill her because she disobeyed you?"

"Not yet. I told her to back off. Too bad she didn't listen. Taking the boy was a bad mistake, her way of trying to get my attention. But it did bring you to me."

Ava swallowed the bile rising in her throat, not sure if she believed him or not, but very sure he would kill the woman who'd gone against his wishes. "That's too bad about your friend. She really wanted me out of the way. Tried to shoot me several times, but she's not a very good shot."

"I know. Tedious, really." He moved closer so she could finally see him, but he was covered in camo and had his face covered with a dark bandana. Holding a handgun aimed at her, he said, "Tell your dog to stay and then carefully clear your weapons out and drop them by the dog. Then you and I can go for a stroll in the moonlight."

Ava did as he asked, her prayers centered on surviving. She had no other choice. The others would find her. And meantime, she planned to do everything in her power to stop this man from killing again.

When she reached into her pocket, she felt something she'd forgotten she'd put there. The black headband Roscoe had found earlier. Making a production of slowly dropping her handgun and the extra magazines, she managed to loop the wide black band over her wrist.

Dropping that down with her weapons, she hoped it would be a sign that she'd been here and that she'd been taken by the Red Rose Killer. Taking one last glance at Roscoe, she gave him a loving stare, then started to walk in front of the gunman.

Find us, boy. Show them that you're never wrong.

TWENTY-ONE

"What do you mean, you don't know where she is?"

Oliver took off his FBI cap and ran a hand over his damp hair, his frown so rigid his temple throbbed in protest.

"She's gone off grid," K-9 handler Lieutenant Nick Donovan said. "No communication for the last thirty minutes."

"That's not good," Oliver said. "Ava knows not to do that. Where's Roscoe?"

"We were about to go search for both of them," Justin Blackwood told Oliver. "So either hop a ride or stay behind, but we're wasting time."

"I'm going."

Oliver limped to an off-road four-wheeler and got in the back seat since the extra front seat was occupied by a K-9 bloodhound. The pain running up and down his spine and hip was excruciating, but he had to find Ava. Something wasn't right.

"I should never have left her," he said to Nick. "I knew better."

"Hey, man, we've all been right here. She got a scent

and she took off. It's what we do. We weren't that far behind."

"Someone should have stayed with her. Where's Buster?" He wondered what had detained the burly Security Forces member.

"On another case but he's trying to get here," Nick replied over the noise of the ATV's motor. "We'll find her, Oliver. Just stay cool and get your head back into this."

Oliver knew his friend was right, so he took a deep breath and asked for updates. After Nick brought him up to speed, he checked in with his agents, relieved that they'd found signs of a campsite and had gathered what few items they could for evidence.

"The choppers spotted someone running toward the river and the dogs went into action when we advanced toward that area," Nick explained. "We found a dirty black hoodie—extra large—a pair of nylon jogging pants and some muddy black tennis shoes. The items were scattered, so the dogs were going wild."

"But you didn't find the person?"

"Nope. Either swam across the river or managed to throw off the scent enough to get away. One of your agents heard a motor cranking up, but we lost the scent in a clearing across the stream."

"And then you heard more barking?"

"Yes. And we realized Ava wasn't checking in."

Nick pulled the ATV up to a clearing and ordered his partner, Annie, down. "This is the last spot where we heard from her. She was onto something."

They got off the ATV and stalked quietly through the dark, low-beam flashlights leading the way. Nick clipped on his night goggles. They'd gone a few hundred yards, finding broken twigs and limbs here and there, when they heard a low growl.

"That could be Roscoe," Oliver whispered, hurrying past Nick and Annie. Annie's ear twitched in anticipation.

They came up on an open area. "Cave," he whispered to Nick.

Ava must have found a cave, and from the looks of it, it was the Red Rose Killer's hideout. Almost exactly like the one Oliver had spotted days ago on the other side of the river.

But this one was in a hidden spot in the middle of a deserted wilderness area that few humans ever saw.

And sitting in front of that cave, guarding what looked like a pile of weapons and equipment, Roscoe stared up at them with hope in his doleful eyes. Then he touched a paw to something lying amid the things Ava had left behind.

A dirty black headband. A Buff, Ava had called these things. Roscoe must have alerted on this. But Ava had left it as a sign, a big clue.

"This isn't Ava's." Oliver looked at Nick and then grabbed one of the weapons from the ground. "He took her. The Red Rose Killer took Ava. But she left something behind so we can find her."

He moved behind her, poking the gun at her ribs each time she tried to stop or turn to face him.

Ava kept her breathing steady to keep her nerves calm. "You know they're out here searching for you, right?"

"What else is new?" Boyd Sullivan asked with a harsh laugh.

"And you know that if anything happens to me, they will find you?"

"They haven't so far. It's really laughable how easy it is to get the jump on the whole Security Forces section. I might have flunked basic, but I know more about this base than any of you imbeciles."

Trying again while she ignored that bait, she asked, "Why are you so fixated on me?"

He stopped and yanked her back. "Isn't that obvious? *He* loves you. He didn't love Madison but he loves you. I want him to suffer."

Ava decided Sullivan's logic was skewed. "But you killed her. You killed the woman you loved."

Anger drew him close. Close enough that she saw his dead soul through his icy blue eyes. "She betrayed me with him. After she swore she loved me." Then he went quiet and still. "I wish I'd never started this, but now I can't stop."

Ah, a crack in his armor. "That must have been horrible for you, killing the woman you truly loved."

Sullivan gripped her arm so hard, pain shot down her side. But Ava steeled herself against what he might do next.

"I don't talk about that," he said, pushing her forward again.

"He didn't know she was with you," Ava said, her heart hurting for the evil that had warped this man.

"Well, he figured it out when they found her, didn't he?"

"He's suffered enough."

"Never enough. None of you have suffered. I'm the one who's been through the worst."

Ava got closer, in his face. "If you kill me, it won't matter one bit. He will track you until he finds you."

"No, he won't," Boyd Sullivan said, taking her by the arm to turn her back around to face him. "Because I'm going to kill you, and after he watches and suffers, I'm going to kill him, too."

Ava swallowed the fear trembling through her body. "You won't do that. You can't keep killing. That will never bring you any satisfaction."

"Shut up."

They'd walked close to a half mile, from her calculations. She prayed that someone would find Roscoe. He wouldn't move until someone came along, and then he'd do his best to follow her trail.

And the trail of a killer.

"Where are we going?" she asked, all the while searching for a way to escape.

"I'll know when we get there," he said.

Ava realized he was stalling. He was waiting for Oliver to show up.

She had to get away, not only to save herself but to protect Oliver, too.

They walked farther down a gully and then back up to a sharp ledge.

"This will do nicely," Sullivan said. "We wait here."

He shoved Ava down against the hard, jagged rocks. "If you make one wrong move, I'll toss you over this ledge."

She didn't respond. She was too intent of figuring out how to push *him* off the ledge.

Roscoe never wavered. The loyal K-9 followed the one scent that he knew with every fiber of his being, that of his partner, Ava Esposito. Even when Nick had called in Chad Watson, a handler who was used to another dog, Roscoe stayed the course.

Oliver remembered Ava always saying that Roscoe was never wrong. He had to believe that, had to cling to that one hope. That they'd find her alive. She'd gotten away from the woman today, even after all the times they'd tried to kill her. Now she had to escape from a madman.

So he prayed for one other thing, too. That somehow they could take down the Red Rose Killer. Then a thought coursed over Oliver.

He'd take Ava alive over capturing the Red Rose Killer.

He didn't want the man to keep killing, but he wanted Ava alive. Period.

When Roscoe stopped and bristled, Oliver and the others stood silent, listening, watching. The very air seemed to still, the humidity so thick Oliver could taste the decay and feel the darkness swirling around them.

Roscoe lifted his nose in the air and held his head up.

The big dog looked back once and then held his head high again.

"We move up," Nick mouthed, Annie silent beside him.

Oliver's whole body screamed in pain. He'd been through all kinds of injuries during his career, but this one cut like a knife through his spine. And yet, he couldn't stop moving because the pain and fear inside his heart hurt even more.

They went off the path and crouched in the heavy bramble deep underneath the tall trees. The woods crackled with a dryness that left Oliver's nostrils covered with dust. Sweat rolled down his forehead and into his eyes, but he had his weapon drawn and his gaze up toward the trees and hills.

Nick flipped his goggles down and then nodded, his fist up for quiet. Taking them off, he offered them to Oliver.

And then Oliver saw them. Ava, sitting on a high bluff beside a man dressed in dark camo, his face covered.

And the man was holding a gun to Ava's side.

Oliver didn't stop to think. He took off around the edge of the hanging ledge, determined to save the woman he loved. When he heard something behind him, he turned and saw a blur of golden fur and felt the rush of wind as Roscoe silently leapt into the air and took off up the steep incline.

Thankful that Chad had ordered the K-9 to go, Oliver followed the dog, each running step slicing a knife-like pain throughout his body. Gritting his teeth, he held steady until he crested the ledge.

But before he could do anything, he watched as Ava rose up and called her partner. "Here, Roscoe. Here."

The big dog barked a reply. Fearful of what Sullivan would do, Oliver shot into the night to distract the killer.

Sullivan whirled, his gun now aimed toward Oliver.

Oliver held his own gun up, but he heard a scream and watched in horror as Ava struggled with Boyd Sullivan. Roscoe leapt up onto the ledge and snarled, his teeth grabbing at Sullivan's camo pants.

Oliver hurried toward Ava and the Red Rose Killer, his gun pointed. "Stop. Let her go!"

The killer screamed in anger, Roscoe still clutching at his pants, and pushed Ava. She fell back, emitting a scream as she went down against the rocky floor of the bluff.

Oliver shot at Sullivan but Sullivan turned and beat at Roscoe with his gun. Roscoe never let go, but then a great ripping sound echoed out over the night. The heavy camouflage material gave way and the killer teetered on top of the ledge, and then with a grunt, his gun firing into the air, Boyd Sullivan fell out of sight and disappeared down into the rocks and bramble below.

Oliver stood there, shocked, and then he started running. "Ava? Ava? Where are you?"

Roscoe barked, looking down below. But then the dog turned to stare at Oliver before turning to run across the bluff's surface.

Oliver watched as Roscoe put his nose down.

The K-9 was touching his nose to the face of the woman who lay still against the rocks. Roscoe whimpered before he turned to give Oliver a plea in the form of a bark.

Oliver heard all of the noise around him and saw the helicopter hovering over them, a spotlight shining like a beacon in the dark. But he kept running toward Ava, the pain in his body forgotten.

When Oliver reached her, Roscoe stepped back and stood silent. Oliver lifted her into his arms, felt her weak pulse and held her there, calling out for the others to get help.

"Hang on, Ava," he said over and over. "You can't give up on me now." When he felt blood on the back of her head, he held her tighter. "Ava, wake up."

"Let us check on her." Chad Watson gently tugged Oliver away.

Soon, the chopper that usually carried Ava and Roscoe to rescue people managed to hover low enough that they got her on a stretcher and took her up so they could get her to the hospital. Roscoe whimpered and came to stand beside where Oliver sat watching, too numb to do anything else.

When Chad came back, he leaned down. "Agent Davison, we need to get you to the hospital, too."

"I'm going down there," Oliver said, pointing to the ravine. "I need to see Boyd Sullivan's body."

Chad shook his head. "Negative, sir. No sign of the Red Rose Killer. He's injured. We found a blood trail, but he's no longer in the area. We're still searching."

A black rage filled Oliver's soul. He let out a grunt full of frustration and failure.

"Don't stop searching," Oliver shouted, trying to stand.

"We won't, sir," Chad replied, calm and in control. "But you need to get help."

Oliver held on to Chad for support. "Yes, get me to the hospital. I'm fine, but I need to be with Ava." Grabbing Chad's protective vest, he said, "You understand, Airman?"

"Yes, sir," Chad replied. "I'll take you there myself."

Ava woke with a soft moan, her mind still lost in the last thing she remembered before Sullivan pushed her. She tried to sit up, to find Roscoe, to see if Oliver was okay.

But she wasn't in the Hill Country woods.

She was in a sterile, dark hospital room.

And her head hurt with all the force of bombs exploding.

"Oliver?" she called, praying he was still alive.

"I'm here," she heard from somewhere in a dark corner.

Then she saw him there, lying on a couch. He stood and hobbled to the chair next to her bed and took her hand.

"You're okay?" she asked, tears burning at her eyes.

"No," he admitted with a weak chuckle. "I hurt everywhere, but they gave me some pain medicine so I'd shut up about you."

She pushed up on the pillow and looked at the contraptions feeding something into a tube in her arm. "What happened? Where's Roscoe?"

"Roscoe is safe and well. Sullivan pushed you and you hit your head. You lost a lot of blood and you have a mild concussion. They told me you might slip into a coma, but I knew you'd wake up."

She held his hand, the warmth and security of having him here giving her strength. "Did we get him? Is Sullivan dead? Or is he behind bars?"

Oliver looked down. "He…he managed to get away, but he's injured. We think he made it to the water and took a boat downriver. We've got people searching and we found several different boats, hidden in various locations."

When she didn't speak, Oliver lifted his head and looked into her eyes. "I'm so sorry."

Seeing the utter dejection in his eyes, Ava asked, "Sorry for what?"

"I let you down. I wanted to end it and I had a chance. I should have gone after him, but I was so worried about you. Roscoe took me to you and I... I couldn't leave you there."

Ava shook her head, thankful that her faithful partner was all right. "You've done everything you can, Oliver. Someone else can take over now. You're battered and bruised and you need to rest. You can rest, with me. With Roscoe. Please tell me you'll do that."

He stared into her eyes, his five-o'clock shadow making him look like a pirate. "I will do that." Then he put his head down against his hands, over her hand. "I'm so tired, and when I thought I'd lost you, I knew I'd been chasing the wrong dream. You're the reason I'm here, and I want to be with you. I'm going to rest, with you and with Roscoe."

"But we won't give up," she said. "We'll keep watch and help the others."

"Yes. But I'm never going in those woods again."

"Me, either," she said. "I think the Gulf Coast is calling my name."

"We'll go there together," he offered. "On our honeymoon."

"Is that a proposal, Special Agent Davison?"

"Is that a yes, Airman Esposito?"

"Yes, yes. Two weeks and I've fallen for you. Forever."

"Roscoe led me to you," he told her between kisses.

"Roscoe is never wrong," she replied with a smile. "He's smart that way," she said, pulling him toward her so she could kiss him. "I'm never avoiding you again."

Oliver held Ava in his arms and kissed her to show her he felt the same way. He couldn't hold back the piercing joy that filled his heart. Ava had renewed his faith in love and hope and all that was good in the world. Whether they took this investigation any further or not, he knew they would stay in each other's lives.

He'd forgotten how to breathe after Madison had died. He'd been carrying around such a heavy guilt, he'd almost been consumed by it. But Oliver had been trying to work his way back to his faith and to God.

And now, because of Ava, he could clearly see the path ahead. That path included being with her the rest of his life.

One week later

The press conference was over.

Ava had watched as Oliver, Justin and Westley handled most of the questions from the media.

Yes, the Red Rose Killer was still out there, but all indications showed he'd left the woods for good this time.

Yes, they had people patrolling the area day and night and the security on base and around the Hill Country had been beefed up.

Yes, they believed the woman who'd been helping Boyd Sullivan had acted on her own, shooting at them to scare them away, that she possibly could have been the shooter in San Antonio and that she could have been driving the motorcycle but wearing Sullivan's pants. Yes, they believed that both the female shooter and Boyd Sullivan had stolen the car and the motorcycle and tried to run Oliver and Ava off the road and kill them.

No, they didn't yet know who the Anonymous Blogger was, but speculation was rampant that the mysterious woman who had disappeared might very well be the blogger.

No, they had not given up the hunt for the Red Rose Killer. They had BOLOs and ABPs out all over the state of Texas and the entire country.

And finally, Heidi Jenks had tried to ask Oliver where he stood in all of this.

"Special Agent Davison, do you plan to stick around and keep up with the search?"

But before Oliver would answer, Heidi's colleague, John Robinson, shoved her aside, stating he was the lead reporter on this case. "When can I interview you, Special Agent?"

"I'll let you know, since I already know everyone else around here has turned you down."

Robinson had stomped off, but Ava noticed Heidi lingering, her lips tightly drawn in aggravation.

"I think you should give Heidi the interview," she said on a low whisper as they were leaving the conference room.

"I haven't decided to do the interview," Oliver replied. "Besides, I'm still not convinced about Heidi. Despite what everyone else thinks, I suspect she may be the Anonymous Blogger. She's the perfect fit."

"She does seem to resent her colleague," Ava admitted. "But then, John Robinson is a bit snarky and annoying."

"And arrogant," Oliver said, grinning. "But enough about them. We have a trip to Galveston to plan."

They got in Ava's SUV, Roscoe eager to go with them, and headed to the Winged Java. But before they got out, Oliver leaned over and kissed Ava.

"I love you," he said. "I know life with me will be

tough. I can't let go of Sullivan and what he did, but I can step back and get my priorities straight while I take a different approach on this investigation. I didn't do that before. Now my future is clear."

"I love you," she replied, her heart swelling because she knew he was sacrificing so much for her. "And I feel the same. I love my work, but at times we'll be far apart. But we can make up for that when we're together."

"And the danger?" he asked, his heart in his eyes.

"The danger is everywhere. We have jobs to do. We have each other. It's a risk I'm willing to take."

"Then it's settled."

He got out and came around to open her door, a gesture that touched Ava. But when they got inside the café, being touched went up several notches to being overwhelmed.

The whole crew was there, smiling and clapping and laughing.

"What's going on?" she asked, surprised to see so many familiar faces.

Oliver sat her down on a chair and, in spite of his still-healing back and leg, got down on one knee, pulled out a little black box and opened it. A diamond ring sparkled and winked at her. When she gasped and looked up, her coworker Chad Watson winked at her, too.

Oliver took the ring and lifted her hand so he could put it on her finger. "For the record, Airman Esposito, I want everyone here to know I'm going to marry you."

"If she says yes," Chad called out.

"If she says yes," Oliver echoed, his eyes on Ava.

They didn't know she'd already said yes, but he wanted her to have this moment.

Ava swallowed the lump in her throat and bobbed her head. "She says yes. She definitely says yes."

Roscoe woofed and stared up at them, a grateful look in his eyes. Because he had known all along. And Roscoe was never wrong.

* * * * *

Lynette Eason is a bestselling, award-winning author who makes her home in South Carolina with her husband and two teenage children. She enjoys traveling, spending time with her family and teaching at various writing conferences around the country. She is a member of Romance Writers of America and American Christian Fiction Writers. Lynette can often be found online interacting with her readers. You can find her at Facebook.com/lynette.eason and on Twitter, @lynetteeason.

Books by Lynette Eason

Love Inspired Suspense

Holiday Homecoming Secrets

True Blue K-9 Unit

Justice Mission

Wrangler's Corner

The Lawman Returns
Rodeo Rescuer
Protecting Her Daughter
Classified Christmas Mission
Christmas Ranch Rescue
Vanished in the Night
Holiday Amnesia

Military K-9 Unit

Explosive Force

Visit the Author Profile page
at Harlequin.com for more titles.

EXPLOSIVE FORCE

Lynette Eason

But the Lord is faithful, who shall stablish you, and keep you from evil.

—*2 Thessalonians 3:3*

Dedicated to the two-legged and four-legged heroes
who put their lives on the line every day.
No amount of thanks will ever be enough.

ONE

First Lieutenant Heidi Jenks, news reporter for *CAF News*, blew a lock of hair out of her eyes and did her best to keep from muttering under her breath about the stories she was being assigned lately.

She didn't mind the series of articles she was doing on the personnel who lived on the base—those were interesting and she was meeting new people. And besides, those had been her idea.

But some of the other stories were just plain boring. Like the stolen medals. Okay, maybe not boring, but definitely not as exciting as some she could be working on. Like finding Boyd Sullivan, the Red Rose Killer. A serial killer, he liked to torment his victims with the gift of a red rose and a note saying he was coming for them. And then he struck, leaving death and heartache in his wake with one last rose and a note tucked under the arm of the victim. *Got you.*

Heidi shut the door to the church where her interviewee had insisted on meeting and walked down the steps, pulling her voice-activated recorder from her pocket. She might as well get her thoughts down before they dissipate due to her complete disinterest.

She shivered and glanced over her shoulder. For some reason she expected to see him, as if the fact that she was alone in the dark would automatically mean Sullivan was behind her.

After being chased by law enforcement last week, he'd fallen from a bluff and was thought to be dead. But when his body had never been found, that assumption had changed. He was alive. Somewhere. Possibly injured and in hiding while he healed. Reports had come in that he'd been spotted twice in central Texas. She supposed that was possible. But what if the reports were wrong? What if he'd made his way back here to the base so he could continue his reign of terror?

The thought quickened her steps. She'd feel better behind a locked door where she could concentrate on the story she was currently working on.

Someone on the base was breaking into homes and stealing war medals, jewelry and cash. Whatever small items they could get their hands on. But it was the medals that were being targeted. Medals of Valor especially. People were antsy enough about the whole serial killer thing. Having a thief on base wasn't helping matters.

She spoke into the recorder. "Mrs. Wainwright stated she hadn't been home at the time of the robbery. However, as soon as she pulled into her drive, she could see her open front door and knew something was wrong."

Heidi's steps took her past the base hospital. She was getting ready to turn onto the street that would take her home when a flash of movement from the K-9 training center caught her eye. Her steps slowed, and she heard a door slam.

A figure wearing a dark hoodie bolted down the steps and shot off toward the woods behind the center. He reached up, shoved the hoodie away and yanked something—a ski mask?—off his head, then pulled the hoodie back up. He stuffed the ski mask into his jacket pocket.

Very weird actions that set Heidi's internal and journalistic alarm bells screaming. And while she wanted to see what the guy was going to do, she decided it might be more prudent to get out of sight while she watched.

Just as she moved to do so, the man spun.

And came to an abrupt halt as his eyes locked on hers.

Ice invaded her veins, sending shivers of fear dancing along her nerves. He took a step toward her, then shot a look back at the training center. Back to her. Then at his wristwatch. With no change in his granite too blue eyes as he gave her one last threatening glare, he whirled and raced toward the woods once again.

Like he wanted to put as much distance between him and the building as possible.

Foreboding filled her just as a side door to the training center opened. A young man stood there, his uniform identifying him as one of the trainers. His eyes met hers, just like the hooded man's had only seconds earlier. But this time, she knew who the eyes belonged to. Bobby Stevens, a young airman who'd recently finished his tech training. He hesitated, glanced at her, then over his shoulder.

Her gut churned with a distinctly bad feeling. With everything that had happened on the base in the last few months, there was only one reason that the man in the hoodie would be so anxious to run when it looked like he would rather do her bodily harm.

She started backing away, her feet pedaling quickly. "Run, Bobby! Get away from the building. Something weird is going on!"

Bobby hesitated a fraction of a second, then took off toward her, looking determined to catch up with her. Her footsteps pounded as she put distance between her and the building and the man behind her.

Then an explosion rocked the ground beneath her and she fell to her knees, her palms scraping the concrete as she tried to catch herself.

Rolling, Heidi held on to her screams and looked back to see part of the building missing and fire spurting from the cavernous area.

And Bobby Stevens lying sprawled on the ground.

People spilled from the buildings close to her, many on their phones. No doubt calling for help.

Heidi managed to get her feet beneath her and scrambled to stand. She raced back to Bobby and dropped beside him, wincing as her knees hit the concrete.

Already, she could hear the sirens.

Calling on her past first aid training, Heidi pressed her fingers against his neck and felt a steady, if slow, pulse. He had a laceration on his forehead and his wrist hung at an odd angle.

His lids fluttered, then opened. His brows dipped and he winced.

"It's all right, Bobby," she said. "Help is on the way."

"What happened?"

"The building exploded, but you're going to be okay."

"Exploded? Why?" His eyelids fluttered. "Hurts." He tried to roll and groaned.

Heidi pressed her hands to his shoulders. "I know. Just be still."

"Hold my hand, please," he whispered. "I'm...cold."

She slid her fingers gently around his uninjured hand. "I'm here," she whispered. "Just hold on." Bobby's eyes closed, but he continued to breathe shallow, labored breaths. "You're going to be all right. Just hang in there."

In seconds, she felt hands pulling her away. First responders had arrived. Heidi backed up, keeping her eyes on the now-unconscious man who'd reached out to her as though she could save him.

"Are you all right?" the paramedic asked her.

She focused in on the figure in front of her. "Um... yes. I was farther away from the blast. It knocked me off my feet, but nothing else. I just ran back to check on Bobby."

"Your knees are bleeding."

She blinked and looked down. "Oh." Blood seeped through her slacks. And now that her attention had been brought to them, her knees throbbed.

The paramedic led her to one of the four ambulances now lining the street. "Let me just check you out and get these knees bandaged for you."

"Yes, okay. Thank you." She drew in a deep breath and let her gaze wander past the crowd that had gathered.

Was the bomber watching the building burn? Could he see the firefighters fight against the raging flames?

She had a bad feeling about this. A feeling that this

was only the beginning of something that might be bigger than any story she'd ever worked on.

And she had a feeling that the man who'd done this would be back.

Because she'd seen him.

First Lieutenant Nick Donovan itched to get his hands on the person who'd just blown up part of the training center. Thankfully, it was an area of the building that wasn't being used at the moment and no animals had been harmed. Airman Bobby Stevens was reported to be in stable condition and was expected to make a full recovery. That was the only reason Nick's anger wasn't boiling over, even though his patience levels were maxed out.

Unfortunately, he and his bloodhound, Annie, would have to wait a little longer to do their part in figuring out exactly what had caused the explosion. Annie was trained in explosives detection, but right now, she couldn't get near the training center, even wearing the protective booties. The area was still too hot, and firefighters were still fighting the blaze. However, Annie and he *could* examine parts of the building that had landed yards away.

Office of Special Investigations, OSI, had arrived and would be taking lead on the case under the supervision of Ian Steffen. Nick also spotted FBI special agent Oliver Davison, who'd been a frequent visitor to the base—not only because of his search for the Red Rose Killer, but also to see his fiancée, Senior Airman Ava Esposito.

Of course, he would show up. At this point, anything bad that happened on the base was suspected of being caused by Boyd Sullivan. And Oliver was one of the most determined people on the elite investigative team formed especially to hunt Sullivan down and bring him to justice. Truth was, they all wanted the killer caught and were working overtime in order to do that.

Nick belonged to the Explosive Ordnance Disposal unit and had gotten the call shortly after the explosion happened. He'd raced from his home and arrived to find the organized chaos he was now in the middle of. If the EOD unit had been called, then someone thought the damage to the building had been caused by a bomb—and they wanted to make sure there weren't any more explosives waiting to go off. Which he would be happy to do just as soon as he could get close enough.

Security Forces with assault rifles flooded the area and stood ready should there be another attempt to attack, although Nick figured whoever was responsible was long gone. But Canyon Air Force Base had an action plan for this kind of thing and it had been put into place immediately.

From the corner of his eye, he caught sight of Heidi Jenks, one of the base reporters, talking to an OSI investigator.

He scoffed. Boy, she didn't waste a second, did she? He sure hoped the investigator knew how to keep his mouth shut. The last thing they needed was for her to write a story before the facts were even determined.

She ran a hand over her wavy blond hair and rubbed her eyes. He frowned. Where was her ever-present notebook? And why did she look so disheveled?

Annie pulled on the leash and Nick let her lead him over to a large block of concrete. She sat. And he stiffened at her signal, which indicated a bomb. While he didn't think the piece of concrete itself was going to explode, it obviously had explosives residue on it. She looked at him expectantly. "Good girl, Annie, good girl." He took a treat from his pocket and she wolfed it down.

He set his backpack on the ground and pulled out the items he needed to take a sample of the cement. Once that was done, he placed the evidence back in his pack and scratched Annie's ears.

"What was that?" a voice asked. A voice he recognized and sometimes heard in his dreams. Against his will.

He looked up and found himself staring at a pair of bandaged knees. The blood on the torn pants had a story to tell. Nick stood and looked down into Heidi Jenks's blue eyes. Eyes he could drown in if he'd let himself. But she was so off-limits in the romance department that he banished the thought from his mind as soon as it popped in.

"No comment."

"Come on, Nick."

"Just something I want to take a closer look at."

She turned away to look at the smoking building. Fire trucks still poured water onto it. It could take hours to put the fire out. "It was a bomb, wasn't it?" she said when she turned back to him.

He pursed his lips. "Why do you jump to that conclusion?"

"What else could it be?" She shrugged. "Why else would you and Annie be here along with other members of EOD? You're going to have to check to make sure there aren't any more bombs, aren't you?"

Nick knew Heidi because he'd read her newspaper articles and some of the stories she'd written. Most people would consider them to be fluff pieces, but the truth was, he could see her heart behind them. And whether he wanted to admit it or not, he liked it. He and Heidi had had a few conversations, and each time, he'd wanted to prolong them. Which was weird for him. He didn't do conversations with people like Heidi. Users who just went after the story without worrying about the fallout. Even though his gut told him she wasn't like that. But she had to be. Otherwise he could lose his heart to her. And that couldn't happen. No way.

"Good deductive reasoning," he told her. "But did you think it was possible that I just wanted to see what was going on?"

"No."

"Hmm. You're right. Annie and I'll have to check for more bombs as soon as we get the green light. And that's not confidential so I'm not worried about you saying anything."

She sighed. "Look, I know with all the rumors circulating, no one wants to talk to me, but this...this is different."

An anonymous blogger had been reporting on the Red Rose Killer, his targets and the investigation. Reporting on things that no one but those involved in the investigation could know. Rumor had it that Heidi was the blogger. As a result, she'd been mostly ostracized from anything considered newsworthy when it came to the Red Rose Killer. But Heidi was persistent. He'd give her that.

He nodded to the torn pants and bandaged knees.

"What happened to you?"

She glanced down. "I got knocked off my feet by the blast."

He raised a brow. "You were here?"

"Yes."

Well, that put a new light on things. "Did you see anything?"

"I don't know. Maybe."

"Either you did or you didn't."

A scowl pulled her brows down. "Then I think I did."

"What did you see exactly?"

She drew in a deep breath. "Like I told the OSI agent, I think I may have seen the bomber."

At Nick's indrawn breath and instant flash of concern, Heidi felt slightly justified in her dramatic announcement. She shrugged, not nearly as nonchalant as she hoped she came across. "Honestly, I don't know if he was the bomber or not, but I sure saw someone who looked like he was up to no good. He had on dark clothing and a hoodie—and a ski mask. Why wear a ski mask unless you don't want anyone to know who you are? Anyway, he took that off right before he turned around and looked at me."

"Tell me everything."

As she talked about the man in the hoodie with the ice-cold blue eyes running from the scene, Nick's frown deepened. "You might be fortunate he was in a hurry to get away."

"I think that's a reasonable assumption." Just the thought of him sent fear skittering up her spine.

"So, he knows you saw him."

"Oh, yes, he knows. OSI is rounding up a sketch

artist for me to work with." She shivered and crossed her arms at the memory of the man's brief pause, as though he'd considered coming after her. Thankfully, he'd been in a hurry, more worried about getting away from the impending explosion. But she had seen his face. Well, some of it. The hoodie had hidden his hair color and some of his features, but she'd be able to identify those blue eyes anywhere and anytime.

"All right, stick close," Nick said. "I'm going to let Annie keep working and we'll see what she comes up with."

For the next thirty minutes, Heidi did as instructed and stayed right with him. Not just so she could collect facts for the story, but because she was just plain rattled. Okay, scared. She'd admit it. She was afraid and feeling decidedly out of her depth.

But watching Nick and Annie work was a good distraction. She felt safe with Nick in a way she couldn't explain, and she couldn't help admiring his strength and confidence, the total focus and dedication he had to his job.

Her father had been like that.

Before he'd died.

A pang of grief hit her and she shook her head. It had been two years and she still missed him like crazy. But he'd been a wonderful example of the ethical reporter she strived to be. She was determined to follow in his footsteps, determined to make him proud. Thinking of her father naturally sent her thoughts to her mother. A strong woman who'd loved her husband, she'd nearly been shattered by his death. His murder. He'd been killed by the big corporation he'd exposed as a front for the mafia. Killed by his best friend, who'd been the CEO of that corporation.

A lump formed in her throat.

Her parents had argued late one night. She'd come over for dinner and fallen asleep on the couch. When she'd awakened, she'd heard the harsh whispers coming from the kitchen. She'd stayed still and listened, hearing her mother begging her father to stop looking, to "give it up." Her father had been adamant. "I'm not looking the other way, Kate. I can't."

"I'm afraid, Richie," she'd whispered. "I'm truly afraid something will happen to you."

And it had. Not even two weeks later, a jogger had found his body washed up against the shore of a nearby lake. Her father had taken a bullet through the back of his skull. Executed. She lifted her chin. But his work would live on through her. The men who'd killed her father had been captured, tried and imprisoned—including the best friend who'd put the hit out on him. But it didn't bring her father back. It was up to her to carry on his work.

Truth, baby girl. Nothing's more important than exposing lies and bringing truth to light. Keep your focus where it should be. Don't step on people to get to the top. Don't excuse people who do wrong no matter who they are—and you'll do just fine.

Her father's words ringing in her mind, she watched as Nick finally stood from the last place Annie had alerted on and tucked a small bag into the larger one he carried. "All right," he said. "I think I'm done here for now."

"Did you find anything else?"

"I'll have to let the lab decide that." He dug a hand

into his front pocket and rewarded Annie with a treat and a "Good job, girl."

His gaze slid to her and he opened his mouth as if to say something, then snapped it shut and gave her a grim smile.

He wasn't going to tell her anything. He didn't trust her. She gave a mental sigh and shrugged off the hurt. What did she expect with everyone thinking she was the anonymous blogger, posting about everything going on in the investigation of the Red Rose Killer? Things no one but the investigative team should know. The blogger had everyone on edge and pointing fingers.

While it was true she was upset she hadn't been assigned the story, that didn't mean she was going around shooting off her mouth about things she shouldn't. The fact was she didn't know anything. Other than what was reported in the papers—and by the anonymous blogger.

But Nick didn't know that. He didn't know *her* other than from a short snippet of conversation here and there. They often ran into each other at the Winged Java café and he always made a point to speak to her—but he kept himself at a distance. Like he didn't want to get too close. For some reason, she wanted to change that.

His eyes narrowed on a spot over her shoulder. She turned to look. "What is it?" she asked.

"I thought I saw something move."

"Everything's moving around here. What are you talking about?"

"In the reserve just beyond the tree line." He strode toward it, Annie on his heels.

Heidi went after him, not about to miss out. Had

the guy that set the bomb off stayed behind to watch the action?

But that wouldn't be smart.

Then again, where was the rule that said bombers had to be smart? "You think it could be one of the missing dogs?" she called after him.

Several months ago, after killing two trainers in the Military Working Dog program, Boyd Sullivan had opened all two hundred and seven kennels and released the animals. While the more highly trained dogs had stayed put, one hundred ninety-six dogs, some PTSD therapy dogs—and dogs with PTSD themselves—had escaped. Most had been found and returned to safety, but there were still twenty-one missing.

Nick reached the tree line and stopped, planting his hands on his hips. Heidi caught up and he shook his head. "No, it wasn't a dog. This shadow had two legs."

"Okay. You see him?"

"No." He sighed and rubbed a hand at the back of his neck. "Maybe I'm just imagining things. Like my nerves are so tight it's causing hallucinations."

"But you really don't believe that, so you want to keep looking, right?"

He slid a sideways glance at her. "Yes."

"Then I'm going with you."

"It's probably nothing."

"I'll just tag along and make that decision myself, okay?"

"No, not okay. Stay here."

"The longer you argue with me, the less likely you are to find out if you saw something."

He shot her a black look and turned on his heel to go after whatever it was he thought he saw.

She shrugged and fell into step beside him, doing her best to ignore the pain in her knees. They were going to be sore for a few days, so she might as well get used to it.

Usually Heidi didn't notice how small she was in comparison to the men she worked with on a regular basis, but being next to Nick made her feel positively tiny. And feminine.

Which was stupid. Okay, not necessarily stupid, but seriously—why was she so hyperaware of him? Why did she notice every little thing about him? Like the way his blue eyes crinkled at the corners when he was amused. Or the way his jaw tightened and his lips flattened into a thin line when he was annoyed. Or how his dark hair was never allowed to grow too long. She shouldn't notice those things. But she did.

Nick was no more attracted to her than he was to the tree they'd just walked past, so she really needed to get over whatever it was she felt for him. The last thing she needed was to set herself up for heartbreak.

"I think he went this way," Nick said, pulling her from her thoughts.

She followed even though she didn't see what he did.

The farther they got from the kennel and all of the action, the more she thought he'd seen a bird or something. She hoped so, anyway. The adrenaline crash was coming now that the danger was over. It *was* over, wasn't it? "You see anything else?"

"No. I've lost sight of him."

"So it was definitely a him?"

"Yes."

Before she knew it, they were standing in front of

her home. "Wait a minute, he came this way?" she asked.

"Yeah, that's what it looked like."

"This is my house, Nick."

"I'd better check the area. Stay put."

"You keep saying that."

"And you keep ignoring me."

This time she listened and let him do his job. With Annie at his heels, he walked around the left side of her home, then the right, which was next to the home that Staff Sergeant Felicity James shared with her husband, Master Sergeant Westley James. Felicity was still a target of the serial killer, but at least she had her husband to keep an eye out for her. Westley was part of the investigative team looking for Sullivan. A team Heidi really wanted to be a part of.

Nick returned with a frown.

"What is it?" she asked.

"I'm not sure. I thought I saw some footprints in the grassy area along your back fence, but I didn't see anyone."

"I see. That's a bit concerning, but it could be from anyone walking back there, using it as a shortcut."

"I suppose. Could be."

"Okay, well, I'm ready to call it a night," she said.

"I don't blame you. I'll wait here and make sure you get inside safely, then I'll head back to the training center. I don't think Annie and I can do much of anything else, but I'll see if OSI wants us to."

"I've given my statement, so they know where to find me if they have any more questions for me."

"Perfect."

He stood there a moment longer, looking down at

her as though hesitant to leave. "Are you going to be all right?" he asked.

"I think so. Why?"

He glanced around one more time. "I don't like that we wound up here while we were following him. He disappeared too easily. Too quickly. If what you say is true, that guy got a good look at you."

"*If* it's true? Really?" She sighed. "I'll be fine, Nick. Good night."

A scuff of a foot just ahead and around the side of her house stopped her.

Nick turned toward the noise. "What was that?" he asked.

"I don't know. Probably nothing." Maybe. Without thinking, she slipped her hand into his.

He squeezed her fingers, then released them. "Stay behind me."

Not quite ready to argue with him, she followed his order as he and Annie led the way. They walked down the sidewalk in front of Heidi's home and were almost to the end of the small property when she saw the shadow skirting around the side of her house. "Hey! Can I help you?" she called.

The shadow took off.

Nick and Annie followed. The fleeing person wove in and out, between the houses, down alleys. Heidi fell back slightly as she realized there was no way she could keep up with Nick's long stride.

She didn't realize he'd stopped until she was almost next to him. Nick had the guy close to being boxed in a corner with no escape. There were buildings on either side of him and an open parking lot too far away from him to flee. He must have realized it the same time she did.

Because he spun and lifted his arm.

"He's got a gun!"

The words were barely out of her mouth before something heavy slammed into her, and she hit the pavement.

TWO

Nick rolled off Heidi and leaped to his feet. He placed himself in front of her as he faced the armed man, disgusted that he'd had no time to pull his own gun—and it was too late to do so now with their attacker's finger on the trigger. "Drop the weapon," Nick ordered.

"Not a chance." The low voice trembled, but Nick couldn't tell if it was from fear or sheer determination not to be caught. The low ball cap and hoodie kept the man's features well hidden. "I'm getting out of here. And if you set that dog on me, she'll take the first bullet. Understand?" He slid sideways, toward the street.

"What are you doing here?" Heidi asked. "Did you blow up the training center?"

But the man wasn't interested in answering, just escaping past Nick. And as long as the man held a gun on him and Heidi, Nick wasn't moving. Also, with the threat against Annie, it was clear the man knew how dogs and their handlers worked. Nick wouldn't knowingly send Annie after him only to have the guy keep good on his threat to shoot her.

Two more steps brought the man to the edge of Heidi's house. He darted past Nick and Annie, his feet pounding on the sidewalk as he headed toward the parking lot. Nick pulled Heidi to her feet. "Are you okay?"

"Yes. I think that's the same guy I saw run from the training center. I couldn't see his face thanks to the hat and hoodie, but it looks like the same one my guy was wearing."

"Stay here. I'm going after him." He left Heidi as he turned and took up the chase once more. He followed on the man's heels. They would soon be at the fence on the other side of the lot and the guy would have nowhere to go.

But he was also armed.

Nick reported his whereabouts into the radio on his shoulder, requesting backup as he pounded the asphalt in pursuit. Heidi stayed behind him, yelling details to the Military Police dispatch.

Was this guy the bomber? Had he been hanging around to watch the chaos his explosion had caused? To gloat? Or was this someone else altogether?

Determined to catch him, Nick pushed himself harder. Annie stayed right with him, lunging at the end of the leash.

The guy disappeared around the building that backed up to the fence.

Nick followed, rounded the building…

And the guy was gone.

Nick skidded to a stop, slightly winded, but he would have gone a little farther if he could have seen who he was chasing. A piece of cloth on a bush caught his attention. He noted it, his eyes darting, looking for any sign someone might have a gun trained on him, while chills danced up his spine.

Footsteps sounded behind him. He whirled, weapon ready. Only to come face-to-face with Heidi. She flinched and he lowered his gun. "Sorry." Nick spun back to the area where he'd lost the suspect. Annie whined and shifted. "What is it, girl?"

Annie looked up at him, her soft, sad eyes asking permission. He glanced at Heidi. "Keep your eyes and ears open, will you? Let me know if anything catches your attention."

She nodded.

Nick slipped his weapon back into the holster and pulled a pair of gloves from the bag on his shoulder. He snapped them on, then reached for the piece of cloth and studied it. Had this been snagged recently? Or had it been there awhile? It didn't look like it had weathered much. He held it out to the dog. "Annie, seek." She sniffed, lowered her nose to the ground, then lifted it to check the air.

"She can track, too?" Heidi asked.

"Sure. It's the same concept, and she's a smart dog. You can hardly train a bloodhound to sit, but tracking is so natural for them, the only training needed is for the handler." A slight exaggeration, but not much. He followed the dog cautiously while he spoke, scanning the area. His radio alerted him to backup closing in behind them and on both sides. The base had been shut down and security was tight. There was no way anyone would be able to get off or on the base for now.

But if whoever had been loitering around Heidi's house lived on the base, Annie would find him.

Annie padded her way to the fence at the far side of the parking lot and sat, looking back over her shoulder at him.

Nick squatted next to the animal and eyed the heavy-duty chain-link fence. "It's been cut." He sighed in disgust at the large opening. "This was his way out. He came prepared. He knew exactly where he was going."

"But where was he hiding? You checked my house."

"I'm guessing he jumped the fence into your backyard when he heard me coming. Once Annie and I left, he simply hauled himself back over."

"My backyard? Nice." She grimaced. "But why would he wait so long to leave the base after setting off the explosion?" she asked. "He should have been long gone by now. Why would he be so stupid as to hang around and take a chance on being caught?"

He glanced at her and shook his head. He had his theories on that, but would keep them to himself for the moment.

"You said he knew his way around the base," she said. "That he was familiar with it. I would agree with that. So, why go this way? Why not simply run back to his home?"

"I said he was familiar with it. Doesn't mean he lives on it."

"True."

"Plus think about it…"

"What?" she asked.

"The dogs."

She raised a brow. "Of course. The base is full of them. He figured a dog like Annie could track him. If he left through the fence and had a car waiting…"

"Exactly. There might be some security footage, but since he kept his face covered, that won't help much."

"He took his mask off right before he turned and spotted me," Heidi said. "But even with the hoodie covering part of his features, I'd still be able to pick him out of a lineup. The guy you just chased? I don't know." She sighed. "Think your forensic people could find some prints or something?"

"On what?"

She shrugged. "I don't know. The fence maybe?"

"He had on gloves, I think." He tucked the piece of cloth into an evidence bag. "They'll try, but I'm not holding my breath." He stood.

His frown deepened and he remembered whom he was talking to. "This better not show up on the front page tomorrow."

Heidi stiffened and her lips turned down. "It's a story, Nick."

"And we don't have the facts yet so don't go printing that we chased the bomber. We don't know who we chased."

"I never said he was the bomber. But I *do* know we chased a guy with a gun."

"Heidi…" He sighed and pinched the bridge of his nose.

Backup arrived then, cutting him off, but he held her gaze for a moment longer before turning his attention to the OSI investigators clamoring for answers.

Standing back from the fence so she didn't trample any evidence, but close enough to watch the action, Heidi drew in a deep breath and tried to calm her nerves. She was glad Nick's attention was off her for the moment, but it did little to calm her.

She'd nearly been killed in an explosion, and someone had been lurking at her house and then held her at gunpoint—all in one night.

She ran a hand over her ponytail, hoping she'd hidden how shaken she'd been, how frightened. Pushing the residual fear aside, she pulled her voice-activated recorder from her pocket and hit Play. Holding the device to her ear, she heard herself call out to Bobby, then the explosion, the aftermath, Bobby begging her to hold his hand, her reassurances.

A tear slipped down her cheek and she sent up a silent prayer for the young man. She'd make her notes, then turn the recording over to OSI.

"Heidi?"

She stiffened at the sound of John Robinson's voice. Great. Of course *he* would show up. And of course, even in the midst of all of the chaos surrounding her, he would hone in on her like Annie on a bomb. No offense to Annie. She grimaced, then smoothed her features before turning to face her nemesis. John, the lead reporter for the Red Rose Killer case—and the bane of her existence at the moment—hurried toward her. She couldn't seem to escape the man.

"What are you doing here?" he asked. "You're supposed to be covering the break-ins and medal thefts."

"I am, John. I was on my way home when…things happened. What are you doing here?"

"Looking for you." He pulled out a pad and paper. "What *did* happen?"

Oh, no. No way was she letting him steal this story from her. "John, you're covering the Red Rose Killer, not everything else."

"I'm covering anything that could be related to him. I heard a couple of MPs speculating that Sullivan was back on base and causing trouble. So, see? This is my story. So…give me details."

"I'm still sorting it all out." She shoved a stray hair from her face. "I'm heading home. I'll see you tomorrow sometime."

"Heidi—"

She waved and started walking away from him.

"What's the rush?" he called. "You got to go get your blog post ready?"

Heidi froze, did a one-eighty and marched back to the man who'd been a thorn in her side from the day he stepped onto the base and into the newspaper office. She stopped in front of him, ignoring the stares from those who'd heard his comment. "Once and for all, John Robinson, I am *not* the anonymous blogger. So stop spreading that lie before I sue you for slander."

A hand curled around her right fist. A fist she didn't even remember making. Looking sideways, she found Nick beside her.

"He's not worth it," he said softly.

Drawing in a deep breath, she made a conscious effort to push down her anger. Nick was right. If she punched John, her career would be over. And she'd worked too hard to let him provoke her into losing everything. But she would *not* let him stand there and accuse her of being the anonymous blogger who was plaguing the investigation.

She pulled her hand from Nick's, and leaving John with his jaw hanging, she executed another about-face and headed toward her house. She was tired. Beat, actually. So exhausted it was all she could do to put one foot in front of the other. Not even the adrenaline sputter from the confrontation with Robinson did much to help her energy level.

Once she reached her home, she slipped the key in the lock, opened the door, and stepped inside.

Peace washed over her as she shut the door behind her. She drew in a deep breath and let the atmosphere calm her. Heidi loved her home. It may look boring and ordinary from the outside, but the inside was all her.

Blues and tans, with a splash of orange here and there, her home allowed her to breathe and cast off the worries of the day.

Except she couldn't stop thinking about Bobby and wondering if he had known the man who'd run from the training center only moments before it had exploded. Or was Bobby just an innocent caught up in a dangerous incident?

A knock on the door sent her temper spiraling.

She yanked it open. "I told you—" She snapped her mouth shut when she saw Nick standing there with Annie at his side. "Oh. I thought you were someone else."

"Robinson?"

"What makes you think that?"

A corner of his mouth tilted up. "Sarcasm looks cute on you."

This time it was her jaw that hung.

"Can I come in?" he asked.

She closed her mouth. "Of course." Stepping back, she let them enter, then shut the door. "Den is to your left."

"Thanks. Your place is similar to mine. Smaller, of course." Base housing for those who didn't live with family members was small. Hers was a one-bedroom residence, but at least she didn't have to do the dorm-style living other airmen were stuck with. "But it sure is nicer than mine. It's...calm and soothing. I like it."

"Thanks. That's what I was going for when I picked out the colors. The days around here can be so long and hectic that I wanted something that reminded me of the ocean. Peace and calm."

He settled on her tan couch and Annie curled up at his feet. "Are you all right?"

"I'm—" She stopped. "I was going to say 'I'm fine,' but I'm not sure that's true. I'm actually stressed and annoyed beyond everything with John Robinson. That man pushes me to the very edge." She shot him a look through her lashes. "Just in case you didn't pick up on that."

"I think I might have."

"Thank you, by the way, for keeping me from slugging him. I don't think I would have, even as much as I wanted to, but I can't say for sure that I would have walked away had you not been there."

"I don't think anyone would have blamed you, but yeah. You're welcome."

"I'll also admit I'm shaken from the explosion and the possibility of being shot, but mostly, I'm extremely tired of everyone thinking I'm the anonymous blogger." She let the last word out on a huff and sank into the recliner opposite the couch. At his startled expression, she wished she could retract the words, but it was too late now.

"And you're not? The anonymous blogger, I mean?"

She didn't have the energy to do more than scowl at him. "No, I'm not. I wouldn't do that. And besides, I don't even have the facts that are being reported in the blog. Every time I read it, I learn something new."

She laughed. "That blogger is someone who has access to information I only wish I did."

His eyes searched hers and he gave a slow nod. "I think I believe you."

She wilted. "Really? You think?"

"Yes."

"Well…thanks. I *think*." She sighed. "If you believe me, do you have any thoughts on who it *could* be?"

"No."

"Not that you would tell me, anyway, right?"

He raised a brow. "I knew Boyd from basic training, but I didn't have much contact with him. I don't know who he hung out with other than what we've managed to dig up during the investigation—and, of course, the victims."

"That's probably a good thing. Not knowing him too well, I mean. You don't want to be on his radar."

"No kidding. So…" He cleared his throat. "Now that we're away from all the craziness, would you tell me one more time what you saw tonight?"

Gathering her strength, she nodded. "I can tell you, but you can also listen to it."

"What do you mean?"

"My voice-activated recorder picked up most everything. I mean, the guy who ran out of the training center didn't say anything, but—" She stood. "Hold on and let me get my laptop. I'll start transcribing while you listen."

"You recorded it?"

"Not on purpose. I was walking and talking into it when I spotted the trainer coming out of the building. And then the explosion…" She waved a hand. "Just listen."

She brought up a blank document on her laptop, then hit the play button on the recorder. He listened while she typed as fast as her fingers could fly. If she missed something, she could always go back and fix it.

When the sound of the explosion came through, Nick flinched and rubbed a hand over his chin. He listened to her comfort Bobby. The screams of the sirens. He listened to it all. When it ended, he hit the stop button.

Since there wasn't a whole lot of conversation, Heidi was able to get the whole thing transcribed in one listen. She'd go back and add in her memories and perceptions later for the article. For now, she'd just lived through one of the scariest nights she'd ever experienced, and she was on the edge emotionally.

To put it simply, she wanted Nick to leave so she could crawl into her bed and hibernate until morning. And maybe cry a little. But instead of sending him on his way, she fell silent, not exactly sure that she really wanted to be alone after all. A knock sounded on the door. "Excuse me."

She rose, and he followed her. At her raised eyebrow, he frowned. "Can't be too careful."

Heidi peered out the side window. "Who is it?" she called out.

"Carl Trees. I'm the sketch artist," the man on the porch stated.

"I know him," Nick said. "He's legit."

Heidi opened the door. "Hi. Come on in." The two men greeted one another, and Heidi led them to the kitchen. "Have a seat at the table. Would you like some coffee or a bottle of water?"

"No, thanks. I'm sure you're tired and ready for this day to be over with."

Carl was right about that. She sat next to him and he turned the laptop so she could see it. "All right," he said, "start with the shape of his face."

For the next hour, they worked on the sketch with Heidi doing her best to get the face as detailed as possible. Finally, she sat back and rubbed her eyes.

"That's him?" Nick asked. He stood behind Carl, looking down at the final rendering.

She studied the image on the screen. "As close as I can remember." The icy blue eyes stared back at her from the screen. "The eyes are spot-on, I know that." Carl had added a hoodie to the man's head, and Heidi shivered. "That's him."

Carl nodded. "Good job. Your descriptions helped a lot."

"Must be the way with words she has," Nick murmured.

"Must be." Carl shut his laptop and rose. "I'll get out of here and get this sent to the powers that be." He looked at Heidi. "If they catch him, they'll want you to point the finger at him."

"I know." She led him to the door. "Thanks for coming over here."

"Not a problem. Have a good night." Carl left, and Heidi shut the door behind him.

Nick placed his hands on her shoulders and turned her to face him. "I'm really concerned," he said.

"About what?"

"You. I think it's important to know whether the guy we chased was the same guy you just described to Carl."

She frowned. "I know. I think it was, but I'm not a hundred percent sure. There was a hoodie involved both times and it looked like the same one. The first time, I locked eyes with the guy running from the training center. They were blue and looked like they'd be right at home in the frozen tundra. The guy at my house had the hoodie pulled low and he kept his head down. I didn't see his eyes, so…" She shrugged and sighed.

"He might not know that. Or think that. I think the man you saw at the training center and the man who pulled the gun on us are one and the same. That's probably why he was here. Waiting on you. The fact that I was with you threw him off, and he decided he'd better retreat."

She grimaced. "I know. I've already thought of that." A shiver swept through her. She'd planned on a relaxing evening and an early bedtime. Now she wondered if she'd be able to shut her eyes.

Nick could tell his words had worried her in spite of the fact that she'd already put two and two together. He almost felt bad about saying something and confirming her fears. Almost. But she needed to be on the alert.

He'd been standing outside her home for the last twenty minutes, debating what he should do. He simply didn't feel right leaving her. Then again, she did live on a military base. If she needed help, all she had to do was holler.

But what if she couldn't?

He pulled his phone from his pocket and let his finger hover over Master Sergeant Westley James's number. After all, the man and his wife, Felicity, lived next door to Heidi. Surely, he could keep an eye on her.

Still, Nick hesitated. He hated to bother him when he had his hands full with the investigation. Then again, it made sense. The man was right next door. Instead of dialing, he pocketed the phone and walked over to Westley's and knocked.

The curtain in the right window opened and Felicity peered at him. She disappeared and the door opened. "Hi, Nick."

"Hey." She wore loose-fitting jeans and a T-shirt that was probably left over from her days as a trainer. Now she spent her time behind the lens of a camera as the base photographer. The change seemed to agree with her. "Is Westley here?"

"I'm sorry, he's not. You want to come in?"

Nick shook his head. "That's all right. I'm concerned about Heidi and wanted to see if he'd be willing to keep an eye on her place tonight."

Felicity frowned. "I'm sure he would, but there's no telling when he'll be back. What's going on with Heidi?"

"We're pretty sure she saw the guy who blew up the training center and that he knows it."

Felicity's eyes widened. "No kidding. Well, I can understand why you want to take precautions. I'm sorry Westley isn't available to help."

"It's all right. I have one more option."

"Who?"

"Caleb Streeter."

She smiled. "He's a good option. And I'll be sure to keep an eye out as well. And so will Westley when he gets home."

"Thanks, Felicity." She shut the door and Nick dialed Caleb's number as he walked back over to Heidi's home. He stood at the base of her porch steps while the phone rang. Nick had just started to get to know the master sergeant who was now running the K-9 training center. He'd spotted him earlier in the midst of all of the chaos at the explosion site, but hadn't had a chance to say anything as he'd been swamped answering OSI's questions.

"Hello?" Caleb croaked.

"You awake?"

"I'd just dropped off. What's up, Nick?"

"I was going to ask if you'd help me out by keeping an eye on a friend's place for few hours tonight."

"Normally, I'd say yes, but I've got to get a few hours of sleep. I've got to be up and at the training center early to start assessing the damage and filling out insurance paperwork."

"How many hours do you need?"

A sigh filtered to him. "At least five. Only had three last night."

"When's your next day off?"

"It was supposed to be tomorrow."

Ouch. He was asking a lot of his friend, but everyone else he could think of was busy. "Okay, I'll take first shift. You get your five hours, then come over here. I'll buy you a steak dinner." He noticed Annie's ears perking up at the word *steak* and smiled.

"For two," Caleb said. "I'm taking Paisley with me." Paisley Strange was the girl Caleb was trying to get to know—and impress.

Nick rolled his eyes. "Fine. For two." He gave him the address and Caleb hung up. He noticed Felicity had come back outside and was sitting on the steps. He jogged over. "Hey."

"Hey. Is Caleb able to help you out?"

"Yes. For now."

She nodded. "Westley's still working. He called and said he was going to be at the office for a while." She sniffed. "Still smells smoky out here."

"It comes in waves depending on the wind. I'm just going to hang around and keep an eye on things for a few hours. Do you mind if I use your rocker?"

"Make yourself comfortable." She stood. "This Red Rose Killer is about make Westley pull out what little hair he has."

"He's not alone."

She grimaced. "I don't understand how Boyd Sullivan can just disappear, show up to create havoc, then disappear again without a trace. It's ridiculous." Her lips tightened.

Nick grimaced. "And a bit embarrassing." He frowned. "The fact that we haven't caught him just confirms some of the conclusions we've come to. He's got help on the inside." He was fine discussing the case with Felicity as he knew she was privy to the information.

"I agree. But still, you would think he would have tripped himself up by now—or someone would have spotted him and turned him in."

"Even if someone spotted him, how would they know? He seems to be a master at disguises. Not to mention the fact that he'll kill to get the uniform he needs. He's smart and he's extremely careful."

"I remember Westley saying that Sullivan doesn't make a move unless he's sure he won't get caught."

"True." He frowned. "But we're not giving up. He *will* get careless and we *will* get him eventually."

"I know. That's what Westley says, too." She offered him a small smile. "Take care of Heidi."

"That's the plan."

"I'll watch out for her, too. Let me know if I can do anything."

"Could I get a bowl of water for Annie? I've got food with me."

"Sure. And a bottle for you?"

"That would be perfect. Thanks."

Once he and Annie had their water, Felicity slipped inside and Nick turned the porch light off. He took a seat in the wooden rocker.

After a long drink, Annie settled at his feet.

Time passed while Nick did as much work as he could using his iPhone. He requested one of the OSI investigators to stop by so he could give him the evidence he and Annie had collected from the bomb site. The investigator would make sure it was delivered to the lab for examination.

Once he had everything finished that he'd needed to do related to the explosion, Nick leaned his head back against the rocker and let his gaze linger on Heidi's home. She'd affected him in a big way. Those eyes of hers had brought forth emotions he'd thought he'd locked securely away a little over three years ago after Lillian Peterson had taken his heart and stomped all over it.

But with one outburst laden with frustration and truth, Heidi had snapped the lock like a toothpick. His heart had reacted and that scared him. He could face down guns and explosives, but a woman who had the potential to hurt him? No way. Normally, he'd run as far and as fast as possible. But he couldn't do that with Heidi. She might be in danger, and Nick simply couldn't bring himself to ignore that and abandon her when he could help.

So now he was completely unsettled.

The streetlamp illuminated a figure heading toward them, soft footsteps falling on the sidewalk. Annie sat up, ears twitching toward the noise. Nick focused on the shadow in the darkness, his hand sliding to his weapon. "Who's there?"

The figure stopped. "Nick? What are you doing out here?"

Isaac Goddard? Nick relaxed. The man was a senior airman and turning into a good friend. "Hey, keeping an eye on Heidi Jenks. She's mixed up in everything that went down here tonight."

"I heard about that." Isaac walked over and leaned against the railing. "Glad no one was seriously hurt."

"Bobby Stevens ended up in the hospital but will heal. What are you doing out here?"

"Just walking. I couldn't sleep."

"Nightmares?" Isaac never talked about it, but Nick knew the man's PTSD, brought on after serving and being wounded in Afghanistan, kept him up most nights.

"Yeah."

"I'm sorry. Any word on Beacon?" Beacon was the German shepherd who'd been in Afghanistan the same time Isaac had been serving and had saved Isaac's life. Now Isaac was determined to bring him home. Unfortunately, red tape and bureaucratic nonsense had delayed that to the point where Isaac was ready to head back to the desert of his nightmares and find the dog himself.

"They found him," Isaac said.

"Wait, what?" Nick sat straighter. "They did? That's great."

"Yes and no. He was found injured and they're not sure he's going to make it."

Nick's hope for his friend deflated. "Oh, no. I'm sorry."

"I am, too. So right now, it's just wait and see." He shook his head. "I can't give up on him, Nick. He's as much military as I am. I was lying there, injured and bleeding, and he came up and settled down beside me. Like he was trying to let me know I wasn't alone."

Nick had heard the story before, but he let Isaac talk. It seemed to help him.

"He stayed right with me," Isaac said. "For hours until my unit buddies were able to get to me and pull me to safety."

"He's a hero, too."

"Exactly." Isaac sighed and rubbed a hand over his face. "Anyway, sorry. Didn't mean to talk your ear off. I'm going to keep walking. Maybe head over to the gym and work some of this energy off."

"Keep the faith, man."

"I'm trying. You keep it for me, too."

"You got it."

Nick watched his friend walk away and sent up a silent prayer for him.

Hours later, when Caleb arrived, Nick was still praying. About a lot of things. But mostly that the night would continue to be as quiet as it had been up to that point.

Caleb yawned and rubbed his eyes. "I'm going to enjoy that steak dinner. I hope this is worth it for you."

Nick looked back over at Heidi's dark home. "It's worth it," he said softly. "Every single penny."

THREE

Thankfully, the night had passed without incident. After pacing for a couple of hours, Heidi had finally checked the locks four times, glanced out the window to see her street quiet and motionless, and fallen into bed. To her surprise, she'd slept well and five hours later awakened with a new sense of purpose.

Before allowing herself to sleep, though, she'd worked on the story of the training center explosion and sent it off to her editor. The man was thrilled with the piece if his email this morning was anything to go by.

The fact that she could have been killed didn't seem to faze him. His "You're okay, right?" tacked on at the end of his gleeful thanks for a firsthand account of the incident seemed to be perfunctory. She imagined him scrolling through her story while asking that, his brain not even registering her response.

It was okay. She didn't need him to care about her, she just needed him to recognize her work. When he'd given the Red Rose Killer story to John Robinson, she'd nearly had a coronary. But she was a good reporter and one day someone would notice that.

One day. As long as she kept working hard and proving herself. And she supposed she could start by figuring out who'd bombed the training center.

To do that, the first order of business was to visit Bobby Stevens in the hospital. Not only did she want to check on him, she'd admit she wanted to get his story. Having him tell his experience at the training center would make for a good story, ending with him being caught in the explosion at the training center. If she approached it that way, her questions wouldn't seem so intrusive or odd—or look like she was working on the Red Rose Killer story.

When she looked at her phone, she found a text from Nick that he'd sent after she'd gone to bed. Caleb Streeter is watching your house. Don't be alarmed if you see him parked across the street. Touched that he'd arranged protection for her, she texted him back. Thanks. Appreciate it.

She called the hospital and learned Bobby was able to talk in between periods of sleep. She hoped to catch him awake.

When she stepped out of her home, she stood for a moment on her front porch. The air still had a smoky scent to it and she shivered even though it promised to be a hot September day.

She glanced around looking for any indication the man from yesterday might be hanging around, but the only person she saw was sitting in a car opposite her home. Caleb. He lifted a hand in a short salute. She returned it and walked over to him. "Thank you for staying out here. You didn't have to do that."

He shrugged. "There's some scary business going down on this base lately. I'm happy to put in a few hours making sure nothing else happens."

"Well, I appreciate it."

"Where are you headed?"

"To the hospital. Thanks again and see you later."

"Sure thing." He took off, his headlights disappearing around the first turn.

Heidi couldn't help sweeping the area once more with her eyes. When nothing alarmed her, she climbed into her car and pulled away from the curb. It wasn't far to the base hospital, but she blasted her air-conditioning. The last thing she needed was to arrive with sweat pouring from her.

Minutes later, she pulled into the parking lot and made her way toward Bobby's room, only to see First Lieutenant Vanessa Gomez near the nurses' station. The petite and attractive critical-care nurse had her dark hair pulled back into a ponytail and was focused on something on her laptop. Heidi walked over and smiled. "Hi."

Vanessa looked up. "Hi, yourself. I read about the explosion in the paper this morning." She frowned. "You were there and wrote the article as well? All last night?"

"Sleep was hard to come by, so I had nothing better to do. I sent it to my editor in time to be printed this morning."

"And you weren't hurt in the blast?"

"I had a scare and got a couple of scraped knees in addition to a few other bruises, but I'm fine. Much better than poor Bobby Stevens. He got the brunt of it, I think."

"At least he's alive."

"There is that." She paused. "Do you mind if I ask you a question about Boyd Sullivan?"

Vanessa's gaze grew hooded. "Depends on what you want to know."

"Just what you thought of him."

"You want to know what I think about a serial killer?"

Heidi wrinkled her nose. "Okay, so maybe I didn't phrase the question right. How do you know him? Why did he target you?"

"Now, that is a question I'd like the answer to myself." She sighed. "I met him one night when he got into a fight. He didn't want to go to the hospital and risk having his superiors find out about it so he asked me if I'd help him. I had a kit in my car and treated him. I was nice to him. He was nice to me. That was it. Or so I thought until I received a note and a red rose. I have no idea why he targeted me or what I did to make him mad." She shuddered and looked around. "But I feel safe here at the hospital. I'm always around people and I take precautions coming and going."

"How scary."

"Yes." Vanessa's gaze slid to the elevator. "Excuse me, I need to grab something from the cafeteria. It's going to be a while before I'll have a chance to eat again."

"Of course. Be careful."

Vanessa shot her a tight smile. "Always."

Once Vanessa was gone, Heidi found Bobby's room number and knocked. When she heard a faint "Come in," she stepped inside to find Bobby sitting up and eating a bowl of Jell-O while a game show played on the television opposite the bed. The remains of scrambled eggs and bacon sat on the plate in front of him.

"Hi, Bobby."

He set his spoon on the tray. "Hey, Heidi." He sounded surprised to see her.

The right side of his face sported a white bandage from temple to chin and his right arm had a cast from elbow to wrist. Other than that, he looked unharmed. "How are you feeling?"

"I have a headache and some other bumps and bruises, but overall, I'd say I'm a very fortunate guy." His eyes narrowed. "You were there. I remember seeing you."

"Yes. I saw the guy come out of the building."

Fear flashed in his eyes. "You yelled at me to run. How did you know it was going to explode?"

"I didn't. I just... I don't know." She shrugged. "Something felt off. This guy came out wearing a ski mask and I figured that meant he was up to no good. He didn't see me at first and took his mask off. When he realized I was there, he was furious, but the way he looked back at the building and decided to run... I really can't explain it."

"When the explosion happened, it knocked me off my feet," he said. "My whole body vibrated with pain—" He reached up and touched the bandage on his head. "You held my hand."

"You asked me to."

He nodded, then winced. "I've got to remember not to move my head." His expression softened. "Thank you for staying with me. I—uh—admit that I didn't want to be alone."

"I understand. I'm glad I could be there for you." She paused. "What else do you remember?"

It was like someone flipped a switch. His open,

unguarded expression instantly shut down. "Nothing much."

He was lying.

"Come on, there has to be something."

"Nope. Just coming out of the building and you yelling at me."

"That part of the building is closed. What were you doing in there?"

He flushed. "I often walk through, checking to make sure everything is secure."

"I see." She paused and he started to pleat the sheet. "So, you have cause to believe something's going on in there that needs your attention?"

"What? No, of course not." He frowned at her. "It's just routine, okay? I do it on a daily basis." He shrugged. "It's quiet in there. Gives me a few minutes to clear my head and just take a break, you know?"

"So that's it?"

"Yeah. That's it."

He reached for the remote, so Heidi switched tactics. She had time to take it slow and pull as much information as she could out of him. In his time. She could be tenacious, but she had to be smart, too. There was more than one way to get an answer from someone. Most guys his age had an ego. "You know, people are going to think you're a hero."

"What? How do you mean?"

"I mean, you've been pretty brave through this whole thing. People might even believe you got hurt trying to stop the guy from blowing the center up."

"But I...well...really?"

"Sure."

"Oh."

"And they're going to want to know how you're doing."

He blinked and some of his chilly facade thawed. "Um. Okay. I guess." His curiosity seemed to take over. "How does this work?"

"I just ask you some questions and you answer. Then I run the article by you and if you approve it, I send it to my editor."

"And if I don't like something in it?"

"We change it so you do like it. I won't print it if you don't approve."

"I see." He thought for a moment. "What kind of questions."

"Questions like…" She looked at the game show he was watching on the television. "How good are you at solving those puzzles?"

His brows shot up and he smiled. "Not very good. I used to watch this show with my mother all the time. She's brilliant and can figure them out with the least amount of letters." He paused. "It's quite frustrating to play against her, actually. But fun, too. I always try to beat her and rarely can do it."

"Sounds like a good mom."

"The best."

"Is she coming to visit?"

He started to shake his head and then paused. "No. It's too far for her. She's in a wheelchair, with MS."

"Oh, I'm sorry."

A shrug. "Been that way my whole life, but didn't stop her from being a great mom. She's already called me several times and I know she'd be here if she could."

"I'm sure she would." Heidi nodded to the television. "Want to watch while we talk?"

Frowning, he tilted his head, then shrugged. "Sure."

Heidi nodded at the television. "Can you solve that one?"

He laughed. "No."

Caleb's phone call informing him that Heidi was leaving her home spurred Nick to action. "Where'd she go?"

"She said she was headed to the hospital. I can't follow her. I have to get over to the training center ASAP."

Hospital? Why?

The trainer who was hurt in the blast. She was going to question him. "Fine. Thanks for your help last night. Let me know when you're planning on that steak dinner."

"Will do."

Nick's next call was to Master Sergeant Westley James. He let the man know he was heading out to find Heidi, who was a possible witness to the bombing.

"Before you go, have you seen the paper this morning?" Westley asked.

"No, I haven't had the time." His gut clenched. What had Heidi done?

"There's a story on the bombing. Heidi Jenks wrote it."

"And?"

A pause. "The story is actually good. Facts and no opinions. Good reporting," he said with a faint smile in his voice, "in my opinion."

Nick paused. Wow. "Um…good to hear that." And a huge relief. "She said that's all she would write. She kept her promise."

Westley huffed. "I've known Heidi for a while now.

At first, I was skeptical of her, but since I moved into Felicity's place next door to her I've gotten a different perspective. She seems to be a good reporter who keeps her word. It's impressive. I'll have to admit that before getting to know her, I never would have believed it possible."

"You're not the only one."

"She's also started doing those personality pieces on enlisted personnel. I've read them and they're good. I've even learned a few interesting tidbits about the people I work with. It's nice."

"I'm glad to hear that." And he was. But he needed to get going if he was going to catch up to Heidi.

"Might change my mind and let her do one on me," Westley said.

"She asked?"

"Yes, but I said no at the time." He hesitated, then said, "She's a reporter, after all."

"Yes, she sure is."

To Nick's relief, the man made a sound like he was getting ready to wrap up the conversation. "All right. I know you're working with the investigative team on this Red Rose Killer case. I was talking to Justin and he said OSI wants you on the bombing as well. The evidence you and Annie found has been sent off and we're waiting to hear back. Until then, you might want to keep Heidi in your sights. If we've got a bomber out there who thinks she knows something, she could be in danger."

"Exactly." Which was why he needed to get moving.

"All right. Stay in touch and keep me updated, if you don't mind."

"Of course."

He hung up and whistled for Annie. She came running and stood impatiently at the door while he clipped the leash on her collar. "All right, girl, let's go make sure that nosy reporter doesn't get herself killed."

It only took him a few minutes to get to the base hospital. He left Annie in her temperature-controlled area of the car and headed inside the building. A stop at the information desk provided him the room number.

Once on the floor, he made a right at the nurses' station and found the room. The door was cracked open and he could hear voices inside.

"Come on, Bobby, please tell me what you know. Do you know who the guy was?" he heard Heidi ask. "The one who ran from the building?"

"No."

The trainer's low voice vibrated with tension.

Heidi sighed. "That explosion was no coincidence. You know as well as I do about all the weird stuff happening on the base. The Red Rose Killer who killed those two trainers, Clinton Lockwood, and then all of the dogs getting out."

Nick pursed his lips. Those dogs. Out of the twenty-one still missing, he would have thought they would have located a few by now. And those four highly trained German shepherds should have come back. But they hadn't. Which probably meant someone had them.

Uncomfortable with his eavesdropping, he knocked.

"Come in," Bobby called.

Nick stepped inside and found the trainer sitting up in the bed and Heidi in the chair next to him. She raised a brow when she saw him. "What are you doing here?"

"Me? What are you doing here?"

"I thought I'd stop by and check on Bobby." She

shot the man in the bed a warm smile and something twisted inside Nick. Something he could only identify as jealousy. But he knew that couldn't possibly be true. His only explanation for the unexpected—and unwelcome—feeling was that he'd had far too little sleep last night. And *every* night since the Red Rose Killer had struck the base and set off a chain of events with the murder of the two trainers as well as of his former Basic Training Commander, Chief Master Sergeant Clinton Lockwood. Since then Boyd Sullivan had continued his reign of terror over those who had any connection with him at all.

Nick cleared his throat. "Do you mind if I join you?"

Heidi shrugged, but Bobby shifted on the bed and wouldn't meet his eyes. Interesting.

"I thought I'd see how he was doing and ask him a few questions about the bombing," Heidi said. "Unfortunately, he doesn't remember much."

"I see. How are you feeling?" Nick asked Bobby.

"I'm all right." The young man seemed grateful for the distraction. "They tell me I should make a full recovery, so that's a relief."

"I'm sure." Nick settled himself in the window seat. "I've got a few questions for you myself, if you don't mind." Without giving the man a chance to answer, he said, "What was your shift at the training center yesterday?"

"Second."

"So, what do you think the man in the building wanted? The one Heidi saw run out?"

Bobby looked away again, over Nick's shoulder and out the window. "I was… I needed a break so I was going to step outside for a breath of fresh air and that's when I saw Heidi. She yelled at me to run." He shrugged and briefly met Nick's eyes. "She sounded really intense, so I ran." He turned his gaze back to Heidi. "You saved my life."

Heidi smiled. Nick ran a hand over his jaw. "So, no idea who the man was?"

"No. I've already said it several times. I've got no idea." The young man plucked at the sheet near his knee. Then he linked his hands and turned his gaze to the television, effectively dismissing them.

Nick frowned. Bobby was lying. He slid a glance over at Heidi and saw her eyes on the man. Her wrinkled forehead said she wasn't buying his story, either.

But why would he lie? Was he somehow involved in the explosion or did he know the identity of the bomber and was too scared to tell?

A knock on the door brought a flicker of relief to Bobby's pale features. A woman in her midfifties entered. The lab coat and blue lettering stitched on her shoulder identified her as the doctor. "What's going on in here?" she asked.

Nick stood. "We're just having a chat with your patient."

"Well, you're going to have to leave. In case you haven't noticed, he has a head injury and needs his rest."

"We've noticed." He turned to Bobby. "Thank you for your time. If you remember anything else, will you give me a call?" He handed him his card.

"Ah…sure. Yes, of course." He stared at it, then set it on the table by the phone.

"Get better, Bobby. I'm glad you're going to be okay," Heidi said.

Bobby's gaze softened when he turned to look at her and, once again, Nick's blood pressure surged. He shook his head and told himself to get a grip. He was not attracted to her. *Liar.* Okay, fine, so he was, but that was neither here nor there. The only reason he was going to keep an eye on Heidi was to make sure she didn't wind up a victim of the bomber—and to make sure she didn't report anything she shouldn't.

Maybe if he told himself that enough times, he'd eventually believe it.

Once outside the hospital room, Heidi turned to Nick and crossed her arms. "What was that all about?"

"What do you mean?"

"I mean, I was in the middle of a conversation with Bobby and you showed up to interfere."

"You mean you were in the middle of pumping a poor, wounded man for information so you could get a scoop on a story."

"I already got the scoop. I was going for the follow-up," she said.

He blinked. Then laughed and held up a hand in surrender. "I can't believe I'm laughing. I should be really annoyed with you."

"So why aren't you?"

His blue eyes flashed with something she couldn't identify. "I don't really know," he said softly.

"That bothers you, doesn't it?"

"In more ways than I'd like."

She waited for him to explain, but he simply sighed and looked away.

"You don't trust me, do you?" she asked, then raised

a hand. "Never mind. Don't answer that. It's as clear as the nose on your face what you think of me."

He gave a short laugh. "You're a reporter. That automatically puts you on the *Do Not Trust* list."

"What happened?"

His brow lifted. "What do you mean?"

"What made you not trust reporters?"

And just like that, his face closed up. "It doesn't matter. It doesn't have anything to do with you or this case, so—"

Her phone buzzed and he snapped his lips shut.

"Sorry," she said. She looked at the screen. "I've got to answer this. It's my boss."

"Of course." The coolness in his voice pierced her, but she swiped the screen and lifted the phone to her ear. "Hello?"

"Heidi, where are you?" Lou Sanders demanded.

"Still at the hospital. I just finished talking to Bobby Stevens, the man who was hurt in the training center explosion."

"Right. Well, forget about him for now. Three more homes were burglarized last night, medals were stolen and you're needed to conduct interviews and cover the story."

Heidi bit her lip on the complaint that wanted to slip out. Instead, she nodded. "All right. Text me the addresses, and I'll get on it."

"Good. I expect something on my desk by the end of the day tomorrow."

"Yes, sir."

She hung up and found Nick staring at his phone. He tucked it into the clip on his belt. "I've got to get to a meeting. Are you going to be all right?"

"I think so. Nothing's happened, and last night was peaceful."

"I hate leaving you alone."

His concern sent warmth coursing through her. He might not trust her simply because of her profession, but he obviously cared about her as a person. How long had it been since someone had been genuinely concerned about what happened to her? A man, anyway. She had friends on the base, of course, and she and her neighbor, Felicity, had gotten pretty close over the last month in spite of the fact that Westley, her new husband, didn't seem to like Heidi very much. Heidi was glad Felicity was willing to give her the benefit of the doubt.

Heidi waved off his worry. "I'll be fine. I'm going to be working on this story, so I'll be talking with people all day. The base is as busy as a hive. If I need something, someone is within yelling distance at all times."

Nick nodded. "Okay, just be careful."

"Of course."

He didn't move.

She raised a brow. "Now what's wrong?"

"What was your impression of Bobby?" he asked.

"He's in pain and he's lying through his teeth. He knows something, and he's scared to tell what it is. I'm not sure why he's scared, but he is."

"Yeah. That was my take on him, too. What makes you think so, though?"

With a shrug, she said, "He never actually said he didn't see the guy at the center. He never asked me to describe the man I saw. He just denied knowing who the guy was. Which makes me think he did see him and doesn't want to say."

"That's impressive, Heidi."

"Thanks?"

"No, I'm serious. You're perceptive. That's how a cop thinks."

She laughed. "Well, I'm no cop, that's for sure—and I have no desire to be one. Too dangerous."

Her wry statement and roll of her eyes seemed to amuse him.

"Right. Because being a reporter has kept you safe and sound thus far."

"I like my job and I like to do it well. Part of that entails being able to read people and to read in between the lines."

"Which tells me that OSI needs to dig a little deeper into Bobby's background."

"I'd say so."

"I'll give them the rundown on our visit with Airman Stevens." With a nod and one last look in her direction, he turned on his heel and headed down the hallway to the elevator.

Heidi sucked in a breath and told her feelings to settle down. Yes, Nick was a good-looking man. Yes, she was attracted to him. And no, nothing was going to come of that because…because he didn't respect her occupation, for one. He was bossy and demanding, for two. And he'd awakened long-dormant dreams of what could one day be. A family. A home with children and a husband who loved her—in spite of her job.

With a groan, she knew this was going to be a long day. But at least the interviews would distract her from thinking about the handsome lieutenant. Maybe.

Nick felt slightly better about leaving Heidi. She was right. The base was teeming with people during the day and she'd be with someone constantly on her interviews.

But still…he couldn't shake from his mind the fact that Heidi could be in danger and it was only a matter of time before someone showed up to do her harm.

The guy who'd run from them—and pulled a gun on them—was still out there.

Unable to just drive away, he waited until she came out of the building and watched as she set off on foot. He continued to observe, noting the others leaving at the same time. No one seemed to be following her and that allowed him to draw in a relieved breath and relax a fraction.

Nick then climbed into his vehicle. Annie welcomed him back with a "woof" and he gave her ears a scratch. He drove to the base command office and found a parking spot outside the building that housed the large auditorium-style conference room. Once he was inside, Annie at his side, the executive assistant to the base commander, Brenda Blakenship, met him in the reception area. After they exchanged salutes, she nodded to the nearest door. "Everyone's here. Captain Blackwood is ready."

"Thank you." This was a last-minute meeting on a Saturday. Obviously, something was important.

When he entered the conference room, the large oval table was full of those investigating the Boyd Sullivan case. He saluted and took his seat next to Security Forces Captain Justin Blackwood. Annie settled at his feet with a contented sigh while Nick studied Justin. The captain was a tall, imposing figure, his blond hair cut with military precision. His blue eyes could slice right through a person, but Nick liked the man. In fact, he liked and respected every person in the room. They made a good team. Which was why he knew they would have Boyd Sullivan in custody soon. They had to. This whole investigation had gone on too long.

Across from him sat First Lieutenant Vanessa Gomez, whose insight into Sullivan could be helpful. It was a long shot, but worth having her on the team. Sitting beside her was Captain Gretchen Hill, who had been temporarily transferred to the base to learn how the K-9 Unit and a large security force were run. She'd been assigned to work with Justin, whose former partner had been killed. Nick briefly wondered how that was going. They both looked slightly stressed whenever they were in the same room together. But it wasn't any of his business. They were professionals; they'd work through any problems. Tech Sergeant Linc Colson, a Security Forces investigator, First Lieutenant MP Ethan Webb, Westley James, Ava Esposito and Oliver Davison rounded out the team.

"Thank you all for coming in," base commander Lieutenant General Nathan Hall said. He stood to Nick's left. "I know it's Saturday, but I wanted us all together for an update. It's no secret that Boyd Sullivan is still out there causing grief. He's a killer who shows no mercy and it's up to us to stop him. Fast. First order of business, I think we need to focus a little closer on Yvette Crenville. I still think she's our link. It's well-known how crazy she was about Sullivan, and he seemed to return the feeling."

"True," Nick said. "But we've been looking into her. What else do you suggest?"

"Closer scrutiny. I want constant eyes on her. I want proof supporting our suspicions. I've done some checking and she's regular as clockwork to show up for work, so it should be easy enough to keep her under surveillance. Any volunteers to trail her and report back her routine, who she talks to, where she goes, et cetera?"

Several hands went up and the lieutenant general pointed to Vanessa. "Since you're at the hospital where Yvette works, you're the obvious choice, but are you sure you're up to it?"

"Yes, sir. I'll have to work around my schedule, of course, but I'm happy to do it when I'm not on the clock. Then again, she *is* the base nutritionist, so I may be able to catch up to her occasionally during the day, to see if she's up to anything suspicious."

"All right, you're on it. The only reason I'm asking is because when Ava and Oliver were searching for Turner Johnson last month, they spotted Sullivan in the woods." Seven-year-old Turner Johnson, the son of a base colonel, had been on a school field trip when he'd disappeared. Ava Esposito and Oliver Davison had brought the child home safely. "Turner talked about the 'bad guy and mean woman.' Unfortunately, he never got a look at her. She had on a black hoodie and stuff. But he was sure it was a woman. So, by process of elimination, we're down to Yvette. If it's her, she's going to be suspicious of anyone in law enforcement. But she wouldn't have any reason to connect you to the investigation," he told Vanessa.

"No, we've talked a couple of times, and she knows I got a rose as well." Yvette had received one the same night as Vanessa.

"But I don't want you doing this alone. I think you're safe at the hospital, surrounded by people, but

I'm going to find someone to partner with you. When I decide who it'll be, I'll let you know."

"That sounds good, sir. I do feel safe at the hospital." Vanessa shrugged. "It might be a false sense of security, but for now, I think I'm all right."

"Good, let me know if anything changes."

"Of course."

For the next thirty minutes, the team discussed the case in detail. With one glaring, depressing fact right in front of them. Boyd Sullivan was still on the loose and no one had any idea where he was or how to find him.

"One last thing," Lieutenant General Hall said. "Our anonymous blogger is still wreaking havoc. This time he—or she—has decided to smear the investigators all over the place."

"What do you mean, sir?" Nick asked.

Nathan tapped his phone's screen and read from the blog, "'Well, folks, it looks like the training center bombing wasn't just a random thing. There's speculation that the Red Rose Killer is somehow involved. That it's possible he's back on base. Lock your doors, folks. I know I'm going to.'" Nathan tossed his phone on the table. "I want this person stopped."

"Whoever it is has mad tech skills," Nick said. "But there's got to be more to it."

"What do you mean?"

"I'm just saying, it's like this person has a bug planted in our meetings. We've talked about everything the blogger's mentioned. As we've noted, these are confidential discussions that are being plastered in the posts. I think it's time to play our cards a little closer to our vests." He looked around. "I'm not saying it's one of us, but I do think it's someone we're trusting."

Justin scowled. "Then from this moment on, trust no one but the people in this room. Discuss nothing, and I mean nothing, about this case with anyone but the people here. Is that understood?"

A chorus of "Yes, sirs" echoed through the small room. "Good. That's it for now. Stay in touch."

Most everyone filed out, but Nathan reached out to Nick. "Hang back, will you? You, too, Justin, Gretchen."

With a raised brow, Nick glanced at Gretchen, who shrugged and shoved a strand of short dark hair behind her ear and then tucked it up under the blue beret.

After the others were gone, Nathan turned to them. "Gretchen, what do you think about pairing up with Vanessa in order to keep eyes on Yvette at all times?"

"I'm happy to do it," she said.

"I know that we had considered Vanessa might actually be Boyd's accomplice. I truly don't think she is, but I'd feel better knowing you were observing. And not only that, it's possible she's a target since she got a rose and a note. I'd like someone watching her back as well."

"Absolutely. I agree."

"What do you think, Nick?"

"I think that's a great idea. We don't need to take any unnecessary chances with anyone's life."

"Good, that's settled, then. Gretchen, why don't you catch up with Vanessa and let her in on the plan?"

"Of course, sir." She hurried off.

Once she was gone, Nick raked a hand over his crew cut. "I think we need eyes on Heidi Jenks as well."

"You think she's up to something?"

"No. I think she's in danger." He didn't bother explaining why he thought that. Nathan and Justin were both aware of everything that had happened last night.

Nathan pursed his lips, then nodded. "All right. Why don't you take on that responsibility?"

"Yes, sir. Happy to."

"Excellent. I still want you to be a part of the investigative team, but my gut's telling me Heidi needs to be a priority. Until we know for sure she's safe, you and Annie stay close to her."

"Yes, sir." He paused. "One more thing. I know OSI is investigating the bombing of the training center and is keeping you in the loop."

"Right."

"Heidi and I saw the trainer who was hurt in the blast, Bobby Stevens."

"How's he doing?"

"Recovering. But he's lying about something."

Justin raised a brow. "How's that?"

Nick told them about the visit. "I think he and Heidi have established some sort of bond, simply because she's the one who warned him to run in time and saved his life. But he's hiding something even from her."

"Hiding what? The identity of the person who set the explosion?"

"Maybe. He claims he doesn't know who it was. I think he does know, but is too scared to say anything. Maybe." He shook his head. "I don't know what it is, but there's something."

"You want to do some digging?" Justin asked.

"I can. I don't want to step on OSI's toes, though."

"I think as long as you agree to share whatever you find out, they'll be all right," the Lieutenant said.

"Of course."

Justin nodded. "See if Heidi will agree to continue to keep that bond with Stevens. Maybe at some point he'll tell her what he's hiding."

"That wasn't really what I was thinking, but I can do that."

"What were you thinking?"

"That someone needs to do an in-depth background check on him."

"They did that when he enlisted," Nathan said.

"I know, sir, but I still think he needs to be investigated. Finances, daily routine, the people he hangs out with and socializes with."

"So, a full-blown investigation," Justin said, rubbing his chin.

"Exactly, sir."

"I'll mention your concerns to Agent Steffen."

"Thank you."

Nick left, satisfied that everyone seemed to be in agreement that Heidi needed protection—and that he was the guy for the job. He told himself that his happiness had nothing to do with the fact that he wanted to see Heidi again and everything to do with the fact that he just wanted to make sure she stayed safe. He'd feel the same about anyone in her situation.

Liar.

He huffed a sigh and decided not to examine any of that too closely.

He'd keep Heidi safe and that would be that.

So, why was he wondering what her favorite flower was?

Nick put the mental brakes on once again.

No flowers, no romance, no nothing. Why did he have to keep reminding himself of that when it came to her? He hadn't had that problem until she kept crossing his path. Now, when he thought about the future, blue eyes and shoulder-length wavy blond hair kept intruding. It was ridiculous. She was a reporter. The one profession that filled him with disgust.

No flowers, no romance, no nothing.

But takeout wasn't included in that list. He'd grab some Chinese and stop by to check on her. Just to be sure she was safe. Chinese wasn't romantic.

Unless he included candles.

"No candles, Donovan," he muttered. "Get your mind off romance and on keeping her safe."

After all, he had a direct order to that effect.

FOUR

"Thank you for seeing me, Mrs. Weingard." Heidi stood on the front porch of the house and smiled at the woman who'd answered her knock.

Children's voices echoed loudly behind her. The young mother nodded and swiped a stray hair from her eyes and turned. "Billy! Stop jumping on the couch and take your sisters upstairs."

"Can we play video games?"

"Yes, for a little while."

Screams of glee at the apparently unexpected treat trailed behind the youngsters as they raced up the steps. A door slammed. Silence descended. "Call me Kitty," the woman said. "And come in if you dare."

Heidi stepped into the chaos. And longing pierced her. Would she ever have a family to call her own? With children who would leave their toys strewn around the furniture and the floor in testament to a play-filled afternoon?

Heidi wasn't getting any younger, and she had to admit that as the months passed, the questions seemed to rear their heads more and more. First Lieutenant Nick Donovan's flashing blue eyes popped into her mind for a split second and she cleared her throat. "You look like you stay busy."

Kitty laughed. "Are you kidding me? I rarely get to sit down, that's for sure." She paused. "But I love them. They're high-energy, but have sweet dispositions. Do you have kids?"

"No, not yet. Hopefully, one day."

Kitty picked up a children's book, two toy trucks and a plastic tiara from the couch. Then waved a hand at it. "Have a seat."

Perched on the edge of the cushion, Heidi pulled her voice-activated recorder from her bag. "Do you mind if I record this? It makes it easier to just transcribe everything later." It also was proof if someone discounted her reporting.

"Sure, that's fine."

"So, can you start from the beginning?"

"Um…like I told the police, my husband was deployed a few weeks ago for his third tour to Afghanistan. He's earned a purple heart and other medals that we kept in a drawer in the bedroom. I'd gone grocery shopping while my kids were at school and when I got home, I found the house torn apart."

"So, this happened during broad daylight."

"Exactly."

"And no one noticed anything at all?"

She shrugged. "No, I think the MPs questioned the neighbors and looked at the security camera footage, but all they could see was a guy in a black hoodie strolling casually out my front door, with his hands tucked in his pockets."

"A black hoodie, huh?"

"Yes."

Like the guy who'd bombed the training center? Sounded like him.

Heidi continued to question the woman, but her mind was only halfway on the interview as she really wanted to know if the training center bomber, the guy who'd pulled the gun at her home, and the person stealing the medals were one and the same. Although it didn't make much sense to her. Why go from stealing medals to bombing an unused portion of the training center? What could be the purpose in that?

Soon, she wrapped up and tucked her recorder back into her purse.

Kitty stood. "Do you think my story will help?"

"I don't know. But it sure won't hurt. The more people who are aware of what is going on, the more likely they are to keep their eyes open."

"I suppose. You know, the thefts are sad and it's infuriating that someone would do such a thing. I'm more angry about the disrespect to my husband and the other soldiers than the loss of the medals. They aren't worth much. Maybe a couple hundred dollars each. But what they represent...that's priceless. And stealing them just makes me mad."

"I agree completely," Heidi said. "Unfortunately, a few of the medals that have been stolen have been passed down through the generations and are worth quite a bit of money. I think the thief is just taking his chances with the value. He doesn't know who has what, but finds something worthwhile to keep stealing more. And, also, a few hundred dollars times a hundred-plus medals is some nice pocket change. In addition to the jewelry and money he finds on top of the medals."

"True. But it sure makes my blood boil."

"I understand. Hopefully, this person will be in custody soon and everyone can relax." On that score, anyway. With Sullivan still on the loose, no one would be relaxing anytime soon. Heidi walked to the door. "Thanks again for meeting with me. If you think of anything else, please give me a call." She held out her card.

"Of course."

"Mom! Can we have some popcorn?"

"In just a minute, hon," Kitty called over her shoulder to her son.

"Thanks! And some apple juice boxes?"

"Yes, I'll bring them in a minute if you won't interrupt again, please."

"Okay."

The door slammed again and Kitty rolled her eyes, but the smile curving her lips said she didn't really mind. She looked tired as most moms with multiple children were, but it was obvious she loved her brood. The longing hit Heidi again, and she had to push it away, yet again. It would happen for her. Someday. Maybe.

Heidi left and headed for the next interview, where she heard basically the same story as Mrs. Weingard's, except the break-in had occurred at night when the newly married couple had gone to dinner. The thief had taken the young man's great-grandfather's Medal of Valor, awarded to him by the President of the United States for his service in World War II. The young groom almost cried as he described the loss, and Heidi's heart ached for him.

Hours later, she decided to call it a day. It had been a long one and she was exhausted from the emotional roller coaster she'd ridden while doing the interviews. She'd done her best to offer comfort and sympathy, and now she needed some space to gather her notes and write the article.

Walking home, Heidi felt slightly guilty once again. While listening to Airman Keith Bull talk about his great-grandfather with pride gleaming in his gray eyes, it had occurred to her that she was doing the story—and the families—a disservice with her lack of focus. They deserved her full attention even if the stolen medals story hadn't been her first choice for an assignment.

So she didn't get the lead on the Red Rose Killer story.

So her boss couldn't seem to see past his own nose—or his obvious favorite, John Robinson—to see her potential.

So John Robinson drove her batty.

So what?

She was a good reporter and she needed to give this story her best. The families deserved that.

Decision made, guilt assuaged, she drew in a deep breath of the night air. As the sun dipped lower on the horizon, the temperature dropped. She loved being outside in the fall. It was time to open the windows and turn the air-conditioning off. And write.

She strode with a little more pep in her step, actually looking forward to transcribing her notes and sending this article to Lou.

Footsteps sounded behind her and she spun. The setting sun blinded her for a moment, but she thought she saw a shadow dart off to the right and slip down the sidewalk that led to more houses off the main Base Boulevard.

Chills swept through her. That was weird. And creepy. And secretive. For a moment, she considered searching for the shadow, but memories of icy blue eyes, exploding buildings and the man with the gun steered her steps toward home. Quick steps. Sure, she could just be paranoid, but that didn't mean someone wasn't following her. One blessing was that there were plenty of people out tonight enjoying the weather. She passed several officers and saluted, thankful for their presence on the sidewalk.

But the darting shadow still bothered her.

A hand on her shoulder spun her around and she let out a startled squeal. She raised a fist and swung it— only to have it caught.

"Heidi! It's just me, Nick."

He released her hand and she placed it over her racing heart. "Wow. You scared me. Seriously?"

"I called your name twice. You started walking faster."

"I didn't hear you. But a few minutes ago, I thought someone was following me." She frowned. "When I turned, he shot off down a side street."

"I must have crossed the street about then because I saw you turn around. Where are you headed?"

"Home."

"Do you mind if I walk with you?"

Was he kidding? "That would be great, thanks." She looked behind him. "Where's Annie?"

"Back at the kennel. She's finished her work for the day so she gets to take a break."

Once they were inside her home, she kicked off her shoes and turned on a lamp. And sniffed. The trash in the kitchen. Great. It wasn't horrible, but it wasn't great.

She'd meant to take it out first thing that morning, but in all of the chaos of everything, she'd forgotten. Oh, well. Hopefully, he wouldn't judge her. "Want something to drink?" she asked him.

"Sure. Whatever you've got is fine."

She returned with two glasses of iced tea. He took his and settled on the couch. She turned her air conditioner off and opened the two windows in the den to let in the fresh air, then took the recliner. "Any progress on finding the man who blew up the center?" she asked.

"No. Unfortunately. And nothing on Sullivan, either. That man is as slippery as a snake."

"As scary as one, too." She shuddered.

"Depends on the snake," he said. "How's the story coming with the stolen medals?"

She shrugged. "I'm talking to the victims. The MPs are tight-lipped about the investigation so I have to get the details from the people who'll talk to me."

"People don't trust reporters. Especially law enforcement."

"No kidding. At least not until it suits their purposes, then they're the first ones to call."

He tilted his head. "How do you live with that? Doesn't it get frustrating?"

"Of course."

"So, why do it? Why pick a career that a lot of people don't have a lot of respect for?"

She sighed. "Because it's in my blood. My father was a reporter and a good one. He was killed while investigating a story and after the shock wore off, the anger set in. I was mad. Livid. It felt like if I could pick up where he left off, I would be carrying on his legacy." She shrugged "I don't know if that makes any sense or not."

"Strangely enough, it kind of does."

His soft words pierced the chunk of armor she'd had to wrap around her heart. "Thank you."

He cleared his throat and nodded.

"And besides," she said, "journalism is a very respectful career. It's just a few who give it a bad name. I'm trying to be one of the good ones."

"I'm starting to see that," he said softly.

"You are?"

"Yeah."

"Well, good. Thanks." They fell silent and she studied him for a moment.

"What is it? You're looking at me weirdly."

"I was wondering what happened to you."

"What do you mean?"

"You're very anti-media, anti-reporters. More so than what seems normal for the average person, I guess. I figure something must have happened to make you feel that way."

Nick looked away. She'd brought the subject up before and he'd managed to avoid answering. He didn't like to talk about his mother's death to anyone. Much less a reporter. Then again, she could easily research it and find out everything she wanted to know and more. Of course, most of it wouldn't be truth. And he wanted her to know the truth.

For a moment, he wondered why he cared. When he couldn't come up with an acceptable answer, he shook his head. "My mother was a Type 1 diabetic. She'd battled the disease from the age of eight. But she did well, got married and had me. My father was a political star and rising through the ranks in Washington when a reporter took pictures of him in a very compromising position with his young and very pretty political assistant."

Heidi's eyes widened. "Uh-oh."

"Exactly. Those pictures wound up in the newspapers and all the media outlets you can think of and his career was destroyed."

"I'm sorry."

His eyes frosted. "Are you? Are you saying you wouldn't have done the same thing had you been in that reporter's place?"

She bit her lip. "I'm sorry it happened. Would I have done the same thing?" She frowned. "I don't know."

"Right."

With narrowed eyes, she did her best to filter her response. "Look, until I'm walking in someone else's shoes, I can't tell you what I would or wouldn't do in that same situation. I *can* tell you that I do my best to act with integrity at all times. I get that not all reporters have the same code of honor, but I do." She paused. "Was the story fact or not?"

"Fact."

She huffed. "Then, yes. I might have done the same thing."

He stood and shoved his hands in his pockets as he checked the locks on her windows.

"Where's your father now?" she asked him.

"Married to that assistant and living in San Antonio. She's sixteen years younger than he is."

"Do you talk to him?"

"No. Not often. He doesn't seem to care."

She winced. "Nick, I'm sorry you had a rough time, I really am. It's no fun being in the spotlight, I get that. Trust me. Probably better than you think."

He turned to her. "You're talking about when your dad was killed?"

"Yes."

"Where's your mother?"

"Happily remarried to a pastor, living in Tennessee."

"Nice."

"It is." She sighed. "But if the story about your father was fact, why are you so antagonistic?"

"Because it led to my mother's death. Indirectly."

She blinked. "Oh. How?"

"The story led to her depression, which led to her not taking care of herself, which led to her insulin issues going out of control, which led to her passing out at the wheel and going over a cliff.

"Anyway, that was one story the papers got all wrong because a diabetic passing out at the wheel and driving over a cliff isn't nearly as sensational as saying she killed herself. And that's the conclusion they immediately came to when there were no skid marks indicating she tried to stop."

With a gasp, Heidi surged to her feet. "That's horrible, Nick."

She sounded like she meant it.

"Horrible is one way to describe it," he said.

"And completely unethical. I'm so sorry. I really am."

He raked a hand over his hair. "I am, too." And why was he telling her this?

"Did you confront the reporter?" she asked.

"I did, actually. He didn't care and there was nothing I could do to make him grow a conscience. There was no way to prove Mom didn't commit suicide— even though the autopsy later revealed that her blood sugar was so low that she probably passed out. But even with that evidence in hand, the paper wouldn't print a retraction or admit they might have jumped the gun and not done a thorough investigation before printing the story. But Mom wasn't suicidal. She was hurt and she was mad at my dad and aggravated with the media up to that point, but she'd just bought us tickets to go see the Rangers play at the stadium that weekend." He gave her a short smile. "We were big fans." He sighed. Enough. He didn't come over here to go down memory lane.

He turned away and once again examined her windows. Maybe just to give himself something to do. "Do you have an alarm system?" he asked.

"Um, no. Why?"

"Because I think you probably need one."

With a slow nod, she let her gaze sweep around her home. "I've never felt unsafe here. This place has been my sanctuary since I moved in. And now..." She rubbed her arms. "I feel like a sitting duck."

"We'll work on that. What are your plans tomorrow?"

She shrugged. "Church, then lunch. Sometimes Felicity and I see a movie if Westley is busy. Other times I ride out to the lake. I'll probably work some in the afternoon after I make my weekly call to Mom and take a nap. And then I have that last interview I need to do with the latest theft victim so I can get this article in to Lou."

"You don't have many friends, I gather," he said softly.

She gave him a sad smile. "Well, I had a few more, but when rumors of me being the anonymous blogger started gaining some traction, a lot of them kind of dropped off the radar."

His jaw tightened. He didn't want to feel sympathy for her. And yet, he did. "We go to the same church here on base. So…come to church with me tomorrow and let's grab lunch after."

Her eyes went wide, then narrowed. "Wait a minute. Is this pity company?"

He blinked. "What?"

"You know. You feel sorry for me, so you're trying to do something nice. Not because you really want to, but because you feel you should."

His jaw dropped and for a moment, he just stared at her. Then he stood and glared, jabbing a finger at her. "I don't do pity company. Sure, I feel bad that you're feeling the brunt of the gossip, but I don't spend time with people because I feel sorry for them." Much. Okay, maybe occasionally, but that didn't apply to this situation. "And if I do," he said, completely negating what he'd just claimed, "I don't volunteer to spend *that* much time with them." Her eyes sparkled, and he cleared his throat—something he found himself doing a lot around her. "Anyway, no. Definitely not pity company."

His glower didn't seem to faze her. She searched his eyes. "I think I believe you," she said. Then grinned.

Having her throw his words back at him sent his anger down the drain. A bark of laughter escaped him and he stepped back. "Well, thank you, ma'am. I appreciate that."

A small smile tugged at her lips. "You're welcome."

"So? Church and lunch?"

"Sure," she said. "Church and lunch."

"Good. I'll pick you up." With that, he left her standing in her den, staring after him, speechless.

The smile on his face died when he saw the Security Forces vehicle parked outside her home. Nope, not pity company. Protective company, yes. Because while he had no plans to fall for the pretty reporter, he was genuinely worried about her safety. He sighed and did a one-eighty. Back at her door, he knocked.

She opened it with a frown. "Are you okay?"

"Yes. I just need to know your favorite flower."

"Pink carnations. Why?"

"Just needed to know. See you tomorrow."

"But—"

"Good night, Heidi."

Her confused huff made him smile again. A tight smile that stayed with him all the way home.

When he stepped inside, he found his grandfather in the recliner, a football game playing on the television mounted over the fireplace. A retired colonel, the man had moved in with him after Nick's grandmother had died last year. He was able to function on his own, but Nick felt better with him there so he could keep an eye on him. And besides, he liked the company. "Hey, Gramps, how's it going?"

"It's going fine. Where've you been?"

"I went over to see Heidi." He'd told his grandfather about the explosion. As much as he could, anyway. Even though the man was retired military, there were still things Nick had to keep to himself. "I was worried about her."

"Uh-huh. You like her, don't you?"

"Did you miss the part where I said she's a reporter?"

"I didn't miss it. So why do you like her?"

"I didn't say I did."

Gramps harrumphed and let out a low laugh. "Okay, boy."

His grandfather could make him feel like a child of ten without even trying. "Gramps..."

"I picked up your shirts from the cleaners. You can wear the blue one tomorrow to church."

Church. Right. "Ah...about church. We have to swing by and pick up Heidi. She's going with us."

"That reporter you don't like?"

He sighed. "Yes, sir, that's the one."

"Gotta find me a woman I don't like as much as you don't like that one."

With a groan, Nick made his way back to his room and shut the door on his grandfather's chuckles.

"Just keeping her safe, that's it," he muttered to the quiet room. Because in spite of the lighthearted banter with his grandfather, Nick's pulse pounded a rhythm of fear every time he thought about her being a target of the man who bombed the training center.

Which meant nothing special, he told himself. He'd be concerned about anyone who'd caught the attention of a man who bombed a building.

But Heidi...

He did like Heidi. A lot.

And while his head argued that it was a bad idea, his heart was jumping all over it.

He had a feeling he was in big trouble.

FIVE

Heidi had found sleep difficult to come by last night, but when nothing had happened by one o'clock, and she could see the MP was still parked outside, she'd been able to fall into a restless doze. By the time her alarm buzzed, she was already up and getting ready.

And questioning her sanity as she slicked pink gloss across her lips. "We go to the same church here on base. So...come to church with me tomorrow and let's grab lunch after."

She rolled her eyes at her reflection and decided she would do. She'd left her hair down and it rested against her shoulders, the strands straightened with the help of her flat iron. Light makeup enhanced her blue eyes and the lip gloss added a subtle sheen to her mouth.

In her day-to-day work life, she looked professional and neat, not made-up. It suited her. So why was she making more of an effort today?

She knew exactly why and his name was Nick Donovan. She might as well admit it.

With a grimace, she turned from the sink and headed for the kitchen for a bagel and a cup of coffee. Her nose reminded her she still needed to take the trash out, but she wasn't about to risk dirtying her nice clothes. She put that at the top of her after-church to-do list. A glance out the window revealed the Security Forces vehicle still parked on her street. She frowned. The man she'd seen running from the training center hadn't liked that she'd seen his face. In fact, he'd been so desperate to get away he'd pulled a gun on her and Nick. Then he'd managed to escape the base perimeter. Would he come back or was his work done? Or had he decided the smart thing to do was disappear? She hoped it was the latter.

While she was on her second cup, her phone rang, and she snagged it. "Hi, Mom."

"Hey, stranger."

Heidi grimaced. "Sorry, it's been crazy around here."

"I know. I've been keeping up with what's happening on the base. They haven't caught that serial killer yet. Boyd Sullivan."

"No, they haven't, but they don't think he's on the base anymore. He was last seen in central Texas."

"And what about the explosion at the training center?" her mother asked.

"Oh. You heard about that, huh?"

"Like I said, I keep up."

What could she say that would be the truth, but not send her mother running to the base?

"We're not sure, Mom. OSI is investigating so we hope we hear something soon. Until then, security is super tight."

"I would hope so. Do you need to take a leave of absence and come here?"

"No, ma'am. I need to stay here and do my job."

"In spite of the fact that it might get you killed?"

"I'm not planning on putting myself in any danger."

"Your father—"

"Dad knew exactly what he was walking into when he started working that story. Now that I'm older, I understand his thought processes. He didn't want to die, but he was doing what he believed in." She paused. "I'm not Dad, but I'm a lot like him. I don't plan to do anything that may put me in danger, but I believe in ferreting out the truth."

For a moment her mother didn't respond and Heidi wondered if she would hang up on her. Then a watery sigh reached her. "On the contrary, my dear, you are just like your father."

"Well...okay."

"And I'm very proud of you."

Heidi snapped her mouth shut. Then let out a low sigh. "Thanks, Mom. I needed to hear that."

"Please let me know if there's anything I can do."

"I will."

"And someone needs to tell that blogger to quit posting. Whoever is writing that stuff is revealing things probably better kept under wraps."

A choked laugh escaped her. "I agree, Mom. They're working on silencing that person."

"Which means they don't know who it is."

"You're very astute."

Heidi could almost hear the smile her mother no doubt wore. "I love you, hon."

A knock on the door made her jump. "I love you, too, Mom. We'll talk later, okay? Give Kurt my best." She really did like her stepfather. Mostly because he adored her mother.

"Of course."

"Bye." Heidi hung up as another knock echoed through her small home. She rose and placed the cup in the sink, then grabbed her purse.

When she opened the door, she blinked. Nick in his military fatigues was one thing, but dressed in civilian clothing, he plain looked *good*. Amazing. She'd seen him at church before in his civvies, of course, but to have him standing on her doorstep put a whole different kind of beat in her heart.

"Hi," she said. "Good morning."

"Morning." He blinked as his gaze swept over her. "Wow. You look different."

"Thanks?"

He shook his head and laughed. "Sorry. I mean different as in good."

Did a little makeup make that much of a difference? Apparently, it did, judging by how his eyes were focused on her. "Thank you. You look different, too. As in good."

She thought his cheeks might have gone a little pink. He cleared his throat. "I think I need to work on my manners. Let's start over." He turned his back to her, walked down the steps, then back up. When he stood in front of her once more, he offered her a slight bow. "Heidi, you look lovely this morning."

And there went her heart. "Thank you." She was sure her cheek color now matched his. And where did that breathlessness come from? She cleared her throat. "Is it okay if I don't say 'you do, too'?"

He laughed. "I'm more than fine with not being called lovely. Are you ready?"

"I am." She locked the door, then shut it behind her. Then she smiled up at him. "But you are handsome."

"Ah, thank you." More throat clearing. "I hope you don't mind that we have some company."

"Not at all. Who? Annie?"

"And my grandfather. Colonel Truman Hicks, retired. He lives with me and decided to come to church this morning."

"Sounds wonderful." She hoped it would be, anyway. "So, how does he feel about reporters after what happened to your mother? His daughter, I presume?"

His eyes narrowed. "Yes, he's my mother's father. Let's just say he's reserving judgment on any reporters, present company included."

"Uh-huh."

At the car, he introduced her to the man who sat in the back seat. He looked familiar, like she'd seen him in the church before, but she wouldn't have placed him if Nick hadn't introduced them. "Very nice to meet you, sir, but I'm happy to take the back."

"I've got better manners than that, young lady. Climb in."

"Yes, sir." She raised a brow at Nick and he shrugged and opened the door for her. Oh, boy, this might just get interesting.

Annie rode in the very back. The colonel stayed quiet the entire ride while Nick did an excellent job with small talk. She figured the colonel was listening and observing, because while he didn't seem to resent her presence, she wasn't sure he approved of it.

So, Heidi focused on Nick and thought she managed to sound halfway intelligent. The sight of a handler walking his dog brought the missing animals to mind. "Any word on the dogs still missing from the kennel?" she asked.

"No."

"What about the four German shepherds? Felicity said Westley was especially concerned about them."

"They're definitely the more trained and special dogs, for sure, but there's been no word or sightings on them. It's frustrating."

"I'm sure."

They fell silent and she couldn't hold back the sigh of relief when the church came into view.

The jaunt from her home to the church had taken all of three minutes. It had felt like at least thirty.

Nick parked and everyone climbed out into the heat that was already starting to steal the oxygen from the air. She was definitely ready for cooler weather.

The colonel went on ahead, his steps confident and sure, his back straight and strong.

"Why'd he retire?" Heidi asked as Nick released Annie from her area. "He seems a little on the young side."

"He is. He'll only be sixty-eight on his next birthday, but a couple of years ago, my grandmother got sick," he said, "and he wanted to give her his full attention so he requested a leave and was granted it. She passed away. Losing my mom and then grandmother was hard for him. Grief knocked him for a loop. He had his forty-five years—and then some—in, so he was able to retire. Since it was just the two of us left in the family, I decided to ask him to move in with me. He didn't argue about it too much. I think he was lonely."

"I see." She walked with him up the steps and into the sanctuary. "You've had a lot of pain in your life."

"Hmm No more than anyone else, probably. Life comes with a guarantee of pain. It's how you deal with it that matters."

"Maybe." He was right, of course. She just didn't want to think about how she'd dealt with the pain life had served her. Avoiding it wasn't exactly dealing with it.

They found their seats. The colonel sat in the front row. Now she knew why he'd looked familiar. She saw the back of him most Sundays. Nick led her to a pew in the middle and slid in. She sat next to him, ignoring the suddenly speculative looks of some of the others around them. "You don't sit with your grandfather?"

"No. Sometimes I have to slip out and I prefer not to do that in front of the whole congregation. He's sat in that seat since he's been on base so he's not about to move. And see that empty space next to him?"

"Yes."

"He puts Gramma's Bible there in her place."

"He likes tradition."

"Thrives on it."

"And no one says anything? What if a new person sits there without knowing the history?"

He smiled. "Then Gramps finds another place to sit. But the nice thing is, most newcomers don't sit in the front row so it's not an issue."

"Cool." Nick came from a long line of love and an impressive family—at least on his mother's side.

Westley and Felicity slid in beside Nick, then looked around Nick to greet her. "How are you doing? Recovering from the blast, I hope?" Westley asked her.

"I still have sore knees, but other than that, I'm doing fine, thanks."

He nodded and started to say something else, then snapped his lips shut as John Robinson approached. Heidi's stomach turned sour, but she kept her face blank, not wanting the reporter to see her reaction.

"Good morning, all," John said. "Thought I'd catch you here. Master Sergeant James, can you give us an update on the Red Rose Killer?"

"I cannot. Have a nice day, Robinson."

The reporter flinched and narrowed his eyes at Heidi. "Lou isn't going to be happy to hear about this. This is my story."

Heidi crossed her arms and raised her chin. "Did I say it wasn't?"

"No, but everywhere I go, you're there." His gaze flicked to Nick. "With someone working the investigation. If you're hoping to scoop me on this—" The music started and he was forced to end his bickering. "We'll talk later."

"Not if I can help it," she muttered as John walked across the aisle and Nick placed a comforting hand at the small of her back. She shot him a tight smile and drew in a deep breath that was supposed to help lower her blood pressure.

It helped. A little.

Security Forces Captain Justin Blackwood and his sixteen-year-old daughter, Portia, entered and quickly found a seat. Portia carried her ever-present iPad and looked about as happy to be in church as she would being stuck in after-school detention. Not for the first time, Heidi wondered what her story was or what went through her head—the daughter of a high-ranking military official. But also the daughter of a single dad. From what Heidi had learned just from keeping her ears open around the base, Portia was the result of a high school romance. She'd lived with her mother until the woman had died about a year ago and then Justin had gotten custody. She'd been living with her father ever since and didn't seem at all happy about that fact.

Heidi couldn't remember seeing a smile on the girl's face and that made her sad.

She let her mind flip from the girl to what she needed to do on the Red Rose Killer. While she'd been honest about not working the story, it didn't mean she just had to ignore it, right? Of course, she had her priorities straight. First and foremost, she needed to figure out what was going on with the missing medals, but if she happened to come across something that could lead them to Boyd Sullivan, then so be it. John would stroke out if that happened, but there wasn't anything she could do about that. That was his problem.

When the second song ended and it was time to sit, she realized she hadn't even been aware of standing. However, she was very aware of Nick's hand still at the small of her back. Which made her wish they'd sing at least one more song.

But it wasn't to be.

She sat and continued her musing even as she tried to focus on the sermon and not on the man next to her. And then it hit home what Pastor Harmon was talking about. Something about loving one's enemies. She slid a glance at John Robinson across the aisle and clamped her lips together. *Lord, don't ask me to love him, please. That's going above and beyond, isn't it?* Then her gaze moved to the man on her right. *But Nick Donovan might be another thing altogether.* However, Nick wasn't her enemy, so she was pretty sure that wouldn't be the correct application of the sermon. Still…

"Are you all right?" Nick whispered.

She started. "Yes, why?"

"You're squirmy and distracted. Like a little kid."

Heat suffused her cheeks. "Sorry." For the rest of the service, she sat still as a rock and forced her mind to stay on the sermon.

Once the service ended, they made their way to the back of the church and stood in line to greet the pastor and exit. Annie stayed obediently beside Nick. "She's really an amazing dog, isn't she?" Heidi said.

Nick leaned down to scratch the hound's ears. "Truly amazing. Not very pretty and the slobber sometimes gets to me, but she's all heart and give. I couldn't ask for a better partner."

"I hate that the other dogs are still missing. I hope someone's taking care of them."

He frowned. "I do, too."

"It's been five months since Sullivan released them. Do you think there's still hope?"

"Of course there's hope, Heidi." But it wasn't Nick who answered. It was Pastor Harmon who'd no doubt heard her remark as they approached him. He reached for her hand and gave it a friendly squeeze. "There's always hope—even when the situation looks hopeless."

Heidi smiled at the friendly and wise man she'd come to enjoy speaking with on Sunday afternoons. "Hello, Pastor Harmon. I know God can use even this situation. Sometimes it's hard to focus on that, though."

"I know. I'm praying those dogs come home soon."

"Thank you," Nick said. "We appreciate that." They

moved on and stepped out into the heat. "Lunch?" he asked.

"That sounds fabulous."

They found his grandfather talking to three officers and making a golf date. When Heidi and Nick approached, his brown eyes turned speculative. "I'm going to skip out on lunch with you two if that's all right. These three need a fourth."

"Of course, Gramps, just call me if you need a ride home."

"One of these guys can drop me off. Y'all mind?"

"No, sir, happy to do it," one of the officers said. Heidi tried to pull his name from the recesses of her memory, but couldn't find it.

Then Nick's hand was under her elbow and he was leading her to his car. "Is the Winged Java okay with you?"

"Sure. I love their potato soup and Caesar salad."

"Perfect."

They were stopped by Pastor Harmon, who called out Nick's name. He stood at the top of the steps, waving him over.

"Go on, I'll meet you at the car," she said.

The parking lot was almost empty. The car was twenty yards away.

He nodded and jogged over to the steps while she headed for the vehicle. The sound of an engine caught her attention and she turned to see a vehicle heading toward her. Black-tinted windows blocked her view of the driver. As he rode toward her, his window rolled down, his right arm lifted…

…and she saw the semiautomatic in his grasp aimed right at her.

* * *

Nick turned at the sound of the first crack from the gun, followed by a *rat-a-tat-tat* that spit up the asphalt near his SUV. "Heidi!" He ran toward her, pulling his weapon. She'd darted behind the vehicle as the weapon fired, but had she been fast enough? "Heidi! Are you hit?"

The silver sedan roared to the edge of the parking lot, then out into the street without stopping. Within seconds, it had sped around the corner.

He turned to see his grandfather on the phone, yelling orders. The MPs would be here soon, but there was no one here to follow the guy. No matter, someone would catch him soon enough. He was on a closed base and wouldn't get far. Nick rounded the side of the vehicle to find Heidi crouching behind a tire. When she saw him, she launched herself into his arms. He held her, his heart thudding with the knowledge that she didn't appear to be harmed.

He pushed her back to look her over. No blood in sight.

"He didn't hit me," she said. "Came close, but I think trying to shoot me from a moving car threw off his aim."

The colonel hurried over, phone still pressed to his ear. "Do we need an ambulance?"

"No, sir," Heidi said, although Nick knew they'd send one anyway. "Let me sit for a minute, please," she said. "My knees are shaking."

He lowered her to the asphalt and knelt beside her. "You're sure you're okay?"

"Just shaken."

"Understandable."

Sirens were already screaming closer, racing down Canyon Drive. Nick tucked his weapon back into his holster as the first Security Forces vehicles turned into the church parking lot. "You'll need to give a statement," he told her.

"I know. I'm just trying to get it together. It's a story, right? I can do this. I can write this from my perspective."

Already she sounded stronger, but Nick was floored. "A story? You were almost killed!"

Her eyes met his as she stood. "I'm aware of that, thanks."

"Apparently not. It's not a story. It's your life!"

"Stop shouting, Nick, and let me handle this my way."

Belatedly, he realized what she was doing. Compartmentalizing. "You know you completely exasperate me, right?"

"Can't say I'm surprised. I think I have that effect on most people I meet."

At least she was responding with a bit of morbid humor. He got it. Most people in law enforcement used sarcasm or bad humor in order to deal with what they had to live with on a daily basis. Heidi had been around long enough to adopt the technique.

He groaned. "Fine."

A hand on his arm pulled his attention from her to his grandfather. "Gramps?"

"More trouble for the pretty reporter, huh?" While the older man looked steady as a rock, his brows were drawn tight and a muscle in his jaw pulsed, revealing his tight hold on his anger and fear.

"No kidding," Nick told him.

From the corner of his eye, Nick spotted John Robinson heading straight for Heidi. Knowing she was in no condition to deal with her colleague, he nudged his grandfather. "Can you head that guy off at the pass? He and Heidi don't get along, and she may deck him if he says something snarky."

With a gleam in his eyes, his grandfather nodded. "My pleasure."

Turning, Nick found Heidi staring at him. She blinked. "Thanks."

"You're welcome. Now, let's give your statement and get some food. I have a feeling we're going to need it."

SIX

When Heidi was done giving her statement to the police, it was two o'clock in the afternoon.

She was conscious that Nick was right by her side through the whole thing. All of it. He held her hand while she spoke to the MPs. He kept his hand on her shoulder when he encouraged her to let the paramedic check her out. And, finally, he took her to the newspaper office and sat patiently in the corner of her cubicle while she typed up the story for Lou.

"Wow, you just can't stay out of trouble, can you?"

Heidi paused and then lifted her head to find John Robinson hovering just outside her cubicle. Nick looked up from the magazine he'd been reading and set it aside.

"Not in the mood, John," Heidi said and turned her attention back to her computer.

"A shoot-out is a pretty big deal. How did that guy get a semiautomatic on the base, anyway?"

"I think that the MPs are probably working on that," she said.

"Really? And you were the one who saw the guy run

out of the training center, too. As well as get chased by a gun-wielding maniac outside your home."

"He didn't chase us. We chased him." She paused, looked up. "What are you implying?"

"I'm not implying anything. I'm just saying it's kind of odd, isn't it?"

"Spit it out, Robinson," Nick said.

"Fine." He jabbed a finger at Heidi. "I think you want to work on the Red Rose Killer so bad that you're setting up these little incidents to make Lou think you're the better reporter. Kind of like a daredevil reporter who'll go after any story no matter what."

Heidi stared at him for a good three seconds, then rose. "Get out."

"You're not going to deny it?"

"No, I'm not. You've made up your mind, and your blinders wouldn't allow you to see the truth if it bit you on the nose. Now, get out of my space and leave me alone."

Robinson's nostrils flared. "You're going to get knocked off that pedestal you've put yourself on. Real soon."

"Is that a threat?" Nick asked and stepped casually in front of Heidi, partially blocking her view.

"No," Robinson said. "A promise." He spun on his heel and left.

Heidi's breath whooshed from her lungs. "What a jerk."

"Yeah. You better watch your back with that one."

She caught his gaze. "Guess I'll trust you to do that while you're watching for the other guy who's out to get me."

He huffed a short laugh. "Right." His phone rang. "I'm going to get this while you finish up."

When he returned a few minutes later, Heidi had just put the finishing touches on her piece and hit the send button. "I'm starving," she said.

"We'll grab some food on the way back to your place. That was Westley. He said they think they've figured out how the gunman got on base."

"How?"

"Looks like he hopped a ride on a delivery truck. Security footage showed him getting out of the back when no one was watching. The weapon was in his hand. Then he tried a few cars until he found one with the keys left in it. Piecing together the footage from different cameras, it's apparent that he drove around base for a few minutes—looking for you, they think—before stopping at the church. And you know what happened after that."

"Did they catch him?"

"No. Unfortunately, he managed to get away. He ditched the car and slipped inside the Base Exchange. With the baseball cap and sunglasses, we weren't able to get a good picture of him off the security footage."

She sighed and nodded. Then stood. "All right. I think I'm ready to get out of here and get something to eat. Do you mind if we just hit the drive-through? I don't feel up to sitting in a café."

"Sure, we can do that. Let's go."

He loaded her and Annie into his SUV and they swung through a drive-through before he took her home. Once inside, he placed the food on the table.

In companionable silence, they worked together, grabbing plates and silverware, and soon, she found herself sitting across from him—albeit a bit tongue-tied. After several bites, she took a sip of soda and eyed him.

"What?" he asked before taking another bite out of his burger.

"Why are you being so nice to me?" she blurted.

He blinked. "Someone just tried to kill you. Should I be mean to you?"

She gave a low laugh. "Of course not. I don't think that would even be in your makeup. But you don't like reporters. That means you don't like me by default."

"Hmm. That's been the general feeling over the last few years."

She raised a brow. "And with me being fingered as the anonymous blogger, that should really make you think twice."

"But you're not the blogger."

"I know that, but I don't have any proof."

"I think you've proven you're not."

"Really? How's that?"

"I'm not blind, Heidi. I've been watching you, and you have integrity."

A lump gathered in her throat. "Thanks, I appreciate that. But you still don't like reporters."

"I have to admit, there's a certain reporter who might be changing my mind."

"Let me guess. John Robinson?"

He choked. Then went into coughing spasms while she pounded his back. "Are you okay?"

"I may take back my statement about liking a certain reporter. She may have integrity, but her wicked sense of humor can hurt a guy."

Heidi grinned. She couldn't help it. His expression

set her heart racing. "You actually like a reporter?" She was proud of the calm, matter-of-fact tone she managed to use. "Judging by your reaction, I'm guessing it's not John."

"No, John is exactly the kind of reporter I don't like."

"So, who might it be?" Seriously? Was she *flirting* with him? The guy who hated reporters? Obviously, she was still traumatized from the day's events and was in desperate need of a good night's sleep.

Now that he had himself under control, his eyes narrowed, but a smile played around the corners of his mouth. "You really have to ask?"

Dropping her gaze to her food, she gave a small laugh even while heat crept into her cheeks. "No, I guess I don't." So. He was inclined to flirt back. Interesting.

And then the gunfire she'd escaped that morning echoed in her mind and she frowned.

His smile slipped away. "What is it?" he asked.

Swallowing the last bite of her burger, she shook her head. "This probably isn't a good idea."

"What?"

She met his eyes. "You know what. Us hanging out. Flirting a little. You being anywhere near me. That's what."

"Why not?"

"Because I might get you hurt. Someone shot at me today. Obviously, this guy is crazy and doesn't care who's in the path of his bullets."

"You were the only one in the path of those bullets. They didn't come close to anyone else."

"This time. What about next time?"

He ran a hand over his eyes. "I'm hoping there won't be a next time."

She bit her lip and nodded. "I appreciate that. But if the shooter and the bomber are one and the same, he's not going to stop."

"Then someone will have to stop *him*. Period."

The flat confidence he infused into his words gave her hope and terrified her at the same time. Because stopping him might mean putting Nick's life in danger. "Nick—"

"It's going to be okay," he said.

She shot to her feet. "Don't say that!"

His brows rose. "What? Why?"

"Because you don't know that it's going to be okay." She jabbed a finger at him. "It might *not* be okay. Sometimes, it's just *not* okay." She paced to the window and looked out through the blinds, hating that she thought to stay to the side so no one could see her. The afternoon sun shone bright—a direct contrast to her moody, overcast emotional state.

He gave a slow nod. "All right. That's true. Sometimes it's not okay."

Crossing her arms, she closed her eyes for a moment while she gathered her emotions tighter. Then she turned. "I'm sorry. It's just my dad used to tell my mom that every time he left to cover a story and she expressed concern or fear. Those were some of his last words. 'Don't worry, honey, it'll be okay,' he said. Well, trust me, it wasn't okay."

"Aw, Heidi, I'm so sorry." Nick rose and stepped over to her, the look of sheer compassion in his eyes making her want to cry all over again.

But she refused. That wouldn't help anything. She

set her chin. "Don't worry about it. I shouldn't have reacted so strongly."

"But some things do turn out okay, right?"

She sniffed and offered him a small smile. "Yes, some things do. Specific things. Like the fact that I'm still alive. And I have you watching out for me. That's definitely okay."

"Good," he said softly. "Because I'm glad you're still alive and I'm for sure watching out for you."

"Thank you. I appreciate it." She sighed. "And now, I need to work."

"Anything I can help you with?"

"Not unless you want to give me the scoop on the evidence you found at the training center."

"Sorry, that's a negative."

Letting her shoulders droop, she nodded. "I kind of figured."

He sighed. "Heidi, it doesn't have anything to do with whether or not I trust you. It's an investigation. There are some things I simply can't talk about."

"I know." She smiled. "It's okay."

When his brow lifted at her use of the words, she shrugged. "You can say those words when it really is or is going to be okay. Just don't say them when you have no way of knowing if it's going to be okay or not. You can't predict the future."

"Got it." He cleared his throat, stepped back and started cleaning up the remains of their lunch. "I'll let you do what you need to do. Work, take a nap and recover, or whatever. Just do me a favor?"

"What?"

"Don't go anywhere alone. Don't make yourself a target. Stay inside and stay safe."

Her jaw tightened at the request. "I won't be a prisoner in my own home."

"Don't look at it as a prison. Look at it as a safe house."

She rolled her eyes. "Nick—"

"Please." He placed his hands on her shoulders. "I don't want to see you get hurt—or worse."

The look of compassion in his eyes had morphed into something entirely different. "Why do you care so much?" she whispered.

"I don't know." He gave a low laugh. "A few days ago, I would have said you were as irritating as a gnat."

"Well, thanks. And now?"

"Now that I'm getting to know you a bit more…well, let's just say I want to continue to be able to do that."

She swallowed. Hard. "Okay."

"So, are you going to be all right if I leave you here alone? And be honest with me. Today was really scary. It's only natural that you might not want to be alone."

"Are you a counselor now?" she teased half-heartedly.

His lips turned up in a sad-tinged smile. "Just a guy who's been through some scary stuff."

She nodded. "I think I'll be all right. I've got coverage on my home, remember?" With a sigh, he stepped over to her and wrapped her in a hug. "I like you, Heidi Jenks."

The thud-thud-thudding of her own heart said she liked him, too.

He pressed a kiss to her forehead and she blinked.

"Call me if you need anything," he said. "Promise?"

Still reeling from the feel of his lips on her skin, she simply nodded.

And then he was gone.

And she was alone…

…with the fact that someone wanted her dead. And she was falling in love with Nick Donovan. She wasn't sure which scared her more.

Nick gave himself a mental slap. He was doing it again. Letting his heart have a say in how he acted. He decided he needed some rules when it came to Heidi.

Rule number one: keep your distance. Emotionally and physically. Which led to rule number two.

Rule number two: stay at arm's length—i.e. not close enough to hug.

Rule number three: definitely no hugging.

New rule number four: no kissing of foreheads.

Seriously, he had to get it together.

He let himself into his home and found his grandfather in the recliner, watching football. "Gramps? What are you doing here? Thought you were golfing."

His grandfather muted the game. "After everything settled down, the others decided to postpone and try again next week. I'm on the schedule. How's your girl?"

"My girl?"

A raised eyebrow was the only response from Gramps.

Nick resisted rolling his eyes. "She's fine. For now."

"Why was someone shooting at her?"

"We think it's the person who bombed the training center. She was there when it happened and saw a guy in a ski mask and hoodie running from the place just before the explosion. The guy didn't realize she was there and took off his ski mask. Then saw Heidi."

"That would explain it."

"Only the hoodie hid his face enough that she was only able to give a partial description. Good enough for a detailed drawing of a guy wearing a hoodie, but nothing more than that."

"Frustrating."

"No kidding."

"So what are you doing back here? You should be watching out for her."

"She's got someone on her place."

"Then what are you going to do?"

"What do you mean?"

"You're standing there, with your keys in your hand and that look in your eyes."

"What look?"

Another raised brow. Nick huffed a short laugh. His grandfather could read him so well.

"I think I'm going to talk to Justin Blackwood and see if he thinks any of this is related to our ongoing investigation of Boyd Sullivan."

"It's Sunday. Supposed to be a day of rest."

"Unfortunately, killers don't seem to care about that. Which makes it hard for the good guys to take the day off."

"I know, boy. I've been there. Just don't like to see you working so hard."

"Wish I didn't have to, but at least I like what I do." He did like his job. He might wish it wasn't necessary, but as long as there were bad guys with bombs, he would do his best to stop them.

He shot a text to Justin, who answered that he was in the conference room of the base command office. The captain agreed to meet and Nick headed back out the door. "Sorry I can't stay and watch the game with you."

"Trust me, you're not missing anything. The Cowboys are playing like they've never seen a football. It's maddening."

Nick gave a low laugh and headed for his truck.

When he pulled into the parking lot of the base command building, he noted several other vehicles he recognized.

Inside, he made his way to the conference room, where he found Justin with Westley, Oliver and Ava. Files were spread across the table and yellow legal pads held copious notes. "Did my invitation get lost in the mail?"

Justin waved him to a seat. "You didn't miss anything. I knew you were with Heidi." He met Nick's gaze. "Is she all right?"

"She is. She's at home resting. Or working. Probably the latter. There's an officer on her house, watching out for her."

"Okay, good." Justin caught him up on what the quartet had been discussing. "Vanessa's been keeping an eye on Yvette but hasn't seen any indication that Yvette is hiding anything or is in contact with Sullivan, but it's only been twenty-four hours. We're going to keep up with the surveillance."

"That sounds wise. If Boyd had anything to do with that explosion, he could be lying low for a bit until the investigation slows."

Justin nodded. "The good thing is, Sullivan's targets have received no more threats. We've got those who've received roses under protection and there've been no movements against them. Heidi still needs protection, though, so we'll keep someone on her."

"Which brings me to a question," Nick said. "Do you think Sullivan is behind the threats to Heidi?"

"I don't know. If Sullivan had a hand in blowing up the training center, then I'd say it's possible. But until we find the bomber, I don't think we can make that assumption."

"So, in the case of the others, Sullivan's biding his time," Nick said. "Waiting."

"That's what I think. He sure hasn't decided to stop."

Nick shook his head. "This shouldn't be taking so long. Why is it so hard to catch him?"

"We've all been asking ourselves that question," Oliver said.

Ava shrugged. "He's smart."

"And rubbing our faces in the fact that he's smarter," Westley muttered.

"He'll mess up," Justin said.

"Right," Nick said, "hopefully before someone else dies."

His phone rang, and Heidi's number flashed at him. "Excuse me while I get this." He slipped into the hallway. "Heidi? Everything okay?"

"I need a favor, if you don't mind."

"What's that?"

"I'm going to do a couple of interviews. MP Evan Hendrix is going with me so I should be fine, but could you pick me up when I'm finished?"

"Yes, of course. Wait a minute. What interviews?"

"For the medals, Nick."

"And you have to leave your house? Can't you just do phone interviews?"

A sigh reached him. "I could, I suppose, but it's really hard to read body language over the phone."

"FaceTime? Skype?"

"Nick, this is my job. I promise to be careful. I'll take every precaution and I'll have Evan with me."

"I still don't like it."

"Sorry. Talk to you later. I'll text you my location, if you can come get me."

"I'll be there." Oh, yes, he'd be there. Because while Evan was very likely a good soldier, there was no way he'd watch out for Heidi like Nick would. And he was going to make sure this type of situation didn't crop up in the future.

Heidi glanced at her watch and pressed a hand against her rumbling stomach as she left the last interview for the day. She'd texted Nick her location and told him Evan needed to leave but would wait with her until Nick arrived.

And true to his word, he stayed as close as a burr.

They walked down the steps of the latest theft victim's home and Heidi placed the recorder in her pocket.

"You're good at that," Evan said.

"Thanks."

"Seriously. You asked great questions, were compassionate about her loss, and didn't lead her to answers that you wanted her to have. You let her come up with her own. I've seen a lot of reporters, even answered some of their questions, but I've never seen one do it the way you do."

Heidi gave him a smile. "That's really kind of you to say so. Unfortunately, not everyone in the business acts with integrity." Understatement of the year? "But my dad taught me that integrity comes before the story. And that if I act in such a way, I'll always be the better reporter—and others will trust me." A flash of grief speared her. "And while it takes years to build relationships and gain the trust of others, lies can destroy that in seconds."

"You're referring to the fact that people think you're the anonymous blogger."

"Yes."

"Do you know why they think that?"

"I suspect because John Robinson spread that rumor." She sighed. "You know, I get that he's ambitious. This job is very competitive and cutthroat and it can bring out the worst in people." She met his gaze. "But it doesn't have to be that way. I want to help catch the bad guys, not tell them what's going on in an investigation by leaking stuff that will help them." She shook her head. "But I don't know how to prove to everyone that I'm not the blogger. Other than to continue doing my job with integrity and honesty." She shrugged. "And hope, in the end, that pays off and people see it."

"After hanging out with you and watching you work, I don't believe you're the blogger."

She squeezed his hand. "Thank you, I appreciate that. Now, pass the word, will you?"

He laughed. "Sure."

Nick pulled to the curb and stepped out. "Sorry it took me so long." He walked around and opened the door for her, a scowl on his face.

"No problem. Evan kept me company." She said her goodbyes to the MP and climbed into the passenger seat of Nick's work truck. She buckled her seat belt and scratched Annie's head while watching her ill-tempered chauffeur settle into the driver's seat. "Are you okay, Nick?"

He shot her a frown. "I'm fine."

"Then why are your eyes narrowed, brow furrowed and smoke curling from your nose?"

"Smoke?"

"Might as well be. What's the problem? Did something happen with the case?"

A sigh slipped from him and the frown faded a bit. "Nothing."

"Nothing's wrong or there's nothing more with the case?"

"Both."

"Liar. Maybe not about the case, but something's definitely wrong about you. What is it?"

"I didn't—" The scowl deepened. "Never mind. It's not important."

She let it slide while a fragment of hurt lodged in her heart. "Fine." Once thing she'd learned about Nick—if he wasn't going to talk, he wasn't going to talk.

Silence dropped between them.

"What are you going to do now?" he finally said as he turned onto Canyon Boulevard.

"Go home and write this story."

"What did the victim have to say about the robbery?"

"The same as all the others. She was out to dinner with her family. When she came home, her house had been ransacked and the medals were missing from a box in the top of her closet. Along with three hundred dollars in cash."

"Doesn't anyone use safes anymore?"

She huffed a laugh. "Guess not."

He pulled to a stop in her driveway. "Thanks for being smart."

Hand on the door handle, she paused. "What do you mean?"

"You called me. You took precautions."

With a sigh she turned back to him. "Of course. I'm not stupid."

"I didn't mean to imply you were. It's just that I guess I didn't expect that. I would have thought you were the type to get a lead on a story and just take off regardless of the consequences. That if you needed to conduct an interview you would just do it without thinking things through."

"Remember the fact that someone tried to kill me today?" She stepped out of the vehicle. "Thanks, Nick. I really appreciate that you think so highly of me. Go home. And don't come back until you can get over your preconceived notions of who I am and are willing to take the time to find out." She stared at him, fighting tears. "Because you really don't have a clue." She slammed the car door.

And then she ran for her home. Once inside, she leaned against the door and placed a hand over her pounding heart. A heart that was more and more drawn to the man who'd just hurt her feelings in a major way. She was so on the emotional roller coaster when she was in Nick's presence. The thought that they might never really get along or move forward into some kind of romantic relationship because of her job pained her.

She sighed and moved into the den. And stopped. Wait a minute. Something was off. She took in the sofa, the recliner, the end tables. What was it? Everything looked fine…except for the throw on the back of the chair by the fireplace. When had she put that there? She kept it on the couch.

Had Nick moved it when he'd been here last? Pressing a hand against her forehead, she couldn't remember. Uneasiness settled in her gut. Had someone been in her home?

Nick slammed a fist on the wheel and Annie whined. He glanced at the animal, and her sad eyes drilled him. If he didn't know better, he'd almost believe she was chastising him for being a jerk.

He sighed. He *had* been a jerk. A colossal one. What had compelled him to say such a thing to her?

Fear.

The answer leaped into his mind. He shoved it away before snatching it back. Fear? Yes. Because if he gave her the power, she could hurt him.

Not to mention the fact that someone was out to kill her.

What if that person actually succeeded?

And he'd pushed her away. Made her run from him. Jerk.

His phone rang and instead of opening the door and going after Heidi, he lifted the device to his ear. "What?"

"Having a good day, I see?"

Justin's voice made him wince and clear his throat. "Sorry."

"Have you seen the latest blog post?"

"No. Why?"

"It claims the bombing of the training center is being linked back to Boyd Sullivan."

"What? We haven't said that officially. It's just been

speculated about. How would they know that?" He slapped the wheel again.

"Just like all the other information this person is managing to get her hands on."

"It's not Heidi."

The line fell quiet. Then Justin cleared his throat. "Are you sure about that?"

Was he? Completely one hundred percent sure? "Yes, I'm sure. As sure as a gut feeling can be."

"Sometimes a gut feeling is better than any evidence," Justin said. "All right. We'll keep looking. Not that Heidi won't still be in the pool of suspects, but—"

The explosion rocked his car, throwing him into the passenger seat. The windshield shattered, raining shards of hard glass down on him.

Ears ringing, he lifted himself up to squint against the flames shooting from Heidi's front window.

SEVEN

Nick pulled himself out of his SUV and let a barking Annie out of her area. Keeping the leash around his wrist, he stumbled toward the house only to fall back when the heat scorched him. "Heidi!"

Sirens were already screaming. Westley and Felicity hurried down their front porch. Westley reached him first and gripped his forearm. "Nick! Are you okay? You're bleeding."

"Heidi's in there!" Horror clawed at him. His lungs tightened against the smoke and the fear. There was no way she could have survived that.

Westley went white and Felicity cried out, covering her mouth with her hand. "No," she whispered. "I don't believe it."

There had to be a way in, a way to save her. Nick raced through the narrow pathway between her house and Felicity's, rounded the corner and stopped. The fence. He'd forgotten about the fence. Scrambling for a way to climb over, he paused.

A noise caught his attention even over the sirens and the roar of the burning home. A cry? A cough?

He followed the fence line and turned to see Heidi sitting outside the fence, staring at her home.

"Heidi!"

She looked up at his call, her face streaked with tears and dirt. He raced over to her and dropped to his knees. Gripping her upper arms, he took in the sight of her, looking for any outward signs of trauma. "Are you all right?"

"No!" She swiped a hand across her cheek, smearing the dirt. She pointed. "Look what he did! Just look! It's gone. All of it." He pulled her to him and she buried her forehead against his chest. Annie whined and tried to shove her face between them. Then she licked Heidi's ear. Sobs broke through and Heidi hugged him tighter and let him hold her.

"Heidi! Nick!"

Westley's harsh cry pulled Nick's attention to the man who'd followed the same path Nick had taken just minutes before. He hurried over to them. "Heidi! Boy, am I glad to see you."

She sniffed and hiccupped, but didn't move from Nick's hold.

"What were you doing out here? Because whatever it was, it saved your life."

She giggled, and Nick frowned. Was she going to get hysterical on him? She said something and he missed it. "What?" She pointed and he followed her finger to a white trash bag lying on the ground. "Heidi?"

"The trash," she said. "I was taking the trash out." Another slightly hysterical giggle. "Taking out the trash—a chore I hate with everything in me and put off until the last possible moment—saved my life. I'll never complain about *that* again." She dissolved into another fit of giggles, followed quickly by gasping sobs. Nick simply held her while her home burned.

His gaze met Westley's. "We have to stop this guy."

"I pulled security footage from the night of the training center explosion and saw the man she saw, but there's no way to tell who he was. By the time Heidi said he pulled the ski mask off and turned, he was out of range of the camera. So far, we've gotten no leads on the sketch Carl worked up."

Heidi had stopped crying and he figured by her stillness she was listening. "He pulled the mask off because he knew it was safe to do so. He knows this base. First we need to investigate every single person who lives on this base."

Westley sighed, but nodded. "That's what I was thinking. I'm also thinking it's going to take a while."

"Then we might as well get started."

Heidi sat in the back of the ambulance next to Nick, who hadn't let her out of his sight. The paramedic had checked her out, then cleaned and bandaged several cuts on his face, arms and hands.

"They're not deep, but your face didn't like the force the glass came with," the medic said.

"I know. It's fine."

"No head trauma that I can see on either of you, so you can count your blessings for that."

"I'm alive," Heidi said, "I'm grateful." But the loss hurt. She wouldn't put on a brave face and pretend it didn't. Her notes, her laptop, her files. Everything. Gone. Either to the explosion and fire or water damage. The only reason she wasn't in a puddle on the floor of the ambulance was because she had almost everything backed up to the cloud. The only thing she might not be able to access was the latest piece she'd been writing. Unable to remember if she'd saved it to her online backup, Heidi gave a mental shrug. She could rewrite it.

A flash to her right cause her to recoil. She blinked and finally focused her gaze on John Robinson lowering his camera. "Really?" she demanded.

He shrugged. "I just follow the stories."

"Right." She wouldn't get into it with him. One, it seemed to spur him to be even more obnoxious, and two, she simply didn't have the energy.

Nick stepped out of the ambulance and stood in front of the doorway so Robinson couldn't see into the back where Heidi was. "Get away from here. Now."

His low command sent Robinson stumbling backward. Heidi leaned to the right to see fear flash in the man's eyes, but his chin was raised. "You have no right to stop me from getting my story."

"You have no right to impede medical treatment."

With a roll of his eyes, Robinson left. "I got my picture. I guess that's all I need. I'd love a statement from the victim, but I'm assuming that's not going to happen."

He had that right. "Thanks, John. I appreciate your concern." She couldn't help it. His lack of professionalism infuriated her. No story was worth sacrificing the human touch, expressing sympathy to one's fellow man. Reporters like him made reporters like her look bad. And she just plain didn't like it.

"I can see the smoke coming out of your ears," Nick said to her when Robinson left, "and it has nothing to do with your house blowing up."

She scowled. "That man gets under my skin. Way

under. I've got to find a way to let him and his actions roll off my back."

"Be a duck."

"What?"

"Your new mantra when it comes to Robinson."

"Oh. Be a duck. Meaning let the irritation I feel for the man roll off?"

"Exactly. Come on," he said. "Forget about Robinson. We've got to get you settled somewhere."

"I guess I'll have to find a hotel."

He frowned. "No way. Not when you have friends."

"I do have a few friends, but I'm not going to put any of them in danger. Not when this guy is going around blowing up houses."

Felicity pushed her way through the gathering crowd. "Heidi!" She rushed forward and hugged her, forcing Nick to drop her hand and step back. "I'm so glad you're okay," Felicity said. "At first, I thought you'd…that you'd…that you were—"

"That I was in the house when it blew?"

"Yes." Another tight hug. "I'm so glad you're all right."

"Thank you." Heidi looked back at the smoldering structure. "At least it was just mostly the front of the house that took the brunt of the blast. It wasn't big enough to take the whole thing down. Or cause damage to yours."

"I'm just glad you weren't hurt." Felicity squeezed her hands, then let her go. "What can I do to help?" She bit her lip. "You'll need a place to stay."

"She can stay with me and my grandfather," Nick said.

Heidi blinked and her mouth rounded as she processed his words. "What?"

"We have a guest bedroom, and the colonel is there most of the time. And he obviously knows how to use a gun so you'd have built-in protection."

"But I—"

"That sounds like the perfect solution," Felicity said. "I'll run back to my place and grab you some clothes to wear. I'm going to assume all your uniforms are gone?"

"Except the two at the cleaners, yes."

Annie whined at his side and Nick stroked her ears. "We'll get to work on this one soon, girl." He looked up at Heidi. "We've got to wait for clearance from the fire department, then we'll go in."

Justin Blackwood climbed out of his official vehicle and approached. "Anyone hurt?"

"No, but not because someone wasn't trying," Nick answered for her. Surprisingly, Heidi didn't care. The two of them talked while she rubbed her still-ringing ears. She just wanted to leave, to be alone and process all that had happened.

After some questions, she finally got her wish and Nick led her and Annie to his vehicle. "Stay here for now. I'm going to get the colonel to come take us to my house." He squeezed her hand and called his grandfather. From the quickness of the call, she assumed the man hadn't asked any questions. "He'll be right here." He glanced at his vehicle. "Thankfully, I was in my work truck. It'll be impounded for evidence. I'll be back with Annie to see if we can determine what caused the blast. Meanwhile I'm sure Justin will check out each camera within a mile of your home and see if there's anyone suspicious."

Three minutes later the colonel pulled to a stop just beyond the scene. He stepped out of his sedan and took in the sight with a shake of his head and concern in his eyes. "Are you two all right?" he asked as he approached them.

"We're fine, Gramps. Just need a ride home."

"Come on, then."

Once at the men's home, Colonel Hicks led the way up the front porch steps and into the foyer. Nick shut the door behind them.

"You're welcome to stay here as long as you need," the colonel told her.

"Thank you, sir."

"Nick can show you where to stow your gear. I'll get the bathroom ready for you."

She followed Nick to the guest room and stepped inside to see a twin bed against the far wall, a dresser next to the door and a comfortable chair under the window.

"The bathroom is just outside the room, off the hall," Nick said. "In the second drawer, you'll find toiletries. We keep them for visiting family and friends. Help yourself to anything you need."

"Towels and washcloths are by the sink," the colonel said from behind Nick.

"Thank you very much."

The colonel led the way back to the kitchen, where he gestured for her to sit. "Coffee?"

"Decaf?"

He laughed. "Of course. Even that keeps me up at night sometimes, though."

With the mug in front of her, she wrapped her hands around the warm porcelain and took a deep breath. Someone had just tried to kill her. And almost succeeded. The thought almost didn't compute. "How did someone get a bomb in my house?" she asked.

"Probably picked a time when no one was watching it," Nick said with a sigh. "If you weren't there, there was no reason to have someone on your home—or so we thought."

"Of course."

His phone buzzed and he glanced at the screen. "Looks like it's time for Annie and me to go to work." He called for the dog and she rose from her spot by the fireplace to pad into the kitchen. "You ready to go catch some bad guys, girl?"

Her tail wagged, and he slipped her into the harness hanging near the door. Then he added booties to protect her paws. He looked over his shoulder at Heidi and his grandfather as he slung his pack over his back. "You two lie low. I'll be back soon."

Nick arrived at Heidi's home to find the place roped off and the crime scene unit working in an organized grid. He showed his ID to the officer in charge and was allowed to pass under the tape.

Annie trotted at his side. Justin was still on the scene and Nick made his way over to him and Westley.

"Glad you're here," Justin said. "Let us know what you and Annie find."

Even though firefighters had put the fire out, just like with the training center, he and Annie started examining the debris farther away from the hot areas. While they worked, Nick thought. What was the best way to catch the guy who wanted to wipe Heidi off the planet? Because failing to do so wasn't an option.

Footsteps behind him caught his attention and he turned to see Westley.

"Find anything, Nick?"

"Some scraps that Annie found interesting. She was most interested in the den area. Looks like he hid a bomb, possibly dynamite or C-4, in the den area. We'll see what the lab says."

"ATF is here once again. Didn't even have to use the GPS this time. We've got to stop this guy."

Probably hadn't had to use it the last time, either. But Nick got the point. Two explosions on base were two too many. "My thoughts exactly."

"Security Forces are going crazy scanning video footage of the training center explosion. And now this." He gave a disgusted sigh and shook his head. "I'll leave you to it. Let me know what you find."

"Of course."

The man left and Nick and Annie went back to work. Once the place cooled down, he and Annie and the ATF investigators would go inside and see if they could find what triggered the explosion. When they had some of the materials, they would be able to compare it to the training center evidence.

However, Nick was pretty sure he knew exactly who the bomber was. It had to be the guy from the training center. He was scared Heidi could ID him and he was going all out to make sure she didn't. He was a guy who wanted Heidi dead and he had to be stopped before he succeeded in getting what he wanted.

EIGHT

Heidi sat curled up in the large chair next to the fireplace and sipped her second cup of decaf coffee. Her eyes had grown heavy as the hours passed. The colonel had finally declared he was headed to bed. The weapon in his hand made her wonder, but she hadn't argued. She wanted the time alone to think. And she'd had that. Now she was tired of thinking and just wanted to go to bed.

But her mind wouldn't let her.

The fact that Nick wasn't back kept her glued to the chair.

Minutes later she heard footsteps on the front porch, followed by voices. She walked to the window to look out.

"...might be back on base," Justin said.

"When did you learn that?"

"Just now. When we were finishing up at Heidi's house, Vanessa Gomez reported that someone was watching her house. When MPs arrived, the person ran."

"Vanessa got a rose from Sullivan. You think he's back to make good on his threat?"

"I do. I don't have proof, though, so keep this under your hat."

"Of course."

"I was on the way home and figured I'd stop by and let you know. Anyway, get some rest. I'll see you tomorrow."

"Thanks."

The door opened and Heidi stumbled back. Nick raised a brow, then frowned. He stepped inside and narrowed his eyes. "Guess you heard that?"

"Um…yes. I guess I did. But I wasn't eavesdropping on purpose. I heard voices and looked out the window."

He sighed. "That's not to go in the paper, understand? We don't need to cause a panic on base until we have more information."

"But you think Sullivan's back."

"There's evidence to indicate he is. Yes."

"Nick, people have to know. They have to be on guard."

"And we're going to let them know. As soon as we're positive. So, please. Nothing in the paper about it until we're sure."

"But you'll let me have the exclusive?"

"Sure."

She nodded. "Okay."

"You wouldn't have printed it, anyway, would you?"

"No, but I figure it doesn't hurt to weasel the exclusive." She took a sip from the mug. "So, how did it go at my house? What's left of it, anyway."

He sighed. "Annie did a good job as always. There weren't any other explosives to be found and we scooped up some evidence that the lab will examine.

Now she's back at the kennel getting some much-deserved rest."

"Good, I'm glad." She stood and began to pace.

"Heidi, what's going through that head of yours?"

She stopped and faced him. "Who am I, Nick?"

"What do you mean?"

"I mean, tonight, just about everything I've worked for has been destroyed. Sure, all my files are safe, but I've been thinking. What if they weren't?"

He took her hand and pulled her over to sit on the sofa, then planted himself opposite her. "I'm not following."

Palming her eyes, she fell silent, then lowered her hands and looked up. "I guess what I'm trying to say is, if I can't do my job—and right now, that's looking pretty iffy—then who am I?"

"You're still you. First Lieutenant Heidi Jenks. And not being able to do your job is just a temporary problem. As soon as we catch this guy, you're back to being a star reporter."

She sighed. "I've never been a star reporter." She shrugged at his frown. "Yes, I'm good at my job. Yes, I can write an excellent article. And yes, I can be like a bulldog with a bone. But I'm not cutthroat. I won't step on someone else to get to that next rung on the reporting ladder. So…what does that make me?"

"Admirable," he whispered.

"But John Robinson," she said as though he hadn't spoken, "now, there's a man who'll go behind your back and do whatever it takes to get a story. No matter the consequences or the fallout."

"He's a jerk."

"Yes, he is. But he also gets the job done. So, is that what I need to be? A jerk?"

"No." He clasped her hand. "Please don't even go there."

She sighed and blinked. "I'm sorry. I'm thinking out loud." She paused. "You don't think Robinson hates me enough to blow up my house, do you? You don't think he would be so desperate to keep me out of the loop on not only the training center bombing, but the Red Rose Killer story, that he'd do something like this to throw me off?"

Nick threaded his fingers around hers. "I don't know, but you shouldn't jump to conclusions until you talk to him. Does he even have any experience handling explosives?"

His touch grounded her. Centered her. Made her very aware of him. "As far as I know, he doesn't have any background dealing with explosives. Then again, I guess if someone's desperate enough, it's not hard to find out what you need to know. He's been awfully territorial. I mean, you saw him at church—and then after my house blew up. He'll do anything to get a story. I think I need to talk to him."

"Look, Heidi, you're a good reporter with good instincts. But don't let your emotions start getting in the way. Get the facts before you act."

Heidi drew in a deep breath. "Of course. You're right."

"Why don't you get a good night's sleep and we'll take care of whatever needs to be taken care of in the morning? For now, I think you need to relax and take some time to regroup."

She nodded. "I think that's a good idea."

He stood and pulled her up. For a moment, she simply stared into his eyes, thought he might say something else, but then he cleared his throat and took a step back. "Good night, Heidi."

"Good night, Nick."

In her bedroom, she drew in a deep breath. Somehow she'd ignored the spark of attraction that had flared when she'd stood in front of him in the living room. She had other things that needed her focus. Not chasing a romance with a man who was so gun-shy around reporters. She pulled her small recorder from her pocket and spoke in detail the conversation she'd overheard. Then with more reluctance than bravado, she grabbed her phone and dialed John's number.

"Hello? Robinson here."

"Did you blow up my house?"

"Did I what? Heidi? What are you talking about?"

"Did you blow up my house? Are you so threatened by me that you want to get rid of me? To kill me?"

For a moment silence echoed back at her. "You're a piece of work, Heidi. I know we're rivals, but for you to accuse me of that is really low. Especially for you."

He sounded so sincere that guilt immediately flooded her. She swallowed. "I'm…I'm sorry, John. I didn't want to ask. I just figure I need to cover all my bases."

"Well, you don't have to worry about me being the one trying to kill you." He gave a short huff. "I'll admit to being willing to profit from all the trouble you're having, but I'm not the one instigating it."

"Wow. Thanks."

"Hey, it's just the way it is." He paused. "But no, I'm not trying to kill you."

"Well, I appreciate that. I'm…sorry I practically accused you of doing so. I know how false accusations can hurt."

"Exactly." He paused. "You wouldn't want to give me an interview, would you?"

She laughed. "Good night, Robinson. I'll see you around."

So, if it wasn't John, it had to be the guy she'd seen at the training center. She picked up the recorder and worked out her thoughts on the machine. It always helped to go back and listen and make sure she hadn't forgotten anything when she worked on a piece.

A light knock interrupted her. She opened the door to find Nick standing there, a speculative gleam in his eyes. She raised a brow. "What?"

He set a glass of water and some ibuprofen on her dresser. "Just in case."

"Ah. Yes, that's a good idea. Thanks."

"Night again."

"Night."

He turned, paused and turned back. "Heidi?"

"Yes?"

"I couldn't help overhearing your apology to Robinson."

She flushed. "I suppose you think I should have waited to confront him in person."

"I don't think it matters. Were you wrong? You don't think he was involved in blowing up your home?"

"It sure sounded like that on the phone. I wouldn't mind having concrete proof, but if I were to go with my gut, I'd say he wasn't involved."

"And you apologized."

"Of course. I try to do that when I make a mistake."

He shook his head. "If I hadn't seen it, I don't know that I would have believed it."

She rolled her eyes. "Thanks."

"No, I need to be thanking you. It was refreshing. I needed to see that—as a reminder that everyone is different and deserves to be judged based on who they are, not based on preconceived notions. Like you said in the car before you slammed the door in my face." She winced and he smiled. "I deserved it."

"Sorry about that. I kind of lost my temper a bit."

"I understand." He drew in a deep breath. "Anyway, thanks. Say, I figure you have tomorrow off since I doubt anyone is going to expect you to work after losing your home. Would you like me to take you into town to shop for some things?"

"I was going to ask Felicity if she wanted to go with me, but I know she has to work tomorrow."

"So, is that a yes?"

She nodded. "It is if it won't inconvenience you any."

"It won't. Maybe getting off the base will help."

She frowned. "Do you think it's safe?"

"As safe as staying here."

"That's not a very good argument."

"True. I'll watch out for you. We can watch each other's backs."

"All right, sounds good."

"Perfect. Good night."

He left and she carried the water and medicine to the end table. She shut the door and got ready for bed, feeling safe in the home of the man who seemed to want to hold her at arm's length and pull her close— all at the same time. She sighed and decided not to get too comfortable. As she'd learned the hard way, feeling safe didn't mean she was.

Nick took a sip of the coffee his grandfather had made and thought about what he'd accidentally overheard. Heidi had actually apologized to Robinson. Since when did reporters apologize? Especially ones who were as competitive as those two. He had a feeling if the shoe was on the other foot, Robinson wouldn't have had the gumption to do the same as Heidi. The reporter who'd covered his mother's death sure hadn't. But Heidi had. To someone she didn't even like, no less.

Nick had to admit, it said a lot about her character. She hadn't known he was listening—albeit unintentionally. When he'd realized she was on the phone, he'd started to walk away, but stopped when he heard her say Robinson's name. He'd been ready to offer his comfort if Robinson lit into her, but it had sounded as if they'd had a civil conversation. Not exactly friendly, but at least she hadn't become upset and hadn't needed his intervention. A strong woman, she could take care of herself.

Except when someone was blowing up her house.

"You okay, son?"

His grandfather stood in the doorway, dressed in his pajamas and long robe with matching slippers. "I'm okay. You look dapper."

"Have to dress a little better when we have company."

"We don't have company often."

"Exactly. Now, what's eating at you?"

Nick raised a brow. "What do you think?"

Gramps laughed. "Yeah, I thought so."

"I don't know what to do about her."

"Take it one day at a time."

"Hmm." He sighed. "I have to admit that I'm worried someone's going to succeed in killing her before I find who it is."

His grandfather slipped into the chair next to him. "I would say that's a real problem."

He met the older man's eyes. "How do I take care of her, Gramps?"

"Don't know what else you can do short of taking her off base and hiding her away somewhere."

"An idea I've thought of, but doubt she'll go for." He paused. "She's getting to me."

"I know."

Of course he did. "I overheard her apologize to someone just now. A reporter. Apologizing. It struck me."

"Right in the heart?"

"Something like that."

"You've wanted an apology from a reporter ever since your mother died and they printed that ridiculous story."

"I guess you're right. And hearing hers…well, I think it just healed something deep inside me."

"You need to tell her that."

Nick smiled. "I will."

His grandfather stood and bid him good-night, then disappeared down the hall to his bedroom.

Sitting at the table in the quiet with only a soft glow coming from the light over the sink, Nick considered the next steps in the investigation. They'd confirmed the training center explosion was deliberate. Residue identified it as C-4. Easily set off with a timer.

"Which explains why he was in such a hurry to get away from the training center," he muttered.

It was obvious the man in the hoodie was after Heidi and pretty determined to shut her up for good. Although, Nick had to wonder what purpose it would serve to kill her now. She'd already talked to OSI and Security Forces and told them everything.

Then again, he supposed it would help if Heidi weren't on the base to accidentally run into the man she could identify. Which, if that was the concern, meant he was on the base frequently. Or lived on it.

There'd been no word from Justin on the progress being made in checking the visitor logs, but Nick knew that was like looking for the proverbial needle in the haystack. He sighed. And running it around in his head all night wasn't going to help matters. But one thing did concern him. Did the person who wanted Heidi dead know she was staying with him and his grandfather? He couldn't help thinking about that possibility.

Nick rose and glanced out the window to see a Security Forces vehicle stationed in front of his home. He knew there was another one at the back.

He took a weapon from his safe, then stepped out onto the front porch. With a wave to the airman in the car, he started his trek around the perimeter of his home.

Nothing caught his attention. There were no moving shadows that made him jump, no mysterious sounds that he needed to investigate. All was still.

Back inside his home, he locked up, then checked all the windows. Still unable to relax—and knowing he wouldn't sleep if he tried—he kept the gun with him and stretched out on the couch, ready to defend his home and protect the woman he was growing to care about way too much.

NINE

Shopping with Nick had seemed like a good idea last night. Unfortunately, in the light of day, Heidi's indecision weighed on her, leaving her embarrassed that Nick had to see her at her worst. Indecisive and incredibly picky.

She finally stomped out of the last store, crossed the street and found a booth in the small café. He followed at a brisk trot and handed her the two bags he'd so chivalrously carried for her. "Hold on to these. I'll be right back."

Fortunately, since it was two in the afternoon, the café's busy lunchtime rush was over and only a few stragglers remained. When he returned, he set in front of her a steaming mug of hot chocolate topped with whipped cream and a caramel drizzle. He'd gotten himself the same, along with a cinnamon roll that he set in between them. "Let's eat."

She blew out a breath and couldn't help the smile that wanted to curve her lips. "Thanks. I'm sorry I'm such a lunatic when it comes to shopping. I'm just so particular and I loved my wardrobe. Before it was incinerated, anyway."

"It's okay. Shopping for clothes can be hard."

"And I don't really need that much. Not with wearing a uniform every day."

"I get it."

"And I'm not used to shopping with a guy. You make me nervous."

He slid around to sit beside her. She'd chosen a corner booth for a multitude of reasons. The most important one being it was away from windows and doors and she didn't have to worry about someone shooting her in the back. "I don't want to make you nervous," he said as he scooted closer.

She cleared her throat. "Ah. Well, that's not helping."

"Why?"

"Because you're a little close." And he smelled really, really good.

"I like being close to you," he said softly.

"You do?" The squeak those words came out on could not belong to her.

"I do. You've gotten under my skin, Heidi Jenks, and I'm really not sure what to do about it."

"I...um...hope you're not asking me for advice, because I'm really not sure what to—"

His lips cut off her words. She froze, unsure what to do. Then instinct took over and she closed her eyes, lifted her hand to cup his cheek and let the lovely sensation of being kissed by Nick Donovan wash over her.

When he lifted his head, the tender expression in his eyes was nearly her undoing. "Well, I suppose that's one thing to do when someone's under your skin," she whispered.

He grinned. Then shook his head. "Like I said, I like you, Heidi. A lot. And I'm not sure it's a good idea."

"Why? Because I'm a reporter?"

"No, you pretty much opened my eyes on that one. I'm not worried about your motives or that you're only out for a story. I've seen your heart. You're very good at what you do and you put others first. It's obvious you care and that's why people respond so well to you."

Tears welled before she could stop them. One dripped down onto her cheek and he swiped it away with a thumb. "Thank you for that," she whispered. "I needed to hear it. I need someone to believe that I'm not the anonymous blogger and that I have integrity. I mean, *I* know it, and usually, that's enough. But this time, I think I just need others to see it, too, I guess. Which is probably stupid."

"It's not stupid," he said. "It's human."

She smiled. "I'm definitely human. With all of the shortcomings and failures that come with it, but I'm trying to rise above those, you know?"

"I know. I'm right there with you."

"You? You seem pretty perfect to me."

He let out a low chuckle. "Trust me, I'm far from perfect."

"Oh, that's right. You do have that whole distrust of reporters thing." She sighed. "But you definitely have a reason to feel that way."

"I told you. I don't feel that way about you." He leaned over and kissed her again. A light, sweet, comforting kiss that she wished could go on forever. It made her forget about the troubles surrounding her, the fear and anxiety, the despair about her lost home… everything.

When he pulled back, he enveloped her in a hug that took away what breath she had left. "I trust *you*, Heidi."

* * *

Nick listened to the words coming out of his mouth with something resembling shock. Had he just told Heidi, a reporter, that he trusted her?

Apparently. And the funny thing was, he did. He'd seen her in action. She was a go-getter and good at what she did, but she didn't step on other people or lie to get her story.

He looked down at her. "Are you all right now?"

"Yes. I'm much better. Thank you."

"Ready to do more shopping?"

She groaned and he laughed. They finished the cinnamon roll and the hot chocolate, making small talk, and Nick realized not for the first time that he could fall for this woman.

And he really shouldn't.

Why not?

Because she was a reporter.

But he trusted her, right?

Until he didn't.

"You ready to go?"

She wiped her mouth with a napkin. "Sure. I guess so."

For the next hour, they continued their shopping, with Heidi a little more relaxed and Nick a lot more conflicted. He liked Heidi. A lot. He'd been honest with that statement. And while he trusted her in the moment he told her he did, he wondered if that would last. Then he was disgusted with himself for his wishy-washy feelings. He should be able to give her the benefit of the doubt.

His gaze followed her reflection in the storefront

glass as they passed a shop advertising fresh fudge. He grabbed her hand and pulled her inside.

"Whoa." She lifted her head and inhaled deeply. "Mmm. The smells in here are intoxicating."

"I have a really hard time resisting fudge—and strawberry shortcake. What's your favorite dessert?"

"Besides chocolate turtle cheesecake? Chocolate turtle fudge."

"Give me a pound of the chocolate turtle and the peanut butter cookie crunch," he told the woman behind the counter.

When he turned back to Heidi, he caught sight of a man in a hoodie just outside the shop window. He was just standing there, his face shadowed by the hood, his hands shoved into the front pockets of his jeans. Nick frowned as he pulled out his debit card and passed it to the clerk. She swiped it and handed it back to him.

He took a second to scrawl a tip and signature. When he looked back, the man was gone.

He sighed. Paranoia was not a good thing. Then again...

Picking up the bags, he nodded to the door. "Ready?"

"Sure." She unwrapped a piece of the fudge and took a bite. Then gave a piece to him.

He chewed and smiled, but his attention was on the window. "Stay behind me, okay?"

Her eyes sharpened and she frowned. "What is it?"

"I'm not sure. Maybe nothing."

"Maybe something. What?"

"A guy watching through the window. Could have been nothing, but it's making me nervous."

"You think someone followed us here?"

He shook his head. "I don't know. I was watching and didn't see anyone, but that doesn't mean someone couldn't have trailed us."

They stepped out of the shop and Nick made sure to angle himself in front of her. People walked on the sidewalk to his right and to his left. Across the street, a family sat outside at one of the tables belonging to the little café.

But he saw no man in a dark hoodie.

While he knew he hadn't imagined seeing the man, maybe he was overreacting. Nevertheless, he gripped the bags tighter with one hand and slipped his other under her elbow as they walked.

"You're making me really nervous, Nick."

"Sorry."

They made it to his car with no incident, but the whole way he felt like he had a target on his back. Or Heidi did. Once they were on the way back to the base, Nick watched the rearview mirror.

"Do you see someone?" Heidi asked him.

"Maybe. A car pulled out of the parking lot behind us." He flexed his fingers on the wheel. Then relaxed. "And it just turned off."

"I'm sorry you've gotten all caught up in this," she said softly.

"Not your fault."

"Maybe not, but I still feel bad about it. When do you think you'll hear something about the explosions? Like whether or not they're related?"

He shrugged. "Probably in the next day or so."

She fell silent and he continued to watch the road, the mirrors, the surrounding area. The shopping center wasn't too far from the base, and soon, he was turning into the entrance.

Back at his house, he helped her unload the bags and led the way inside.

He found his grandfather talking to Felicity James. She stood. "Hello, Heidi, I just stopped by to check on you."

Heidi set her bags on the end of the sofa and gave her friend a hug. "Thank you. I'm doing all right. I'm just in the process of replacing my wardrobe. I'll be sure to get your clothes washed and back to you soon."

"There's no hurry on that. Any news on who was responsible for the explosion?"

"No, not yet."

She nodded. "Well, I brought a casserole and pie for you guys for dinner. I won't stay. I just wanted to check on you."

"Thanks, Felicity, I appreciate it."

"And…"

"And what?"

"Have you seen the latest blog post?"

Heidi groaned. "Seriously? There's more?"

"Yes. Westley and Justin are fit to be tied. This anonymous blogger is causing everyone on the investigative team a lot of grief. Are you sure you don't know who it is?"

Heidi froze. "What are you saying?"

"Nothing. And I'm not accusing. I just thought maybe a name might have occurred to you, or—"

"Westley told you to come over here and ask me this, didn't he?"

A flush crept up her friend's neck and into her cheeks. She groaned. "Yes. I'm sorry."

"It's not Heidi," Nick said from behind her.

Felicity stilled, then looked past Heidi to meet Nick's eyes. "I don't think so, either."

"Then convince your husband and tell him to leave her alone. Please."

Biting her lip, Felicity gave a slow nod. "All right. I'll do my best."

"Thank you."

She rose. "Well, I guess I'll take off. Heidi, if you need anything, you'll call, right?"

"Of course. Thank you."

"No hard feelings?"

"None toward you." She scowled.

Felicity gave her a small smile, then left. Heidi's shoulders wilted. An arm slid around them. "She means well."

"I know." She sniffed. And then she followed her nose into the kitchen. "That smells amazing."

"Guess we know what we're having for dinner."

"So," the colonel said, "who's up for a game of Scrabble?"

Heidi grinned. "I love that game. And I'm good at it, too."

Nick raised a brow. "Hmm. We'll see about that."

"Is that a challenge, First Lieutenant?"

"It is, First Lieutenant."

"You're on."

It was a fun evening. They played two games and ate half the casserole and the entire apple pie before calling it a night.

On his way to his room, Nick cupped her cheek. "I'm glad you're here, Heidi." He paused. "Let me clarify. I'm not glad for the reason you needed a roof over your head, but I'm glad Gramps and I were able to provide this one."

"Thanks, Nick." He smiled, and she watched him disappear into his room before slipping into hers.

She lay in bed and stared at the ceiling. She'd enjoyed today. She'd actually had fun in a way she hadn't had in a very long time. Scrabble had been her dad's favorite game and playing tonight had resurrected memories she'd thought she'd tucked away forever. Good memories, but still painful because they brought home how much she missed her father.

But Nick's grandfather was clever and smart. He'd won the first game before Heidi had trounced them in the second. Nick had simply shaken his head and declared the tiles had been against him. "How am I supposed to come up with a word with six vowels and a Z? No one can win with that."

His good-natured grumbling had endeared him to her even more, and she'd been astonished at how fast the time had flown.

While she'd been granted more time off due to the explosion, Heidi planned to get back to work on the story of the stolen medals first thing in the morning.

Fatigue pulled at her and she gave in to it. Feeling safe and well guarded, Heidi let her eyes close.

Only to have them fly open after what seemed like seconds, but according to the clock, was two hours. One in the morning. What had awakened her?

She sat up and listened.

Voices.

Nothing that sounded alarming, but the reporter in her perked up. She rolled out of bed and pulled on a new pair of jeans and a lightweight sweater she'd purchased on the shopping trip with Nick.

She opened the window and the voices sharpened. "...just sitting here. I say you need to call the trainer. It's probably one of the still-missing dogs. Call Westley James. He can be here in no time."

Heidi shoved her feet into the tennis shoes next to her bed, grabbed her recorder and notebook, and hurried into the living area, where she found Nick standing in the foyer, hand on the doorknob. "I'm just going to see what's going on," he said. "You can go on back to bed."

Heidi laughed. "Right. Let's go."

"Heid—"

She slipped around him, turned the knob and was on the porch before he could blink. She thought he might have emitted a low growl, but she was more interested in what was happening over near the entrance gate. Since Nick and his grandfather lived in the end unit of the row of houses, they were closest to the gate entrance.

Which explained why she heard the commotion. With her voice-activated recorder in her pocket, notebook in hand and a protesting Nick right behind her, she hurried to see what was going on.

Nick pulled up beside her when she stopped near the growing crowd of onlookers. "What is it?" she asked the airman nearest her.

"A dog showed up."

"One of the working dogs that are still missing?" Heidi asked.

"That's what they're trying to figure out. Master Sergeant James should be here soon as well as Rusty

Morton." Rusty was one of the trainers from the K-9 center.

Rusty arrived first, followed by Westley and Felicity. "What do we have here?" Westley asked.

A young airman stepped forward. He was one of the guards who monitored the base entrance gate. "Sir, I was on duty when I noticed this dog just outside the gate. He simply walked up and sat down as though waiting for someone to let him inside."

"Does he have a collar?"

"I didn't get close enough to check, sir."

Westley nodded and approached the open gate. "That looks like Patriot." The German shepherd watched him, ears up, tail wagging. "He's friendly like Patriot." Westley murmured, "Stay."

He reached for the tag and Heidi moved so she could see while describing the scene into her voice recorder. Nick stayed by her side and she thought he was looking everywhere but at the action in front of them. It hit her that he was nervous about her being out in the open.

But she was surrounded by people.

"His tag says Poco." Westley looked back at Rusty. "Call him."

"Poco! Come!" The dog's ears twitched, but he didn't move.

"Try Patriot," Westley said.

"Patriot, come!" The dog bounded over to the trainer, who scratched his ears. Rusty looked up. "This is Patriot, all right."

Other than his coat needing a good brushing, he looked healthy enough to her.

Rusty looked up. "Someone's been feeding him. Or he's found a well-stocked trash can. Not sure what made him come home, but I'm glad he's here." Westley nodded. "This gives me hope. Patriot's one of the best. One of our superstar dogs. If he found his way home, then maybe the other three will, too." He spotted Nick in the crowd and waved him over. Heidi stayed on his heels. Westley's brows rose at her presence, but she simply shot him a smile. He turned his attention to Nick. "I want to meet with the investigative team as soon as possible. We need to go house to house and see if anyone has noticed who's been taking care of this dog. Tell them his name is Poco since that's what the person would have called him."

Heidi's jaw dropped. "It's one in the morning. You're going to wake people up?"

"We do what we have to do in an investigation. You know that."

"Of course."

Zip it, Heidi.

Heidi stepped up to Westley. "Where do you think he came from?"

"I don't know. We're working on finding out."

"So, if Patriot got off the base, then did the other dogs get off, too?"

"Working on that, too. Wish I had the answers to those questions."

"And why is he wearing a different collar?" Nick asked. "Someone changed it."

"So, this guy has been missing for months and now he shows up out of the blue," Westley said. "He's on the skinny side, but not starving so he's getting food from somewhere." He ran a hand over the dog's coat. "Needs a good brushing."

"Someone's been taking care of him," Heidi said.

Westley examined the dog's paws. "And probably someone who's fairly close to the base. He didn't walk too far to get here. Paws are in fine shape."

"What's being done to find the other twenty dogs, sir? Especially the three others that Nick said were so special?" Heidi held her pen over her notebook.

"We've got people looking for them."

Heidi wasn't going to be deterred by his vague answer. "Looking where, sir?"

"Off base." He quirked a smile at her, not at all fazed by her persistence. "Is this going to be the headline in the morning?"

She shrugged. "Of course. It's news."

"Yep, I guess it is."

"Are you planning to offer a reward for the safe return of the other dogs now that you know it's possible they could be nearby?" she asked.

"We were hoping it wouldn't come to that, but it's possible we're going to have to do that. That's enough questions for now."

He started to walk away, but she kept up with him. "Just a couple more, if you don't mind." She didn't give him a chance to answer. "Has anyone discovered Sullivan's motive in releasing the dogs a few months ago? Have you figured out what reason he could possibly have?"

Westley sighed. "Come on, Heidi, you've already asked me these questions. I didn't have answers then, and I still don't. I wish I did. Now, that's enough. I've got a case to work." He turned to the young man who'd clipped a leash on the collar. "All right, Rusty, get him to the vet and have him checked out, will you? The rest of you fan out and let's see if anyone's going to admit to missing a dog named Poco. Someone put that collar on him, and I want to know who it was. Don't let on that he's a base dog. Just act like he's a stray."

Rusty left with Patriot, while several members of the investigative team who'd been called in left to begin knocking on doors.

Westley nodded to Nick and Annie. "Are you still on Heidi duty?"

"I am."

Heidi duty? She grimaced, but let it go. Already, she was forming the article in her head while she continued to watch everything play out.

She finally nudged Nick. "Come on, let's go. I want to get the reaction of the neighbors being questioned at one in the morning."

He frowned. "I don't like that we're out in the open like this."

"I don't like it, either, but honestly, I'm not going to let this guy keep me from doing my job. I've got a story to write and I need something to put in it." She scanned the area and, across the street, spotted two MPs on the front porch of the closest house. She headed that way and heard Nick's exasperated sigh. "Fine, I'll go and watch your back."

"Thanks." Although, she knew he might not spot a sniper. That worried her, but what was she going to do? Put her life on hold until whoever was after her was caught?

She grimaced. It might be the smart thing to do, but..." My dad wouldn't let this stop him," she said softly. "He'd go right into the fray and get the story."

"But—"

She cut off his words and shot him a sad smile. "I

know. But he ended up dead. That's what you're think-ing, aren't you?"

He shrugged. "Thinking, yes. Saying, no." He ab-sently scratched Annie's ears and the dog leaned into him.

"It's okay. I can say it." She sighed and shook her head. "I just can't sit back and do nothing."

"I know. Let's just be careful."

"You're still sticking with me?"

"Those are the orders."

"Right." She looked at the ground. "Of course."

He tilted her chin to look her in the eye. "And if they weren't orders, I'd request them."

"You would?"

"I would."

"Why?"

"Because."

With another roll of her eyes, she did her best to hold back the smile that wanted to spread across her face. "All right, then. Let's go."

They approached the nearest MP speaking to the sleepy-looking woman who'd opened the screen door. She shook her head. "I don't know anyone who owns a dog named Poco. Sorry. Can't believe you woke me up for that." She slammed the door.

Heidi shook her head.

They walked to the next home and for the next hour they got the same response—and several more slammed doors.

Nick cupped her elbow and brought her to a stop. "Are you ready to head back yet?"

With a sigh, she nodded. "I guess so. This is look-ing pretty pointless."

Nick turned her back toward his house. "What would you think of leaving the base? Going into hiding until all of this is resolved?"

"What do you think I think about that?"

"Right. I kind of figured that would be what you thought."

She bit her lip. "I can't hide, Nick. Even though that's my first instinct, I just can't do it. This guy wants me scared and cowering."

"No, I don't think he does."

"What do you mean?"

"I think he just wants you dead, Heidi, and that's what scares me."

TEN

"Come on, Heidi," Nick said. "There's nothing more to do here tonight."

She looked up from the little black notebook, then tucked it into her pocket with a sigh. "I guess you're right, but I've got some good stuff to work with."

"I suppose you're going to write this up for tomorrow," a voice said from behind Nick. He turned to see John Robinson looking at Heidi. That man was as annoying as a sandstorm.

"No, John, I'm going to ignore it—and my job. What do you think?"

The man's eyes flashed and he stepped closer to Heidi. "I think you'd better watch your step or I may have to go to Lou."

Nick ventured forward. "Hey, Robinson, you're out of line. Watch your space."

John looked back over his shoulder at Nick, then brushed past Heidi. She stumbled back a couple of steps and Nick reached forward to grasp her forearm. "You're dangerously close to assault, Robinson."

"Sorry, sorry." He held a hand up. "I stumbled." He smirked and stalked off.

Heidi stood glaring after the man and Nick turned her toward his house. "Forget him for tonight. Let's go home."

"Yeah. I've got a story to write."

Nick's heart rate finally returned to normal after he shut the door on the outside world. And whoever wanted her dead. He'd been blunt with her a few minutes ago, but the truth was, he was scared for her. His immediate attraction to her the first time he'd met her months ago had sent him scurrying. There'd been no way he'd allow himself to be drawn to a reporter.

But now that he'd gotten to know her, all he wanted to do was protect her.

"You know you're not making this easy," he said, keeping his voice low so as not to wake his grandfather. Nick had sent the man a text just in case he woke up and wondered where they were. No return text said he'd probably slept through everything.

"Making what easy?"

"Keeping you safe."

"Oh." Her brows drew together. She went to sit on the couch and he followed her.

"Someone has shot at you and blown up your house, Heidi."

"I'm aware, thanks. But you know what I've noticed?"

"What's that?"

"Everything he's done has been so that he had a way to escape. The bombing of the training center? He had his escape plan in place. The shooting at the church? He was in a speeding car that got away. The bombing of my home? Same thing. He had it rigged to blow either at a certain time or when he could set off the explosion with a remote. A cell phone or something."

Nick frowned. She was right.

Heidi continued, "And he always seems to target me when there aren't many people around."

"So, you think if you're surrounded by people, you'll be all right?" he asked.

"It seems to look that way. Tonight, I was around a ton of people and he didn't try anything."

"I'm not sure that logic works."

She raked a hand through her hair. "I don't know. I just know that I can't hide." She stood and paced the room till she stopped by the mantel. "I'm taking precautions, I'm being careful. I'm not stupid and I don't have a death wish, but I won't hide."

He nodded. "I can't say I don't understand because I'd probably feel the same way if I were in your shoes."

"Really?"

"Yes. Didn't say I liked it, but I do understand."

"Thank you."

Standing, he held out a hand to her. She took it and stepped forward. "I'm headed for bed. You should do the same."

"I know. But I still have to write the story about Patriot's return. I'll see you in the morning?"

"I have an early meeting with Westley and Justin about the Red Rose Killer. What are your plans?"

"I have a meeting with Lou at eight thirty. Then I have to write up my latest personality piece." She smiled. "You wouldn't want to volunteer for a spot, would you?"

"Me? No, thanks."

"I figured, but I had to try."

"Go to bed, Heidi. We'll catch up tomorrow." Instead of letting her go, he pulled her close and slanted his lips across hers. It was an impromptu action that surprised him. And yet, he didn't regret it. The kiss lasted a few seconds before he ended it with a hug.

When he finally let go of her, she looked…bemused. "I hope that was okay."

"Oh, it was more than okay," she replied. "Confusing, but a good kiss."

He chuckled, then sighed. "I don't mean to be confusing. The more I'm around you, the more I like you. The more I like you, the more I question my sanity."

"Well… Thanks?"

Grimacing, he raked a hand through his short hair. "That didn't come out right. I'm conflicted about you, but not enough to stay away from you. How's that for honesty?"

Her eyes glittered up at him. "I like honesty. And I like you, too." She patted his cheek. "Good night, Nick."

And then she was walking away from him. He waited until he heard her door close before he went to bed. "Lord, don't let me mess this up. Protect Heidi from whoever is after her. And, Lord? Please, protect me from myself."

Morning came faster than Heidi would have liked and she found herself scrambling to beat the clock. Fatigue pulled at her as she got ready, and for the first time since taking the job at the base, she considered calling in sick. After everything that had happened, she didn't think Lou would give her any grief about it, but the thought of John Robinson had her pushing forward. Which was silly. Why did she even care what he thought?

She didn't, really. But she did care about her job and what her boss thought. Once she was dressed for the day, she reached for her recorder and the little black notebook and frowned when she couldn't find the recorder. She'd used both last night and had them in her jeans pocket. She'd only used her notebook last night to write the story about Patriot's return because she had everything she'd needed. She hadn't bothered to check the recording.

Where had she put it?

A glance at the clock sent her scurrying. No matter, she'd have to find it later. She stopped. But what if it was just lying around somewhere and someone picked it up? *No, please no.* She'd recorded her thoughts on just about everything she'd written in her little black notebook. If someone found it…

She scoured her room once more and when she came up empty, she gave a groan of frustration. She'd *really* have to find it later. But for now, being late wasn't an option. She slipped out the door and climbed into the rental her insurance company had delivered late last night.

Her own car had been parked in the driveway and had taken a hard hit when the house had exploded. Most likely, it would be declared a total loss. She tried not to be too depressed about the fact that her house, her car and all of her belongings were gone, but kept reminding herself that she had survived and no one else had been hurt. Doing her best to be grateful for that, she parked and made her way inside the newspaper office. She called out greetings to the few coworkers she passed as she headed to Lou's office.

He looked up at her knock. "Heidi! I didn't expect to see you this morning."

She frowned. "I emailed and told you I would be here."

"I got it, then saw John this morning and he said he wasn't sure you'd make it."

Anger seethed inside her. "John has no idea of my schedule. Please don't rely on his word."

Her boss gave her a shrewd look. "Everything okay between you two?"

Heidi gave him a tight smile. "Just fine, sir."

"Hmm." Heidi thought that sound held a world of skepticism but didn't bother to address it. She would handle John Robinson without dragging her boss into the fray. Only as a last resort would she bring her troubles to him.

"I'm here, sir," she said.

"Just wanted to say great job on the piece you sent last night. That was some mighty interesting stuff."

"Well, thanks, I appreciate that. I just happened to hear the commotion outside and joined in."

"I liked the dog story, too. We'll run that one tomorrow."

She frowned. "Wait a minute. Isn't the dog story what we were just talking about?"

He eyed her. "Are you losing it, Jenks?"

"I didn't think so until right now. Exactly what story are you talking about, sir?"

"I'm talking about the one you sent on how you overheard a conversation between two high-ranking investigative officials and their speculation that the serial killer is back on base. And how he was targeting everyone on the base now. I can't believe the guy actually called in and gave them a heads-up that he was going to start killing again and officials have covered it up." He leaned back and crossed his arms. "You're a sneaky one, aren't you?"

"Sneaky? Overheard?" She sputtered. "Wait a minute, I didn't write anything like that."

"I don't know where you got the information from, but it's good. Just the kind of investigative reporting I like to see. Funny, I figured Robinson would explode when I told him I was printing it, but it didn't seem to faze him."

Panic rose within her. She leaned forward. "I didn't do a piece on the Red Rose Killer. Or the fact that he was back on base."

It was his turn to frown. "What are *you* talking about? You sent it about five hours ago. It went out in this morning's paper—and let me tell you, it was a chore to get it out on time. I know it's not a huge paper, but it's still a lot of work."

He picked up the paper sitting on the desk beside him and handed it to her. Heidi stared at the front-page headline—and her byline—in horror. SERIAL KILLER BACK ON BASE.

"I didn't send this! I didn't even write this. And it's not even true! No one said Sullivan called in with more threats. No one's covering anything up. Those are lies." She didn't have to read the article to know she didn't write it. "Lou, please tell me this isn't happening." She couldn't help reading a few lines, and her heart dipped into her shoes. "No, no, no, no, no. Oh, no. No one on this investigative team will talk to me ever again. I've

got their trust now and this piece is going to kill it." Not
to mention Nick. Oh, Nick…he would think… "How
did you get this? From my email account?"

"Yep."

Heidi stood and paced in front of his desk. "I don't
understand. How can this be?"

"Heidi, calm down. Are you telling me that you
didn't send it?"

How many times did she have to say it? Placing
her palms on his desk, she leaned forward and looked
him in the eye. "That's *exactly* what I'm telling you."

"Then you're telling me I just printed an article that
can get me sued?"

She paused and bit her lip. "Yes. Maybe. The information is mostly accurate, but it wasn't supposed
to be announced in the paper. I wasn't even supposed
to know it. But the other parts are pure fiction." She
slumped into the chair and covered her eyes. She was
so done. No, she wasn't. She hadn't done this. How
had this happened?

"How did this come from your email account, then?"

She narrowed her eyes. "John Robinson. He did this.
Somehow, someway, he got that information and used
it. He wants me off this paper and thinks he's found
a way to make that happen. If no one will talk to me,
what kind of reporter will I be?"

Lou scoffed. "What? Even if Robinson is inclined
to do so, how would he get into your email?"

"I don't know, but he's resented me from day one.
He was the only reporter on staff before the paper expanded to include me. All of a sudden, he had to share
stories. I guess he doesn't like that." She picked up the

paper again and settled back into the chair to read, ignoring the feel of his eyes boring into her.

The more she read, the sicker she came. "You have to do something," she finally whispered. "Print a retraction, something."

"But you said most of the information is accurate?"

"Yes, but some of it's not. It's going to cause panic on the base. The true elements are part of an ongoing investigation. As soon as Nick reads this, he's—" She bit her lip and fought the tears as she pictured his reaction. His feeling of betrayal.

"We'll fix the parts that are false, but the rest of the story stays."

"You realize this is just going to be fuel for the fire. Everyone is *really* going to think I'm the anonymous blogger now. They'll believe that not only am I releasing confidential information, I'm making stuff up. And I'm not! I only came by that information by accident and—"

Lou's tight jaw said he wasn't happy. At all. "All right, I'll talk to Robinson, but unless you have proof…"

"The proof is right there in front of you," she snapped. "I have to find Nick."

"Heidi—"

Her phone rang. She snagged it and lifted it to her ear. "Nick, I'm so sor—"

"This isn't Nick," the voice said. "This is Mark Hanson. You interviewed me about the stolen medals."

"Oh! I'm sorry, I thought you were someone else. How can I help you?" She was only half listening as her mind raced with how to explain this to Nick when she couldn't even explain it to herself. She'd jumped to the conclusion that John was behind the article, but could it be someone else? She couldn't imagine who.

"I've thought of something else you can add to the story," Hanson was saying. "I think I may know who the thief is."

He now had her attention. "Who?"

"No," he said, his voice now a whisper. "I think he's following me. I've got to go. Meet me in the alley behind the Winged Java in fifteen minutes and I'll tell you everything."

"No. Let's meet inside the cafe."

"I can't. He might see me! If you want the information, be there." He hung up.

She looked at her boss. "We're not done. I want a meeting with you and John Robinson as soon as possible."

"I'll talk to him. Where are you going?"

"To find out who the medal thief is and then to find Nick to explain that I didn't write that article and have no idea how John got that information—" She stopped. Yes, she did know. When he'd bumped into her last night. He'd lifted her recorder from her jeans pocket and listened to it. And wrote that piece.

She spun on her heel and raced out the door.

Nick set the paper aside and pinched the bridge of his nose. Betrayal, hot and swift, flowed through him. He stood and threw his mug across his office. The ceramic shattered and spilled coffee to the floor.

Annie jumped to her feet and barked. He settled a hand on her head. "Sorry, girl. Didn't mean to scare you."

Justin appeared in the doorway. "Nick?"

"I can't believe she would do this." He tossed the paper onto his desk as though it might bite him.

"I saw the article this morning," Justin said. "Before the meeting."

"And you didn't say anything?"

"Wasn't sure what to say, to be honest. I know the blogger posted that we suspected Sullivan was back on base, but that was just conjecture on her part. That article, though, is about a direct conversation people will be more inclined to believe. But the other stuff…that's just not true. I figured you may have told her some of the facts she got right, and she made up the rest."

"I didn't tell her. She overheard Westley and me discussing it." Nick pressed his palms to his burning eyes and let out a humorless laugh. "She promised not to write it." His gaze met Justin's. "And I actually believed she wouldn't. And the stuff that's not true?" He shook his head. "I'm an idiot." He stood. "I'm supposed to be protecting her." That was going to be interesting. How he would manage to do that and keep his anger at her under control at the same time, he wasn't sure. It would be a huge test of his will.

"I put someone on her so you could be here for the meeting." Justin cleared his throat.

"I know. That's not what I meant. I'm supposed to be protecting her and right now, I don't even want to be around her." He glanced at the man leaning against the doorjamb. "I thought she was different."

"I did, too. I've never seen an article by her that wasn't well researched and well written. This one, though? It's like a different person wrote that piece."

"Well, it wasn't. Her name's right there under the headline."

"Yeah. Doesn't make sense."

"Oh, it makes sense all right." Bitterness, so potent he could taste it, rose within him. "I made a huge mistake trusting her. A reporter!" He slammed a hand on his desk and Annie woofed again. "Apparently, I'm as dim-witted as they come. I guess I just have to learn things the hard way."

"Ask her about it before you take her apart. She may have an explanation."

Nick reached for the phone. "Oh, you better believe I'm going to ask her. I'm going to find her right now." If anyone would know where she was, it would be her boss.

When Heidi pulled into the parking lot of the Winged Java, she noted it was busy and crowded. Probably why Mark wanted to meet her in the alleyway behind it. She pulled around the side of the building, down the sidewalk and around back. Putting the car in Park, she looked around trying to spot the man. When she'd interviewed him two weeks ago, he'd been eager to tell his story and hadn't seemed like he was holding anything back. But if he'd decided he knew the thief, then she was going to find out.

She sat in her car for the next several minutes, watching, noting that it was a pretty deserted area. Which made her feel a little nervous. She hesitated. Was she doing the right thing? Her dad would have gone after the story. He would have met anyone, anytime, anywhere. But she wasn't her dad. She'd promised to be careful. This wasn't being careful.

She cranked the car and backed away from the alley.

A shadow to her left made her jerk. Then her window shattered and glass rained down over her.

With a scream, Heidi hit the gas. The vehicle lurched forward and slammed into the side of the building.

A hard hand grabbed her ponytail. Pain shot through her head and down the base of her neck when her attacker yanked her from her car. She let out another scream and threw an elbow back. She connected and her attacker let out a harsh grunt.

His grip relaxed a fraction and Heidi lashed out with a foot, connecting with a hard knee. In a dark hoodie, the man cried out and went to the asphalt.

And she was free.

Until he lunged forward to wrap a hand around her ankle.

"Hey!"

The voice registered in her mind. Nick. Relief flowed through her, but she was still in the attacker's grip.

"Let her go!" Nick yelled.

The attacker's other hand reached inside his zippered hoodie, causing Heidi to scream. "He's going for a gun!"

In the next instant, somehow she was free.

The release of her ankle threw her off balance and she fell hard to her knees. Pain shot through her. She'd probably reopened the healing wounds, but at the moment that was the least of her worries.

Nick had his grip locked around her attacker's wrist and was wrestling him for the weapon.

ELEVEN

Nick's grip slipped and he clenched the muscles in his hand while he brought a knee up to the man's midsection. It was a glancing blow and did little damage other than to distract him a fraction. But it allowed Nick to get him on the ground.

In his peripheral vision, Nick saw a boot lash out. It connected with the side of the man's head and he went still, those icy blue eyes glazing over. The weapon fell from his hand and Nick scooped it up to aim it at him, then glanced up to see Isaac and Oliver. "Thanks. Can one of you check and see if he has any more weapons on him?"

A quick but thorough frisk by Oliver found him weapon-free. And glaring. Nick glanced at Heidi, noting her pale face, but set chin. "You okay?"

"Yes. Thanks."

He turned his attention back to the man on the ground. "Well, it's good to finally meet you," Nick said. Unfortunately, he didn't recognize him. Without taking his eyes from his captive, Nick asked, "The MPs on the way?"

"They are," Oliver said.

"Thanks for your help."

"Glad to do it," Isaac said. "What's the deal with this guy?"

Heidi stepped forward and looked at her attacker. "I recognize him. He's the one who blew up the training center—and probably my home."

"And shot at you in the parking lot of the church?" Nick asked.

"Possibly that, too."

The man on the ground moved as though to get up. "Stay put." Nick gestured with the gun.

The man stilled.

Two Security Forces vehicles pulled into the parking lot, lights flashing. The MPs approached, hands on their weapons. One covered the man and cuffed him while the other took the perp's weapon from Nick.

"What happened here?" that officer said.

"He attacked me," Heidi said, pointing to the blue-eyed man. She explained that he was the one she'd seen running from the training center just before it exploded.

"So, you're the one," one of the MPs said. "Let's go."

"Wait a minute," Nick said, stepping forward. "I'm part of the investigative team looking for Boyd Sullivan. We're not sure the bombing has anything to do with him, but do you mind if I ask this guy a couple of questions?"

"Go ahead."

Nick faced the cuffed assailant. "Why did you blow up the training center?"

"I didn't."

"Yes, you did," Heidi said.

"And if you don't cooperate, you're going away for attempted murder," Nick added.

The ice in those blue eyes melted a tad and a flicker of fear darkened them. "Murder! I didn't murder anyone."

"But you tried." At first, Nick didn't think the guy was going to talk. "Look, we've got you dead to rights here. We've got witnesses who saw your attack on Heidi. And she saw you come out of the training center just before it exploded. We've even got security footage of you." He snagged a handful of the hoodie and gave it a not-so-gentle yank before he dropped his hand. "This will match up to what's on video. You're going to go down for that. If you cooperate, you might get off with a lighter sentence. What's your name?"

The guy licked his lips and his shoulders dropped. "Airman Lance Gentry. And I really didn't mean for anyone to get hurt. The place was supposed to be empty."

"Right," Heidi said. "You didn't mean for anyone to get hurt. That's why you shot at me in the church parking lot."

He scowled. "Once I knew you could identify me..." He looked away. "I got scared," he said. "I had to get rid of you because I can't go anywhere on base without fear of being recognized. I can't live like that. If you were out of the picture, even if someone thought I was the guy, you wouldn't be around to confirm it." His eyes darted to the MPs listening to the exchange. "Guess I'm done now."

"Why are you doing all this?" Nick asked. "We know you went after Heidi because she could identify you. But why blow up the training center? That was the catalyst for all of this."

"Money. Why else?"

Nick exchanged a confused glance with Isaac and Oliver.

"Someone paid you to set the bomb?" Isaac asked.

"Yeah."

"Who?"

"I don't know his name, he didn't say. But he knew I needed money so he'd obviously done his homework on me."

"How did he contact you?"

"Knocked on the door at my house."

"Do you live on base?"

"Yeah." He looked down and scuffed his foot.

"But why stay here? Why take the risk of being caught? Especially since you knew Heidi could identify you if she saw you?"

Gentry lifted his head, nostrils flared. "He still owes me the other half of my money. I had to stay until he paid me. I've been looking for him, but haven't come across him yet. But he'll be back. I was just waiting for him to put in an appearance, then I was going to grab my money and get out of here."

"You could have lain low."

"Can't find a guy when you're not looking for him. I had to be out and about on the base. But every time I set foot outside my house, I was afraid someone was going to spot me."

Nick pulled his phone from the clip on his belt and tapped the screen. He pulled up the picture he kept on hand and showed it to the prisoner. "Is that the guy who came knocking?"

Gentry's brows knit and he frowned as he studied the picture. "That's Boyd Sullivan."

"No kidding."

"No, that's not him." Nick sighed and lowered the phone. "Wait. Let me see that again." Nick obliged. "You know, it's possible that could be him. The eyes look the same, but his hair was red and he had a beard."

"That doesn't surprise me. The man is a master of disguises."

"Whoa. Seriously?"

"Seriously," Nick said. "What else can you tell us? Did he say why he wanted the training center blown up?"

"When I asked, he just said he needed a distraction. He needed attention focused on something other than him."

Isaac gave a light snort. "Is he really that stupid to think that we would turn our attention to the explosion and off of him?"

Nick shrugged. "Well, it was one more thing to deal with. And it used resources and cost money. Sullivan is angry. He's out for revenge on those he feels have wronged him in some way. If he can cause us grief or inconvenience us in any way, he's going to do it."

Oliver nodded. "You've got a good read on him."

"I do."

"We done here?" The MPs were ready to get their prisoner to booking.

"We're done for now," Nick said. He turned to Heidi. "Done with him, anyway."

Heidi swallowed at the pure ice in Nick's eyes. She'd thought Gentry had a cold stare. He had nothing on Nick. "Can we talk?"

"We can," he answered in a clipped tone.

"Where?"

"Where we won't be overheard."

"Are you going to yell?" she asked him.

"Probably."

"Then let's go back to your place."

He eyed her with a flicker of confusion before his gaze hardened once more into unreadable chips of blue. "Fine. My grandfather is out today volunteering at the food bank."

She started for the rental, then stopped. "I guess they'll need my car for evidence."

"They will. You can ride with me."

Not sure she wanted to, she nevertheless didn't argue and climbed in. The ride to his home was made in silence. Heidi almost broke it but decided against it.

When he still didn't speak as he led the way inside, Heidi got an inkling of just how livid he really was. Once in the den, he didn't sit. He simply crossed his arms and faced her, his jaw like granite.

"How did you know I was in trouble?"

"I didn't. I called your boss and asked him to tell me where you were."

"I'm sure glad of that." His glare hadn't lessened with the small talk. "I didn't write that article," she said.

He scoffed and shook his head. "And now you're going to lie to my face?"

Heidi bit her lip and sighed. "I have a feeling who did, but it wasn't me."

His frown deepened to the point she wondered if he'd ever be able to smile again. "How is that even possible? It's in the paper. With your byline."

"John Robinson is how it's possible," she spat. Just saying his name made her want to gag.

"Really? You're going to blame this on him? Your editor published it!"

"Because he thought it was from me! He didn't know I didn't write it."

Nick paced in front of the mantel and raked a hand over his head.

Heidi sighed. "I'm sorry, Nick. I—"

"How?"

"How what?"

"How did he get that information? That was a conversation between you and me and I asked you to keep it quiet. I didn't share that with anyone else who could have passed it on to Robinson."

"My recorder is missing. I think when John bumped into me last night after Patriot was found, he lifted the recorder from my pocket. I haven't had a chance to confront him, but I'm going to do that right now." She headed toward the door and stopped. "But I don't have a car."

"That's okay. I'm not planning to let you face him alone. You almost decked him one time. I think this time I need to come along to keep you from killing him."

Nostrils flaring, she gave him a tight nod. "I think that might be a good idea."

TWELVE

Nick didn't think he'd ever seen her so mad. Actually, the last person he'd seen this angry had been his grandfather when the story about his mother ran. When a person was this angry, it was hard to think straight.

That was why he was going along.

To make sure she didn't do anything that would get her court-martialed.

It didn't take long to track down Robinson. He was at his desk at the newspaper office. When he looked up and saw Heidi bearing down on him, Nick thought he saw a flash of fear in the man's eyes before he lifted his chin in defiance.

Heidi stopped at his desk. "I'd like to speak with you, if that's all right."

Admiring her calmness, Nick decided to stay back and let her handle it. At least until she decided to do him bodily harm.

John cleared his throat and rose. He grabbed his jacket and slipped into it. "Actually, I was just on my way out the door. I just got word that someone was arrested for the training center bombing—and that it's somehow related to the Red Rose Killer."

"Right. I was there."

Robinson froze. "What do you mean you were there? How were *you* there? How many times do I have to tell you that this is *my* story?"

"Then why do you have to steal my notes to get a story printed? Why are you trying so hard to discredit me?"

He flinched. "I don't have to stand here and listen to this garbage." He reached for his car keys and Heidi moved fast, swiping them from the desk. They hit the floor and skidded under the chair. "Hey!"

"You're not going anywhere until you tell Lou what you did." She crossed her arms.

"Are you nuts? You can't just come in here and act like this."

"Like what, John? Like a woman who is confronting a man who is not only a liar, but is willing to do just about anything to ruin her career?"

"I'm not—"

She stepped forward and Nick tensed. His phone rang and he shut it off, unwilling to have any distractions at the moment. He might have to intervene.

But Heidi didn't lift a hand, she simply thrust out her chin. "Yes, you are. You stole my recorder, listened to my notes and picked the one thing that would be sure to bring the hammer down on my head—and possibly my career. All you had to do was make sure those working the investigation wouldn't talk to me. How did you get into my email account?"

"Heidi, you're delusional. I don't know where you're getting all of this, but I've got to go."

"It should be easy enough to prove," Nick said.

Robinson stilled. "What are you talking about?"

"I'm talking about getting one of our IT people over here and letting them examine your computer. If you hacked into Heidi's account, it can be found. If you didn't, then no worries."

Robinson's face went bright red. "This is ridiculous! Get out of my space!"

"Have someone come over and check it out," a voice from behind Nick said.

Heidi spun. "Lou?"

Her boss shrugged and met Nick's gaze. "I don't want to think one of my reporters would do such a thing. Have someone come over and prove he didn't do it. That way, we'll shut everyone up."

"Lou." John rubbed his hand across his lips. "Really? You know I wouldn't—"

"Right. I do. But she doesn't. I'm doing this for her, too."

"Thanks, Lou," Heidi said.

"Don't thank me. You're going to feel pretty foolish when we prove you wrong."

She huffed. "I'll take that chance."

John's jaw got tighter. "Fine!" he exploded. "I did it."

Heidi blinked, her shock holding her silent for a moment. Had John actually admitted it? Nick nudged her and she snapped her mouth shut. Her shoulders slumped. "Why?" she whispered.

John groaned and dropped back into his chair. "Because I'm afraid I'm doing a lousy job on this story and just last week, I overheard Lou saying what a great reporter you were and I thought if I offered some kind of proof that you could possibly be the anonymous blogger—and were reporting false information on top of that—then Lou would get rid of you."

"So you were jealous?" She gaped, then shot a look at her boss, who looked ready to stroke out at any moment. Her gaze swung back to Robinson.

He shrugged.

Heidi turned again to Lou, who gave a disgusted grunt and shook his head. "I'm disappointed in you, Robinson."

"I know, sir. I'm disappointed in myself."

"I should fire you."

Robinson flinched. "Sir…" He lifted a hand as though to argue his case. Then he dropped it. "Whatever you decide, sir."

"Don't fire him," Heidi said.

All eyes turned to her. "What?" Lou asked.

"You don't have to fire him."

"I can't let him get away with this."

"I agree. But…can you just take appropriate disciplinary action and let that be it?"

Lou stared at her for a few seconds before shaking his head. And Nick watched her, his expression a cross between pride and disbelief—and what she thought might be a smidge of admiration mixed in.

She shrugged. "Don't ask me to explain. I can't. I just know I don't want him fired."

"I'll print a retraction, then—or something," Lou said. "Actually, Robinson will. He'll print a confession."

"No," Nick said. "We don't want the paper's reputation to suffer."

"Then how are we going to fix this?" The man looked ready to explode.

"I think," Nick said, "you could have Heidi write a piece about how her email was compromised by someone she trusted, someone who's had a grudge against her and wanted to smear her name and the readers will buy it. Not only is it true, but with everything that's been happening to her—and the fact that she's been reporting on it—the readers will also be sympathetic that she's being targeted. Of course, she will talk about grateful she is for her boss's support and the support of the paper overall."

"I like that," Lou said.

"She can also point out how the paper holds to the highest standards of professionalism."

"Because that's true, too," Lou grunted. He turned his glare on John. "Get out of here until I can calm down long enough to think straight. I'll call you later and let you know what I've decided."

"Yes, sir." He shot a look at Heidi. "I'm sorry. That was lower than low and completely unprofessional. I'm sorry and, if I get to stay, it won't happen again, I promise."

Heidi nodded. As John left, she let out a low, slow breath and ran a hand over her hair. "Wow. I did *not* expect that."

"I don't think any of us did," Lou said.

She looked at Nick. "Can someone really tell if he hacked my email?"

"Probably. Truthfully, I have no idea. Are you ready to go or do you have something else you need to do here?"

She raised a brow at Lou and he waved a hand at her. "Go find a story." He headed for his office. "Preferably who the thief on this base is," he shot over his shoulder. "And I'm not talking about a recorder and story thief, I mean the guy stealing the medals!" His door slammed and Heidi flinched.

Then she cleared her throat. "What now?" she asked Nick.

"I think we should go back to my place and you should rest."

"Or write up my article you just assigned me."

He shot her a wry glance. "Sorry."

"No. It's brilliant. Thank you."

"Of course."

He took her hand and led her out of the building. She took a deep breath and looked around. "It's nice not to be looking over my shoulder and wondering if someone's going to try and kill me."

A low laugh escaped him. "I'm sure." Then he frowned. "But Sullivan is still on the loose. And if Gentry is to be believed, Sullivan had him blow up the center as a distraction, which means Sullivan still has plans. Evil plans, no doubt."

"So, what do we do?"

"We do what we can to find out who's stealing the medals." He looked away, then back at her. "Heidi, I—I apologize."

"To who? For what?"

"To you. For jumping down your throat about the article."

She shook her head. "You don't have to apologize for that. Your reaction was completely understandable."

"No. I knew better. Deep down, I really didn't think you'd do that, but when I couldn't find a better explanation…"

Heidi squeezed his hand. "Really, Nick. It's okay."

"Let me make it up to you."

"Hmm. Okay. How?"

"You feel like Mexican tonight?"

"That sounds good."

"So, I'll pick you up at six?"

She smiled. "How about we just meet at the front door?"

He laughed. "That works."

His phone rang, and he raised it to his ear. After a moment a dark look spread across his face. "I understand," he said into the phone. "Thanks." He hung up.

Dread curled through her. "What is it?"

"Lance Gentry just escaped custody."

"What? How?"

"He attacked one of the MPs escorting him, got his weapon and took off on foot. They chased him and lost him in the woods. They're bringing the dogs out, but if he manages to get off base, he's as good as gone."

"He lives on base. He knows how to come and go without detection."

"Yeah. Which means we're back to looking over your shoulder."

THIRTEEN

Nick tugged at his collar and studied himself in the mirror. He couldn't believe how nervous he was. They'd decided to go ahead with dinner—and keep looking over their shoulders.

Gramps appeared in the bedroom doorway. "You look good, boy."

"Thanks."

"So why do you keep fidgeting with that collar?"

Nick dropped his hands. "Because I don't know what else to do with myself."

"She's come to mean a lot to you in a short time."

"She has. It scares me."

"Because she's a reporter?"

"Partly. I'm having second thoughts about this. I keep second-guessing myself. And her."

"It's your nature."

He huffed a short laugh. "I come by it honestly. When that story came out in the paper, I can't tell you how betrayed I felt. That feeling was not a good one and it never once occurred to me that she didn't write it."

"I can see why you're struggling, but you just have

to talk through those times. But there has to be trust. If you can't trust her, you can't build a life with her."

"I know, Gramps."

"I know you do." He paused. "Your mother would like her."

A lump started to grow in the back of his throat and Nick cleared it away. He rubbed a hand over his eyes. "I think so, too. That's part of the struggle. I want to marry a girl Mom would approve of."

"I know, son. But truly, you can't go wrong with a girl who likes Mexican food."

Nick laughed, appreciating his grandfather's attempt to lighten the moment. "Maybe not."

His grandfather's expression sobered and his eyes narrowed. "She has a kind heart, Nick. Be gentle with it. But don't date her if you don't think you can work through the angst you still have about her."

Nick shook his head. "I think I'll talk to her, see what she's thinking. See if I learn anything new. I don't want to get hurt, but I don't want to hurt her, either. Maybe spending some time alone will help."

"Aw, you'll be all right. Now, let me get this for you." Gramps reached up and adjusted the collar, then patted Nick on the shoulder. "You look great, kid. She won't know what hit her."

Together, they walked out of the bedroom and into the foyer.

Heidi was pulling her coat off the rack. Nick stopped dead in his tracks when she turned and smiled. He gulped, wondering what happened to all the oxygen in the room.

His grandfather slapped him on the back. "I may have been wrong in my assessment."

"What do you mean?" he asked.

"I think it's you who doesn't know what hit him."
He hugged a startled Heidi. "Go easy on him, honey.
He's out of practice with this dating stuff."

"Gramps!"

The old man laughed and strode into the den to turn
the television on.

Nick blinked at her. "You look amazing."

"Thanks. So do you."

"So…uh…are you ready to go?"

"Whenever you are."

He helped her on with her coat and opened the door.
Her light vanilla-scented fragrance followed her outside and he breathed deeply—only to stop when he
came face-to-face with Justin Blackwood. Nick saluted, as did Heidi. "Sir?" Nick asked.

"Sorry to interrupt your evening, but we just got
word that Bobby Stevens was attacked in the hospital."

Heidi gasped. "Oh, no! Is he all right?"

"He's wounded and under sedation right now, as
well as heavy guard, but the doctor says he should
be able to talk first thing in the morning. He's not to
have visitors until then." He paused, his gaze on Heidi.
"Because I want you there, I'm going to read you in on
something that I need to stay out of the papers."

"Yes, sir."

"OSI Agent Steffen has been digging into Stevens's
background, financial records, et cetera. At first, he
couldn't find anything that set off any alarm bells."

"At first?" Heidi asked.

"As they kept digging, they expanded their search
and found some interesting deposits into his mother's
savings account. His name isn't on the account so it

took some convincing to get a warrant for his mother's banking. Which is why it's taken this long to get back to you on Stevens."

"His mother has MS," Heidi said. "She's in a wheelchair." She cleared her throat. "I guess that has nothing to do with what you're saying. Sorry."

"It has everything to do with it. He told you about her?"

"He did."

Justin nodded. "That's exactly what I'm talking about. You saved his life and you have a rapport with him. I'm guessing he's being paid to keep his mouth shut about something and I want to know what. Between the two of you, I want you to drag every scrap of information you can out of him. He knows something and it's time we knew it, too."

"Yes, sir," Heidi said. "I'm happy to talk to him. I'm glad he's going to be okay."

"Me, too."

"Captain?" Nick asked.

"Yes?"

"Why didn't you just call?"

"I did. You didn't answer your phone."

Nick sighed and pulled it from the clip. "Sorry, sir. I'd turned it off during a meeting. It's back on ring now. If you need anything else, I'll hear it."

Justin nodded, climbed into his vehicle and left.

"Poor Bobby," Heidi said. "I have a feeling he was up to no good at the training center the night it exploded, but he doesn't deserve this."

"I'm not sure I have quite as much sympathy." Nick took her hand. "Let's grab dinner and then get a good night's sleep. Tomorrow's going to be a long one."

* * *

By eight thirty in the morning, the hospital was a beehive of activity. And so was Heidi's brain. Determined to get some answers, she led the way to Bobby's room even while her mind relived the dinner from the night before. It had been nice—and weird. Nick had seemed a bit distant, as though he wanted to be there, but wasn't sure if he should be. She chalked it up to distraction due to the news about Bobby and the fact that Gentry had escaped. But they'd kept the conversation light, touching on a variety of topics before finally landing on the case of the stolen medals.

"Why do you think the thief's doing it?" Nick had asked. "They can't be worth that much."

"Some aren't, but there are a few that are. I think this guy doesn't know who has the ones worth money so he's having to break into every home and just grab the ones he can—along with any jewelry and cash he can find—and get out."

"I suppose."

"A lot of these families are multigenerational military. Some World War II medals are going for hundreds of thousands of dollars."

"That's crazy. It's not the piece of metal that should be worth anything, but the heroism behind them."

"I agree. Unfortunately, our thief doesn't."

"And he might be able to pass one or two off as worth more than they are. There's no telling."

"Right."

Now Heidi stood in front of the door that would lead her to the man who could possibly help them figure out who the thief was. And she wasn't leaving until he told them.

The security officer at the door stood and eyed them until Nick flashed his badge. He nodded and returned to his chair, his posture alert, eyes moving over each person in the hall. Heidi was glad to see him taking his responsibilities seriously.

"Hi there, may I help you?"

Heidi and Nick turned. A nurse in her early forties stood next to a cart with an open laptop.

"We're here to see Bobby Stevens," Nick said.

"I'm sorry, he's still pretty weak. I just came out of his room. The doctor upped his pain medication and he dropped back off to sleep. You might want to give him a few hours or come back after lunch."

Heidi frowned. "We were told he'd be able to talk this morning."

"Well, that person was wrong. Sorry."

Heidi sighed and exchanged a shrug with Nick. "All right, thanks. Guess we'll come back later. If I give you my number, will you let me know when he can talk?"

"Sure." Heidi gave it to her and the nurse moved to the next room.

Nick blew out a low breath. "Great."

"I have my laptop with me," Heidi said. "I guess I could head down to the cafeteria and get some work done on a couple of articles."

"We have a team meeting at eleven that I could make. Justin excused me from it so we could be here, but if we're not going to be able to talk to Stevens until after lunch, then I guess I'll head over there."

"All right. Go get caught up and come back and fill me in."

He quirked a smile. "A lot of it will be classified, sorry."

"I understand. I'll take whatever information you can give me and try to be happy with that. I'll let you know you when the nurse calls."

"Sounds good. I'll catch up with you later."

Nick arrived at the meeting ten minutes early. He slipped into the room and took a seat near the door, hoping Heidi would be safe while working in the hospital. If her attacker was smart, he'd be long gone by now, but the fact that Sullivan still owed him money meant he might still be hanging around. And that worried him. Only the fact that the hospital had security would allow him to focus his full attention on the forthcoming discussion.

Justin entered the conference room and set his briefcase on the table. "Nick, I'm surprised to see you here. Weren't you going to speak with Bobby Stevens?"

"Yes." Nick explained and Justin nodded.

"All right, you can head back over that way after the meeting."

Gretchen and Vanessa entered and took their seats at the table. Once everyone was accounted for, Justin opened by bringing everyone up to speed on the arrest and escape of Lance Gentry. "We managed to ask him some questions before he escaped. Not that I'm happy he's still out there, but I think he's given us everything he knows about Sullivan. There's no security footage at his home, so we're just going to have to believe that Sullivan showed up there. I believe it happened the way he described it." He looked at Vanessa. "Why don't you give us an update on Yvette Crenville?"

Vanessa shook her head. "We've been watching. Tag-teaming it, so to speak. So far, there's nothing.

She's gone to work, shopped for ridiculously priced health foods at the base market and spent any spare time doing yoga at the base gym. If she's an accomplice, we can't find any evidence of it."

Gretchen nodded her agreement.

"All right. I'm not ready to give up on her just yet. Keep up what you're doing and give us another report at the next meeting."

"Yes, sir." Gretchen nodded.

Vanessa also agreed.

"Let's move on to our next steps in finding Boyd Sullivan."

For the next two hours, they went over the case files, reviewing notes, interviews, and making more plans to track the man down.

Nick's phone rang just as they were wrapping things up and he motioned to Justin that he needed to take the call.

In the hall, he swiped the screen. "Hey, Heidi, everything okay?"

"That's sad."

"What?"

"The first question out of your mouth is asking if everything's okay."

He gave a low laugh. "Sorry, I guess it's become a habit at this point."

"I guess."

"What can I do for you?"

"The nurse just called me and said we should be able to talk to him in the next few minutes. I'm going to head to his room."

"Perfect, I'm headed that way."

* * *

Heidi tossed the remains of her snack into the trash and headed for the elevator. Once on the floor, she went straight to Bobby's room and showed her ID to the officer on duty.

"You might want to wait a minute before going in," the officer said. "The doctor's in there."

"What? The nurse just called and told me to come on up."

"Oh, well, he'll probably be done in a few minutes."

"I'll just stick my head in and let him know I'm here."

With a frown, she shoved open the door. To find a man in a white lab coat standing over Bobby Stevens, holding a pillow over his face.

She screamed and launched herself at the man, slamming into him. Heidi went to the floor while he stumbled back into the IV pole, cursed and landed beside her. Then he was on his feet. Heidi tried to get up, but at the last second, saw the hard fist swing at her. She rolled and his knuckles grazed her jaw. A flash of pain shot through her face and she lost her balance, falling to the floor once more. She landed on her backside with a grunt.

The door swung open and the officer ran in. "What's going—"

The attacker slammed a fist into the officer's face. His head snapped back and he crumpled to the floor. As the officer rolled, the man jerked the door open and bolted into the hall.

"Bobby?" Heidi gasped. Once again, she surged to her feet, ignoring the throbbing in her jaw. She hurried to Bobby's side. When she got a good look at him, she flinched at the sight of his new wounds. He had a puffy right cheek and a bruised eye. She went to him and grasped his hand. "Are you all right?"

Bobby nodded, breathing hard. "Yes. I'd just dozed off when I felt the pillow over my face. But yes, I'm okay."

Hospital personnel swarmed the room. A nurse was kneeling next to the fallen officer. She looked up. "We've alerted security."

Nick stepped inside. "Heidi? What's going on?"

It didn't take long to fill him in. He touched her chin and she pulled back with a wince. "That's gotta hurt," he said.

"Yes, but, thankfully, it was just a glancing blow. I'll have a bruise, but nothing's broken."

"Did you see who it was?"

"No, not really. He was dressed like a doctor in a white coat but had on a baseball cap and sunglasses when he turned around. And before you ask, it could have been Lance Gentry, but I can't say for certain."

Once the officer was removed to receive more care and the doctor had checked out Bobby, he nodded to them. "You can have ten minutes. Then I want him resting again."

"Yes, sir," Nick said. The doctor left and Nick placed a hand on her shoulder. "Let me talk to him first, okay?"

"But the captain said…"

"I know what he said. Just go with me on this, will you? For now?"

She huffed and eyed him. He was up to something. "Fine. For now."

"Thanks." Nick opened the door and she followed

him inside. Nick stepped up to the man's bed. "Bobby, who did this to you?"

"I—I don't know. It's all a little foggy."

"Maybe the attack is foggy, but I doubt the name of your attacker is," Nick said. "Who was it? Was it Lance Gentry?"

He flinched and then his expression shut down.

"Come on," Heidi said. "Without naming who it was, what happened with the previous attack? We know what happened this time." She rubbed a hand across her still-throbbing jaw.

"The previous attack?"

"Yes. When you got the bruises to your eye and cheek."

"I was asleep," Bobby said, his eyes locking on Heidi's. "When I woke up, I couldn't breathe. Someone was holding a pillow over my face—just like this time. I started flailing, trying to grab something, anything, to make him let go. My hand landed on my mug of ice and I managed to crack him in the head with it. He let go long enough for me to push the pillow off. Then he punched me. A nurse heard the commotion and ran in. The other guy bolted out and down the hall. This time was like an instant replay."

"Let me guess," Nick said. "He was wearing a hoodie."

"No, but a hat and sunglasses," Bobby muttered.

Leaning against the sink area, Nick hooked his thumbs into his pockets. "Why are you protecting someone who tried to kill you?" he asked.

Bobby huffed and crossed his arms. He looked away while his teeth worked his lower lip.

"Because he's scared," Heidi said softly. She stepped

forward and took the young man's hand. He was probably just a few years younger than she, but she felt a lot older. Almost maternal in the way she wanted to not only help him, but smack him upside his head and demand he cooperate.

She controlled the second compulsion and squeezed his fingers. "Come on, Bobby. You're not helping yourself here. You're a victim of the bomber. Someone tried to kill you. Twice. Why won't you tell us what we need to know? What was Lance Gentry doing there?"

His fingers trembled in her grasp and a tear slid down his cheek. He quickly swiped it away and Heidi pretended she hadn't noticed. "It's...I...if I tell, he'll kill me."

"Looks like that's his goal anyway," Nick said. "Let me just share something with you. We know Lance Gentry set off the explosion in the training center. He's been trying to kill Heidi because he knows she can identify him. Guess what? He knows you can identify him, too. We had him in custody, but he escaped. So, if he's the one after you, he's still around to come back and finish the job. And it looks like he's pretty determined. What are you going to do when you get out of here? Run?"

"If I have to. Look, Lance Gentry isn't trying to kill me. He never knew that I saw him at the training center."

"Then why protect him?"

"It doesn't matter," Bobby said. "Don't you understand? I can't tell you anything."

Nick's nostrils flared. "Are you really that stupid?" He all but shouted the question and Bobby sank into the pillows even while his eyes flashed a defiance that hadn't been there a few moments earlier.

Heidi rose. "Excuse us, Bobby, I need to have a word with First Lieutenant Donovan." She raised a brow at Nick. "Outside, please?"

"Heidi—"

She gripped his forearm and all but shoved him from the room. Once the door shut behind them, Nick frowned down at her. "What are you doing?"

"Trying to get the name of his attacker, but if you keep shouting at him, he's just going to close up tighter and tighter."

"I'm not shouting."

"You are. And you act like you've never questioned someone before. Can't you read his body language?"

He smiled. "Yes, ma'am."

"Ah." She gave him an assessing look. "I thought you were up to something. You planned this, didn't you?"

"And you played the good cop perfectly." He paced three steps down the hall, then back. "But I'm getting impatient. Go see if your more gentle approach works better. We know that Lance Gentry is the guy who attacked him. He knows we know. I want to know why he's protecting him."

"He seemed sincere when he said Lance never saw him."

"He's lying."

Heidi shook her head. "I don't think so. He has this tell when he lies. He rolls his eyes away from you, then looks down."

"Okay. Then if it wasn't Lance trying to kill him all this time, who is it?"

"I don't know."

"Then use those investigative skills and go find out." She grinned. "Stay tuned."

"I'm going to have hospital security come cover the door while I grab some coffee. You want one?"

"I'd love one," she said.

He stopped at the nurses' station to arrange the security and she reentered the room. Bobby had shut his eyes, but opened them when she sat next to him. "Look, Bobby, I know this isn't easy. I get it. I do. You say Lance Gentry isn't the one who attacked you, that he never knew you were there. Then where is all this coming from? You might as well tell us because we're not going to stop asking. What are you hiding? You were there at the training center before the explosion."

"Of course I was. I was taking care of the dogs."

"That's what you said before. But there weren't any dogs in that part of the building, Bobby. Your story makes no sense."

He looked down and pleated the blanket with his fingers, then smoothed it out over his thighs.

Heidi sighed. "They found the money in your mother's bank account."

He froze. "What money?"

"Really?" She stared at him and his face crumbled. "What did someone pay you for? To keep quiet about the bombing?"

"No." His swift denial—and the fact that he met her gaze when he said it—had her believing him. Almost.

"Then what?" He sighed and rubbed his eyes. She pushed a little harder. "It's all going to come out in the long run," she said. "You might as well tell us what you know and catch a break legally."

"Do I need a lawyer?"

"Depends on what you were taking the money for."

Bobby hesitated only a moment before he said, "You were right. I was taking it to keep my mouth shut."

"About what?"

"About who was stealing the medals."

Finally. "I kind of thought so."

"I know who's stealing the medals, and he paid me to keep quiet."

"Then how does Lance Gentry fit into this and why would you protect him?"

"Because I saw him at the training center, and he saw me. He has a certain reputation and if he knew I blabbed about him, he'd come after me."

Heidi wanted to do a facepalm right there. "If you had told the MPs who he was, they could have caught him and you wouldn't have had to worry about him."

He laughed. "Right. Like he wouldn't have been released on bail or something." He shook his head. "I couldn't take the chance. But if you caught him and he escaped, then he's probably a long way away by now."

She was done with the Lance Gentry subject. "Who's the guy stealing the medals?"

"Roger Cooper. He's a senior airman. He's stealing the medals and hiding them in the kennel. The empty areas. I walked in early for my shift one afternoon because I needed an extra cage and we store some in that unused portion of the training center. He was there. When he saw me, he pulled a gun and said he'd pay me to keep my mouth shut. I agreed because I needed the money. Sometimes, he'd pass the medals off to me and I'd hide them for him when I went in to work."

"Where?"

"Different areas of the training center. Always away from the dogs, though, because you never know when someone's going to be around."

Heidi nodded. "Anything else you want to add?"

"No."

"So it was definitely Cooper who tried to kill you?"

"It was him. I saw him."

"Then you're going to press charges."

Fear flashed. "I don't know—"

"If you don't, he'll go free. And then he really will kill you. You do understand that, right?"

The man wilted against the pillow and gave a short nod followed by a wince. He lifted a hand to his head. "I understand. I just want all this to go away."

"Good. I'm sure OSI Special Agent Steffen will be by to take your statement." And conduct an arrest, but she kept that to herself. "You need to tell him everything you told me, okay? It needs to be officially on record."

"I get it. I will."

"Good." She stood and walked to the door. "I'm sorry it's ending this way for you, Bobby. I don't think you're a bad guy. I think you just got caught up in something a lot bigger than you. But you have the opportunity to turn this around and do the right thing. I suggest you take it."

A deep sigh filtered from him. "I know. I will. I actually feel better already now that it's off my chest."

When Nick returned with her coffee, she patted Bobby on the arm and they said their goodbyes. Two officers now stood guard outside the airman's room. She filled Nick in on the conversation with Bobby and he shook his head. "You're amazing."

"No, I just connected with Bobby when I saved his life. And he's really not a bad guy. I hope he can get his life straightened out at this point."

"His air force career is finished."

"I know. And so does he. He's just afraid. He's been afraid for a long time, but I think he feels better now that he's manned up and told the truth." She drew in a deep breath. "How's the officer who was hurt?" she asked. "Did you hear?"

"I checked on him. He has a fractured jaw, but he'll be all right."

"Wow, he really took a hard hit."

"He did."

She cleared her throat. "Okay, so what's next?"

"We look for this Roger Cooper character and see what we can shake loose from him."

"No, *I* look for Roger Cooper," Heidi said. "This is my story, Nick. Roger doesn't have anything to do with Boyd Sullivan."

His eyes narrowed. "Why don't we fill Justin in on what we know and see what he says? Although, if you think about it, my orders are to protect you. So if you're going looking for Cooper, that means I am, too."

FOURTEEN

Nick returned to the car after searching for Cooper and slammed the door. "Another negative." Annie nudged the back of his head from her spot behind him and he reached back to scratch her ears.

"Great." Heidi sighed and rubbed her eyes. "And nothing from Justin?"

"Nope. They've got the MPs out in force looking for him and Gentry, but so far they don't have any solid leads as to where either could be."

"I get that Lance Gentry might be hard to find since he knows if he shows his face on base, he'll be caught, but how is it that no one has seen Roger Cooper lately? It's like he's dropped off the face of the planet."

They'd been tracking down Roger Cooper's known associates, asking information. Nick figured the easiest way to keep Heidi safe was to go along with the hunt. He had hopes that Justin and the Security Forces would find the man first, but it looked like none of them were going to find him.

Now they had only a couple of hours of daylight left. Nick really wanted them to locate the man before the sun went down, but he wasn't holding his breath.

"What did Captain Blackwood find after looking into Cooper's background? Has he said when he'd have something?" she asked.

"Shortly."

"Okay, what now, then?"

"Let's grab something to eat. A drive-through." The longer he could keep her in the car, the easier it was to keep her out of danger. Between Gentry and Cooper, things could get deadly fast. He shuddered at the thought.

His phone buzzed. "Hold on. Justin just texted. He said Senior Airman Cooper has a spotless record. Which is why no one's thought twice about him being out with the flu the last four days."

"Does he live on base?"

Nick texted the question to Justin. "No. And the officers sent to his home said he wasn't there."

"Then he's hiding somewhere," Heidi said. "Close by if he's the one attacking Bobby at the hospital."

Nick nodded. "I'd be inclined to agree with that statement."

"Any local relatives?"

"No." He scrolled the text. "According to Justin, he has a sister in El Paso and a brother who's married with three kids, living in New Mexico."

"So he's not with them."

"Nope. Local authorities have already checked just as a way to cover their bases. He's here—somewhere. Justin's put a BOLO out on him." He stood. "I want to head to the kennels."

"Why? Aren't they already searching them?"

He shook his head. "I asked Justin if we could do it. With officers tied up searching for Gentry and Cooper, until I know for sure that Stevens is being straight with us, I'm not causing a scene or going on a wild-goose chase."

"Yeah. I see what you mean."

"So, let's go see what we can find."

With Annie in the back, Nick drove to the training center and parked close to the door.

He climbed out of the SUV and put on his backpack, then got Annie from her area and put her protective gear on. She sat and let him do what he needed to do with no protest. She knew she was going to work and her body quivered with excitement. Once they were ready, he scratched her ears, then looked at Heidi. "Stay behind us, okay? I don't know how safe this place is."

"Okay."

With Heidi behind him and Annie beside him, he pushed aside the yellow crime scene tape and led the way to the warped steel door. "I think the opening is big enough to get through. I don't know if you know the layout, but the door is higher than the ground floor. Once you're inside, you have to walk down three steps, okay?"

"I've been in there before. I know what you're talking about."

"Good. Let me go in first, then Annie, then I'll help you in if you need it."

Placing one foot carefully on the door, Nick had to climb over it and stop. The steps down had been destroyed and lay in crumbles two feet below. He hopped down. "Annie, come. Jump."

The dog scampered over the door and into his arms. He gave a grunt when she landed. "I think you've gained a few pounds, girl." She swiped a tongue across his face.

As always, her absolute trust in him never ceased to send a pang through his heart. Nick set the sixty-pound animal on the dirty, sooty floor and wiped the slobber from his cheek. He then turned back to warn Heidi. "Watch it, the steps are gone."

"Got it."

With his hands holding her waist, he helped her through the opening. She placed her hand on his shoulders and he lowered her to the floor beside Annie.

"Thanks," she said.

"No problem." Even in the dim light of the broken building, she took his breath away. He didn't remove his hands from her waist immediately.

And she didn't step away from him.

"Heidi…"

"Yes?"

"I…uh…" What was he going to say? That he must be going crazy because he was crazy about *her*?

"Nick?"

"Yes, sorry." He dropped his hands and stepped back. He took his flashlight from his belt and clicked it on. The small windows lining the top edge of the wall just beneath the ceiling let in the waning natural light, but they needed the flashlight to illuminate the damage.

"Wow," she whispered as she looked around. "This is awful."

"No kidding."

"Why blow up this part of the kennel?" she asked. "I'm assuming Sullivan chose the location to bomb. Odd, I wouldn't think he'd care if he set off a bomb that killed people. It's almost like he picked an area that would cause damage, but wouldn't kill anyone. Human or animal."

"I don't think he cared whether he killed anyone or not. He probably picked this area because it's easy to get in and out of without being noticed and he could get the distraction he wanted."

"True."

They walked through the lobby and into the hall that would lead them to the large kennel area. "Where would you hide a bunch of medals if you were going to do so?" Nick asked.

"Someplace inconspicuous. Where no one would think to look—or accidentally stumble upon."

"That sounds about right. So, where is a nice inconspicuous place in a training center? The kennel?" He flashed the beam over the walls and then along the floor, looking for a path. There were large pieces of concrete and rubble that made the going slow down the hallway, but they kept at it until they reached the kennels. The outer door stood open. "It's not that bad back here. The bomb must have been set to go off near the entrance. It took the brunt of the blast. This is just soot from the smoke, and lots of standing water."

"Did they say what the bomb was made from?"

"C-4," he told her. "Annie found RDX, which is a common ingredient in the explosive."

"Where do you think he got it?"

"No telling. It's used with construction projects or demolition." He shrugged. "Could be from anywhere. And it's fairly stable. Like you have to set it off with a detonator."

"But you can attach a timer to that detonator, right?"

"Sure."

"Or use a remote to set it off?"

"Yes."

A noise behind them stopped him. "Did you hear that?" he asked her.

"I did. You think someone else is in here, too?"

"Shouldn't be," he said. "Unless one of the other investigators decided to come check it out, too."

"Or Roger Cooper's been hiding out here the whole time."

He nodded. "That was my next thought. Then again, it could just be the building shifting. It might not be safe. Hang back while I check it out, will you?"

"Not a chance."

"Heidi—"

"Nope."

He sighed. "Then at least stay behind me."

"I can do that."

Heidi did as he'd asked, but noted that Annie resisted the change in direction, pulling on her lead, wanting to go ahead.

"What is it, girl?" Nick muttered. "Go on. Show me what's got your attention."

A good handler always paid attention to his dog and Heidi realized that Nick wasn't just good, he was incredible, always completely in tune with Annie when they were working. The animal darted ahead to the end of the leash, sniffed around a pile of crates and then sat. Nick froze.

"What is it?" Heidi asked.

"Head for the entrance where we came in."

"Nick—"

"Just go! Now! Get out of here!"

One of the crates flew off and a figure rose from beneath it. "Don't move," he said.

Heidi stepped back and her heel caught against a piece of broken concrete. She fell back, landing hard on the debris, her phone skittering behind her. Her back protested the sudden stop and her palms scraped the floor, stinging. Gasping, she stared up at the man who held a weapon in one hand and something else in the other. A cardboard box sat beside his feet.

"Roger Cooper, I presume?" she asked, blindly reaching for her phone. She couldn't find it.

Nick stepped in front of her, hands raised in the surrender position. "Put it down, Cooper. It's all over for you."

"It's not over yet. At least not for me. But looks like you two showed up at the wrong time."

"Or the exact right time," Heidi said, ignoring the fear thrumming through her. Her fingers searched blindly for the phone, but she couldn't land on it. "We've been looking for you."

"I know. Everyone's looking for me."

"So you decided to hide out here?" Nick asked.

"Not exactly hiding."

"You're getting the medals so you can run, aren't you?" Heidi asked.

"Smart girl." His eyes flicked to Nick and Annie, then back to Heidi. "Only now, I've got to come up with a plan to get rid of you two."

"What are you doing with the bombs?"

"Insurance. Looks like that's going to pay off."

"So you're going to blow us up?" Heidi asked, hating the quiver in her voice.

"Not if you cooperate."

Nick shifted more fully in front of her. "What do you want us to do?"

"Walk. That way." Roger Cooper pointed with the hand he had clamped around the firing button, thumb hovering, ready to press it. Nick shuddered, his mind spinning for a way to get it away from the man. Tackling him might cause him to press the button.

Heidi moved, her foot catching on the rubble, and she stumbled against Nick. He caught her and pushed her behind him. Her hands landed on the small of his back, just under the Kevlar vest.

Her touch stirred his protective instincts in a way he didn't think he'd be able to explain if he had to. But one thing was for sure. Cooper was going to have to go through him to get to Heidi.

Nick eyed the man. "Is that the button that'll set that explosive off back there?"

"Yes, so don't try anything funny."

"Wouldn't think of it. What is it? C-4?"

"Like you don't know."

"So, what's the plan now?"

"I'm going to blow the place up. Some of those medals are worth a fortune, but it's obvious things are heating up and the investigation is getting too close. It's time for me to make my exit." He waved the firing button device. "Thanks to the guy who blew this place up the first time, I can now blow it again and everyone will think the original bomber did it."

"No, they won't," Heidi said.

Cooper frowned. "Why not?"

"Because the other bomber used a timer, not a firing button."

"It doesn't matter. It'll confuse the issue for a while and I'll be long gone."

Heidi's fingers trembled against his back and Nick couldn't help wondering where his backup was. He'd give anything to use his radio. Thankfully, Cooper hadn't told him to lose it yet.

"All right. New plan." Cooper licked his lips and his eyes darted over the training center. They hardened when they landed back on Nick. "Go to the kennels."

"What?"

"To the cages! Now!"

Annie gave a low growl and took a step forward. The man lowered the weapon to the dog and Nick placed a hand on her head. Annie calmed, but her fur still bristled. Nick took a step back and grasped Heidi's upper arm. "Go on," he said.

Heidi moved toward the kennels, making her way through the rubble once more. Nick stayed behind her, between her and the gunman. Would Cooper really do as he threatened? Maybe. He didn't seem to have any hesitation when it came to trying to kill Stevens. He didn't think the man wanted to die, but the uncertainty kept Nick from jumping him.

Once in the room with the kennel cages lining the walls, Cooper motioned to Nick. "Throw me your radio."

When Nick hesitated, he lifted the weapon and aimed it at Heidi. Nick tossed him the radio. Cooper gave it a hard kick and it skittered across the floor and out of the room. "Now your phone."

Nick complied.

Roger waved his hand with the firing button. "Get in."

The doors hung open, the locks swinging from the hooks.

"What's the plan once you lock us in the cage?" Nick asked, stopping just short of entering the chain-link kennel.

"I get out of here."

"And blow us up," Heidi whispered.

The sound of sirens caught Nick's attention. And it caught Roger Cooper's as well. He paused and flicked a glance over his shoulder. That was the distraction Nick needed. He struck, launching himself at the man's hand and knocking the firing button to the floor.

FIFTEEN

Heidi bolted for the device while Nick and Cooper wrestled for control of his weapon, but Cooper's foot caught the small box and swept it from her reach.

The men rolled into her path and Heidi jumped back to avoid being hit. Only she moved a fraction too late. A boot landed on her calf and knocked her feet out from under her. She went down hard for the second time.

"Give it up, Cooper," Nick ordered.

The man didn't stop his desperate quest to escape. Over her shoulder she could see his hand reach for the firing button and then he screamed. Heidi flinched and rolled to her side to see Annie's jaws clamped down on the man's leg. He thrashed and kicked with his other leg, but Annie held fast—and Cooper didn't give up his attempts to gain control of the device.

Heidi scrambled toward it just as his hand landed on it and Nick's fist smashed into Cooper's face. He screamed again, but managed to clamp his fingers around the device.

And his thumb came down on the red button.

The explosion rocked the area. Nick rolled, covering

Heidi with his body while the ceiling tiles fell. When the building settled, smoke and dust filled the room. Coughing, gagging, Heidi tried to drag in a breath. She shoved at the heavy weight pinning her to the floor. "Nick. Move," she gasped.

He groaned and rolled. Pain engulfed her left arm and blood flowed from the wound. She clamped a hand over it, wondering how bad it was. "Nick, are you okay?"

He'd taken the brunt of the falling tiles. His vest had protected him some, but one had caught the back of his head and a river of blood trickled from his scalp. He coughed. "Yeah." He winced and lifted a hand to the back of his head. When he saw the blood on his fingers, he grimaced, then wiped his hand on his pants. "What about you?"

"I think so. Other than you crushing my lungs, I think I'm mostly unhurt." She looked around for Cooper. "He's gone."

"Annie!" Nick hauled himself to his feet and stumbled to the animal, who lay on her side. She whined and Nick settled down beside her, running his hands over her. "I think she's all right. Stunned, like us, a few cuts and scrapes, but okay." Annie proved him right by lurching to her feet. She shook herself and Nick gave her one more check before he turned to Heidi. "I'm going after him."

"I think he went toward the exit."

"He'd have to." He helped her to her feet and his expression changed when he saw her arm and her hand covered in blood. "You said you weren't hurt."

"I said *mostly* unhurt." She looked at the wound. "Looks like I can use a stitch or two, but I'm not worried about that right now. Let's go. We have a thief to catch."

Without questioning her further, he looped Annie's leash over his wrist and held his weapon in that hand. "Let's try this again. Stay behind me, all right?"

"I'm here."

She stayed with him as he led the way toward the exit. The bomb had been more in the back this time, not the front, so there was no added rubble to trap them.

Until another explosion rocked the training center.

Once again, Nick pulled her to the ground while the ceiling fell down around them, along with part of the flooring above.

"Nick! What's going on?"

"Unbelievable," he muttered into the side of her neck. "He set that one off to trap us. To give him time to get out."

"But I heard the sirens. Law enforcement's here. He can't get away." She pushed herself to her feet, coughing, wheezing. "It's hard to breathe in here."

"I know. Pull your shirt up over your mouth and nose. It might help filter some of the dust." She did so while he pulled a bandanna from his pocket. "Here, use this."

"No, you use it. My shirt's working fine."

He wrapped the piece of cloth around the lower part of his face, then checked on Annie. She was panting and probably could use some fresh air and water just like he and Heidi. He rummaged through his pack and pulled out two bottles of water. And Annie's bowl. He handed a bottle to Heidi, who drank half of it. When Annie had her fill of the second bottle, Nick finished it off and tossed it aside. Then he reached into his pack and pulled out a mask that he fit over Annie's muzzle. It would filter some of the dust for her. "All right, let's figure out how to get out—or at least let someone know we're in here." He scrambled over the added debris and made his way to the huge pile blocking their exit.

"I don't have my phone," Heidi said. "I lost it when I fell. Do you think we could find your radio?"

He hated the fear in her voice. "I don't know. I think it was probably buried in the first blast. My phone, too."

"What are we going to do?" she whispered.

Nick gripped her fingers. "We're going to stay calm and get out of this, okay?"

She gave him a slow nod. "All right. Tell me what I need to do."

"Let's take care of your arm, and then we'll have to assess the situation." Using supplies from his first aid kit he carried in the pack, he bandaged her arm. "That should hold you for now."

"It's fine. Thank you."

Together, they approached the pile of debris and Nick ran his hands over the mixture of tile and cement. He grabbed a piece and pulled. It slid loose and he tossed it aside. "I think we can try to dig our way out."

"They know we're in here, right?"

"They know. They'll be looking for us."

"They might think we're dead."

"Possibly. But they'll bring in search-and-rescue dogs and they'll alert we're here."

She grabbed a rock and shifted it. Debris tumbled, kicking up more dust. Choking, she shoved the rock aside and lifted her shirt to breathe through it. "Is that true or are you just saying that to make me feel better?"

"It's true." Nick stopped what he was doing and tore her shirt to make a mask. He tied it around her nose and mouth and went back to working.

Then she stopped. "Wait a minute. We can get out through the kennel. We can crawl out the little doggie door and into the dog run."

Nick shook his head. "It's a good idea, but won't work. They keep those doggie doors locked as a security measure and only open them when there are dogs in the cages."

Her shoulders slumped. "Oh." Then she shrugged. "Okay, then. Back to digging."

For the next several minutes, they moved more of the debris, working quickly. Nick's head pounded a fierce rhythm, but the fact that they seemed to be making a little progress helped him push through the pain. Until nausea sent him to his knees.

Heidi dropped beside him. "Nick?"

"I'm okay. I just have to rest a second."

She pulled the water bottle from her pocket and held it out to him. "Drink."

"I'm fine."

"Quit being stubborn and drink it."

He did and then handed it back to her with a grunt. "I only agreed because I have another bottle in my pack. That one's yours, okay?"

"We'll split it if we have to," she said.

"We'll see." He paused. "I owe you an apology."

"What? No, you don't."

"Actually I do. I want to apologize for getting you into this. I should have left you outside the building while I investigated."

She huffed a short laugh. "You really think you could have talked me into that?"

"I should have tried, anyway."

"Rest easy, Nick. You would have failed."

He laughed. "You're very stubborn."

"I know. How are you feeling?"

"Better, thanks." He rose and spotted a steel rod about five feet long. "Let's see if this does anything."

Nick started to insert the rod in between two rocks, then stopped to grab Heidi's arm. "You hear that?"

"No. What?"

The distinct sound of barking.

Annie's ears perked up and she rose from her spot on the floor. She gave a low woof through the mask and stepped over the debris. Nick worked the rod like a crowbar and managed to send more tile and concrete falling from the pile to the floor. Then he pressed it into the small opening and sent the same rolling down on the other side. A whoosh of stale air hit him in the face and relief flowed through him. "Hey! Back here!" he yelled.

The barking intensified and Annie answered with three short barks of her own.

"At least she'll lead them this way," Heidi said.

Nick continued to roll the remnants of the ceiling from the pile. Workers started in on the other side and soon, there was a hole large enough for Heidi to crawl through. He helped her scramble through it and then picked up Annie. "Got a dog coming through. Some-one needs to catch her. She's got on her boots so she can walk."

"Hand her through," a voice called. He thought it

might be Isaac Goddard. Ignoring his throbbing, swimming head, Nick passed Annie through the opening, then crawled up to shove his head and arms through.

Hands grasped his wrists and pulled.

And he was finally on the other side. Isaac greeted him with a slap on the back. Justin and Westley were checking Annie out. A paramedic was trying to get Heidi to go with him. Only she shook her head. "Not until Nick's free."

"I'm here, Heidi."

She spun and ran over to throw herself in his arms. He grasped her tight. "We made it," she whispered.

"I know." He glanced at Justin, whose brows rose at the sight of Heidi in Nick's arms. Nick ignored the look and instead asked, "Did you happen to catch the guy responsible for this? Roger Cooper."

"He's outside," Justin replied. "Wrapped up nice and tight, with his rights read to him and everything."

"How did you know it was him?"

"He tried to run with a big ole box of medals. We figure he's the one who's been breaking into houses and stealing them along with whatever cash and jewelry he could find."

"You figure right."

"He set off the explosions, too," Heidi said.

"And we found more on him," Justin explained. "C-4 and firing buttons. The bomb squad is here and is going to search the building for more."

"Do you need Annie and me?" Nick asked.

"No." Justin clapped him on the shoulder. "You and Heidi are going to the hospital to get checked out, Annie's going to the vet, and then you've got a couple of days off to recuperate. Annie might the best bomb dog on base, but she's not the only one."

"I don't need a hospital, sir," Heidi said.

"Doesn't matter, you're getting one."

"Yes, sir."

Nick knew he'd get the same answer if he protested the hospital so he simply kept his mouth shut.

"Anyone find Lance Gentry yet?"

"Not yet," Justin said. "But we got a lead he stole a car. We've got a BOLO out on it. I'll let you know as soon as he's in custody."

"Thanks. You'll have to leave a message. My phone and radio are buried in there somewhere."

"I'll have a phone delivered to the hospital. Until Gentry's caught, you don't need to be without one. Now, we need statements."

It didn't take long to finish up their statements. Annie headed for the base veterinarian and Nick and Heidi were transported to the hospital. A young airman met them there. "I was told to deliver this to you." He handed Nick a phone.

"Thanks."

"You're welcome."

He left and Nick watched Heidi as they rolled her into the adjoining examination room, suppressing the urge to race after her.

"All right, sir, let's get you transferred to the bed and take a look at that head."

His attention only slightly diverted by the nurse, Nick decided to do his best to cooperate and hurry this whole unnecessary checkup along so he could rejoin Heidi and—what?

What would he say when he saw her? While the

nurse shaved a small patch at the back of his head for the two stitches deemed necessary, Nick silently planned the words he'd say to Heidi—if he could gather his nerve. When his phone rang, he grabbed it, grateful for the interruption. Ignoring the glare from the nurse, he answered it.

When the doctor removed the bandage Nick had applied at the kennels, Heidi got her first look at the wound on her arm and grimaced. It wasn't pretty. But once it was cleaned and re-bandaged, she was ready to go. "I have a couple of articles to write," she told the nurse. "I need to get going."

"You'll be out of here soon enough," she said and left the room.

Heidi leaned back with a groan and closed her eyes. She was exhausted, but couldn't shut her mind off. All she could think about was Nick—and ceilings caving in.

Being trapped with him had been scary enough. If he hadn't been there with her—

She shuddered.

The door opened. "That was fast," she said, not bothering to open her eyes since she assumed it was the nurse.

Tender fingers on her cheek brought her eyes open. Nick stood there, gazing at her with a look on his face that made her pulse pick up speed. "Nick?"

"I don't know how it happened," he said.

She swallowed. "What?"

"You got under my skin."

"Oh. I think you mentioned that once upon a time."

"In a good way."

"I like you, too, Nick."

He laughed and leaned over to kiss her. His lips on hers sent her pulse into overdrive. Warmth infused her and she realized she could get used to this on a daily basis. He pulled away with a pained groan and lifted a hand to his head.

She sat up. "Nick? You okay?"

"Yeah, I just can't kiss you bending over like that. Makes my head pound."

"Hmm. Makes my *heart* pound."

"Ha. Mine, too." He sighed and hugged her to him. "What am I going to do with you?"

"Oh, I don't know. Maybe take me out on a date?"

His laughter rumbled beneath her ear. "I think that can be arranged."

"Just not a shopping date. No shopping."

More laughter. "I like shopping with you."

"Hmm. Well, it wasn't too bad, I suppose. The fudge part was great."

"Wow. Thanks."

"Okay, how about this?" she said. "No bullets or bombs allowed on the date. Just fudge."

"Definitely. That's one rule I think we can follow now that Lance Gentry, Roger Cooper and Bobby Stevens are all under lock and key."

"They found Lance?"

"Justin called while I was getting looked at. They caught Gentry at the airport trying to board a plane. Someone recognized the car he'd stolen and called it in."

"Well, that was stupid of him."

"It was only a matter of time before he messed up."

She sighed. "Good. I'm glad he's no longer a threat

to anyone. I still feel kind of sorry for Bobby, though. I think he just got mixed up with the wrong people and couldn't find a way out without disappointing his mother."

"I think you may be right, but unfortunately, there are consequences for our choices."

"True."

The door opened and the doctor entered. "Oh, hey, Nick."

"Porter Davenport, good to see you." The two men shook hands. "How's my girl here?"

My girl?

"Your girl?" the doctor asked. "I see a lot has happened in the two weeks since we last had lunch," he said as he turned toward Heidi.

She bit her lip, intrigued by Nick's sudden and interesting shade of red even as happiness suffused her. "Um, Heidi, this is Porter Davenport. He and I have been friends for a while now."

"Nice to meet you," she said. She liked being referred to as Nick's girl. A lot. And it looked like he wasn't going to be shy about letting others know he'd staked his claim. Wow. That was a lot to think about. And she would. Later. In the privacy of her room, where she could ponder what the future might hold.

Right now, she was ready to get out of here. She had articles to write. She could think about her feelings toward Nick later. Like whether or not she loved him. The thought made her mouth go dry and her throat constrict. Oh, boy. Love? Maybe.

"Let's find out."

She gasped. "Find out? Find out what?"

The doctor stepped over. "Find out how you are."

"Oh. Right. Thank you."

He checked her eyes, her breathing and her pulse one more time. When he straightened, he nodded. "Pulse is a little fast."

No doubt. Heidi's flush deepened and she met Nick's wicked gaze. "Well, it's been an interesting few hours," she murmured.

"I heard what happened at the training center," Porter said. "Another blast. Unbelievable."

"No kidding," Heidi said. "And technically, it was two more blasts, but who's counting at this point? Fortunately, everything took place in that area that's deserted. It'll have to be completely razed and rebuilt, but at least no one was hurt this time."

He smiled. "Well, it looks like you two were incredibly fortunate. A few bumps and bruises, but no lasting damage. I'd say you definitely had someone watching over you."

"God just wasn't ready to take us yet, I guess," Heidi said.

Porter raised a brow and nodded. "I guess not." He turned and shook hands with Nick again. "And I, for one, am very glad of that fact." He backed toward the door. "Nice to meet you, Heidi. Take care of that arm and get some rest."

"I will. Thank you."

He left, and the nurse returned with her discharge papers—and Nick's. By the time they walked out of the hospital, the sun was creeping up over the horizon.

Nick wrapped an arm around her shoulders. "Are you hungry?"

"Starved."

"Feel like going on that date now?"

She laughed. "What? Now? No way. I'm a mess. I need a shower and a nap."

"All right, how does pizza sound?"

"For breakfast?" She shrugged. "As long as it's delivered."

"Of course."

"Then that sounds amazing."

He pulled out his new phone and placed the order at the twenty-four-hour pizza place while they walked.

The cool morning air was refreshing and Heidi breathed in. "I'll never take being able to breathe clean air for granted again," she said when he hung up.

"I know what you mean."

It didn't take long to reach his home. "Is your grandfather here?"

"No, playing golf." He glanced at his watch. "His tee time is in fifteen minutes, I think. He texted me a little while ago."

"You didn't tell him what was going on?"

"No, just that we were working. I'm sure he heard about the explosions at the training center. Again. But he's used to my hours and doesn't get stressed about it when I'm gone."

"That's nice. And he's really gotten into the whole golf thing, hasn't he?"

He smiled. "It's good for him. The first few months after my grandmother died, he didn't really know what to do with himself, but he's adjusting—and learning to enjoy life again."

Once inside Nick's home, they both took the time to clean up and change before meeting back in the kitchen. Nick started to pull plates and glasses from the cupboard when the doorbell rang. "That was fast."

"Not fast enough." She darted for the door and Nick laughed. "Why don't you get that?"

She returned with the pizza box in one hand, a slice missing a bite in the other. Chewing, she set the box on the table. "Mmm...so good."

Nick laughed. And laughed again.

SIXTEEN

One week later

Heidi walked into Lou's office and took a seat in the chair opposite her boss. "What's up?"

Lou pursed his lips and set aside his reading glasses. "It's been a long few months with this serial killer on the loose."

"I know. The whole base is still on pins and needles." They both knew this, so where was this going?

"I've come to a decision, and Robinson isn't going to like it."

She frowned. "Okay." Since when did Lou run his decisions by her?

"You've really proven yourself over the last few weeks. Your personality pieces are really popular, you caught the person stealing medals from the homes, helped catch the person who bombed the training center and almost died for your efforts."

So, he'd noticed. "Well, I didn't catch the person all by myself. I had a little help there."

"Whatever. I think it's time you were rewarded for your efforts," he said.

"Rewarded?"

"Yep. I'm making you senior reporter. I may be gruff, but I'm honest and I want this paper to reflect integrity. If our readers don't trust us, they're not going to read us."

"True." She managed to get the word out, but "senior reporter" kept echoing in her mind.

"And Robinson messed up in a big way. Thankfully, because of your and Donovan's willingness not to bring to light Robinson's deception, the people are none the wiser. But I can't risk it happening again. I trust you, Heidi. Unfortunately, I don't trust Robinson. He's going to have to work his way back to that."

"Sir—" Heidi's mouth opened, then closed. What did she say? Stunned, she couldn't find any words.

"So, do you want the job or not?"

"Or course, but John's not going to be happy about this. Working with him may be…uncomfortable." To put it mildly.

"Robinson will do what I tell him or he'll be looking for another job. He should be on his face with gratitude that I didn't fire him."

"I agree with that."

"Good. Now get out of here and go find me that serial killer."

Nerves tingling, excitement growing by the second, Heidi stood and rubbed her palms down her uniform pants. "Yes, sir."

She paused and Lou looked up. "What is it?" he barked.

"Thank you, sir. I really appreciate this opportunity."

"I know you do. Now scram."

Heidi did so, her heart light. And the first person she wanted to tell was Nick. She texted him. Can you talk?

Sure. His immediate response made her smile.

A second later, her phone rang. "I got promoted," she blurted on answering, and told him everything.

"No way. Heidi, that's amazing!"

"I know!"

"Let's celebrate."

"Okay, when and where?"

Once they had it set up, Heidi checked her schedule. "I've got to run. I'm meeting Vanessa Gomez at the hospital. She's agreed to let me interview her."

"I'll be honest, I'm nervous about you being so close to this serial killer case. It was one thing when you were just on the base where Sullivan might be also, but you're not one of his targets. Being actively involved in reporting on Sullivan might change that. I have to admit, it scares me. A lot."

"I'm careful, Nick. You know me."

"Yeah, I do."

She laughed. "Don't sound so morose." Turning serious, she said, "I promise, Nick, I'll be careful. No stupid moves on my part that put me in danger. Trust me, I've got too much to live for."

She hung up and headed for the hospital. It didn't take her long to find the cafeteria where Vanessa had agreed to meet. Heidi saw the woman sitting in the back, in a corner where she could watch the comings and goings of everyone in the place.

Heidi slid into the seat opposite her. "Hi."

"Hi."

"Thanks for agreeing to talk to me."

"Sure. I'm so sick of Boyd Sullivan and everything

he's getting away with. If talking to you will help catch him faster, then I'm all for it."

"Okay, then just start at the beginning. I'll record your story, if that's all right."

"It's fine." Once Heidi had everything set up, she nodded. Vanessa drew in a deep breath. "Back in April, I received a rose in my mailbox. Along with a note saying, *I'm coming for you.* I was shocked. I simply had no idea why Boyd would target me. I only saw him a couple of times on base, and one of those times, I actually helped him out. He was kind. I was nice and professional and did him a favor."

"What kind of favor?"

Vanessa ran a hand over her hair. "Boyd got into a fight with someone. He was pretty beat up and came to me because he needed some stitches. He didn't want to go through official channels because he knew he'd be reprimanded." She shrugged. "At first, I was going to say no, but I was drawn to him. I felt sorry for him."

"You had a romantic thing going on?"

Vanessa recoiled. "What? No! Don't print that!"

Heidi held up a hand. "No, I won't, I promise. It's just that's what it kind of sounded like."

"Well, that's not it. When I say I was drawn to him, I just meant that Boyd reminded me so much of my brother, Aiden, that I simply couldn't refuse. I mean, if Aiden ever found himself in a similar situation, I would hope there would be someone there for him, you know?"

Interesting. "I understand. So, what was it about him that reminded you of your brother?"

"I'm not really sure I can put my finger on it. Maybe

an intense restlessness or a boiling anger with no outlet or release."

"That would make sense. The anger part at least."

Vanessa frowned. "I guess. But one can be very angry without becoming a serial killer."

"Yeah. Too bad Boyd Sullivan didn't get that memo."

"Indeed. Now—"

An announcement over the PA system stopped her. She listened, then stood. "I'm sorry, I have to go. That's an emergency. If you have more questions, feel free to call me later and we can try to get together again when I'm not working."

With that, she was gone. "I do have more questions." But they could wait.

A hint of familiar cologne tingled her nose seconds before the kiss on the side of her neck made her smile. And forget all about stories and serial killers and busy nurses.

"Hey, you," Nick said. "Can I sweep you off your feet and take you to lunch?"

She turned to kiss him, a slow, leisurely melding of their lips that she wanted to go on forever. Except they had an audience. She pulled back, but couldn't resist one last quick peck. "You've already swept me off my feet, but you can certainly do it again."

"Come on out by the fountain. Annie and I have something we need to ask you."

"You can't ask me here?"

"Nope."

"All right, then."

He led her out a side door to the beautiful fountain surrounded by a three-foot brick wall. The fountain was set in the middle of a small grassy area that had a peaceful parklike feel to it. Annie settled into a shady spot and put her head between her paws. But she never took her eyes off Nick.

Heidi spotted a bouquet of flowers sitting on the wall and gasped. "Nick? Pink carnations?"

"Yes." He picked them up and pressed them into her arms.

She sniffed them and smiled. "Thank you. This is so sweet."

"That's not all."

"What else is there?"

"That thing I wanted to ask you."

"Ah...right. Okay."

"Heidi, you make me laugh. I can't believe how much you make me laugh." He cleared his throat. "I like that about you, Heidi."

"Well, thank you. I like a lot about you, too. In fact..." She paused. Did she dare say it? She drew in a deep breath. "I may even love some things about you."

He kissed her. Then drew back. "Stop doing that."

She blinked. "What?"

"Distracting me or I'll never get this said."

"Oh. Sorry."

He cleared his throat again. "Annie keeps looking at me."

"What does that have to do with anything?"

"A lot." He dropped to his knees in front of her and her heart stopped. Then pounded hard enough to echo in her ears.

"Nick?" she whispered.

"I have a confession to make—I'm an idiot."

"It happens to the best of us sometimes." She paused

while he laughed. "I'm teasing," she said. "What are you talking about? You're not an idiot."

"I've been trying to think of the words for days now, but I can't find the exact right ones."

"For what?"

"You deserve better. A better place to be proposed to, a better, more romantic guy with the right words, a slow, drawn-out proposal with all the bells and whistles, but the truth is, Heidi, I'm impatient—one of my many flaws you'll learn about, I'm afraid—and I need to say this before I explode. I'm in love with you and I want to marry you. Am I crazy in hoping you feel the same way?"

Tears had started dripping down her cheeks by the time he reached the words, "I'm in love with you and I want to marry you." She sniffed. "You're not crazy," she whispered. "Not about this, anyway. This is a beautiful place. And I don't need bells and whistles, I just need you."

"Oh, good." His shoulders lost their military rigidness for a brief moment. "That's a relief." He dug into his pocket and pulled out a ring.

Heidi let out a gasp. "Nick?"

"It was my mother's," he said. "And her mother's before that. I'd be honored if you'd wear it. But if you don't like it or it's not your style, we'll go find something else."

She swallowed and took the ring from him. "It's gorgeous." The white gold setting held a teardrop diamond that was dainty and feminine. She loved it. Because of the history behind it but mostly because of the man who gave it to her. "I'd be proud and honored to wear it."

"Really?"

"Yes, Nick, really."

He kissed her, long and hard. Then set her away from him, but let his fingers trail down her cheek before he dropped his hand. "Want to go eat lunch and celebrate?"

She couldn't stop the grin. "I do."

"Just the words I can't wait to hear again in a church setting."

They rushed out to Nick's vehicle and Heidi climbed in and Nick let Annie into her area. Heidi glanced at her in the rearview mirror.

And thought the dog was smiling.

* * * * *

Willow Emery approached her brother and sister-in-law's two-story home in Brooklyn, New York, with a deep sense of foreboding. The white paint on the front door of the yellow-brick building was cracked and peeling, the windows covered with grime. She swallowed hard, hating that her three-year-old niece, Lucy, lived in such deplorable conditions.

Steeling her resolve, she straightened her shoulders. This time, she wouldn't be dissuaded so easily. Her older brother, Alex, and his wife, Debra, had to agree that Lucy deserved better.

Squeak. Squeak. The rusty gate moving in the breeze caused a chill to ripple through her. Why was it open? She hurried forward and her stomach knotted when she found the front door hanging ajar. The tiny hairs on the back of her neck lifted in alarm and a shiver ran down her spine.

Something was wrong. Very wrong.

Thunk. The loud sound startled her. Was that a door closing? Or something worse? Her heart pounded in her chest and her mouth went dry. Following her gut instincts, Willow quickly pushed the front door open and crossed the threshold. Bile rose in her throat as she strained to listen. "Alex? Lucy?"

There was no answer, only the echo of soft hiccuping sobs.

"Lucy!" Reaching the living room, she stumbled to an abrupt halt, her feet seemingly glued to the floor. Lucy was kneeling near her mother, crying. Alex and Debra were lying facedown, unmoving and not breathing, blood seeping out from beneath them.

Were those bullet holes between their shoulder blades? *No! Alex!* A wave of nausea had her placing a hand over her stomach.

Remembering the thud gave her pause. She glanced furtively over her shoulder toward the single bedroom on the main floor. The door was closed. What if the gunman was still here? Waiting? Hiding?

Don't miss
Copycat Killer by Laura Scott,
available April 2020 wherever
Love Inspired Suspense books and ebooks are sold.

LoveInspired.com

LISEXP0320

Annalise's heart beat so fast her stomach churned with
nausea and an icy chill filled her veins. Bert was dead?
The security guard with the great smile who loved to tell
silly jokes was gone? And what two women had been
killed? Who had been in the office at the time of this…
this attack?

What were these killers doing here? What did they
want?

The sound of distant sirens pierced the air. The big
man cursed loudly.

"We were supposed to get in and out of here before
the cops showed up," the tall, thin man said with barely
suppressed desperation in his voice.

"Too late for that now," the big man replied. He
turned and pointed his gun at Annalise. She stiffened.
Was he going to kill her, as well? Was he going to shoot
her right now? Kill the girls? She put her arms around
her students and tried to pull them all behind her.

More sirens whirred and whooped, coming closer and
closer.

"Don't move," he snarled at them. He took the butt of his gun and busted out one of the windows. The sound of the shattering glass followed by a rapid burst of gunfire out the window made her realize just how dangerous this situation was.

The police were outside. She and her students were inside with murderous gunmen, and she couldn't imagine how this all was going to end.

Don't miss
48 Hour Lockdown *by Carla Cassidy,*
available March 2020 wherever
Harlequin Intrigue books and ebooks are sold.

Harlequin.com

HIEXP0320